He'd once im...

He'd wondered what she would feel like to his touch. Taste like to his lips. He wanted to know all of her.

As if the years had not passed them by. As if the journey they'd traveled had been the same. He could not change what had come before, but tonight she would be his.

They gradually migrated to the center of the room, and Rachel stepped into his arms as if she had always belonged against him. As if her thoughts lay parallel with his.

"Why are we doing this?" she whispered.

"When I find the answer, I'll let you know." Chastely, he bent and kissed her lips. Tasting. Testing. Challenging.

Then he angled his mouth and took a little more.

Their breaths mingled.

"Stay with me." There was a husky tenor to his voice, a strange desperation. "Stay with me until dawn."

She looked up into his shadowed eyes. "I will."

Avon Books by
Melody Thomas

ANGEL IN MY BED
A MATCH MADE IN SCANDAL
MUST HAVE BEEN THE MOONLIGHT
IN MY HEART

MELODY THOMAS

A Match Made in
Scandal

AVON BOOKS
An Imprint of HarperCollinsPublishers

This is a work of fiction. Names, characters, places, and incidents are products of the author's imagination or are used fictitiously and are not to be construed as real. Any resemblance to actual events, locales, organizations, or persons, living or dead, is entirely coincidental.

AVON BOOKS
An Imprint of HarperCollins*Publishers*
10 East 53rd Street
New York, New York 10022-5299

Copyright © 2005 by Laura Renken
ISBN-13: 978-0-06-074231-7
ISBN-10: 0-06-074231-3
www.avonromance.com

First Avon Books paperback printing: September 2005

Avon Trademark Reg. U.S. Pat. Off. and in Other Countries, Marca Registrada, Hecho en U.S.A.
HarperCollins® is a registered trademark of HarperCollins Publishers Inc.

Printed in the U.S.A.

10 9 8 7 6 5 4 3 2

For my wonderful father and brother,
the engineers in my family.
I appreciate the hours you spent with me
on the phone talking in terminology
I will never understand,
but which my characters surely do.
Love you both.

Chapter 1

London
1873

With a sigh of frustration, Rachel Bailey thrummed her fingers on the polished banister, the diaphanous froth of her emerald skirt whispering with her movement. Perfumed currents of air mingled with cigar smoke drifting from the ballroom below. She turned, her fan dangling from one wrist, an empty dance card on the other.

She'd tried not to care that so many here found her an intellectual oddity or had excluded her from their social circles.

Especially tonight.

For Cinderella had nothing on Rachel, except perhaps the eye of the handsome prince, or in this case the talented recipient of one of the most prestigious awards in all of Great Britain. A civil engineer could garner no higher honor than the Gold Telford Award, an honor that she would never receive because of her gender, but one that Ryan Donally most aptly deserved.

From the gilt-edged balcony of the Palace Hotel, overlooking the ballroom, she watched him, his tall, dark form easily recognizable among the colorful assemblage. Music floated high above the spacious floor to resonate against the dome-shaped roof, elaborately paneled in Venetian mirrors. All about her, the ball was in full swing, the swirl of colors arcing across the polished floor like a rainbow.

Incredibly handsome, Ryan was suited to the petite blonde he held a little too intimately in his arms, Lady Gwyneth Abbott. His future wife, if one was to believe the rumor running rampant among the crowd. She was a jewel of elegant architecture in vermilion silk and upswept blond hair wrapped in a diamond tiara. The two conversed, his vital energy mesmerizing, his open smile reflecting an animated conversation that drew more than Rachel's attention.

Ever since they'd been children, Ryan had garnered attention wherever he went. He mastered crowds as easily as he gathered accolades, his charisma a reflection of his Irish good looks. Now, having amassed a fortune in the iron-ore industry, Ryan himself had since become an international conglomerate separate from his family—and separate from her—a far reach from the uncouth boy who used to throw spiders in her hair when they were children.

Theirs had always been an impossible relationship. He was her curse.

And the very reason she had returned to England.

Drawing in her breath against her tightly laced corset, Rachel knew she was naïve to think she could walk back into his life tonight after everything she'd done to him, and not feel panic.

They had not spoken since Kathleen had died four years ago.

She had to find a way to speak with him. She *needed* to talk to him.

"The woman in my brother's arms is the Earl of Devonshire's niece," a masculine voice murmured next to her ear and startled her.

John Donally had managed a soundless approach and caught her staring at Ryan. "And of whom are you speaking?" Rachel plucked a fluted champagne glass off the tray of a passing footman.

"You know of whom I'm speaking. I understand that she's the earl's ward and that she's sought after among the *ton's* bachelors. But she has eyes only for my brother. She's quite beautiful."

And Ryan's brother, with whom she usually managed an excellent rapport, only jammed the knife a little deeper into her heart. Rachel truly didn't want to know that the girl was flawless as a snowflake. Sipping champagne, she welcomed the wet effervescence against her senses. "Did Lady Gwyneth make him cut his hair?" she asked, for lack of anything charitable to say. She'd noticed Ryan's trademark queue missing.

"I doubt it, colleen." Johnny crossed his arms. "But you can always inquire."

"I would very much like to talk to him. He's not been in London for a week."

"He's been in Bristol. They returned last night."

"They?"

Ryan's older brother peered over the balcony, his dark curly hair catching the light from the Venetian chandelier. "He and Lady Gwyneth, and the girl's sister," Johnny said. "He just purchased property there."

"Can he really want to marry her, Johnny?"

"What do I know about Ryan's heart? Since Kathleen's death, he's kept his emotions locked away so tightly none of us have been able to make sense of anything he does." Slipping a hand into his pocket, Johnny turned. "He's not the same man he used to be. Don't be lulled into thinking otherwise."

"Does he ever speak of Kathleen?"

Johnny folded his arms and leaned against the balustrade. "Why have you come all the way from Ireland to be here to-night, colleen?"

"Despite everything else he's done these past four years, Ryan still chairs Donally & Bailey Engineering." She studied the champagne bubbles in her glass, realizing they were perfectly formed spheres and, if she held them to the light, they glittered. That such perfection could result from the nasty by-product of massive chaos and organic upheaval was the essence of true chemistry.

Rachel swiveled her glass in the light and blinked as Johnny's handsome face suddenly came into focus over the crystalline rim. Realizing he might construe too much from such unusual whimsy, she sipped. "You have to admit the award is well deserved. He's required reading at Edinburgh and Göttingen."

"And naturally, you're filled with admiration for his talents." Johnny plucked the glass from her fingertips and set it on the table beside the richly gilt Corinthian column. "Methinks you've imbibed enough, colleen."

"Shouldn't you be dancing with your wife?" She recaptured her glass, prepared to do battle for one more taste. "What will she be thinking to see the two of us all alone up here, cozy as lovebirds grappling over my champagne flute?"

His dark eyes filling with mischief, he deftly snatched the glass from her hands and set it on the tray of a passing footman. "She'll be thinkin' that we've known each other all of our lives, Rachel." Taking her elbow, he forced her gaze from the glass of spirits disappearing down the back stairway that led out to the hotel kitchens. "She told me to find you and drag you onto the ballroom floor if need be. Neither of us thinks you should be watching the world from up here. It's time to play for once."

Swallowing a groan, Rachel allowed Johnny to lead her

down the marble steps into the man-made rainbow of silks and satins, where she immediately sank within the bright colors. "You don't need to hold my hand," she whispered. "Metaphorically speaking, of course."

"I do if I intend to dance, literally speaking." Johnny placed his fingertips at her waist, then bent to look into her face. "You're not thinkin' you've forgotten how to waltz, are ye?" he asked, stepping with her onto the floor, his movements carefully precise.

There was nothing that put the starch into her spine like the fear of failure. "I think that you're treading hazardous waters. I could ruin your two perfectly good feet before the clock strikes midnight."

"But this does provide me the opportunity to hold a beautiful woman in my arms. With my wife's permission even. How fortunate am I?"

Rachel let herself fall into the easy step of the waltz. "You've blarney for blood, Johnny Donally," she said. "But I thank you for it just the same."

She was grateful that, even after all the mistakes she'd made with her life, anyone in the Donally family could still be her friend. Yet they had remained staunchly so. Most of them anyway.

Except Ryan.

Even as her throat tightened, her eyes remained dry. Life had taught her the uselessness of tears and the dangers of emotions that crept into the orderly world she'd created for herself as one of only two female civil engineers in the world. But the cracks had begun to form after Kathleen's death four years ago and widened when Rachel hit her twenty-ninth birthday last month. She didn't know what to do with the impractical, feminine part inside that had suddenly reawakened.

She needed desperately to rectify her past with Ryan.

Long ago, she'd watched as he married her best friend. And Rachel knew if she left tonight without telling him anything in her heart, she would never have another chance.

In a few months, he would be out of her life forever.

"Do you actually drink this stuff, Donally?"

Havana in hand, Ryan turned from the arched doorway where he'd been standing for the last half hour watching the ballroom. Lord Devonshire entered the billiard room from the terrace, and Ryan regretted the demise of his solitude.

"The Engineering Society could have afforded a better stock of champagne, don't you agree?" Devonshire rebuked.

Ryan held up his tumbler. "Compared to stock Irish whiskey, everything else is tame, my lord." He tipped back the glass and relished the burn down his throat before setting down the glass to rack the pool balls. The billiard room had emptied when the orchestra began to warm up again for the last set.

Like every man present, his lordship wore a black formal swallowtail coat, white cravat, and gloves. This was not the kind of event men like Devonshire usually attended. Ryan's professional peers were commoners, but tonight the earl and his family had come as his guests.

"You're not dancing?" Devonshire stood in the archway, looking out onto the ballroom floor.

"Your niece's dance card is full." Ryan took the cue stick he'd leaned against the billiard table. "I had my requisite two dances. Do you play billiards, my lord?"

Devonshire continued to watch the dancers with interest. "No," he said absently.

Ryan chalked a stick. Smoke curled from the ash tin in which he'd stubbed out his cigar. He listened to strains of the waltz. Laughter. His own disorganized thoughts.

He knew who had caught Devonshire's attention. Ryan

had been watching her for most of the night. Even when he'd been dancing with Gwyneth, he'd glimpsed Rachel on the balcony overlooking the ballroom. He'd returned from Bristol yesterday to learn she'd been in London over a week.

"Miss Bailey's presence tonight is curious. She is not the kind of woman I'd expected to find dabbling in the engineering profession."

Ryan fixed his gaze over the cue stick. "Why is that, exactly?" He cued the white ball, sending balls scattering over the table.

"A woman who looks like she does should have more appreciation for the finer talents of her sex." Chuckling into his glass, Devonshire froze as he looked across the rim and into Ryan's gaze.

For a moment, the earl's eyes flickered as something in Ryan's expression wiped the smirk from his face.

Ryan potted the orange ball into the left pocket. "Is there a reason for this conversation?"

His lordship picked up the red ball. "You must be aware that my niece wants an autumn wedding," Devonshire said. "Clearly, whatever it is that you talk about whenever you are alone, she is agreeable to a future as your wife."

"Clearly the size of my bank account makes her more tolerant of my inherent faults."

Ryan continued to observe Devonshire's darkening color with calm interest. The man treated those he considered beneath him with contempt, which was every man present that night. Yet, they both knew where they stood in their business relationship. Devonshire needed his money. Their personal relationship had yet to be defined.

"There you are, Uncle." Devonshire's younger apple-cheeked ward stopped beneath the archway. Her face flushed, she was breathless. "I have been looking everywhere for you. They have started a new waltz."

"Beatrice," Devonshire snapped. "Have you forgotten your bloody manners?"

The girl's blue eyes rounded on Ryan, blond ringlets framing her plump face. "Please allow me to steal my uncle away, Mr. Donally." She lowered her lashes and curtsied, her pale blue skirts whispering with her movement. "Gwyneth put his name on my dance card so that it would be filled. I was only hoping that perhaps—"

"Where is your sister now?" Devonshire looked out onto the ballroom floor.

"She's dancing, of course. *Her* card is always filled."

Devonshire glanced down at her. "Consider that her card is always filled because she doesn't go flitting about like some silly schoolgirl, Beatrice."

Turning away, Ryan lifted up his jacket from the chair where he'd laid it earlier.

"I'm sorry, Uncle," he heard the girl murmur.

"Go to the withdrawing room and straighten your hair."

"Yes, Uncle."

Ryan kept his gaze focused on his sleeves as she fled the room. Devonshire looked over his shoulder at him, a hint of iron in his gaze. "We've an agreement, Donally."

Adjusting his silver cuff links, Ryan regarded the elder with a tight smile. "Your servant, as always, my lord." A crisp bow implied the opposite.

Watching Devonshire leave, Ryan walked to the arched doorway and leaned a shoulder against the wall. One hand in his pocket, he was conscious of a sour taste in his mouth that the strings of a waltz and the gaiety on the dance floor could not dispel. His entire life, he had gone horns to horns with men like Devonshire, who thought they owned the world and the people around them by virtue of their birth. In the process, he'd made enemies. Let there be no mistake—Ryan knew Devonshire was one.

Ryan's gaze came to an abrupt stop on the lone feminine figure standing on the outskirts of Johnny's crowd, and every other thought in his mind fled.

Rachel Bailey had been his adolescent obsession.

His curse.

The only woman in the world who could beat him at croquet, outscore him in arithmetic, and probably knew more about him than any other being alive.

A glimmering wash of candlelight set her apart like some ethereal Madonna, etching her profile in revealing shadows and light. Devonshire knew not the woman he besmirched with the insinuation that Rachel Bailey had returned to London for some other purpose than seeing Donally & Bailey receive the award tonight. She lived and breathed D&B, toeing the line between good and evil like one born to the task of martyrdom. She'd been working out of their office in Dublin for four years.

He had always had a way with women. The smart ones avoided him, which proved that Rachel had always been smarter than most. Yet, even as she'd chased after his oldest brother for most of her youth, she had always managed to cloud Ryan's vision and ruin his judgment. Then somewhere between the years he had given her her first openmouthed kiss and graduated at the top of his class in Edinburgh, he'd met Kathleen.

Silent, Ryan simply stood now, watching Rachel, until some inherent resonance of his thoughts turned her head and, for a dragging moment, he waited for her to see him through the press of people. She was searching for someone, he realized, as she looked out across the dance floor—and the restlessness he'd felt all night returned.

Growing up, he'd known just where to place a spider in her hair, or how to knot the strings of her pinafore to the barn post so tight that she had to undress to escape. Old habits died hard, he realized. As he withdrew his gloves from his pocket and absently began to apply them to his hands, he thought about her hair, wondering if it still flowed to her waist in a fiery wave of sin. He began to shoulder through the crowd, only to find his way blocked as people stopped to congratulate him for the reward he'd received. His eyes on Rachel, he worked the crowd as efficiently as he did everything else in his life.

The crystal chandelier hanging in the center of the ballroom illuminated the throng of dancers. Rachel stood for perhaps five seconds more, searching the faces before she turned and attempted to squeeze her way through the crush. Lady Gwyneth had yet to leave the dance floor. But Ryan was nowhere to be seen.

She secured a new glass of champagne from a footman, too hot to care that she had little in common with the people in the room or that she disliked crowds immensely. Stopping in front of a console table festooned with an enormous fuchsia arrangement, she paused to consider an austere rendition of Queen Victoria staring down at her from the wall—and wondered how the most powerful country in the world could have a queen at its helm and be so completely archaic when it came to a woman's station in life.

"Your Majesty—" She raised the champagne flute to her lips.

A gloved hand reached over her shoulder and slipped the glass from her fingers. "Has anyone ever told you that you drink too much?" Ryan stood behind her, nearly scaring the wits out of her, looking even better up close than he had dancing.

"Practically your whole family."

He set the glass on the table. His dark eyes faintly challenging, he merely held her gaze. "Can you still dance?"

Her heart hammering, she watched his fingers curl around her palm and deftly turn her into his arms before leading her onto the dance floor. "Truly, Ryan," she managed to quip, as he swept her out onto the ballroom floor, "you can be quite full of yourself at times."

"Not anymore." He grinned, a portrait of sheepish charm. "I'm a reformed man."

"You're half-right," she scoffed, remembering that he was the one who used to spy on her swimming naked in the pond behind her house. "You're a man."

His gaze touched hers. There it was. That hint of friction between them, a slow-growing heat that would eventually spark. She'd just forgotten how hot. Nervously looking around at the gilded ballroom and the thousand candles that flickered like golden stars, she fell easily into step. "Tonight, I'll even let you lead."

"Jaysus." He laughed quietly, his eyes briefly marking her lips before he looked at a spot over her head. "What are you doing out of Ireland?"

"I am expanding the Rathdrum project," she said.

He remained silent.

"I wrote to you a few months ago. Twice."

"I've been out of the country, Rache."

"Johnny told me tonight you were in Bristol this week."

He lowered his gaze and looked at her. Her flush was surely caused by the champagne she'd consumed. He didn't reply, and she added, "My room is in this hotel." Her words almost sounding like a blatant invitation to frolic, she cleared her throat, wondering why it was so hard to say what she'd come to tell him. "I mean, we can talk over lunch. In the dining room, of course."

"I don't know, Rache. Venturing to London to see me. Now inviting me to lunch, all in one week. I might get the wrong idea and think you're trying to seduce me."

As usual, he was behaving poorly. "Don't flatter yourself." She lifted her chin. "My grandmother could seduce you. You're that easy."

A startlingly white smile swept across his tanned face. "How is Memaw these days?"

"She reads about you in the scandal sheets, Ryan."

He didn't seem too worried that he was a regular topic these days in both the financial and scandal columns of every newspaper in Great Britain. "Then I can only imagine what Memaw says about me," he mocked gravely.

Rachel could feel the heat of him against her body, the wild scent of clover and sunshine that seemed to emanate from the fibers on his shirt. Looking to a point level with her eyes, she saw that he wore the Telford medallion on a ribbon around his neck, tucked snugly between the fine lawn of his white shirt and his waistcoat. She thought of thrusting her hands into his clothes and retrieving that medal.

"Maybe if you're nice, I'll let you take it out and play with it." He leaned nearer until his breath brushed hot over her ear. "You always did like my toys better than yours."

"At least there are some things about me you've not forgotten," she said, miffed that he could read her mind with such ease.

"Are you seeing anyone?" he asked after a moment. His assessing gaze roamed over her. He arched a dark brow. "Are you in love? Do you have a life outside D&B?"

"Of course, I do." Her response burst out too quickly. All he had to do was look at her to know that she was lying. "I teach at a girls' school outside Dublin," she said as an afterthought, then added, "And I fence."

He peered down at her. "How long have you been fencing?"

"Three years. David is my instructor."

A corner of his mouth lifted. "How is my illustrious brother? Is he still a priest?"

"Oh, please, Ryan. You don't have that many siblings left who still talk to you on a regular basis. Must you besmirch him?"

"You're all heart, Rache." He laughed, sweeping her through a turn and out the doors onto the terrace. "Some things never change. At least I don't have to worry that the years in Ireland have turned you into a cream puff."

They came to a stop.

Ryan had danced with her outside the glass doors before slowing beneath the bough of an overhanging tree. Strains of music continued to play into the night.

"Why the letters?" he asked. His expression was so eloquent of his entire implacable personality, she thought he sounded angry. "Why the renewed interest in my life? I thought we'd said all there is to say to one another."

"Why haven't *you* come to Ireland? That ferry goes two ways." Heart pounding, she crushed her skirts in her palm. She could retreat no farther in her life than she'd done for the last four years. "I know you have every right to hate me."

"Look at me," he said.

A hand reached around and gently pulled her chin, turning her. In the shadows, she heard the whisper of Ryan's sleeve at the same time her muddled senses registered that he slid something over her head. Warm bronze settled between her breasts.

"Take the medallion back to Dublin. You've earned it, too."

She shook her head. His hand folded over her smaller one. "For once, just bloody accept something I want to give you."

"Damn you, Ryan." Her heart too complex, she could say no more.

"Is that sentiment open to discussion?" he asked, lowering his hand.

He leaned against the stone wall at his hip, looking very nice in black tails and trousers. Shadows and moonlight at his back. His jacket pulled at his shoulders, his lounging pose altering perceptibly as he turned his head and looked at her.

"No." She laughed in maudlin disgust.

Rachel's gaze encompassed his dark, fathomless eyes, now focused on hers intently, and his mouth, which she'd kissed long ago and suddenly yearned to do so again. He was more handsome than any man had a right to be, and his touch spoke to something so deeply buried that he must surely read it in her eyes. He'd been married to her best friend. He'd loved Kathleen. She'd loved Kathleen as the sister she'd never had, and she suddenly felt traitorous to that loyalty. But she was finished living the lie that had become her life.

"I said some things to you once that I regret. Things I should never have said at Kathleen's . . . at her funeral—"

"Don't, Rachel." Ryan left her gaping at his back. He stopped at the edge of the terrace and, with his hands on his hips, looked out across the goldfish pond.

His reaction was so incongruous in the midst of her turmoil that Rachel's brain lagged behind her body's response. "You can't just turn your back. This is important."

He put his hand on his waist. As he turned, she glimpsed the silver clasps of his suspenders where the jacket had pulled away from his hip. "If it's a confession of the past you want to make, I forgive you for everything you think you ever did."

"You don't even know what sins I've committed."

"How bad could they be?" He faced her directly. "You go to Mass twice weekly. You haven't murdered anyone. If you don't count your penchant for drinking, smoking, swearing, and indulging in chocolate, you're practically a candidate for sainthood."

"Sainthood? I accused you of killing my best friend." She swallowed, remembering all the wretched things she'd said that day. Kathleen had died in childbirth, and Rachel had blamed Ryan. She'd been unkind and horribly selfish in her grief.

Worse, she had done things with her own life that had brought shame on her family. She was not who Ryan thought she was.

"A few weeks ago, I turned twenty-nine. Did you know that?" Rachel went to stand before him. "You asked why I came to London." She was aware of her own cascading emotions, the constriction in her chest that seemed to grow as if she had opened the floodgate, and it was no longer possible to hold the waters back. "You see, I've spent so much of my life working to achieve the kind of status that, frankly, you and Johnny have. That my father had. On one level I needed you to know that I was worthy of the position that I hold at D&B in Dublin. As you've noted, I've committed myself to this course to the exclusion of all else in my life. I made choices. Heaven only knows my mistakes. I want to see Mary Elizabeth. I want to see you."

Ryan merely continued to watch her, with hooded eyes now wary.

She folded her hands around the medallion. The strange sensation of having come to the end of the road brought with it a familiar, disconcerting feeling of uncertainty. "This is about making amends for our past," and her entire life, she realized. "I once said some horrible things to you. You didn't deserve my anger that day when you were already grieving. You can say that you don't remember, but I know you do. I was wrong. Then I disappeared from your life, and we never had a chance to talk . . . about anything."

The moonlight only amplified the shadows behind her mood as she gathered her composure. A box hedge and trellis shielded them from the ballroom. Inside, the music ceased to play. Soon the last dance would begin. Ryan should be inside. The crowd would be looking for him.

Finally, his head shook. "You've been thinking about that day all of these years?" A note of disbelief tinged the question. He made her feel like a fool.

Maybe all they'd really ever shared was their love for Kathleen. Perhaps there *was* nothing in their past, and she'd lived these years stagnant in some foolish long-ago memory when he'd kissed her in the darkness beneath the elm tree. "Why are you making this so difficult? You always do that to me!"

"Me?" He was arrogantly astounded.

"Yes, you. I'm trying my best to talk to you. To tell you . . . things. Important things."

"Important?" The silence became onerous. "You waltz back into my life again? For what? To clear your conscience over an event that happened almost four years ago? Everything you said that day to me was the truth." His dark eyes flickered with a raw emotion she had not seen in years. "Kathleen died because of me. You don't know how many ways I killed her. So don't bring up that day to me again."

"I'm sorry."

In the shadows of the hedge, his voice had gone quiet. "You don't know who I am. You never did. You've lived in your own world, the musical troubadour flitting about with dreams bigger than a man's soul. You've been very good at getting what you've wanted."

"Stop." Rachel hated the tears that welled. She hated that he made her incapable of rational thought. He didn't know anything about the last few years. "Please . . ."

"Please . . . what, Rachel? You're godmother to my daughter. I haven't kept you from seeing her. I don't want to hear your bloody confessions because you're twenty-nine years old and have now decided to return to England under some assumption that you need to correct the past so that you can sleep at night."

"You're impossible, Ryan Donally! I don't even know why I'm trying to talk to you."

"Hell, Rache." He flung out his arms. "There's nothing new about that."

He wasn't going to get off that easily. She could take some of the blame for their estrangement, but not all. How could she have been in love with him her entire life and he still be so blind? "I came back to see *you,* Ryan," she whispered.

She took his hands. Capable hands. They'd built bridges and roads. They'd held her after her mother died. "That's what I'm trying to tell you. I tried writing you."

She'd tried in so many ways these past months to tell him what was in her heart.

"Jaysus, Rachel. What are you doing?" His voice was a rough whisper.

She felt his tumult. The moonlight fell full upon him. She sought his eyes to discern his thoughts, placated by nothing she saw within those dark depths.

Then she did what her heart was telling her to do. What she should have done long before now. Long before her twenty-ninth birthday. Long before she looked into the mirror and realized how much of her life she'd thrown away on grief or pride.

She drew his mouth to her lips.

And kissed him.

The instinct to touch him was as natural to her as breathing. She heard the husky timbre of her name on his lips, fueling hope that had died with the passing years. Her body curved against the long length of his, and she felt every hardened contour. She slid her hands up the warm flesh of his neck to tangle in his hair. Then his hands framed her face, and he tore his mouth away. "I can't do this," he rasped. "I can't."

The words jolted her senses. He followed her chin with his hand and turned her face to his. "There can never be anything between us." His palm gentled. "Go home, Rachel."

She stepped away from his hand. If she could stop herself from reacting, she could accept his calm as some noble gesture to spare her further humiliation. Instead, she felt only the bleak reality of his rejection. There was no honor in her actions. She should never have opened this wretched gate to the past.

Worst of all, Rachel resented that Ryan had more respect for her than she had for herself. More self-control. A burst of self-anger rescued her from shame. "She cannot possibly love you, Ryan."

For an awful moment, neither of them moved, and it seemed as if her heart caught in her throat. For she had not meant the words the cruel way they sounded. Inside, the music had commenced, a resounding finale befitting the end of a successful celebration. "Is that your ever-impressing opinion of my character, Rache?" Droll amusement touched his mouth, and, despising his blatant mockery of her feelings, she gave him her back. "I believe it is," he said, with a ghost of a laugh.

He walked past her down the flower-bordered path.

She sank onto the stone bench, devastated more than she could have imagined possible.

The medallion in her hands drew her gaze, and she traced the Latin lettering, a rush of familiar feelings tumbling through her mind. Truly, in her best imitation of a failure, she could not have bungled this night more, she thought, wiping the wretched tears from her cheek with one hand. She was furious at him and his own lack of logic concerning his life, convinced that he was stepping off a cliff and didn't even know it. He was a fool. But then who could ever tell Ryan anything? Certainly not her. She couldn't offer him anything.

Drawing in a deep ragged breath, she looked up.

Her wet gaze stopped abruptly on a young blond-haired man sitting on the stone wall. Her spine jolted her upright. Wiping the heel of her hand across her cheek, she came to her feet. He had not been there previously, but by his manner, it was obvious he had witnessed the entire humiliating affair!

"Though I do prefer Covent Garden for its entertainment, I've found tonight very interesting." He folded his arms and stretched his legs out in front of him. "You must be the notorious business associate of that very same man who intends to wed my cousin," he said, coming to his feet. "The very person I've wanted to find."

He was neither exceptionally tall nor exceptionally broad of shoulder. He was handsome, and his clothes were tailored, as exclusive as the fat diamond stickpin in his cravat. "I couldn't help but overhear your conversation."

"I'm sure that you could have if you'd tried a bit harder to walk away."

She stepped around him, only to have him block her way. "Allow me to introduce myself." He bowed, then handed her his card. "I'm Lord Gideon Montague Viscount Bathwick, Lord Devonshire's son, who is here as Ryan Donally's guest. My illustrious cousin . . . as you probably suspect . . . will be occupied with her own plans for the night. So here I am left to fend for myself among the other lost souls of the night," he said with casual deference, as if he had a right to impose himself or to imply that she was lost.

"You and I have something in common, Miss Bailey."

"I seriously doubt we move in the same circles to have anything in common."

She was too humiliated by what he'd seen. Too angry. Johnny appeared on the terrace from the direction of the ballroom. He halted when he saw her, his gaze shifting to the man blocking her path before joining them. "Bathwick . . . my lord."

"Johnny Donally." Lord Bathwick turned, clearly annoyed by the interruption. "How old-world of you. Are you coming to the rescue tonight?"

"Are you all right?" Johnny stood beside her, a protective hint of steel behind his query. But Rachel needed no one to defend her. She only wanted to leave.

"Please, Johnny, me boy," Bathwick mimicked Johnny's slight accent. "Some of us are still gentlemen and, despite your brother's conceit, there are some things left in Britain that he does not own. I merely wanted words with this very enchanting D&B board member."

"You've had them. Now leave," Johnny said.

Bathwick's gaze homed in directly on Rachel as he passed. "When you are ready to talk. Another time then, Miss Bailey."

Rachel held on to Johnny's arm to avert an open dispute, but watching Bathwick leave, she could only wonder what Ryan had done to make this man hate him.

Chapter 2

"Who is Lord Bathwick to Ryan?" Rachel asked Johnny the next morning.

Having slept only a few hours last night, she'd arrived early at D&B with an aching head. Strange that the sky could be so blue, the day pleasantly warm—and so utterly discordant with the world order of things. She reached her hand across the desk and shut the blinds. She could still hear the traffic on the street outside.

"I suggest you stay away from him, colleen," Johnny said, leaning with his palms on the drafting table as he continued to pore over the plans she'd brought with her from Ireland. He'd removed his jacket and rolled up his shirtsleeves, the color's starkness a contrast to his tanned forearms. "Lord Bathwick is not a friend to Ryan."

Rachel smoothed the corners of the plat and looked up to gauge Johnny's silence. "Reading the financial news in the broadsheets of late, I've noticed that a lot of people seem to feel that way about Ryan," she prompted, refusing to be put off.

"Ryan went through a very public and ugly battle in his acquisition of Ore Industries a year ago. Devonshire and son, Lord Bathwick, no longer own the company."

Yet Devonshire had agreed to a betrothal between Ryan and Lady Gwyneth, she thought, recognizing that Lord Bathwick had not seemed pleased about that last night.

Like everyone else in London, Rachel had read the betrothal announcement in that morning's broadsheets—a titanic society event judging by the amount of space dedicated to the bride's pure blue pedigree. Ryan had stepped into a little fiefdom, worthy of his own growing financial kingdom. Last night, when she'd thrown herself at him and made such a fool of herself—he'd known there could never be anything between them.

"D&B is certainly a smaller firm compared to the worldwide giant, Ore Industries," she managed. "D&B must be of little importance to Ryan, now."

"Don't count on it." Johnny shook his head. "He still sits at the head of this board."

Johnny continued to lean both palms on the drafting table, and she returned to the diagram they had been discussing most of the morning. A flood had taken out the bridge near Rathdrum two years ago. The Irish division of D&B had received the contract to repair that bridge. Except that wasn't why she was there. "We have nearly finished," she said. "But the flooding will only be abated in the future with this levee. I want to be the one to build it. Not as the person who sits in the Dublin office and oversees the running of various departments, but as the project engineer for the job."

Johnny slanted her a glance. "It isn't done, colleen."

"I refuse to be a figurehead in this company any longer, Johnny." She was in no mood for lectures on professional protocol or anything remotely associated with the fact that she was a woman in a man's business. She'd spent years of her life in the field and auditing classes to complete the necessary mathematics, physics, and engineering requirements it took to become an engineer, and much more to understand the internal machinations of the company she'd inherited from her father. Rachel only knew that she'd staked her reputation and her financial survival on this entire venture.

"Hundreds of people are depending on me to put food on their table. I just need your approval to send it through the committee for funding."

"I don't have the authority to approve this. You know it as well as I."

"I don't know any such thing, Johnny."

"Ryan is the only one who can approve this as it stands. I can tell you, he won't."

She steeled herself against the unexpected urge to argue with him, for there was truth to Johnny's statements about women in the engineering profession, she reluctantly conceded. She could put Allan Marrow's name as the project head and send the report through the committee as she'd done on many occasions before. But she'd made many decisions about her life before coming here, wanting to take a stand on them all. Indeed, she was finished hiding behind the wall of perpetual anonymity when it came both to her proficiency as an engineer and her heart, believing that she and Ryan not only shared a desire to see Donally & Bailey thrive but something else as well. Something that had always been present between them from the days they'd been children.

She'd set out for London with an elaborate dream, wishful illusions to conquer the love of her life, never thinking that Ryan didn't feel even a miniscule drop of similar feelings for her. She'd danced with him like some belated Cinderella—only the slipper he held in his hand today did not belong to her.

"So be it then." She rolled up the top diagram, careful not to crease the fragile paper. She understood bargains made with the devil. She'd been making them for years.

"Will you tell me what happened last night?" Johnny peered down at her.

Her braid fell forward over her shoulder. "I don't know what you mean."

"When my brother takes me from a dance with my wife and tells me to go out to the terrace and make sure that you get to your hotel room for the night, it leaves me a little concerned, colleen."

Rachel's spine stiffened. Leave it to Ryan to come up with the worst possible rationale for her confession and think her foxed.

A steam whistle sounded from outside.

Rachel tipped open the blinds and looked out the window that fronted the drafting room. The D&B office sat off the bank of the Thames. In another month, the London climate would prevent the window from staying open, though the stench coming off the Thames was far less, now that the embankment had been completed.

The door in the outer office opened, and she heard the low mumble of voices.

"The painters are here," Johnny said, rolling up the rest of the papers she'd scattered over the drafting table and handing her the tubes. "You don't want to be here when they begin work."

"Are you leaving?"

"I don't work all the time." Johnny took his jacket from the stool next to hers. "Moira and the children are taking me to Lords for the cricket match this afternoon. Have you seen Mary Elizabeth yet?" He shoved his arms into the jacket sleeves.

She had wanted very much to see Kathleen's daughter, but she had not pursued the quest. Children in general made her uncomfortable, and that particular one scared her to death as much as the thought of facing Ryan again after last night.

"Brace up, colleen. Ryan may not even be home," Johnny

said, lifting his satchel from the floor. "But you need to talk to him about the project. Not me."

She let go of an exhalation. "He probably wishes I'd just go back to Dublin."

Johnny turned. Wearing the dark coat, with his brown eyes and hair the color of Ryan's, he studied her briefly, as if unsure what to say. "The wedding will take place in October at Devonshire's estate," he said quietly. "I should have told you last night."

Rachel said nothing more. For that was that—as Memaw would say—the sound of her heart breaking as it crashed into a thousand pieces against her ribs. She hated weakness, especially in herself. She hated feeling like a shrew, when she went out of her way to be nice—at the very least not mean— believing in her heart that what went around in this world would come back around and smile on her with benevolence. Fate was indeed keeping score, but not in the way that she'd hoped.

Rachel remained on the stool, her skirts spread primly over her legs, her leather half boots moving in agitation beneath the hem. Ryan might not be interested in her—he might not even be able to abide her—but whether he willed it or not, as the daughter of an original charter member, she sat on the board of this company, and, for the first time in her life, she felt qualified to share in company decisions. He would have to accept her in that capacity at the very least. For she was not folding up and going away.

"You are reckless this morning, Mr. Donally."

"Indeed, Jacques." Breathing hard, Ryan tested the grip of his foil with a slice through the air, his eyes narrowed on the fencing master through the mesh of his mask. "Let's go at it again."

Two steps, he met the other man's riposte, the *click* of their foils the only sound in the glass studio. He'd been working out for over an hour. Tempered by his fickle mood, Ryan had awakened early, something he rarely did, especially since he'd returned to his country estate and not his London residence last night. He'd not fallen asleep until dawn.

Circling counterclockwise to his opponent, Ryan struck the other's weapon in a steady forward thrust. He had taken up fencing last year, as a way to alleviate the restlessness that seemed to be the driving force in his life. Jacques had come to him at the recommendation of Lord Ravenspur, his sister's husband.

Ryan moved with the agility of a man who had not yet lost his reflexes, countering with graceful steps. They went around the floor twice more before the Frenchman nicked him again, this time in the chest. "You are dead, Mr. Donally. I've skewered your heart."

Ryan snatched off the mask. "No, Jacques." He tossed the foil to one of his footmen standing at the glass doors. "That untrustworthy organ was skewered sometime ago." He removed the protective leather vest and accepted a towel from the other man's outstretched hand. Even with the glass doors opened to the cool air, sweat dampened his shirt and hair. Looking out across the expanse of rolling green yard that stretched to the woods, he drank from a pitcher of water a servant brought him.

"I understand a betrothal between you and Lady Gwyneth was announced this morning, sir," Jacques said, joining him by the window. "My congratulations. She is beautiful. I am envious, *oui*?"

Ryan slapped the towel around his neck, aware of an irritation he felt without quite knowing why. "Thank you, Jacques."

"Da!" A little girl's voice sounded from across the room.

His daughter's nanny could barely restrain the squirming three-year-old.

"You know your way out, Jacques," Ryan said. "I will see you again next week."

He walked across the vast room to greet his daughter. His knee-high boots clicked on the polished floor. Miss Peabody set down the wriggling ball of energy.

"I thought you would sleep the morning away." He swung his daughter into his arms, and, giggling, she flung her arms around his neck.

"She should not be allowed to sleep so late," Miss Peabody said.

Holding his hand against his daughter's baby-fine curls, he pressed his mouth against her hair. She smelled like sweet clover. "Has she eaten, yet?"

"No, sir. Boswell said you wished to take your meal with her."

"I wants to fish and ride my pony, Da."

Ryan looked over her head at the gray-haired nanny. "Was she coughing again last night?"

"No, sir. I left the door open between our rooms to make sure. It was my opinion that she should not have been allowed to play so long outside yesterday, sir," Miss Peabody said pointedly to the elderly man who stood like a military sentry at the door. "But Boswell seems to have a difference of opinion on that matter."

"Were you ill yesterday, poppet?"

"It hurted, Da."

Ryan surveyed her face. "What hurted?"

Mary Elizabeth held up a finger, the single digit revealing the sore where a splinter had been removed last week.

"Maybe I should throw that bad finger back where it came from," he said. "What do you think?"

"No." She laughed, her favorite word of late.

"We'll lunch outside." He glanced at Boswell, sure that his trusted valet of ten years would edify him with a list of complaints against Miss Peabody the moment they were alone. "Pack her fishing pole," he said, handing his daughter to him. "I wish to have a word with Miss Peabody."

"Yes, sir, Mr. Donally. I'll see that Amy dresses the tyke for an outing."

Mouth pursed, Miss Peabody remained behind. Ryan watched his daughter disappear around the corner. Still sleepy-eyed, she'd plopped a thumb in her rosebud mouth, her blond curls bouncing with Boswell's gait.

Ryan turned to the nanny he'd hired only two months ago because he was told she was the most sought after in London. "I was informed that Mary Elizabeth woke up last night crying. When I came home, her room was dark."

"She's almost four years old, sir—"

"I don't care if she's forty. It's not so much trouble to leave a light in her room."

The woman's chin lifted, but there was a noticeable set to her jaw. "She rarely wakes in the night when you are not here, sir."

Ryan didn't believe his daughter had nightmares because she wanted attention.

"Catering to her fears will only teach her to cry at night," Miss Peabody stated. "If you leave her alone, she will learn quickly enough—"

"I pay you salary enough to see that you're a nanny, not a heartless taskmaster. I warned you once before she's always to have a light on in her room."

"Mr. Donally," his butler interrupted. Carrying a packet, he stopped behind Peabody. "A courier from D&B arrived and brought this. She told me that it is your mail."

"She?" Ryan took the packet, turning it over in his hand.

"Yes, sir. She is in the salon awaiting you."

Ryan wondered who the hell Johnny or Stewart would send over on a Saturday? Women weren't couriers. He thought of

Mary Elizabeth waiting for him. "Pay her and send her on her way."

"I don't think she'll leave, sir." His butler's voice lowered discreetly. "She's not dressed like any courier. And she's . . . bossy."

"Jaysus." Ryan started to roll his eyes, aware that he was going to have to go downstairs.

The harsh rustle of taffeta betrayed Miss Peabody's intention to leave. Ryan turned, abruptly stopping her with a look. "Is there anything else, sir?" she asked.

"I don't care who you are, Miss Peabody. If you want to stay in this household, don't question my authority again. Is that clear?"

Her mouth sagged open to speak, but she only nodded, as Ryan turned on his heel and left her standing alone in the corridor to contemplate her future as his employee.

Coming to a dead stop downstairs in the salon, Ryan gripped the towel around his neck. Still in his shirtsleeves, he was clothed improperly for guests. He did not expect to see Rachel and, in any case, her own unchaperoned appearance in his home made his lack of dress irrelevant.

She sat with her back straight on a blue-and-white-striped settee. She had not yet heard his approach, and he moved into the airy room. The crystal lamp on the table next to her chimed a musical cadence to the air stirred by his movement and, as her eyes fell on him standing in the doorway, she rose to her feet in a subtle rustle of fabric.

A long moment passed as they considered each other in silence.

"And after six days of hard work, he retires to the country castle and rests." She smiled nervously.

"I think the official day of rest is the seventh."

"Since when have you ever done anything the official way?"

He cocked a brow. Now that they had gotten the initial awkwardness out of the way, Ryan assessed her more thoroughly. His eyes slid down her body. The virginal severity of her high-necked white blouse contrasted with her copper hair; barely tamed in a braid that ran down her back and touched her bottom. She looked primly spinsterish and free from the nonsense frills and frippery that the women he seemed to be acquainted with embraced in fashion. No one would ever find Rachel Bailey wearing feathers or waxed fruit. She'd always liked that about herself.

She thought herself sensible.

Sensible like the hen in the fox's lair, forbidden to him all his life. After last night, his first instinct was to tell her to go away.

Yet he watched with a strange sort of possessive energy as her hazel eyes went over his belongings. Artwork lined the richly paneled walls to the high ceilings. "Everything is still as beautiful as I remember." She offered him a tentative smile.

He almost felt sorry for her—but not enough to put her out of her misery.

"Why do I get the feeling that you're following me around, Rache?"

"You've already shown that you aren't very good with apologies," she said, for lack of any articulate explanation to describe why she had thrown herself into his arms last night and kissed him. "I wish I could tell you that I was drunk. I wish I *had* been drunk."

"Because you did something spontaneous? Out of character?"

"It was an accident. I don't know why I kissed you. I apologize, and I do hope that you will try to be some sort of a gentleman and allow me to forget it ever happened. I promise, it won't happen again. Ever. Unless, maybe, I've overimbibed."

Cocking a brow, he didn't know if he should feel relieved or insulted. He leisurely dropped his gaze to her mouth before leaning into the doorway, at once suspicious. He couldn't remember a moment in his life that she'd ever apologized to him for anything, and now he'd received two formal apologies in as many days. He had to give her credit for brass, though, showing up here today, all alone.

But Rachel never did anything without a reason. "I thought you'd be on your way back to Ireland by now."

She peered around him and up the stairs. "I hope I'm not intruding."

He took in the satchel she carried. "And I'll wager your annuity that you know well enough you're disturbing me. How did you get out here?"

"The train takes a half hour from London. Once at the station, I hired someone from the livery to bring me. I actually came for two reasons," she forged onward.

"Couldn't you have waited until Monday at the office?"

Her full mouth tilted at the corners. "Do you lop off the head of trespassers then?"

"I'm partial to red hair. If you're nice, I could spare you."

"*How* nice?"

His gaze dipping to her lips, he considered telling her that she asked a dangerous question. Then, looking away, he wondered what the hell he was thinking?

The butler appeared and saved him from a response. "Would the miss care for coffee or sherbet, Mr. Donally?"

"Have you eaten lunch?" Ryan politely inquired. "You've come a long way to visit me. The least I can do is feed you before I send you back."

"Do make an exception today. Won't you?" She sighed, all pretense gone. "I really do need to talk to you."

He could have. He'd made exceptions before when people had come here with demands on his time, but there was something about Rachel being in this house, close to him, playing nice. If they talked business, they'd argue, and, as he stood looking at her framed by the feminine walls in what used to be Kathleen's salon, as soft and pretty as any Monet subject, he discovered that he didn't want to spend this time arguing.

"What is your second reason for coming out here?" he asked.

"I wish to see Mary Elizabeth."

"You want to see my daughter?"

"Don't sound so surprised. I'm not as indifferent as you think I am, Ryan." She turned the satchel and flipped open the lid when he didn't reply. Withdrawing a worn photograph with frayed corners, she held it out to him.

It was a picture of Mary Elizabeth holding a rabbit. Ryan moved into the room and slid it from her hand. The photograph had been taken at a family gathering two years ago; he couldn't even remember the occasion. But he was surprised Rachel carried a memento of that occasion.

"Who sent you this?"

"Brianna." Rachel drew a tight breath and bent over the satchel, sounding remarkably discombobulated for a woman always so self-assured. "I have another."

He watched her ruffle through her satchel. Miss Organization was nervous as hell. His gaze touched the braid down her back. The scent of spiced apples wafted off her as if someone had dumped an apple pie on her head, and he suddenly wondered how any woman would want to smell like something someone should eat. He was still looking at her, trying to answer that question, when she glanced up and caught him staring.

Her expression froze. Then narrowed guardedly, as if she'd captured him committing some sin. His entire life, she always had a way of making him feel like a naughty altar boy who had just peeked up someone's dress.

"How are your skills at fishing?" he asked.

"Now, that all depends on what I am fishing for?"

"Fish." A slow smile tilted the corners of his mouth. "The kind that devours helpless creatures wrapped around hooks and dangled mercilessly in the water."

"The way you devour your competition?"

A little girl's voice sounded from up the stairs, and Ryan turned. He jogged up the staircase. His daughter, her hand grabbing each spindle in her careful descent, reached for him, and was in his arms when he turned to look back down at Rachel.

"Mary Elizabeth plans on catching dinner for tonight. Don't you, Mouse?"

"I likes to fish." His daughter beamed. "And ride my pony."

Ryan watched Rachel's eyes shift from his face to Mary Elizabeth's.

"This is what I do on Saturdays," he said, descending the stairs one foot at a time until he stood in front of her. "Meet your goddaughter. Say hello, Mary Elizabeth."

Mary Elizabeth plopped a thumb between her rosebud lips. Ryan's mouth touched her temple, but his eyes remained on Rachel. "How old are you going to be soon, Mouse?" he asked his daughter, as he considered Rachel's apprehension.

His daughter held up four digits. "This many." She demonstrated.

Rachel could not have been more nervous.

Children were a foreign element in her life. Like lacy clothes and dainty bonnets.

And this particular child belonged to Ryan.

"She has your eyelashes," Rachel breathed.

"My eyelashes?" he laughed.

"I was always the first to admit you should have been born a girl."

"Did you hear that, Mouse?"

Mary Elizabeth giggled and buried her face against his shoulder.

"She's . . . truly beautiful, Ryan."

He was looking at her from over his daughter's downy head. "If you catch a fish, she'll probably be impressed enough to talk to you."

"Lord." Rachel laughed. "It's been years since I've held a rod in my hands."

"Indeed?"

Heat spilled into her cheeks. Flustered but determined to maintain the fragile peace they'd created, she merely smiled. "But then my skills were never on your expert level, Ryan Donally."

"Then you do have skills?"

Ryan made no move, except to touch her with eyes that looked to have the power to delve into her thoughts and know her innermost secrets. Eyes that always had the power to make her burn. "It's been a long time since I've played . . . at anything."

"What do you say, Mouse?" He turned a casually wicked eye from her to his daughter. "Should we rescue her from her life of toil?"

Rachel sighed. More likely, she needed to be rescued from them, she realized.

Chapter 3

"There's another one!" Mary Elizabeth squealed from her place on the loamy bank, but whatever it was she saw, shot up the stream when a rock splashed in the water.

"Maybe you shouldn't throw rocks at them," Rachel suggested.

"I wants the black one!"

Ryan leaned against a tree at the edge of the glade, a piece of straw between his lips, and watched Rachel tread barefoot in ankle-deep water, her copper skirts hiked to her knees and tucked in at her waist. "I think that one is already swimming for the ocean," she said, dangling a hook and worm in the water before casting the line beyond the rocks.

That afternoon, he'd almost felt sorry for Rachel when Mary Elizabeth convinced her that all the big fish were hiding in the middle of the stream—until she'd stripped off her shoes, stockings, and her bloody petticoats, and waded into the stream.

Ryan admired tenacity.

To a point.

A flash of leg showed beneath her skirts. Folding his arms, he drew in a breath and looked up at the sky, needing to find solace. Anything. She'd been inordinately cooperative and nice all afternoon.

And he'd been watching her frolic with his daughter like some bloody wood nymph. Rachel, who had always been the prim and proper, Miss Holier-Than-Thou, the closet opera singer, the girl who had thrown his toy soldiers into a hot kiln and melted them all. She'd been obnoxious or pretty, depending on his mood or hers—but he could always count on her to be nice when she wanted something from him. Like the time she'd brought him crumpets and weaseled his favorite goldfish from him.

His gaze ranged across this secluded world he owned. A river meandered peacefully through the parkland surrounding his estate. Two hundred acres of parkland surrounded his Georgian manor house. Another ten thousand acres spilled out over sheep and cow pastures. He owned three houses in England, including the one he'd just purchased in Bristol. He came home to this one because this was where he found his peace. Apart from contracts and business.

Eight years ago, he took over the board of directors at D&B. But the greatest extent of his wealth came from his investments in the iron-ore industry. He had always managed to accomplish the impossible, including the unfriendly acquisition of Ore Industries just a year ago, the most publicized of his moves in the last few years. Few people knew that Lord Devonshire had been his target. Devonshire, who had sat at the head of that board like a bloody king, who thought no one could touch him.

To stop his financial bleeding, Devonshire had negotiated a betrothal between his ward, as high-society as one could get and still breathe the air, and the Irishman who had taken Ore Industries out from beneath him.

Indeed, a betrothal with Lady Gwyneth Abbot offered something far more valuable to his future than merely a wife. Ryan wasn't marrying Lady Gwyneth for love. He'd buried that part of his soul with his wife almost four years ago.

At least he'd thought so until Rachel's declaration last night at the ball.

Except, he didn't want her here.

He didn't want to be ten years old again or sixteen or twenty-two, when he would look at her and wonder what it would feel like to shove his hands up her skirt. He didn't want to be that young again and bloody vulnerable, for he had lived too long giving no quarter. He had relied too often these past years on the fight in or out of the boardroom of his life to settle differences. He was too old, and it was too late to change now—even if he had wished to do so, which he didn't. He wanted Rachel to go back to Ireland.

"Mr. Donally." One of his servants approached.

Ryan pushed off the tree to take the message she delivered, then squinted looking toward the house. His solicitor stood on the terrace. "Don't go too far, Amy," he said, tossing the straw to the ground, "in case Miss Bailey should be in need of help."

"Yes, sir." She dipped into a brief curtsy.

For once, Ryan was relieved to forsake pleasure for business.

Flashes of blue appeared above the sprawl of tree limbs as a puff of wind carried the overhead cloud bank south. Rachel watched a pair of robins dart between banks of honeysuckle that seemed to be growing everywhere. Earlier a servant had approached and given Ryan a message.

"I eated a worm once," Mary Elizabeth said.

Rachel looked down at the little girl. They sat cross-legged and barefoot on the comforter, a meal of chicken sitting between them. "What did you say?"

"Fish eats worms. Birds eats worms." She shrugged as if it were perfectly natural to eat what birds and fish ate.

Rachel wondered what a sane adult might say to that.

"Was it any good?"

She squinched her face. "I likes custard better," she confided, and, on another melodramatic sigh, added, "Uncle Christopher gots a dog. Cousin Richard and Daniel gots three cats. But the cat eated Chrissy's bird, so Uncle Johnny buyed Chrissy another one. She's this many." Mary Elizabeth held up four fingers. "When I'm four I wants a puppy, but Da says no puppies cause puppies make too much noise and piddle on the floor."

Mary Elizabeth wore a starched white pinafore over a pink dress that had not fared well on the muddy bank. Rachel helped her remove it. "I see."

The subject moved quickly to guinea pigs, squirrels, mice, and ponies, which she couldn't ride yet because her da said she was too small. While she talked on and on about pets, Rachel studied her upturned face. Her emotions grabbed and tightened.

She understood the solitude. Certainly, she understood the loneliness.

Rachel had been an only child until Kathleen had come to live at the house. Her only pet had been a goldfish that Ryan had given her. She'd adored that silly fish as if it could really talk to her. They'd spent many a night staring at each other through the glass, and before the fish had died, she was sure it knew every detail of her life.

"Are you my fairy godmother?"

"I am your godmother."

Mary Elizabeth touched her braid. "It's all right," Rachel said, when the little girl pulled her hand away from her hair as if caught doing something wrong.

They both stared at each other.

Rachel spied Ryan in the distance talking to a man. Behind him, his monolithic stone house stood like an unerring tribute to wealth and power against the bright colors of the fading day. A beacon of prosperity. His life was completely separate from hers on so many levels that her humiliating scene last night only made her feel all the more foolish.

Later, Mary Elizabeth fell asleep. For a long time, Rachel stared down at the little girl, her hand tucked beneath her cheek, wondering how one child could retain so much energy and look so peaceful in repose. With an indrawn breath, Rachel was thankful she could relax without fear that she'd turn her head and lose Ryan's daughter. She'd been worried all afternoon that Mary Elizabeth would fall into the stream or scrape her knee or hit her head.

The sun laid breezy, patchwork shadows over the ground. Ryan had been gone nearly an hour, and, irritated by his absence, she stood and walked to the stream.

She dug her hand in the bait tin and retrieved another worm, eyeing the plump brown body with disgust. Rachel was adventurous, but not so much that she'd ever eat a worm. After easing herself into the water, she carefully worked her way over the rocks to where the stream was deeper. She'd removed her stockings and petticoats the first time she'd slipped and fallen that afternoon. She had never been a fisherman and had made a mistake taking lessons from a three-year-old who could probably fish as well as she could fly. Fish had scattered in the wake of Mary Elizabeth's enthusiasm. But Rachel didn't want to quit the day a failure, so began casting her line. She'd learned late in life to swim but had never been entirely comfortable with heights and water, which was strange since both components were such a big part of her job, and she was normally quite fearless.

She would have to be to endure Ryan the way she did. He'd been content to sit back and watch her all afternoon, floundering in unfamiliar territory with his daughter. Probably laughing, she thought. Then remembering how he'd held his daughter that afternoon on the stairs, some of her ire departed. She'd never imagined him a father.

There were two sides to Ryan Donally, she realized, reeling in the line. The father part of him was in essence an echo of the boy she'd grown up with. The other side of him was the man she would have to deal with when she spoke to him about her project. The man she'd faced last night at the ball.

A twig snapped.

A tall shadow fell over her. She turned and found herself looking into Ryan's eyes. He stood on the stream bank above her. For a space of time, neither spoke.

"I didn't mean to be gone so long," he said.

Rather than be benevolent in the face of his abandonment, Rachel decided to use it to her advantage. "I thought you didn't perform acts of business on the weekends."

Ryan hunched on the balls of his feet in front of her and rested one elbow on a knee. His boots creaked. "I have a dinner engagement tonight." His mouth smiled. "My playtime is over. And so is yours."

"Mine?" She flushed at his blatant dismissal. "You have a lot of nerve leaving—"

He set a finger against his lips. "How long has Mary Elizabeth been asleep?"

"Thirty minutes." Turning, she worked on reeling in the line, her head bowed over the pole, her shoulders stiff.

Ryan's gaze remained on her back.

He'd been watching her for the good part of the last ten minutes, and his gaze lingered where her braid had unraveled in a curly mass down her back. The light had turned her hair into a disheveled sunburst around her shoulders, and she looked wanton framed against the sky, out of place in his thoughts.

"Are there really fish in this stream big enough to eat?" he heard her ask.

"I don't know," he said, peering at her standing in the water. "I've never caught any."

Water sloshed as she approached him on the bank. "Do you mean to say I've been at this all afternoon, and there are no fish to catch?"

"That's one of your better qualities, Rache." He smiled. "You're persistent."

"Persistent?" A worm smacked him in the chest. In a flash, she'd clearly forgotten she'd been having fun until five minutes ago. "Move out of my way."

His brow cocked when it looked as if she might throw something else at him.

"You are *such* an arrogant ass sometimes, Ryan."

"Is that right?"

"You left me with a rambunctious three-year-old for an entire hour. Something could have happened! What if she'd fallen in the stream?"

"Rache?" With his forearms resting against his thighs, his shoulders pulling at the fine lawn of his shirt, he leaned forward. "Were you afraid?"

"Of course, I wasn't afraid," she scoffed. "But it's freezing in this water." Holding the pole in one hand, she struggled to get out of the stream. "I can no longer feel my toes."

Ryan peered into the stream at her bare feet. Her skirt was wet up to her knees, and somehow his eyes continued to slide upward. She'd removed her waistcoat. He could see the swell of her breasts beneath her damp blouse. A tiny bow on her chemise flirted with his senses. She was dressed like a spinster and still somehow managed to remind him of his favorite vice. He raised his gaze and found her watching him with narrowed eyes.

Hell, with a body like hers she ought to have more sense

than to parade herself half-naked in front of him, he thought, his lips curving into a slow smile that wasn't nearly so polite anymore. "It would be a shame to lose your toes," he agreed, without moving out of her way so she could climb out of the stream.

"Get out of my way."

"Or what?"

She threw a handful of grass and dirt at him. "Or you'll need a long, hot bath."

He dodged another handful of dirt and caught her wrist. Their eyes grabbed and held. If she had contemplated another unorthodox use of the dirt in her hand, she clearly thought better of it, for there was something in his gaze that convinced her he was capable of retaliation. "Do you want to tell me what is going on with you?" he demanded.

"At the moment, I don't like you very much, Ryan Donally." She jerked away, and he fell forward, barely catching himself to avoid tumbling into the water.

"Dammit, Rachel." He came to his feet, brushing off his hands. "I'm not really fond of you too much at the moment either."

"You invite me to fish in a stream that has no fish. Then leave on business when you tell me you don't do business on Saturdays. Now you have a dinner engagement and *your* playtime is over? I should offer you and Miss Snowflake my heartiest congratulations."

She ruined the moment by attempting to climb out of the stream and slipping.

Hands on his hips, Ryan stood on the bank and watched her struggle. The more things changed, the more they stayed the same, he realized as he remembered one of Memaw's many pearls of wisdom picked up from some witty philosopher she was fond of quoting. "Would you like some help?" he politely inquired after she'd ruined her skirt.

Her eyes nearly green behind a fringe of dark lashes, and with an inherent suspicion of his motives bred from their years of childhood war games, she straightened.

Smiling to himself, he knew there had been times in her life when he'd been nice to her, and still things inevitably went wrong, like when he was standing knee deep in the pond behind her house inviting her to swim. She'd walked into the water and stepped into a hole. She'd accused him of nearly drowning her when he'd fished her out, but he was damned if she didn't learn to swim before the week ended.

That memory seized his thoughts. "I won't drop you, Rache," he said.

She glared. "No thank you."

"You're ruining your skirt."

"I can manage on my own."

Ryan lowered his hand, but there was nothing indifferent about the quiet tone in his voice as he lifted his daughter in his arms. "Yes, I believe you can, Rache."

Performance had always been elemental in the Bailey household. Her father had been a domineering son of a bitch. Rachel had learned early to put on her own shoes, to dress herself, and never need anyone. Capability was her middle name.

Indeed, she could manage to get herself out of the damn stream.

Wrapping her hair into a bun, Rachel watched her clothes taken away to be cleaned and pressed. Ruined, she was sure, because of Ryan. Left only with her chemise and a robe that nearly dragged to the floor, she departed her lofty chambers.

It was a nuisance. A damned nuisance to have to discuss business with him at all, much less without benefit of her clothes. In a spasm of impatience, Rachel flicked at the pyramid of fruit that had been set on the table, especially when he seemed quite ready for her to be on her way back to London.

She found him a few moments later, leaving the nursery. He stopped in his tracks when he saw her. His eyes narrowed as he noted her attire. Holding her satchel beneath one arm, she snapped the belt tighter around her waist, daring him to say something rude. Neither of them had ever been modest around the other, and she didn't know why her appearance seemed so off-putting. The robe covered her completely. She even wore slippers that covered her bare feet.

"Is she asleep?" Rachel looked past him to the room he'd just exited.

"She's supping," he said. "You're welcome to say your good-byes if you're brave enough to venture in there all alone."

Folding her arms around her satchel, she observed him coolly. "Truly even you weren't born with the gift of father-hood. If you can learn, so can I."

"Are you saying you want to learn to be her father?"

His tall calf-hugging boots gave him the advantage of an-other inch of height, and she tilted back her head, refusing to fall victim to his poor humor. "I'm saying that my ineptness comes from inexperience."

"You aren't inept, Rache." He strolled past, leaving her to stare at his back.

"What is that supposed to mean?" Rachel followed his long-legged stride.

A white shirt was tucked inside the black trousers he still wore from that afternoon. "It means that you did all right to-day, Rache. I was proud. Honestly . . ." He held up his hand, their mutual signal denoting absolute truthfulness on threat of death.

Rachel stared at his raised palm, wondering if he even realized the ease in which he'd slipped into their old habits. Then, before she could say something nice, he said, "I've asked Boswell to bring up your clothes the moment they are dry and pressed."

"And if they aren't reparable?"

His eyes slid over her, and she felt more of their camaraderie slide away with that gaze. "Then I hope you have a cloak to hide the mud stains." He turned to the looking glass in the hallway and examined his face as if to determine whether he might need a shave. "If you wear my robe outside, people will misconstrue what we've been doing today."

"No doubt that is a common occurrence for you, Ryan."

He scraped a hand across his jaw. "You read too much gossip, Rache."

"Are you saying all that gossip isn't true?" she couldn't resist asking. "What about that Italian countess"—she wagged her hand in an airy arc—"last year while you were in Venice?"

Ryan shifted his gaze from his reflection to look at her with eyes the color of midnight. An amused concession touched her in that glance and affected her so unexpectedly her stomach fluttered. "Now, that was true." His fingers plucking at the buttons on his shirt, he strolled into the adjoining room.

She checked herself with an effort, aware that it was she who was being nosy. She was the one who had fallen in the mud. She was the one who had something important to discuss. Struggling to repair her composure, she followed him. "We need to talk," she said to the silence, as she realized he'd entered the adjoining dressing room. She peered around her at the masculine quarters, a private study. The ceiling was high. Bottle green velvet curtains matched the upholstered chairs. Bookcases lined the back wall behind the mahogany desk. Potted plants in brass receivers thrived in all corners.

Braving the next few moments, she withdrew her project folder from her satchel. "Will you look at my proposal for the levee project I brought with me from Ireland?"

He returned to the doorway with a towel in his hand. His hair was damp. For a long time, he said nothing. "D&B has a feasibility team for that, Rache."

"*I* have a feasibility team," she said with an emphasis on I. "Besides, this job is in David's parish," she hedged. "I'm not waiting months for some committee to reevaluate the report my people have already done."

"Did my brother put you up to this?"

"He didn't put me up to anything. But it's solely because of him that D&B receives the support that we do." She held the project report in her hand, but Ryan didn't take it. A lock of hair fell over his forehead. "It's a simple project, Ryan."

Despite his unwillingness, he took the report and thumbed through the papers. The clock behind her ticked away the seconds. She studied her silk sleeve. Pretended interest in the carpet.

"Allan Marrow's name isn't on this report," he finally said. "Who is the senior engineer in charge of this project?"

"I am."

His mouth flattened, and he dropped the folder on the chair beside the door. "So, you think by going directly through me you can avoid the usual formalities in committee? For instance, the fact that you are heading the project will be revealed. You want this consideration by virtue . . . of what, Rache? You need me for once, so now you're here in London playing nice? Is that what your performance was about last night? Today—?"

"No." Her stomach lurched sickeningly. "It's not like that, Ryan."

"Then why don't you explain it more clearly. Because I'm

a little mystified. You're not supposed to be heading projects. Any projects. Your job in Ireland is to oversee the fiscal accounting of that division. You are not supposed to be working in the field. That was our agreement when I gave you the division."

"If I can do the job—"

"Jaysus, Rachel." Pulling his shirttail from his trousers, he turned into the dressing room. "You've been in this business long enough to know the problems. Hell, you understood the problems when you spent years auditing classes to become something you knew could not sell in this industry. I may as well hand the competition the key to our doors. The broadsheets will tear you to pieces, Rache."

Gripping her satchel, she drew a deep breath. "Why?"

"Because the public loves a good scandal."

"Ada Lovelace, Lord Byron's daughter and an eventual countess, was a famous mathematician. She once worked on a calculating machine."

"Does it work?" Ryan returned to the entryway. "I'd like to own one."

She ran her tongue over her lips. "Women are in every industry. Lady Somilier is a civil engineer who worked on a water irrigation system in South Africa with her husband."

His shirt hanging open, Ryan braced both palms high on the doorframe. "Is that right?"

"Which brings me to my final point," she said. "I've allowed you to make business decisions for this company on my behalf quite long enough. It's time I take my official place on the board. I want my proxy back from you." She lifted her chin, well primed to embark on this final crusade. "It's time I took on a bigger stake in the running of this business. I believe I *do* own a large percent of this company."

He threw out his hands and turned. "Thank you for reminding me."

She padded irately into the dressing room, following him. "I have just as much right to be part of the decision-making process as you or Johnny. More so because my father was the original founder of this company."

"Really?" He balanced himself against the wall as he thrust his foot into the bootjack "And all these years I thought it had been a joint venture between your father and mine." He shoved the second boot into the jack. His shirt outlined his shoulders. "How long will you remain in London acquainting yourself with this part of the company?"

She glared at him as he sat and removed his socks. "Long enough for you to approve my levee project with my name as the lead engineer. A week? Two weeks? How long do you want me here?"

His eyes narrowed. Rachel knew Ryan hadn't made it to the top of his form because he was soft. She knew the incredible speed with which he could mobilize forces and have her removed from her position in the company. Period. He knew how to dismantle corporations. In the last eight years he'd done it a hundred times to his competition or to those affiliates that did not make a profit. He would do it with her if he learned how involved on the engineering side of the business she secretly was. Or how much financial trouble the division in Dublin had fallen into this past year.

"Are you trying to complicate my life on purpose?" His voice sharpened with the accusation. "You're twenty-nine years old, with pangs of mortality knocking at your back door, so you've decided to return to my doorstep and remind me what a complete—"

"Don't you dare insult me, Ryan Donally."

"Let me tell you a little secret that I'm sure you don't remember since you chose not to be around at the time." He threw his shirt on the floor. "But I've already seen twenty-nine. Two years ago, in fact, and, trust me, you'll survive this crisis." He had the gall to laugh at her, but his eyes remained sober. "Just like you always do."

She did not want to dive into his mind any more than she'd already tried to do since her arrival in London. "You are a man who has done and always will do and say as you please. You should have been born a king. At the very least, your Napoleonic qualities make you an excellent dictator worthy of a medal."

"Thank you, Rache." He bowed at the waist. "I believe that I'll take that as a compliment coming from your beautiful lips."

"Get out!" she demanded.

Ryan's eyes swept downward to where the robe molded itself against the curves of her bosom, his ire quickly surmounted by amusement. "And where, madam, do you intend that I should go?"

Rachel lowered her arm. And opened her jaw, ready to crawl into the floorboards.

Except shock had frozen her. Her stunned gaze traveled past his abdomen, up the width of chest and tanned column of his throat. Reason fled to the back of her brain. Her gaze reached the bow of his mouth and higher, to his eyes. The shock was abrupt. They stared at each other beneath the white heat of anger, their gazes locked, his eyes so dark they were nearly black behind the thick fringe of his lashes.

Then he moved and she was suddenly pinned to the wall, his hands on either side of her head as he looked down into her face. And Rachel felt a jolt of arousal, a shock of crystal-perfect awareness of him so pervasive she could not breathe.

"*Now* what do we do?" His expression slipped behind the impervious mask of the carefree sinner Rachel knew so well and hated.

"I haven't spent the last few years working as hard as I have simply to hide any longer because you find a woman on the board inconvenient." Her words came out breathless and heated. "I'm sure I will be seeing you again soon enough, Ryan."

"Tell me"—he leaned his nose toward her hair—"are you sure that's safe? All alone in the same room with you smelling like something I want to eat?"

"Oh!" Her awareness of him, of his words slammed against the hedonistic desire to scrape her palms over his chest. "You are a bully, Ryan Donally." She dipped beneath his arm. "And you aren't getting rid of me that easily. It's time that you learned to share."

Ryan remained with his palms pressed against the wall and listened to the hurried rustle of her robe. The door slammed. Knocking his forehead against the wall three times, he swore as he attempted to rein in one muscle in particular.

Only Rachel was capable of frustrating him to the point of violence. Ryan folded his arms and, turning, leaned his back against the wall. Only Rachel could make the scent of apples and cinnamon synonymous with sin. Only Rachel could arouse his temper to the point of desertion.

Ryan realized the monstrous incongruity of his sudden surge of lust and anger—which at the moment felt the same—after years of emotional self-control. The least he could have been able to accomplish with his monumental will and determination was last more than twenty-four hours before he wanted to shove his tongue into Rachel's mouth.

"Would you like a brandy, sir?" Boswell calmly inquired from the doorway.

He peered at his trusted, nearsighted valet and frowned. "See that Miss Bailey doesn't get a notion to walk back to London, until *after* she's dressed."

But the order was no more than an effort at self-preservation. He would send her back naked if it meant getting her out from beneath his roof tonight.

Chapter 4

❝Are you sure Mr. Donally knows I spent the night?"
Rachel asked, as Boswell set a coffee tray on the table the next morning when she arrived downstairs for breakfast.

"Yes, mum. He was informed when he returned home."

"He is here?"

"He returned just before dawn, mum." There was a cheerfulness in his voice that disconcerted her. "He was quite put off by it all, mum."

She was sure that her overnight presence in this household violated every tenet of moral etiquette, but it wasn't as if she and Ryan were lovers, though she had seen him naked once a long time ago. And he'd seen her in a worse state of dishabille than the heavy robe she'd worn in his room last night. She'd never been an outwardly prissy type anyway. She'd rarely worn a real dress until she was well into her middle teen years.

"He doesn't like me very much, Boswell."

"Quite the opposite, Miss Bailey," he reassured her. "I've never seen him so angry."

Rachel flushed, and said, "And this is a positive sign?"

"Mr. Donally doesn't get angry, mum."

Rachel laughed. Of course he got angry. He'd always been hot-tempered around her. Shrugging aside Boswell's logic, Rachel stirred cream in her coffee and brought the cup to her lips. Mary Elizabeth was on her morning constitutional with Miss Peabody. They would be back in an hour. Rachel had watched her briefly from her window that morning.

Taking a deep breath, she inhaled more than coffee aroma and looked at the fresh spray of flowers adorning each end of the polished table and three console tables between the glass doors that looked outside. A massive sideboard sat against the wall. "Why doesn't Mr. Donally just stay at his house in London?" Rachel asked.

"He usually does when he remains in the city for more than a few nights, mum. But for now he has more privacy here for himself and his daughter."

Rachel idly flipped through the newspaper Boswell had brought her. A courier had delivered it from the train station earlier. Beyond the window, the early-morning sky was a crisp, bright blue. At home, she was always up before dawn. She had already been awake for three hours.

Last week, she had kissed Memaw good-bye and made her way to London on the Holyhead ferry. She had not stepped foot in England in four years. This morning, Boswell had found her a pair of boy's trousers, shirt, and boots. She saddled one of Ryan's fancy thoroughbreds and rode to the chapel where Kathleen was buried.

Now she was eating in Ryan's fine dining room on beautiful china; yet, the glittering morning held nothing that spoke of home or familiar things. She could not sit there forever thinking useless thoughts, staring at the sky beyond the windows, and wondering where Ryan had gone last night. Her clothes had taken too long to dry. The last train to London had departed the station at seven, so she'd been left with no choice but to spend the night. She wasn't a complete stranger there. She had visited Kathleen three times after she'd been married and Ryan had been away. Boswell had put her into the blue room where she'd stayed before.

"The newspapers aren't always kind toward Mr. Donally," Rachel said, folding the broadsheet and shoving it away.

"No, mum."

Not that he deserved kindness, she thought, having read the financials on a daily basis for years. Ryan raided companies for profit. He would take them over, break them up, and sell off their weaker assets. His contacts extended across the Atlantic as well as the Continent. The London *Times* had once accused D&B's charismatic chairman of taking his corporate genius and pillaging the less fortunate for profit. The British *Globe* called him a vulture. *Vanity Fair* labeled him one of the most eligible men in Great Britain.

But to her he was still just an arrogant Irish nincompoop.

Finally, she finished breakfast. Ryan was still asleep. Annoyed that he could sleep so late when her entire future remained uncertain, she paced in her room before again leaving the chambers. She explored the house, opening doors and looking inside the rooms. At the end of the corridor she found a glass studio. Three pairs of French windows opened from the studio to the terrace. A summer breeze filled the room. Fencing gear lined the wall in braces and brackets. She stepped into the room. David had taught her to fence years ago, and she practiced regularly. But nothing she had in her possession compared to the splendors she found in this room.

Rachel lifted a shiny foil from its brace on the wall. Felt the steel in her hand and tested its weight. She stood in momentary riposte, foil extended. She feinted and lunged at imaginary targets, slashing the air with each step backward and forward. Sunlight glinted off the thin edge of steel, and she flicked at the protective knob at the end. There were other ways to slay the dragon that was Ryan Donally, she decided, as an idea popped into her head.

Smiling to herself, Rachel grabbed a second foil, walked out of the room, down the long corridor, and stopped in front of Ryan's door. Holding her ear to the solid wood, she listened for noise. He didn't sound awake. No one was moving inside.

Rachel knocked. When she heard no response, she carefully opened the door. Sheer draperies billowed gently, and Rachel could see the lake behind his house. Honeysuckle filtered through the other essence Rachel breathed, leaving no doubt in her mind the masculine inhabitant of these chambers. She moved farther into the room.

A kneeling bronze Venus sat on one of the console tables that flanked each side of the four-poster tester bed. Ryan lay on his stomach, his head resting on one arm pillowed beneath his cheek. His back was bare to the waist where the sheet had twisted around his hips. His shoulders were wide. His muscles were defined in corded delineations that crossed his upper arms and back, unmarked, save for the scar slashed across one defined biceps—a wound he'd received when he was younger, in a fight against the local village thugs who made some comment about the Irish.

Even in sleep, Ryan's body emanated strength, a contrast to his peaceful repose. His lashes looked like smudges against the flesh. His jaw and cheeks were dark with the beginning of a beard. The last time she had seen Ryan in any state of undress, he had been swimming with his brothers in the pond behind his house. He had been fifteen. Gazing at him now, she felt a rush of heat in her face. But she was in no mood to drink him into her senses or her memory when he was the complete cause of her misery.

"If you look any harder, Rache, I don't think you'll like

what you find." His eyes were open, and he was looking at her from beneath the careless toss of his bangs. Not that she blamed him for his anger. She had no business in his private chambers.

He pushed himself up on one elbow, his dark hair disheveled and in his eyes. As if he noticed her attire for the first time, one brow shot up his forehead. His gaze dropped to her mouth. "Have you been drinking?" he demanded.

"Truly, Ryan." With only one look into those coffee-colored eyes, he made her feel like a blushing virgin, a love-struck ninny, and lush all rolled into one. When she was neither a ninny or a virgin. "I've seen you undressed before."

"That was a hell of a long time ago. And I was bloody swimming in ice water."

"What difference does that make?"

His amused gaze slid over her face and down her boy's shirt. "If I told you, you would only slap me."

"Then tell me, won't you?"

He flopped on his back and scraped a palm over his jaw. He was laughing, she realized, gaping at him. He opened one eye as if it hurt to look at her. She'd shocked him. She'd never shocked him before, and she watched him, the two fencing foils in her hand lowered to her side. The sheet barely covered his lap, drawing her eyes downward to his hard belly. He was so beautiful, unquestionably male—more potently sexual than she was used to dealing with in those men who surrounded her in her day-to-day life. More than she remembered in him. The smattering of hair on his chest tapered to a dark line down his abdomen to disappear beneath the covers that covered the lean span of his hips. No part of him was lacking.

He was looking at her hard when she finally raised her gaze. Narrowing his eyes, he seemed to penetrate the very fabric of her soul to scorch her heart, the sensation stunning her because it was not something she could control, and it heightened the sense of danger he aroused in her, reminding her of her own survival.

They had no future, not in the sense she'd thought she'd wanted when she arrived in London. Ryan didn't love her. She suspected he could be every bit as ruthless with her when it came to his personal and professional life as gossip implied.

Yet, strangely Rachel understood Ryan's drive to marry above his station, had always understood him since they'd been children. The Irish were not welcome into a society that held to such staunch elite segregation of cultures and faith. Ryan had battled the establishment his entire life.

In return for Ryan's wealth, Lady Gwyneth would give his daughter something that he, with all of his riches, could not, she thought with the crystal-clear knowledge that she could never offer Ryan what he so single-mindedly sought.

A true place in society.

No one would ever shun Mary Elizabeth or scorn her because she was the wrong religion or a descendant of Celtic *primitives*. She would be welcomed to society and someone's home, never suffering the perfidy society inflicts on those who live beyond the confines set by the elite. Everything that Ryan worked for in his life was within his grasp.

Indeed, she and Ryan had both set about conquering the world to the exclusion of all else. Today's fight only lent more importance to her own quest, especially now. For when she left London this time, D&B would be all that she had left.

"Have you invaded my chambers to end your misery, Rache? Or mine?" he finally asked, a warning surely aimed at the look he'd glimpsed in her eyes. "I should warn you, the blade is blunted."

She waggled the end of one foil in front of his nose. It was an effort not to smack him. "If I win, you send my report through the committee for funding, and my name goes on it as chief engineer."

"Is that right?"

"Are you afraid you might lose?"

"Hardly," he scoffed, awake and fully aware of her presence. He raised his brows. "Can't this wait?"

"This is important to me, Ryan."

"*Sleep* is important to me."

"It's already well into the day. The sun has been up for over three hours."

"Jaysus." He flung off the sheets.

Rachel retreated an alarmed step, expecting him to appear naked beneath. He wasn't. Not completely. He wore loose-fitting silken pajamas that clung to his hips. Padding past her across the chamber, he walked into the dressing room. "When this is over, promise me you'll leave London and go back to Ireland, Rachel."

"When I win you'll accept me as an equal in this company."

She could hear the splash of water, drawers opening and slamming shut. She set her hand on the back of a high-backed chair where his shirt lay discarded from last night. The masculine trace of his familiar cologne tugged at her senses—as well as something subtly more invasive. Expensive French perfume.

"I can't wait for this." Ryan returned to the doorway wearing black pants tucked into tall boots and finishing the last of the buttons on his shirt. "You must have faith in your instructor."

"I have all the faith on my side. He's a priest, Ryan," she said, tossing him a foil, which he snatched easily out of the air. She would personally skewer him. "Bare feet and in the grass. First strike wins."

"Why bare feet?" Ryan asked when he and Rachel suited up in their protective leather vests and mesh helms.

Rachel stood in ankle-deep grass, her foil poised, her wild hair restrained at the back of her neck with a thong. Miss Pride and Prudent had always thrived beneath the unfortunate notion that she could do anything better than he could.

"Because it makes us even," she said behind the mask. "You're taller than I am."

"I'm still taller." Raising his foil, he stepped backward into his stance.

"Yes, but I learned to fence barefoot in the grass, the first time David stepped on my toes." She bent in the *en guarde* position, and he could see the flash of her white teeth behind the mesh. "My advantage on the grass in exchange for your height."

"Not bad, Rache."

They faced each other.

Eyes dazzling in the morning light, she smiled. "I hope you have your nib and standish ready."

Rachel lunged two steps, and he barely parried her attack. Behind the mask, his eyes narrowed. This time when his gaze held hers, there was something else in his eyes. It was a rare occurrence when Ryan underestimated anyone.

"On your guard, Ryan."

The *click-click* of foils marked the beginning of the contest, and Ryan countered her advance. He hadn't considered that she might actually *know* how to fence. Her timing was impeccable and her steps close to the ground. Her body moved like a dancer's, all grace wearing pants. The leather vest stretched across her breasts, drawing too much of his attention. They went around the garden once. He parried her riposte and stepped aside as she slashed her blade up against his, whirled like a ballerina, and landed with the foil extended, ready to impale him through the heart.

They were both breathing hard.

The morning was already hot, and he could see a bead of

sweat trickle down her collarbone. "Are we fencing or sword fighting, Rache?"

"Does it matter?" She tossed back her head. "Either way, you're going to lose the match."

They walked a slow circle. No flowery scent dripped from Rachel, he realized as he inhaled a trace of cinnamon off her hair. "I wouldn't want to end your hopes so quickly."

"I've noticed that about you. You're all heart and soul."

"Interesting that I look at you and think the same thing," he said, admiring the way her hips filled out her breeches. "Single-minded and mercenary as well. And I don't mean that as a compliment."

"What do you know about what it takes to survive, Ryan," she snapped, mounting a renewed attack. "It galls me that I have no recourse but to come to you."

He slapped down her foil. "At the ball, it didn't seem to gall you. Indeed, you appeared quite willing."

"Consider my offer retracted."

"I never considered it at all."

"Damn you, Ryan Donally." She slashed out at his foil.

"For someone who has been an intellectual snob her whole life, you're using a lot of profanity, Rache." He *tsked*.

It was one of his most prized attributes that he should be able to goad her into losing her dignity. She struck with force. Only this time he was prepared. He parried with a single swift blow. So far, all he had done was tease her. Some part of his mind remained impressed with her grit and will, even as she tried to defeat him, her pride roaring around her with all the vibrant colors of life that had always separated her from him. She crossed over with her foil and might have scored the victorious point had he not recognized the move. When they broke apart this time, their lungs heaved with the exertion.

Butterflies flitted over the neatly manicured flower beds.

Behind his mask, Ryan's attention moved lower down her body. He was conscious of a growing burn of sexual awareness between them, like a shot of whiskey running in his veins that had not yet reached his head.

He had not had a mistress in nearly five months, and he recognized that the heat from his bout of abstinence had thrust him into territory he had no intention of traveling. Not now. Not in the future. He had no time to be preoccupied and no desire for the entanglement Rachel's appearance back in his life presented. Hell, he didn't even want her there, but by every indication, this match wasn't going to end until she dropped.

"You ask the impossible, Rache," he said. "You want professional recognition in an industry that would never honor you publicly as an engineer. I can't toe the line and risk the reputation of the company by putting you in charge of any project."

"Naturally, you would say that, Ryan. When you think I'm going to beat you."

"Hell, Rache, you couldn't beat me on your best day. You could try for the rest of your life, and you still wouldn't come close."

"No wonder I hated you so much growing up!" She attacked.

"You're a liar." He lunged, and she evaded. "You hated me so much you followed me everywhere. I'd look around, and there'd you be, like a sticky shadow that clung to my every movement. You couldn't be one of the boys then. You can't be one now."

"I did not follow you anywhere."

"What is this fight really about, Rache?"

Their eyes remained locked, flaring with the collision between past and present.

"You've forgotten what it's like to have to work for something, Ryan."

"Do not tell me that, Rachel." She countered his riposte, but Ryan was finished worrying about hurting her. He was finished with this fight. "I have bloody worked for everything in my life. I've been bullied and bloodied by people who would as soon knock out my teeth as acknowledge my existence. Not anymore, Rache."

"And I do not feel sorry for you in the least." She leaped atop a rock, and he followed her retreat. "You're like this huge forest fire, Ryan." Her foil swung up, and she met his lunge. "You suck up everything in your path with this enormous energy that surrounds you. You dominate and absorb without looking at what it is you just conquered. You sweep into a room, and people notice. My entire life, I've never been able to compete with that."

"Compete, Rachel?" He slammed his foil across hers. "When have you given me anything but your contempt?" He backed her into the garden. "When have I ever looked at you and not seen another man in your eyes? Tell me, Rachel."

"When was the last time you looked into my eyes?" She tore off her mask. "When?" Her eyes held to his. She made him look now. "There is no other man there, Ryan. If you had just looked a little harder all those years ago."

He tore off his mask, his eyes furious. Silence fell between them, an awful pause. Rachel's heart beat against her ribs.

"If I had looked harder? You were in love with my fooking brother. There was never any *us*." He advanced on her. "Never any you and me. You made that clear."

"You kissed me, Ryan." Rachel surrendered no ground. "Then you went off to Edinburgh, never once writing to me."

It was shocking how childhood fantasies could catapult one's reason to the moon.

She knew all six of the Donallys, had grown up with Brianna and Ryan, the two youngest. But Rachel had always had a crush on Ryan's oldest brother, Christopher. He'd been eleven years her senior, and she'd fallen quite madly in love with him the first time he'd ridden into the yard of his house wearing his military uniform. All the girls had. Some men just naturally wore scarlet well.

To her, Ryan had always been the unruly Donally son who taunted her, flaunted the rules in her face, daring her to follow, who would sneak out at night and visit the vicar's twin daughters. When she and Kathleen weren't spying on him, they were shadowing him everywhere. Then Ryan had gone off to school.

"You married my best friend!" Her blade shattered Ryan's near the handle.

For a moment, both were too stunned to move.

Then Rachel lunged with her foil to finish the fight. He stepped aside, grabbed her wrist, and spun her against his chest, wrapping a forearm beneath her breasts. Her heart pounded. Spooned against him, she couldn't attack him, but before he could regain any momentum, she grabbed his arms, bent, and sent him over her head. He landed squarely on his back at her feet. The wind slammed out of him.

"Ryan!"

Staring up at the flawlessly blue sky, he remained unmoving. She dropped the foil and fell on her knees beside him. "Are you all right?"

"Jaysus," he rasped out. "Where did you learn that?"

"I don't know."

"Next time bloody warn me."

"So you can win?"

The fight still was not over. They both saw her foil lying in the grass at the same time. She dove for the hilt. He managed to grab her ankle and reel her in beneath him. "Get off me!"

Straddling her squirming hips, he laughed. "It looks like no one wins."

"You'd like that, wouldn't you?" She bucked against him.

His weight bore down upon her, one muscled thigh between her legs as he grabbed her flailing hands and pressed them into the soft cushion of grass. She lay pinned by her hair beneath her shoulders. Ryan had stilled, his heartbeat thumping against her chest so hard she could feel it even beneath the leather vest she wore. The fight they waged now had shifted—or maybe it had merely settled into what it had always been between them. She didn't know. His expression had become dangerous and ablaze with tension. She swirled in the dark, liquid splendor of it. Dizzy.

"Maybe I should scream," she rasped.

"Maybe you should." Their breaths, ragged and broken, mingled and blended. "At this moment, I don't know which one of us needs to be rescued more."

She became acutely aware of his body, aware of the thickness of him between her legs. The heat of him, his smell, and taste, everything amplified by the pillow of grass at her back. His eyes touched her lips, then slowly returned to rake her gaze. Energy as hot as lightning flared between them. She did not think to shrink from the look in his eyes as she lay beneath him, barely daring to breathe.

He threaded his fingers into her hair, tilted her head back, and slowly lowered his lips to hers. Haltingly at first.

A whisper. A taste.

Her hands came to rest on his shoulder, and paused, the uncertainty of his actions overpowering. The musk of him filled her senses with an earthy, pagan sensuality. There was danger in surrender, yet he'd yielded a groan to her mouth. Then his tongue dipped between her lips. Liquid heat roared through her veins and brought an echoing sound to her throat. He took still more and more of her mouth, the kiss no less than a primal act of possession.

A long luxurious kiss that made her body throb with pent-up longing and the memory of another hot kiss so long ago.

His face abraded hers. She wrapped her arms around his neck. Pleasure coiled and built in her belly and between her legs where he lay. He slid his fingers into her hair, bracing her face between his palms. He continued to kiss her deeply, taking and giving air as she sought to breathe him into her soul, helplessly affected by the husky timbre of her name on his lips.

"Jaysus, Rachel . . ."

While she was still lost in the silky cloud of languor, he had pulled away, opened his eyes, and looked down on her. She felt his breath upon her lips. Her lashes raised. Storm clouds were a safer refuge than what she saw in his eyes. "What are we doing?"

Startled, she awakened. "Get off me." She shoved against his chest. "Please."

With that, he pushed himself to his feet and braced his palms on his knees as if pained by his ribs. A lock of damp hair screened his eyes. He stared at her, started to say something, then looked up as his daughter hailed him from the direction of the pagoda. "Mary Elizabeth is coming. I don't want her to get the impression we are trying to kill each other," he said as he bent and swept up the two foils, broken hilt and all. "Your clothes should be ready when you return inside. I'll order the carriage."

Watching him, she knew he was also aware that something terribly momentous had just occurred. Something . . .

"Will you be departing for your London residence tonight?" she asked, without looking at him.

She had received his itinerary from Stewart before leaving D&B.

"I'm engaged tomorrow, Rache."

His shadow blocked the sunlight. "Fox hunting, I suppose, with your new friends?"

"Nothing quite so invigorating. But then I've caught the only fox worth chasing in England."

Rachel knew he was referring to Lord Devonshire's beautiful niece. Looking away, she expected a cultured "*cheerio*" to lighten the slight Irish brogue he'd worked so hard to rid himself of through the years.

"I have meetings to attend Tuesday and Wednesday as well."

"Then I will attend them with you."

"Would you believe me if I told you my business has nothing to do with D&B?"

She wrapped her arms around her ribs. "Only if I trusted you."

He turned away.

Then on an oath, faced her again and offered his hand. She didn't understand her desire for him, didn't understand her wanton actions in the middle of his garden, where anyone could see them. She raised her gaze past his outstretched palm. He was contemplating her, his eyes no longer hooded, finally retracting his hand when he realized that she wasn't going to accept his help.

"Suit yourself, Rache."

He bowed with courtly gallantry, then left her sitting beside the petunias, her emotions still tangled and feeling like a dismissed kitchen maid.

Chapter 5

"Miss Bailey?" Light spilled onto the porch as the door opened wider and a gray-haired man stepped outside. "Whatever are you doing out in weather like this?"

Water poured from the eaves behind her and splattered across the walkway. Rachel stood with her cloak clasped to her, her black skirt visible beneath. The scent of lemon wax emanated from the warmth inside the house. "I'm sorry to bother you, Mr. Williams," she said from within the hood of her cloak. "But I must speak to you."

He peered over his spectacles, a broadsheet tucked beneath his arm. Holding the door open, he stood aside. "Would you care for coffee or tea?"

"No, that isn't necessary." She smiled a brief greeting to the young maid standing in the corridor as she handed over her dripping cloak. "I won't be here long." Her glance took in the puddle on the waxed floor. "I apologize—"

"Nonsense, Miss Bailey. Please come inside and get warm."

Mr. Williams closed the door; then she followed him into his cluttered library. He had been her father's solicitor and her man of affairs in London for ten years. He handled her business with efficiency. She'd trusted him. She trusted that her questions, concerns, and interactions would always stay between them.

"Won't you sit?" he asked.

Rachel sat in the proffered chair. The room smelled of musty tomes and cigar smoke. It was a masculine room, similar to her father's study. Her skirts whispered with her movement. Williams settled behind his desk and waited for her to speak.

Her hands tightened on her reticule. She had returned from the country Sunday and spent most of her hours since at her desk tabulating figures, deciding how much longer she could float the project in Rathdrum before the contracts were paid. She wasn't going to ask Ryan for anything else. She had to solve this problem herself, or her credibility as a leader would be forever tainted. No one would ever believe her capable of pulling together a job if she allowed the Rathdrum project to fail. Ryan would close down the Irish division for good.

"Mr. Williams." Clearing her throat, she forced her fingers to relax and withdrew the sheet of paper she'd been working on. Behind him, a wagtail clock ticked away the minutes until noon. "I wish to sell off the last of my inheritance. It isn't much, but it will give me what I need."

He contemplated her. His arm reached across the desk, and he took the paper.

"I have an estate in Carlisle that will fetch a goodly sum. I wish to sell the house and the land. I haven't been there in years, so it really doesn't matter." She slid another sheet of paper across the desk. "These are the names of a few people over the years who have contacted me about a possible sale. Perhaps they are still interested."

The last of her ties with England would finally be cut.

"But that is your childhood home, Miss Bailey. Your father built that house."

"My home is in Ireland now. That estate is the only valuable asset I have left. It's an unfortunate circumstance that I need the money."

"You have Donally & Bailey."

She suddenly thought of Ryan. Mr. Shark of London Town, wealthy industrialist and personality of the moment, who wielded so much control over her life.

"I want to understand the business side of this partnership I have with Ryan and Johnny. What would it take to buy up controlling interest in D&B stock?" she asked.

"Unfortunately, a prohibitive cost, Miss Bailey." Williams sat back in his chair and folded his hands over his stomach. "You neither have the capital nor the means."

Folding her hands tightly in her lap, she looked away. "How is it that Ryan does not own this company outright? He has bought up most of his family's shares."

"All of that changed when he went public with Donally & Bailey five years ago. Ryan put everything he owned back into the company for working capital just to keep it afloat. He could have personally retained the majority stock in the company, but he did not."

Ryan did that? "I don't understand," she said after a moment, "but doesn't the lack of a majority shareholder make a company vulnerable to attack?"

"As set down by the company charter Ryan created, there are two kinds of stock, Miss Bailey. Preferred company stock, which is owned equally by you, Ryan, and John Donally, and common stock, which is bought and sold on the market. By charter rules, the two founding families together will always own 51 percent of D&B. None of you can sell your stock except to each other, and no common stock holder can hold a board position without majority board consent. In this case, since all of you own the same percentage, you each possess one vote."

"But common stock held by the public accounts for 49 percent of company shares. So, conceivably, once I obtain my proxy back from Ryan, I could purchase enough common stock to own a majority in the company. I could appoint who I wanted to the board. Even set new policy."

"Even if you possessed that capability, the instant you tried, Mr. Donally would stop you. Unlike you, he does have the means to buy common stock. He would never allow anyone else to take control of the board of directors of this company."

Drawing in her breath, she disregarded the helplessness she so disliked. But she had to find a way to keep her Irish division afloat. "I want you to obtain the list of shareholders. Such a list is public. Am I correct?"

"Miss Bailey—"

"I only want the list, Mr. Williams." Rachel rose to her feet in a *shush* of airy skirts. "That is all."

It wasn't as if she had the power to do anything else at the moment.

Mr. Williams stood. "Where would you have me to send the information?"

"I'm staying at the Palace Hotel."

At least she would be for a few more days.

Ryan didn't want her in London, and she didn't particularly want to be there either.

She had not seen him since he'd kissed her. Two days to be exact. She knew he'd returned to London last night. His house was less than a quarter mile from her hotel, and she'd accidentally passed it during her evening constitutional before she realized where she was and turned around. Gaslights snaked around the quiet street and had glowed in the mist, leaving a shine on the damp brick walkway. But she'd seen his carriage parked out front, cloaked by the shadows of huge elms, and knew he was there.

"I thank you for seeing me today, Mr. Williams."

"I am, as always, your servant, Miss Bailey." He walked around the desk and opened the library door. "I was a good friend of your father's." The clap of their steps on the wooden floor filled the narrow hallway. "I would have had you here during your stay had my wife still been alive."

"How have you been doing since she passed on?"

"We were married thirty-two years." A smile tipped the corners of his mouth. "How does one do alone after that?"

Rachel didn't know. She didn't know about love, or husbands, or even that much about fathers and daughters. Her father had spent twelve years of his life mourning the son who had died with his wife in birth, never thinking that Rachel had lost her mother. Then she'd spent the remaining years of his autocratic existence seeking validation from a man who would rather find oblivion in a bottle than pride in his daughter. It was no wonder that Christopher Donally had become her white knight, her paragon in scarlet—until she'd realized that the only person capable of saving her life was herself.

Rachel stepped onto the porch. The rain had lessened to a sprinkle. "My son is a full barrister now," Williams said. "I'll be a grandfather again next month."

"Congratulations." She held out a gloved hand, and he grasped it firmly. She was happy for him.

Hands sliding into his pockets, he glanced over her shoulder at the cab awaiting her return. The driver stood beside his horse. "I will get back to you about the estate. Good-bye, Miss Bailey."

"Thank you."

Good-byes always sounded so forever to her, and she could not reciprocate in kind. Rachel returned to her hotel later that afternoon, buried in the hood of her cloak as she swept up the stairway to her second-floor room. Her steps were quiet in the long corridor, her focus intent as she reached the doorway of her room and let herself inside. Her maid, Elsie, had fallen asleep on the settee. Rachel leaned her head back against the door.

Now, it was done. She had severed her ties to England.

Rachel closed her eyes and, with a sigh, rested her head back against the porcelain tub. Champagne bottle in one hand and a cigarette in the other, her arms rested on the smoothly curved sides. Fragrant cinnamon-and-apple-scented steam wafted from the water, and she let the ambiance of the moment capture her. Somewhere she heard knocking on one of the doors in her suite. Unfortunately, she was more sober than she realized, and she opened her eyes, purely maddened to have absolutely no peace in her life.

"Tell whoever it is to go *bugger* himself, Elsie," she yelled, perturbed that anyone would disturb her privacy. "I've paid for this room through the rest of the week. If I want to sing, I will."

Her voice was hardly that bad anyway. Taking a long sip from the champagne bottle in her hand, she sank lower into the tub. She was a woman on her own. Independent. She didn't need anyone else to make her complete. Bubbles crackled around her ears. Tilting her chin, she inhaled from the cigarette; then, flinching, she glared at the burning tip. This newfangled fad was gawd-awful terrible, she thought as she ground the thing out in the ash tin. She'd tried to enjoy tobacco but could see no appeal in what was the current rage among enlightened women. She closed her eyes and, this time, slid beneath the water.

"Miss Bailey." Elsie was standing beside her tub when Rachel came up for air. Twisting her hands, her young maid lowered her voice. "A Mr. Donally is here to see you, mum."

She couldn't imagine what Johnny would be doing there. He and Moira were attending the opera tonight. "A Mr. *Ryan* Donally, mum," Elsie whispered.

"Ryan is here?" Rachel sat up. Water sluiced down her breasts and over the rim of the tub. "At this time of night?"

"It's only six o'clock, mum."

"Lord." Rachel set down the champagne bottle and struggled to get out of the tub. Maybe she'd drunk more than she thought. The world tilted ever so slightly off its axis. "Why is he here?" Water sloshed over the floor as she stumbled from the tub.

"I don't know, mum"—her maid helped Rachel to hurriedly dry off and slide into her wrapper—"but he is very nicely attired."

Rachel bent over the tiny pearl buttons on her wrapper and struggled to work each through a hole as Elsie applied a comb to her hair to pick out the tangles. "Does he have anything with him?" she asked. "Like a large packet of papers?"

"I didn't notice, mum."

Rachel moved in front of the glass and attempted to clear it of steam. Her hand squeaked on the mirror. The bath had flushed her face pink. Her hair fell in dripping tangles to her waist. He'd seen her in a worse state.

"Never mind about my hair, Elsie. Where is he?"

"In your sitting room, mum."

Rachel padded barefoot out of the tiled room into her suite, tripped on the edge of a carpet, and hastily straightened. She was too worried that he would tire of waiting and leave. Then she wondered if he'd heard her tell him to go bugger himself.

Ryan stood with his hands in his pockets in front of the large window facing the street, the white lace curtains opened to St. Paul's distant dome. He had not removed his overcoat, and his hat and satchel sat next to hers on the table beside him. His coat was unbuttoned, to reveal a formal jacket with tails and black waistcoat. As he turned and saw her, she glimpsed a flash of silver buttons. He was dressed very much as he had been for the ball last week, and his very masculine presence filled the small distance between them. His eyes went over her.

He was remembering their kiss as she was.

"I'm sorry about what happened this weekend between us." His voice came to her, oddly humble for a man who practically owned the world. "I shouldn't have kissed you. It was . . ."

"Out of character?" She peered at him. "An accident?"

He shook his head and looked away. "That happened in full view of my staff."

Rachel rubbed her fingers against her temple. She didn't feel sorry for him, but her shoulders began to shake as an odd mood struck her. Obviously inebriated, she decided, as she couldn't help laughing. She looked up when she sensed his approach. "How many times have we apologized to each other this week?" she asked, aware of the heat of him.

"I believe you hold the winning number," he magnanimously conceded.

Rachel leaned back against the doorjamb. She still disliked him immensely. "And I believe it is a sign that we have unfinished business between us," she challenged. "Why did we never finish that kiss all those years ago?"

"Perhaps because you slapped me?"

"Or maybe I slapped you because you thought it was all a joke?"

"Or maybe you were young, and your father would have had me keelhauled."

Sometimes Rachel disliked logic.

Drawing in her breath, she accepted that the truth didn't take away the reality that she was in love with him and that he was to be married in October. Johnny had told her Lady Gwyneth was the woman he wanted. What she felt for Ryan and what he probably felt for her on a physical level might be electric; but they both knew it would proceed no further than it had a few days ago.

She watched his gaze go over the white lace-and-lavender sitting room that looked as if an overzealous demirep had decorated it. "Nice room," he said.

"This is the Palace Hotel bridal suite." She hiccupped and, suddenly perturbed at him for coming to visit without notice, lifted her chin. "Surely you don't think I would have accepted this room on purpose? It was all Johnny could find for me."

A black-gloved hand tipped her chin. "How much have you had to drink?"

"None of your business." She removed his hand from her chin. "If I want to drink myself under the table, I will. With or without your approval."

"How much?" he asked Elsie, who was standing behind her.

Elsie dipped into a curtsy, her mobcap bobbing over blond curls. "Perhaps a half bottle of champagne. She hasn't eaten, sir."

"Excuse me"—Rachel waved a hand in front of his face—"but I *am* in the room."

Ryan stepped past her into her bedroom, as if he had been there a hundred times. She could only stare, before her feet leapt to follow him past her four-poster bed and canopy drawn back to reveal disheveled covers. "Do you have anything *nice* to wear tonight?"

He walked to her wardrobe and flung open the doors, his gloved hands holding each edge. Rachel shut the doors and, crossing her arms beneath her breasts, braced her back against the panels. "What are you doing?"

"You're going with Johnny and Moira to the opera."

"I am?"

He strode to the end of her bed, his coat batting at his calves. "Every D&B and Ore Industries board member will be there tonight. Do you want to be included or not?"

Rachel stared at him in disbelief. Hands on his hips, he brought his gaze back around to her. There was a frown in those dark eyes. He was a bastard for not telling her about the opera sooner, and knew it, too.

"Why didn't you say anything before?" she asked.

"I'm saying something now."

He strode to her trunks and flung open the lid. Her ball gown was suddenly in his hands, and she lifted her gaze as he walked back to her. "Why?" Her voice whispered.

"You're on the board," he said. "I'm not going to bloody let you sit alone in your room again tonight getting drunk. You're going out this evening. I've already spoken to Johnny. He will be here later to pick you up."

"How do you know what I've been doing or not doing in my room at night?" Rachel snatched her gown from him. He had no right to come into her room like some Roman Caesar and dictate to her.

Ryan reclaimed the shimmering gown and handed it to Elsie. "See that this gets pressed. I've already warned the staff that you may be down." A glance at Rachel, and he added, "She'll need coffee, too. Turkish coffee. Black. Never mind—" His dark eyes caught the light in her room as they came to rest on her face and held her pinned with subtle humor. "I'll see dinner brought up. You need to do her hair."

"How do you want me to dress her hair, Mr. Donally?"

"Never you mind, Elsie Tompkins," Rachel snapped. The girl was positively young and quite as flaky as dishrag paper. "It's not that difficult. We'll manage."

"Yes, mum." The dress clasped to her bosom, Elsie hurried out of the room, leaving Ryan alone with her.

Neither moved.

Muted noises from the busy street two floors below pulled somewhere at the back of her mind. She watched as he returned to the adjoining salon. She heard the click of a metal clasp. He reappeared with the folders she'd left at his house. Her levee project folders.

"Your project is sound, Rachel." When she didn't take the folders, he dropped them on the bed. "I've never questioned your talent or dedication. You're an excellent engineer. If you were a man, you could find a place for yourself in any firm in the world."

"But if you put my name on the report, D&B will never be hired for another job in Ireland," she continued for him. "You have to consider our stockholders."

"That is my job, Rachel. You should have known better than to ask special consideration when you knew I could give you none. My decision would be no different for Johnny if he did something that was not for the good of the company." Ryan jammed his hands into his pockets. "We can agree about the unfairness of it all until we turn blue, or you can accept your position at D&B as is and get dressed to attend the opera with Johnny."

Rachel stared down at her arms folded against her breasts, aware that her long hair had dripped water on the floor and she was naked beneath the thin wrapper.

He'd come there when he needn't have come at all. And found a seat at the opera when there was none to be had. She'd inquired. It seemed wrong to throw away tonight on an emotional broadside that would only leave her listing in deeper water. She was twenty-nine years old, after all. She could manage her life—and her heart.

"Everyone I know has already seen that gown on me."

"You don't know that many people, Rache." His voice was filled with gentle humor. "Do you have anything else suitable to wear then?"

She shook her head. "It's not that I don't wish to drape myself in lavish gowns. I just don't socialize on the grand scale you do." The top of her head barely reached his shoulder, and she raised her gaze. "I didn't even know you liked opera."

One corner of his mouth lifted. "I find the required sponsorship of such functions a necessary part of my life."

"You've become too pragmatic, Ryan. Where do your passions lie?"

"Fencing?" he said. "I've discovered I have a passion for the sword."

Rachel almost rolled her eyes. But he'd softened her mood.

"I'll see that dinner is brought up here," he said, turning away, and she leaned her head tiredly against the armoire at her back.

He returned a moment later, satchel in hand, to the doorway between her bedroom and sitting room, an elegant portrait in black—hair, eyes, and clothes—against the frilly white lace and lavender behind him.

"Do you even know what *bugger* means?" he said in that superior way that annoyed her. Rachel had no idea how wanton she looked at that moment, the vibrant red of her hair in the same brandy-colored sunset that brushed her cheeks to a glow.

"Make sure you eat something, Rache." Beneath the quiet of his words, an order again. "And be on your best behavior tonight."

He settled his hat on his head, one corner of his mouth tilting slightly.

Ryan let himself out of her room before he did something he would regret, like attempting to dress her—or God forbid kiss her again or take her to bed, the demon in his mind taunted. He strode down the long hallway, almost running to escape.

"Ryan?" He heard Rachel's voice, and turned just before he reached the stairs.

She stood in her doorway, shadowed by sultry lace and dusk, her girlish pink wrapper not as thick as she probably thought it was. He could see her legs limned against the thin cloth, and far more as his gaze climbed over the gentle swell of her hips. A hasty glance behind him told him that they were alone.

"Thank you for talking to me," she said.

Before his tongue could catch up to his mind, she shut the door. Leaving the hallway filled with the scent of her presence and reminding him all over again that an adolescent obsession was more dangerous to him now that it ever had been years ago.

He should have kept his hands off her this weekend. He probably shouldn't even have come to the hotel, if the heightened state of his body was any proof of his folly.

He had left a meeting at Whitehall earlier in the day and returned to his office at Ore Industries. For some reason when he sat down at his desk, he'd pulled out Rachel's project files. She had left them outside his dressing room the night they'd argued. Her grand, unexpected entry back into his life had caught him cold. He was not prepared to see her as a civil engineer, which he discovered he now did. He was not prepared to feel anything for her—not any part of her—yet, he had kissed her.

Ryan never did anything impulsively. Spontaneity was dangerous—and still he'd found a way to get her a seat at the opera, even if it was his seat in his personal box he was giving her. Johnny would see to her welfare and, in all good conscience, Ryan couldn't exclude her. But neither was he going to sit with her. Or trust himself to be near her, inhaling her like she was dessert. He only knew he was due for a diet.

Ryan stopped a hotel maid and ordered dinner and coffee brought up to Rachel's room. Noise from the lobby filtered up the staircase. He peered over the banister, did a mental survey of the boisterous crowd below, and descended the stairs into the busy lobby, where the famous Four Seasons plaster figures peered from each corner of the foyer. This hotel was not far from Covent Garden and was always crowded on show nights. Only an exclusive invitation could get one inside the restaurant tonight. Such invitations were issued only to the largest sponsors of the arts.

His height easily distinguishable, Ryan reached the lobby and paused as he glimpsed Lady Gwyneth standing near the entrance to the restaurant. He glanced at the large dome clock on the wall above her head and considered that he was supposed to meet her in a half hour at Cassavas for dinner. She stood as if holding court over her admirers. Three of those men sat on boards of international banking firms; another owned a shipping business, and the fourth sat on the board of a South African diamond mine. None was older than thirty-five, and all probably represented more accumulated wealth among them than the economic output of Ireland last year.

They were Ryan's peers.

He suddenly caught himself studying the tableau like an architect examining a design he knows to be flawed. It was a world that had always fascinated him. One that surrounded him. Tonight it all suddenly seemed lackluster.

Gwyneth looked up and glimpsed him standing near the stairs. Her rich skirts flowering over her legs like a tinseled garden of flame, she stood among her minions, chatting gaily. A pearl-encrusted tiara folded into her hair and matched her smile as she touched the man beside her and pointed. Ryan recognized Lord Bathwick. The others in the group turned.

His satchel tucked beneath his arm, Ryan squeezed his way through the crush, pausing here and there to greet a business associate or acquaintance as he made his way to the crowd of men surrounding his betrothed.

"Ryan—" Her generous blue eyes smiled at his approach. "I told you he would come here if I sent him a note. Did I not?" she said to the others.

The men surrounding her departed in deference to his arrival. His manner easy, his hand appeared dark against her willowy waist. "What are you doing here, Gwyneth?"

"Hey, old chap." Marquart slapped him on the back. "We missed you at Lords on Saturday. If you leave your lady betrothed unattended, do not get vexed when she decides to pay mind to others."

"I believe you only missed him for part of the occasion," Lord Bathwick replied to Marquart. "He was merely fashionably late." His gaze touched the stairway, then the satchel beneath Ryan's arm. "Are you here on business or pleasure, Donally?"

"Maybe we should all ask that question." Lord Marquart laughed. "It seems your meeting with the Commons Select Committee adjourned early today."

"Or mayhaps they changed the meeting venue to someplace cozier," Bathwick replied, the grin on his mouth reaching no higher than the corners of his lips, the animosity between them nothing new. "I am told this is a favorite meeting place for those fellow countrymen unhindered by the moral decay of our society."

"Is your father allowing you to stand in his stead tonight?" Ryan asked.

"I am not here as a member of Ore Industries if that is bothering you, Donally."

"Truly, Ryan, you could be a little nicer." Gwyneth wrapped her arms around his and leaned against him. "Do let's not be jealous." Her breathy whisper touched his ear. "I refuse to remain at home with a new gown and bored out of my wits awaiting your arrival. Gideon is merely entertaining me before the opera tonight. I wanted a spot of sherbet." She regarded the crowded doorway to the restaurant. "And we cannot get inside tonight." Her mouth pouted. "The reception is by invitation only, and not one of us has an invitation."

"It's what her ladyship wanted," Marquart replied. "We met them outside."

"I am wearing a new gown, Ryan." Gwyneth turned in a circle, then executed a flawless curtsy that had every man straining to glimpse the swell of flesh above her décolletage. "I wore it for you, and I'm angry that you have said nothing."

"I believe that it is the most beautiful gown in all of London," Lord Marquart deferred.

"Only because of the woman inside the gown," Sir Boris replied.

"At least I am not ignored by everyone."

Ryan's mouth quirked faintly. Clearly, in her element, Gwyneth turned to flirt with his new head of accounting at Ore Industries. She put her considerable skills to work in her attempt to capture the attention of every man present, but should have exercised more prudence in public. Ryan didn't like possessive women and despised the notion that anyone owned any part of him. He disliked in equal proportion finding himself distracted and, tonight, having arrived in a singularly unpleasant state of mind already, he had no desire to play the jealous suitor.

He reached into his jacket and pulled out an engraved invitation. "Enjoy yourself, my lady," he said, presenting the gift to Gwyneth.

His gaze touched Lord Bathwick's. And, as Ryan made his way out the front door of the hotel, walking away from a night of entertainment with one of the most beautiful women in England, he found himself caught by an indifference he didn't entirely understand.

The next hour Rachel was fully occupied with combing the tangles from her hair. Elsie had returned with her dress a few minutes ago, and it now lay pressed and on the bed. Her door into the adjoining salon was shut, and Rachel looked through the strands of her hair, frustrated that her maid had vanished.

"Elsie?" Rachel stretched around the vanity.

She set down the ivory comb. She'd dressed in her stockings and underclothes. She wore her stays beneath the pink robe loosely belted at the waist. She was going to be late if Elsie did not get in here and help her with her hair.

Rachel left the bedroom. None of the lamps in the room had been lit. The bathing room connected to this suite, but the door was closed.

She walked into the salon. "Elsie?"

"I believe she is not here, Miss Bailey."

The masculine voice jolted her around. Her hand against her heart, she searched the shadows. A man stood against the wall, as faintly familiar as he was arrogant. He was tall, with graying hair at his temples and dressed as Ryan had been that evening.

"What have you done with my maid?"

"I believe she found it prudent to wait outside. Don't worry, Miss Bailey," he said, stepping into the shaft of light that angled from her bedroom, and she recognized Lord Devonshire from the Telford Ball. "If I wanted to rape you, I wouldn't do it within hearing distance of the lobby." His brown eyes, set too deeply in his face, did not camouflage the look that entered his gaze when his eyes slid over her. "I knew you looked familiar when I saw you at the Telford Ball," he said, nonplussed by her alarm or the threat that she might scream anyway. "You've a very titillating past."

Her heart racing, she knew there was no possible answer to that, and forced herself to hold his gaze. He held up the champagne she'd been drinking earlier and sloshed some into a glass. "This is better than what the Engineering Society served. I compliment you on your taste." His eyes went over her body again, and she closed the robe more tightly. "Sit down, Miss Bailey. I only wish to talk. For now."

"Why would you possibly want to talk to me?"

"I'm very particular about my new soon-to-be relatives as I am about losing what belongs to me." His feet made little sound on the carpet as he walked nearer. "One might even argue that I have a bias against poverty."

Rachel moved around the small desk at her back, only because it put up a barrier that separated her from him. Her gaze fell on the packet someone had leaned against the crystal lamp. "That envelope contains two tickets back to Ireland."

He appraised her over the rim of his glass. "Quite frankly, I couldn't care less about what you've done in your past or with whom. It's Donally who interests me."

Her alarm escalating, she felt her grip on the desk tighten. "You mean it's his money that interests you."

"A bigger fortune than you could possibly know." He sat in the leather chair facing the desk and propped his leg over the other. "Should I go to the scandal sheets with what I know about you, it would be obvious to everyone how you received the authorization to take an exclusive engineering exam. The fact that you scored the second highest in a classful of men would be irrelevant under the circumstances. How do I know this? you are asking yourself. I'm on the university board of trustees in Edinburgh. I actually knew your father when he was a physics professor there. I knew who you were when you audited classes there."

Rachel forced herself to breathe. She felt faint.

"And why you were quietly removed from the university."

"Why are you doing this, Lord Devonshire? I've done nothing to you. Why would you come here and threaten me. That is what you are doing, isn't it?"

"Before you harp on my cruelty to you, let me tell you what I am offering Mr. Donally compared to what he will lose with you."

"I don't know what you are talking about," she whispered.

"Don't take me for a fool, Miss Bailey." He set down the glass and stood. "I don't play games. I certainly won't with you. At least not verbal ones." Pressing his palms on the desk, he leaned toward her. "Half the people downstairs saw Donally leaving this hotel earlier. Some of us were even present when he danced you out onto the hotel terrace at the ball, and rumors abound that the two of you have known each other a long while. Now he's not attending the opera tonight, and it is widely speculated that he has given his seat to you. My niece came home in tears tonight and has locked herself in her room. But that is neither here nor there. Men take mistresses all the time." He waved his arm in casual dismissal. "Tiffs happen. He won't leave everything that I offer to him. Certainly not if I should tell him the truth about you."

Rachel looked from his hard fingers pressed against the desk to his equally hard face and managed with considerable difficulty not to smash a fist into his face or retreat.

Devonshire pushed off the desk. A flicker of something like admiration showed briefly in his eyes. "Donally and I make excellent bedfellows as it were, more alike than you know, Miss Bailey. We both will do exactly what it takes to get what we want. I've nominated him for his orders. Other than military heroes, such honors are typically awarded for services rendered to society, irony indeed for someone who's been denied entrance to the very echelon of society that he's served." He strolled to the door. "He will not make a fool of me. I hope I am making myself clear."

Rachel did not move from her place behind the desk. Her mouth was dry. He was threatening Ryan, and she could do nothing. Tears burned behind her lids.

"Scandal has brought down kingdoms. Think what it can do to both of you."

Chapter 6

"There has never been a more opportune moment to acquire any company. They're primed to be acquired. . . ."

The conversation droned in the background of Ryan's thoughts, behind the storm outside the window, and the one inside him. He stood with his hands clasped at his back as he watched the rain beat on the glass. Eight stories on the street below the Ore Industries boardroom, a solid sea of black umbrellas bobbed in and out of the traffic stopped on the street. Even from this elevation, he could hear the sound of horses and carriage wheels meeting the pavement, a bobby's whistle.

Rachel did not attend the opera. She had not shown up at D&B for three days. Ryan had finally gone to the hotel only to learn that she'd checked out. He knew only that she'd returned to Ireland.

Behind him sat the eight-man board he'd put into place since his conquest of Ore Industries became final eleven months ago. Men that he had personally handpicked to help manage this corporation. "It shouldn't be difficult to close the deal in Paris," a voice replied, and he recognized Sir Boris was speaking. "They aren't willing, but they've weakened enough financially that they will not be able to put up much of a fight. Valmonts, with all its lucrative connections, is as good as ours."

"Who did the initial analysis?" Ryan asked without turning.

"I did." Sir Boris leaned forward.

Ryan met his gaze in the glass. A strange-looking man with protruding brown eyes that never quite focused on a person, he was the best financial asset Ryan had ever hired. Those eyes never missed a bloody thing. "Valmonts used to build the finest locomotives on the Continent until the price of iron outpaced their profits. We will make a huge profit selling off its assets and taking over all contracts."

"See that the man in charge of the team is current on international law," Ryan said, finally turning to the younger man who sat scrawling notes to his left. "Put the team together, Brendan."

The younger man's face lifted. This was the first assignment he'd received since Ryan had brought him over from D&B.

"And for God's sake don't make a hash of it," Ryan said. "I don't want a repeat of what happened in Spain last month."

Ryan turned to face the room. Banked on two sides by expansive glass, the office allowed gray light to flood the room. Johnny sat apart from the group at one end of the table. He'd been invited to take part in the meeting, something Ryan had not known until he'd walked through the door that morning. Cigar smoke was thick in the air. Devonshire, the only member present who sat in the House of Lords, lounged to the left of Ryan's seat at the head of the table. Devonshire owned the foundry that had given Ore Industries its start. Ryan kept him under his thumb for personal reasons.

"The preliminary papers have been drawn up to begin acquisition of D&B," Ryan's financial advisor said, as they moved to what was obviously the main topic of the afternoon, the reason Johnny had been summoned.

Ryan walked to the end of the long conference table and scraped up the file, flipping it open. "This is not an issue on the agenda today."

"You were given a briefing yesterday, sir."

Then the briefing sat in a folder in his satchel, a satchel that Rachel now had.

Ryan had accidentally taken hers when he'd left her hotel room the other night. In the approaching darkness, her satchel, with its monogrammed *RB*, had looked like his, with *RD*.

His gaze lifted to Devonshire. "Is this your doing?"

"D&B is essential to our expansion," Sir Boris answered for Devonshire.

This was nothing Ryan did not know.

Devonshire watched him with interest. "Acquiring D&B is a matter of economics. We need its assets. The acquisition will make Ore Industries the biggest iron ore supplier and construction firm in the world."

Except Ryan knew the mechanics of a merger as well as an acquisition. Hell, he dismembered companies every year. Ripped their internal guts out. Took what he could to make a profit and sold off the rest.

Yet, knowing that this moment was inevitable didn't make it any easier to accept.

Everyone present knew that D&B could become a part of Ore Industries, or, as a competitor, the entire company would go down. Ryan couldn't have it both ways. He had known that from the beginning, when he'd pursued Ore Industries a year ago.

"Think, Donally." Devonshire tapped his cigar in the tray at his elbow. "When this is finished, you will no longer have the stigma of the firm's Irish label with which to contend. There will be no more Donally & Bailey. That will also be a positive to consider as we continue to expand overseas."

Ryan dropped the folder on the table. Getting rid of the Irish label was essential in a competitive overseas market, but hearing the statement from someone else made it all seem sordid.

"Choose whom you want to bring from D&B," Devonshire said, looking down the long table at Johnny as he spoke. "There is a place for you at Ore Industries, Mr. Donally."

"And for most of your staff," Sir Boris said.

Ryan leaned both palms on the shiny surface of the table and took in the group of men gathered, men whom he had appointed to their positions because they weren't afraid to act. Softness was not a character trait found in any one of them.

"My brother isn't the only member of the D&B board of directors," Ryan finally said into the silence, reading Johnny's mood with unerring accuracy.

"Miss Bailey will be treated as any other stockholder." Sir Boris sucked on a pipe, his blue eyes magnified behind his spectacles. "Her shares will be absorbed, and she will receive dividends accordingly."

"It's convenient that you have planned this little coup when Miss Bailey is no longer in London," Johnny said to the men present.

"I'm sure that Miss Bailey is savvy enough at her job," Devonshire said. "She heads your Dublin division. But if the extent of her misconduct should become public knowledge, you understand the ramifications."

Ryan shifted his gaze. The information took a moment longer to register. "What are you talking about?"

"I've done my own inquiries on the elusive R. Bailey," Devonshire said. "It's rumored that she has more than a professional relationship with your junior engineer, Allan Marrow, and that she is the brains behind the company in Dublin. Last year, D&B was awarded the contract to rebuild the bridge over the Avonmore River near Rathdrum. The project was delayed. Now Dublin will not honor the contracts until the project is completed. Our guess is someone learned she has put herself in charge of said project because someone made a mistake. That fact would come out should she fight the council in a public forum. Whoever is refusing to pay the monies owed is probably counting on pocketing the money himself, knowing she could not take it to court."

Ryan met Johnny's stare across the long length of the table. "Is this the kind of blather she has had to deal with over there?" Except Ryan knew there was more.

Had she not run into financing trouble, she probably would have begun building the levee project on her own as well, he realized.

"You and I need to talk privately," Johnny said.

"As you can see, Miss Bailey is a liability." Sir Boris slid a brown packet toward him. "She will need to be removed, or the Irish division becomes a fiscal liability to us all. Pending government payment of the contracts, you can bring in work-ers from Liverpool and Wales. Cheaper wages will help us make a profit—"

"Rachel will never let you replace her people," Johnny said.

"If Miss Bailey isn't cooperative, we have ways to force the issue." Devonshire relaxed as he surveyed Ryan over his cigar. "A leak here and there about Miss Bailey—"

"The meeting is over." Ryan's dark gaze swept each man present. If he wrapped his hands around any throat, it would be Devonshire's.

He looked at the satchel at his elbow, thinking of his own and wondering what else might be in there. He had unread folders inside. As the meeting concluded, and those around the table stood, Ryan said, "A moment, your lordship." Without looking up from the papers in his hands, he stopped Devonshire. "Wait for me in my office, Johnny," he told his brother. He didn't care how overbearing the command. "I'll need to talk to you."

Devonshire ground out the cigar in the ash tin and waited with his legs outstretched beneath the rosewood table. He was watching Ryan as if he couldn't discern whether he was furious or simply distracted by the folder sitting next to his fingertips. "The decision about acquiring D&B is a long time in coming," Devonshire said. "With the pending deal in France making financial headlines, it's time to act."

"Exactly what would you leak to the scandal sheets that would possibly profit any of us, Devonshire?"

His lordship shoved away from the table and rose. "Your concern about her was quite noted the other night when you were seen leaving her hotel in full view of most of London. Maybe you should consider how she could damage *you* instead. Miss Bailey is not what you think she is." Devonshire walked to the door, an austere figure in black. "We're expecting important guests tonight for dinner," he said. "If they like you, there could be talk of a political future ahead of you."

"Don't overrate your importance in my life, Devonshire." Ryan's indolent façade was carefully back in place, and he waited for the man to turn. "You're here only because I allow it to be so."

Something ugly went over the man's face before he raised a polite brow. Then, dismissing himself, Devonshire opened the door and left it swinging on his way out.

Ryan shut the door to his office.

Johnny stood with his back to the rosewood desk as he looked out the window. Dark rivulets slithered down the glass as the rain picked up streaks of coal dust that layered the city's rooftops. "Her train left for Liverpool three days ago." Without turning, Johnny held up a missive. "She said her grandmother hadn't been in the best of health, and had decided to return to Ireland."

Ryan walked to his brother and took the note. Unlike his bold scrawl, Rachel possessed meticulous penmanship, with prissy g's and m's that an excessively orderly person who rose every day at the crack of dawn would write. A complete contrast to the decadent taste of spiced apples that lingered in his senses.

His fingers crushed the missive.

"Rachel hasn't any family other than her grandmother," Johnny said.

"I'm aware of her plight." He tossed the missive into the refuse container.

Johnny's dark eyes settled on Ryan. "Are you going to allow Ore Industries to acquire D&B?"

"*I* am Ore Industries, Johnny. We have spoken on this matter before. Ore Industries and D&B cannot coexist in the same environment."

One was the past. The other the future. Ryan always looked to tomorrow. He always had. This was no different. Johnny knew that.

Yet, as Ryan stared outside at the distant dome of St. Paul's and a city bound by its history, he set his hands on the waistband of his trousers, suddenly caught by the past. "Tell me how involved Rachel is in production."

"She took over the Rathdrum project after the chief engineer made a costly mistake in his assessment on the soil sampling. The train tracks had to be moved farther inland. The error cost D&B six months while Rachel completed the reassessment herself."

"And the levee?"

"The levee is in the final phase. Maybe she was tired of

working behind Marrow. I suspect she has been bolstering him up for two years. She surrounds herself with competent foremen. I doubt Marrow has ever functioned in any capacity without her."

Hell, Ryan scoffed to himself. *Rachel just has that effect on men.*

By Ryan's estimation, she had left the day after she was supposed to attend the opera. That reeked of running away to him, especially after he thought they had reached an understanding of sorts. But then he had told her he wouldn't grant her special privileges concerning her levee project. Still, the part of him, which didn't feel angry as hell with her, worried.

"Jaysus," Ryan said, his tone acerbic. "The Dublin division has been nothing but a nightmare of charity work since its inception." A hand on one hip, he exhaled before reining in his temper. "I should have known why she came back here."

"Do you honestly believe Rachel came back to London because of that project?"

"Do you think I did something to send her fleeing from England?"

"Didn't you?"

His tall form unyielding, Ryan walked past his brother to gather what he needed off the desk. "She is a big girl, Johnny." He stifled the impulse to tell his brother to go to hell.

His entire life his family surrounded Rachel as if she was God's gift to sainthood and perfection. He was sick to death of dealing with the same rehashed arguments, of looking through perfect fences as if he somehow corrupted everything he touched. "Our whole damn family has filled her head full of dreams she thinks are attainable.

"She wasn't content with quietly managing the Dublin division. All of you have set her up to fall. Not me. And hell,

Johnny, it's a bloody long way to fall. You know what I have to do." He lifted his coat from the back of the chair where he'd laid it earlier.

Johnny sat against the desk. "Are you going to Ireland?"

"For the moment?" Ryan adjusted the collar on his coat. "I'm going home to my daughter. Her birthday is in four days, and I'll be damned if she will spend it alone again this year."

It certainly hadn't taken Rachel very long to forget his daughter either. On his way out, Ryan ordered his secretary to cancel his dinner engagement for that night.

"Miss Rachel! Miss Rachel!" Little Kyra Blakely called from the street as David lifted Rachel out of the cart he'd ridden in to fetch her at the docks.

She turned as another little girl flung herself against Rachel's skirts. "Did you bring back licorice?" Cynthia's favorite. Her blue eyes peeked out from behind raven curls.

A half dozen children playing ball in the yard across the narrow spit of green ran to where Rachel had lifted the little girl into her arms. She always brought home gumdrops or licorice when she'd been away for more than a few days. Fortunately, David made a detour past the candy store on the way home from the docks.

Rachel lived on Dublin's southern fringes, in a picturesque hamlet that rested at the juncture of Old Military Road near Glencree. She spent her free time with her grandmother, living outside Dublin proper because it allowed her, for the most part, to live in anonymity. The fact that she was the granddaughter of a former village elder gave her a certain acceptance she might not have had otherwise for a single woman who seemed eccentric in her ways. At twenty-nine and an obvious spinster, she was allowed more freedom than the younger girls. Though she'd received marriage proposals

from almost every bachelor or widower from Enniskerry to
Glencree at one time or another, most people recognized she
would never marry. Her last proposal had come from the
kindly constable in need of a wife who could be a good
mother to his nine children. The little girl she held in her
arms was his youngest. No one understood what Rachel did
for a living.

Frankly, no one understood her. No one really knew her
either.

Yet the village children seemed to adore her for some reason. Perhaps because they venerated David and trusted that if
he respected and loved Rachel, then she must be worthy of
their affection as well. Or maybe because she had trained
them well with gumdrops, for they all came running as if she
were Saint Nicholas in skirts. And suddenly she was thinking
about Mary Elizabeth, about cats and dogs, and eating
worms. Her thoughts jerked to a stop as though the child's
name was a yawning crevice in her heart for more reasons
than anyone could ever know.

"Come, little one." David lifted Cynthia from Rachel's
arms so Rachel could procure the anticipated treasure from
the back of the cart. Removing a red tin, she flipped off the
lid and doled out one to each child, finally slipping a gum-
drop beneath David's tongue.

"And one for you, Father Donally."

"Ah, *Rachel* me love. You know the path to my heart,
you do."

David was as full of Irish blarney as they came. Surrounded
by laughter and noise, Rachel smiled into his darkly handsome
face, cradled by a moment's return of strength and peace.
David, with his starched white collar and black attire, was familiar, his presence imbuing her with a sense of emotional
safety, a barrier that separated her from the last few weeks.
Carefree and dashing, with a roguish tilt to his mouth, he

looked perfectly at ease in the company of children. A dimple creased one side of his mouth as he smiled at the little girl in his arms, his teeth a slash of white against his darker features.

"Now, off with ye," he said to the child. "Miss Rachel has come home to see Memaw. What did I tell you all about making too much noise around her window?"

"Nonsense!" a huffy female voice called from the upstairs window behind Rachel. "If I get so old as to complain about a child's laughter, then you can put me in me grave, David Donally. Now quit your playing paddy fingers with my granddaughter so I can see her."

Rachel shaded her eyes against the afternoon sunlight. "Memaw, you are supposed to be in bed."

"I'll bring in your trunks," David said, a lingering smile on his lips. "Be sure and tell her how beautiful she looks."

"I heard that wicked blarney," Rachel's grandmother sniffed. "I stubbed my toe, and this man makes me into a convalescent just so he can keep me home."

"You injure my heart, Memaw." David laid a forlorn palm across his chest. "You'll get me in trouble with such outrageous accusations."

"Balderdash! I'll not be havin' ye reading your rites over me yet. Go away and leave me to some peace."

"A stubbed toe?" Rachel eyed David suspiciously. "You told me she hurt herself."

"A stubbed toe can be serious, colleen. You'd not have had me take any chances? She would have jumped in the cart herself and gone to pick you up. The doctor still thinks she should not be out of bed since her spell last month."

"Has she gotten worse?" Rachel grabbed a handful of her skirts and hurried through the door Elsie held open for her and up the stairs to her grandmother's room.

Memaw sat in a fat chair with her foot wrapped and propped on an ottoman. It was her favorite place in the entire house to sit. She'd settled her robust frame among the plush yellow pillows and had set about knitting. In the mornings, sunlight flowed through the windows like an amber breeze. The scent of freshly watered flower beds pooled in the room and mixed with the laughter of children outside the window.

She was a tall woman, several inches taller than Rachel's grandfather had been. Her hair, once a deep, vibrant auburn, had faded to a recalcitrant ginger and straggled from her cap in curly waves as lively as the expression that greeted Rachel upon her arrival.

"Memaw," Rachel dropped to her knees beside her grandmother's chair. "What have you done? This was more than a stubbed toe."

"Absolutely nothing." She sniffed. "I stepped into a puddle of water. It's that madman of a priest who wrapped my ankle and insisted that I stay off my foot." Bright periwinkle blue eyes looked out at Rachel from behind the multitudinous wrinkles that crinkled when she smiled. "David plots to keep me bedridden. You have returned earlier than expected," Memaw said, over the sound of her knitting needles.

They continued to talk over trivial matters, the warm weather, flowers blooming in the garden outside, the ball she'd attended in London. Her grandmother fished for information Rachel wasn't ready to give. What must Ryan think of her running away? Perhaps he was thinking it for the best. She and Ryan could return to managing each other through special courier and keep their contact restricted to business.

Her life had been a series of avoidable and bad mistakes. She wanted only to forget the foolish side of her that had reared itself so unmercifully these last weeks and return to her world of numbers, plats, and diagrams.

She would not think of Ryan Donally ever again. He must know the kind of man Devonshire was. Ryan was not blind and stupid.

Besides, she had her own problems with which to contend.

"Are you truly all right, Memaw?" Rachel finally asked, bringing the corner of the blanket to her cheek. Her grandmother always knitted from the softest wool. When Rachel was a little girl, she'd carried a woolen blanket this very same blue until she was five.

Until Ryan had called her a baby and dropped it into the hog pen.

Oh, how she'd hated him for weeks after that!

And just that fast, her composure fled. Her throat tightened. She felt the horrible swell of tears behind her eyes. The menace of failure. "Come here, child," Memaw's soft voice penetrated her heavy thoughts. "Come sit beside me for a moment."

Rachel looked up to see that Memaw had set aside the knitting. Her blue eyes softened as she patted her lap.

"Oh, Memaw . . ." Rachel dropped to her knees beside her grandmother and let the soft leathery hands cradle her head. "I don't want to cry. I feel so foolish and childish."

"He's marrying someone else, I know." Memaw's quiet whisper reached around Rachel's heart and held. "We tried to warn you before you left for London. But your going had purpose. Everything happens for a reason, Butterfly."

The sound of her childhood name brought a bout of determination. "How did you know?" Rachel sat back on her heels to regard her grandmother. "How did you know how I felt about him?"

"Don't you be forgetting I was there when he wed Kathleen." The blue eyes regarded Rachel with serious attention. "I think most of us knew then how ye felt."

"Oh heavens." Rachel buried her face in her hands. Put baldly, her sentiment seemed so melodramatic and made her into a pathetic spectacle. She shook her head, half-laughing and half-weeping, her long braid falling forward over one shoulder.

In truth, Rachel no longer knew how she felt. Physically attracted yes. Who wouldn't be to perfection? Mentally, Ryan stimulated her interest in worldly things, and she was in awe of his professional ability. She'd followed his career for years. His papers had been the mainstay of her education. But she and Ryan didn't exist on the same emotional plane. He didn't care about the same things that she did.

He'd always been dictatorial, quick-tempered, and careless of moral convention. Yet he also made generous grants to the university he'd attended. He gave to poorhouses and orphanages. She'd lost the ability to understand him. For how could a man who loved his daughter with such great affection coexist with the same person who pillaged companies and destroyed people's lives? Nor did he respect her as a professional, or he wouldn't have tucked her away in Ireland with that pathetic upstart Allan Marrow to head the engineering division when she was so much smarter than any ten men. He had never come to Ireland to see what she'd done.

With newfound resolution, Rachel sat back on her calves. "I'm a big girl, Memaw." She wiped at her cheeks, understanding how foolishly she was behaving. "We should be talking about you."

"Nonsense." Memaw lowered her voice, her palm gently cupping Rachel's cheek. "When that tyrant isn't here, I get along just fine."

Rachel laughed. "I'm glad that you only stubbed your toe." She smiled, her heart filled with love for this old woman, who was more beloved than her own parents ever were. "Now that I know you're all right." She took Memaw's hands. "I do need to check on the progress in Rathdrum. I'll have to leave in a few days."

"You let that rascal Marrow attend to Rathdrum," Memaw

said adamantly. "There are bandits and scallywags along that road."

David leaned in the doorway, his arms folded over his chest. He looked as if he'd been standing there a long while. "Then David will need me to protect him," she said, a smile on her lips. She and her grandmother went through this argument every time Rachel took the road to her project site.

"Pious man that I am," he said.

"Balderdash." Memaw sniffed. "Pious, indeed. The devil's own, I think you are, encouraging her the way that you do."

"I have to go, Memaw. You know that." Climbing to her feet, Rachel brushed her skirts. The silly flow of tears was gone. She walked to the door, but David stopped her. He stroked his thumb over her cheek to grab the remnant of moisture as if to tell her that Ryan was not worth the tears. "Leave it to you to force me up the mountain and throw me off the cliff with no pretentious words of condolences," she said.

"That is what I do best." His teeth flashed white. "I put your trunks and other belongings in your chambers. Go clean up."

The evening was cold and gray as Rachel found her away among the row of lonely moss-covered gravestones, most of which sat outside the consecrated grounds of the local church. The low mist lay thicker beneath the boughs of two huge oaks, a peaceful area reserved for those unblessed souls, though why heaven couldn't be big enough for all souls, Rachel could never understand.

There were raindrops, like a spangle of stars, on her midnight blue sleeves, and the chilly air had whipped up the color in her cheeks. She had wrapped a shawl around her hair and shoulders and clutched it tightly beneath her chin, aware as a distant church bell rang for the evening service. She had not come to this place in a long time, though she sometimes attended services here, especially since this old church was between Glencree and Dublin.

Despite her rigidity, there was a moment when she felt the poignant grief that any child should be condemned to die at all. Certainly never her own infant daughter.

Rachel used to be a great believer in providence. If a person was good, didn't step over the line, followed rules, and worked hard, she would achieve her dreams. Rachel's journey had cost her dearly.

At Edinburgh, she was one of two women allowed to audit classes. Her father had once been a physics professor there. When she'd left London to begin a new life, she'd attracted the attentions of a university administrator who was also her engineering professor. She'd run from Ryan directly into another man's arms, wanting desperately to be loved. Two years into their relationship, he married someone else.

Someone respectable with noble feminine attributes. Men didn't marry their mistresses, after all. Rachel didn't know how much Lord Devonshire knew—or the official reason given to the university for her departure from Edinburgh. She had gone to live in a dormitory for wayward girls just outside Dublin.

Closing her eyes, she inhaled the scent of the damp earth. It rooted at her feet and touched her senses with plaguing memories.

She had been jealous that Ryan's child could be loved by so many when hers had died unloved except by her. She had said terrible things to Ryan at Kathleen's funeral. Her eyes shut, the memory of her own grief suddenly vivid. Despite Kathleen's frail health, she'd wanted to give Ryan a child so badly that she'd gambled away her life. In her mind, Ryan had allowed it to happen. And if Ryan was guilty of blaming himself for Kathleen's death, Rachel had been guiltier of adding to that blame, so deep had been her anguish, losing her baby and Kathleen all within weeks of one another. Rachel had walked away from the most important person in her life—as she had always walked away.

A twig snapped. David stood in the shadows beneath the heavily foliaged trees, his dark eyes unreadable in the twilight. "I thought I would find you here," he said.

"Don't let anyone ever tell you that absolute power doesn't corrupt," Rachel said, thinking of the man she'd thought loved her all those years ago marrying his wealthy, flawless debutante, then thinking about Ryan. "Because it does."

"Tell me about your heart, colleen."

Darkness was falling over the small cemetery, and Rachel looked up at the sky. Her heart lay in pieces. "I know now I cannot ever be with Ryan," she said. "I'm not a suitable wife for obvious reasons. But for just one moment . . . Truly, I don't know what happened to get me up and pulling myself to London the way I did," she managed with self-effacing humor, turning as she once again let her gaze fall on the small grave at her feet. "Do you think she went to heaven? Despite my own sins?"

David walked to her side. She could see his black shoes in her peripheral vision. His height, like Ryan's, dominated his presence and hers. "Yes, colleen. She is there."

David took her back to Memaw's cottage in the donkey cart, though she could have returned faster on foot. Supper was nearly ready when he opened the back door and escorted her into the warm kitchen. "I'll see you at the table in ten minutes," he said.

Leaning on her toes, she kissed his cheek and knew that he'd remained in the doorway watching as she walked toward the stairs. A glance over her shoulder told her that the smile on his handsome face a moment before had changed to a troubled frown. She didn't like him to worry about her. "I am not some delicate piece of porcelain that needs careful handling," she said from the stairway. But David, Memaw, and even Johnny all seemed to conspire in some way to fret over her.

"It is my responsibility to worry, Rachel."

Rachel hurried up the stairs. She'd often wondered why David Donally had taken the cloth. Nine years ago, he'd returned from a stint with the Foreign Service, retired his guns, and left England forever. He'd never spoken of his past. Or about that gold band he wore on his right hand. Nor hinted at the events that had led him to this path. Yet Rachel had seen him fight. He was as lethal with a sword as he was with his hands. David might not be what he seemed, but he was a good man with people, and the parish loved him. If it was the past he was running from, then they'd both found their sanctuary in a small part of Ireland. He'd looked to God to cure his ills and perhaps his conscience.

She looked to her job.

With that thought in mind, she threw open her trunks, found her satchel, and, removing it, laid it inside another trunk she'd take with her tomorrow. All of the paperwork, the topography maps, drawings, everything on Rathdrum she needed was inside. But for now, all she wanted was to visit Memaw and David, to make them quit mourning as if they were at her wake and not her homecoming.

Chapter 7

A week after Mary Elizabeth's birthday, Ryan stood at the iron gates of the Dublin D&B office fronting the Grand Canal. A fluffy green canopy of leafy branches filtered the midafternoon sunlight and laid a dappled carpet over the brick walk. Even though summer had officially arrived weeks ago, a chill breeze pulled at Ryan's long coat. He looked up and down the lonely street bereft of most of the traffic that plagued the next block. His gaze stopped on a spotted dog that sat on the corner of the street and thumped its tail lethargically.

"Hey, boy." Ryan held out a gloved hand.

The dog waggled up to him. Absently patting the hound's head, he opened the gate and walked through a landscaped garden before climbing the steps to the door. A bell tinkled upon his entry.

"Mr. Donally." The girl sitting at the desk came to her feet, spilling a jar of ink. "We . . . none of us were expectin' ye, sir. Mr. Marrow is in a meeting. I'll tell him that you are here."

She was pretty, with bright green eyes and reddish hair

confined in a bun. A book on the principles of physics sat on her desk. "Is Miss Bailey's office upstairs?" he asked.

"Yes, sir. On the second floor. But she isn't here."

Ryan took the stairs. "Send Marrow to me." His voice matched his brisk manner.

People stationed at various desks lifted their heads as he passed, their whispers following him down the corridor. He carried Rachel's satchel. Her nameplate on the first door drew his attention, and he stepped inside. The office was small. A well-ordered desk sat in front of a large sunny window. Textbooks filled the rosewood-and-gold-filigree bookcases that backed the west wall. Plants flourished in the sunlight and added life to the stark simplicity of the décor and the orderliness that surrounded him.

Ryan walked to the window to peer over the colorful buildings that skirted the narrow street below.

Her scent permeated the room. It was in the leather furniture, the simple yellow drapery that framed the windows, the carpet runner on the floor. The Telford medal he'd given her in London hung from a silver chalice that the Architectural Society had awarded him a year ago. Photos lined the wall, perfectly centered. He recognized most as having come from the D&B office in London. But there was more, and he moved his gaze over photographs of half-finished bridges and ornate buildings, all featuring a lone feminine figure in skirts, standing proudly among men carrying shovels and picks.

A spark of pride momentarily overrode every other thought. She'd shed new light, not only on her capabilities as a leader. Rachel was a fighter.

And even without the torture of swimming through veiled mists of libido-inducing spice, she was like a kinetic force, a vortex of moving energy channeling his focus. She had become a permanent fixture in his thoughts and a tack in his foot. He'd felt every step that had taken him closer to her in Ireland with a sense of anticipation.

Ryan returned his attention to the plate-glass window and watched a carriage rattle past on the street below. Watched like an irritated supplicant standing before the altar of his transgressions. He didn't like what he'd come to Ireland to do.

He wanted to find her and make sure she was all right. Then he wanted to shake her until her teeth rattled. That was his problem. He didn't know what to do with her, hadn't known since the second he'd seen her at the ball. Except he didn't want to look at her and feel his pulse quicken. He was thirty-one years old, for chrissakes, not some bloody green kid who didn't know what to do with a woman.

"Mr. Donally," a man's voice rasped as if he'd been running.

Ryan turned to see Allan Marrow standing in the doorway of the office, his hands filled with papers. With wavy brown hair and a height equal to his six feet, Marrow looked older than Ryan remembered. His eyes went over him, and he was suddenly wondering if he had ever put his hands on Rachel. "We were not expecting you," Marrow said. "Miss Bailey isn't here. She left three days ago for Rathdrum."

"Did my brother go with her?" Ryan asked.

"Yes, sir. Father Donally took her."

Ryan withdrew a packet from inside his coat and moved to the desk. "The contracts have been paid." He dropped the envelope. "This is a receipt for a bank draft deposited today in the Bank of Ireland."

"I don't understand, sir. We were told—"

"You wouldn't. You haven't been in this business long enough."

Ryan had gone first thing upon his arrival to the authorities at public works, where he promptly set the matter straight about the Rathdrum project. The past three days, he had put his own men in contact with the necessary officials in Wicklow County. The monies for the project had already been paid and were in Dublin, held illegally by a council member. Ryan left no doubt in any stunned official's mind that he would personally bring charges against everyone on the council if all funds, as stipulated by the original contracts, were not released. Two hours later Ryan carried a draft out of the offices.

"Tomorrow two of my corporate accounting officers will arrive to audit your books." Flipping open the lock on Rachel's satchel, he withdrew the order to allow the audit. "I expect they'll be given every courtesy."

"Is there a discrepancy, sir?"

"I hope not." Closing the satchel with a *click*, Ryan regarded the younger man.

Devonshire's words about this man and Rachel pulled at him. Evidently, the explosion of emotions carried over into his voice, for the man paled when he spoke. "I'll give you an hour to get home and pack your personal belongings," Ryan said. "I've hired a carriage to take us to Rathdrum. And Marrow . . ."

"Yes, sir."

"How is Mrs. Bailey feeling?" He slid the satchel off the desk. "I understand that she had a fall."

The cab driver who had dropped him off at the gates told him as much.

"I believe she is as ornery as ever." Marrow suddenly cleared his throat. "Of course, I mean that in a polite way, sir."

Ryan managed to hide a grin. "I know how you mean it, Marrow." Memaw had taken his head off more than once. But then he'd been brash in his youth. "Do you need a ride to your quarters to pack?"

"Yes, sir. If you want me to be ready in an hour."

"See that the bank receipt is given to accounts." Ryan strode past Marrow, the satchel at his side. "I'll be outside."

Ryan walked past his official photograph, mounted on the wall in the corridor, and down the stairway. He was suddenly thinking of his older brother with a stab of irritation and didn't want his antagonism toward David's relationship with Rachel to color his judgment. She was closer to his entire family than he was.

Yet, unexpectedly, he discovered he held little true animosity, only a clumsy sense of the inevitable and, worse—a vague hint of remorse.

What he had to say to Rachel he could say to them both.

Ryan didn't leave Dublin at once, and, as he stood on the front porch of Memaw's house, surprised he'd been able to find it after so many years, he discovered he was as nervous as a recalcitrant schoolboy. His coat collar pulled up against the chill, one hand buried in his pocket, he stood half in the shadows of an ivy-laced trellis. Kathleen had visited there twice before Mary Elizabeth had been born. He had not been with her.

There was a familiarity in the surroundings that did not exist in the houses he owned in England. He had stayed beneath this roof often as a child on the occasions that he'd left Carlisle, where he'd grown up. His father's parents were buried somewhere here in this land of saints and scholars between Dublin and Kenmore. His mother had been English and disinherited by her family when she'd married his father, an Irishman.

No one answered the summons on the door, and Ryan stepped off the porch and looked up at the window above the door. Memaw's wrinkled face was framed in the glass, her pale orange hair visible in the shadows. Ryan didn't know what to expect from the woman who had been so close to him after his own mother had died. He'd always found a strange sort of refuge here, away from his father.

"Ryan Donally?" Memaw shoved open the window and yelled down at him. "What are you doing here, young man?"

"Hoping an ornery old lady has a few hours to spare," he said, behind a grin.

"I'm not so old that I cannot hear all the commotion you're making on my door. Step into the light and let me see you. My eyes are good, but they're not young."

Ryan stepped out from beneath the shade. "You're still looking like a spry seventy-year-old, Memaw. You haven't aged a day since I saw you last."

She cackled in glee. "And how long ago was that? Tell me about your daughter. Rachel said she is the image of her beautiful mother."

"That she is," Ryan agreed, noting the people leaning out windows up and down the block.

He heard his name whispered among the villagers as if they knew who he was. He was surprised when some waved and smiled. Most were simple people who lived simple lives. This was not an unfamiliar world to him, only a world he had left years ago.

"Well, are ye goin' to be standin' out on my walkway all day?" Memaw smacked her hand on the sill. "Come inside and let me see how much you've grown."

Any other woman, and Ryan might have been amused by that.

"And bring Marrow in with you." Memaw returned to the window. "He'll be wantin' to sup. We've got his favorite stew cooking."

Ryan turned to assess the young engineer he'd left waiting in the carriage, only to see that Marrow had already heard the words. He hurried past Ryan through the door—as if he'd been there a hundred times before.

"Miss Bailey," the project foreman called from his seat atop a wagon. The older man had reined in the horse on the ledge that overlooked the gulley where she had been making inspections most of the afternoon. Six burly men in red woolen shirts sat behind him. All nodded politely. "Will ye be needin' a ride into the village?" he asked.

Slogging her way up the rocky incline, Rachel reached the grassy plateau and shaded her eyes with her hands as she looked into the craggy, bearded face of her foreman. She held a tool belt in her hand. Her working uniform consisted of heavy boots and trousers, a shirtwaist and long-sleeved coat. Most of the men who worked for her were used to seeing her on the site and no longer gawked at her strange attire. They all thought her perpetually strange as it was. "I have work to finish, Mr. O'Roarke."

"The work will be here tomorrow, Miss Bailey."

"We already discussed this an hour ago."

He pushed his sleeves up his thick forearms. "But most everyone has gone into the village."

Rachel dusted off her hands. "No doubt, you have been well coached by Father Donally to keep an eye on me." They all knew better than to tell her what she could or couldn't do. "I don't expect any of you to stay here tonight. Go enjoy yourselves."

She'd been up at daybreak to walk the work site, and was exhausted. "Mr. O'Roarke," Rachel called, as he turned to slap the reins. "Tomorrow, please check on the supplies I ordered before leaving Dublin. They should be here."

Rachel walked along the riverbank and took the wooded path that led to her work tent. The sky was clear, the forest warm in the dying light of the day. She was not supposed to be at the base camp after dark, and most of the men who worked for her were protective enough of her welfare to see her escorted into town. After all, she paid their wages—she would continue to do so until she'd depleted her funding. The Rathdrum annual fair had changed her plans. There were no rooms to let within miles of the town.

Rachel swiped the back of her dusty hand across her forehead and dipped beneath the canvas doorway of the tent. Wooden chairs and tables were spread around the living area. She and Elsie each had a cot. Her cook slept in another shelter out back. Rachel welcomed the solitude at the Rathdrum site, the sense of independence and authority that followed her around. Her presence had even ceased to scandalize the village elders. Especially in the weeks since she'd contributed a substantial donation to the local poorhouse, the parish, and built the main street that now went through town, if only so she could drive a wagon to the D&B building.

Removing the old beater hat from her head, she tossed it on the table beside her satchel. She'd wrapped her hair beneath the thick-rimmed helmet and now shook it free of the tight bun, before rummaging in the small dresser for the bottle of aged whiskey that she kept hidden from David.

"Are you planning on skipping the entire festivities tonight?" David's cultured Irish voice said from behind her.

"Mother Mary and Joseph, you scared the daylights out of me, David Donally." Her heart pounded her ribs. "I thought you returned to your parish this morning."

Wearing his black priestly garb, David stooped his tall frame beneath the entrance and stepped inside the tent. His white collar lay against the tanned column of his throat. "Why aren't you dressed?"

"Truly, Father," she mocked with a deliberate, flirty smile, "I'm not undressed."

David had the grace to look embarrassed. "A lamentable

bit of poor wording. Do you have something"—a lazy white grin worked its way across his mouth—"more festive for the occasion in town?"

"I like my attire." She sat at the table and lit the lamp, before blowing out the match. "Go away, David. I have work to do."

"The town residents will expect to see you there tonight. Your men will expect to see you there. You have to make an appearance."

As expected, David took everyone's side but hers. Men always stuck together, she realized. He wasn't going to let her stay at the camp alone.

Rachel jiggled the latch on the satchel, turning the case upright and into the light, curious as to the difficulty. On closer inspection, she noted the initial, *RD*, on the gold clasp rather than *RB*. The sight made her pause. She hadn't noted the oddity of the latch when she'd packed her satchel before leaving Dublin. She hadn't used the satchel at all since she'd gone to Mr. Williams's office and asked about her inheritance.

Pressing the clasp, she finally worked it off the catch. A vague trail of clover and aged leather rolled over her senses. Alarmed, Rachel pulled out a handful of folders and felt her stomach tighten. The notes were definitely Ryan's bold scrawl. He'd always scribed his R's with daunting flourish, nearly arrogant in perfection. She slid the papers from their encasement, realizing that somehow Ryan must have picked up *her* satchel by mistake when he'd left her hotel room the night of the opera. And she had taken his satchel filled with contracts, agenda notes, and reports.

David stood behind her. His sleeve brushed her shoulder, and she caught the pleasant scent of soap on his skin as he lifted a sheet of paper to the light. It was Ryan's itinerary for the week, every line filled to overflowing.

"My brother is a popular man." He peered down at her. "Is this what you want with your life?"

"Yes." She snatched back the paper. "I want to be busy."

Rachel shoved everything back into the satchel as if she'd violated consecrated ground by laying her hands all over Ryan's things. He would want this satchel back as soon as possible. "I wanted to prove I could be as professional as Marrow or any other man at D&B. Do you think I was wrong for asking Ryan?" she asked without turning.

"What does my answer matter? You are already doing Allan Marrow's work."

"I have too many secrets as it is, David." Rachel sighed and dropped into the chair. "Mr. Marrow has a meeting with the political powers that be in Dublin tomorrow morning. If they don't pay our contracts, we will have to close the project."

Rachel shoved the last folder inside the satchel and scraped her knuckle across something sharp. She pulled out the injurious object. The D&B logo emblazoned a solid gold money clip with a single red ruby at its center. Her jaw dropped open. She thumbed through the thick stack of currency notes. "Who carries a thousand pounds? Ryan must be completely mad."

"Aye." David lifted the clip from her hands. "But the good Lord appreciates his generosity."

"That's thievery." Rachel gasped. "The money isn't mine."

"If my brother wishes to complain about his generous donation, he's welcome to do so in confession." David strode to the tent opening and threw back the canvas edge. "It would do his soul good to meditate over his sins. Especially since he decided to convert to the Anglican Church three years ago."

"Where are you going?"

The last rays of the sun spilled around his tall dark form. "Outside to wait for you." He raised a brow that matched his lively deep indigo eyes. "Unless you wish for me to go through your trunks and find something for you to wear."

No doubt he would, too.

Elsie appeared from the private area of the tent separated

by a canvas divider. Two short blond braids curved around the shells of her ears. "I took the liberty of laying something out for ye, mum."

Frowning, Rachel neither protested nor cooperated exactly. She latched the clasp on Ryan's satchel. "I can't go, David."

"Yes, you can."

"David . . ." She twisted around in the spindle chair.

"Pack up Elsie as well. I'll be outside waiting."

"Oh, *yes*, sir," Elsie squeaked dreamily, her cornflower blue eyes wide on David as if he were Saint Jude himself. "I shall love to go."

Glaring at David, Rachel swore that he and Ryan were exactly alike.

Ryan descended from the carriage and brushed at his sleeves, stretching his legs as his gaze sought the distant village rooftops. Marrow climbed down behind him, and they both eyed the throng of carts lining both sides of the narrow road. The faint sound of fiddlers and pipes hinted at a festival in progress.

"The crowd is here for the annual fair," Marrow said from beside him. He and Marrow had spoken little on the trip from Dublin, and Ryan turned as if he'd forgotten the man was with him. "Quite a pack it is, too," the man added, when Ryan did not reply. "I had forgotten that it would be here this time of year."

Ryan observed the distant village with a faintly ironic eye as he considered his lack of timing and considerable bad luck of late. Turning, he flipped two coins to his driver. "We'll need a place to sleep for the night," he said. "Go back down the road and secure a room. I don't care what it costs."

He had no idea where Rachel or David might be. He

couldn't reach the base construction camp until he found another way around the town.

Already he was looking for her.

Somewhere a bonfire colored the darkening sky a shimmering orange. A cold breeze whipped through the canopy of trees overhead. Ryan's clothes were damp. The rain had fallen ceaselessly since leaving Memaw's early this morning.

He'd ended up spending the previous night at the cottage, ensconced in Rachel's bed amid a canopy of lavender and lace. Who would have guessed that Rachel had such a romantic side to her life?

"When was the last time you were in Ireland, sir?" Marrow asked, as they walked some distance without speaking.

A drunken couple bumped Ryan's shoulder. "Ten years," he said. "Just before Miss Bailey's grandfather passed away."

"You are somewhat renowned here," Marrow said. "Your name is anyway."

"Why is that?"

"Donally & Bailey feeds a lot of people here."

Narrowly avoiding a pair of overloaded hay carts in his path, he smothered a curse as he stepped in a pile of questionable substance. Like a fool, he was garbed in a charcoal black coat and black trousers as he moved among the wagons, carts, and carriages toward the outskirts of the crowded village. A full moon sat like a bright chalky eye on the mountainous horizon, an ethereal orb against a velvety backdrop. It was a night made for mythical gnomes and fairies if not for the bloodsucking mosquitoes that swarmed around him in droves.

By the time Ryan reached the village he was in the foulest mood and regretted not removing his coat or changing his clothes to something more auspicious, certainly less conspicuous. His shoes alone cost more than most people there made in a year. The music had grown louder, the crowd thicker, the din in his head a buzzing annoyance that boded ill for the object of his hunt.

A buxom woman sashayed up to him carrying a tray laden with cream tarts, a bold smile, and overstated femininity amplified by her low-cut blouse. Leaving Marrow to handle her bold advances, Ryan shouldered through a group of men and followed the booth-lined street that spilled into the open field. The smell of roasting boar mixed with taffy and high meadow grass.

Troubadours roamed the crowded lanes singing of love lost. A roistering party of gamblers threw dice off the path. Beyond the street, thatch-roofed cottages rose up white in the night. Ryan followed the music, and it was there, amid the honeysuckle and thyme, that Marrow caught up to him. A younger crowd had gathered around the bonfire to watch a spirited rigadoon led in time by a quartet of fiddlers and lutes. For a moment, as his gaze scanned the people for a familiar face, Ryan bent to wipe his shoes on a rock. A man spat a long stream of tobacco juice across his path, grinning brashly when Ryan turned his head. Two front teeth were missing.

"Sir . . ." Marrow said above the noise, pointing, and dragging Ryan's gaze from the apple-faced varlet. "I see Miss Bailey."

Ryan followed the direction of Marrow's hand. The crowd had parted just enough for him to glimpse the high-stepping dancers near the bonfire. Impatient, he still didn't see Rachel, didn't expect to see her dancing, and started to turn away when everything inside him paused on a breath. He slowly straightened.

Rachel was among the circle of dancers.

Except she didn't look like Rachel at all.

Not the Rachel he knew.

The weighty mass of her hair, no longer bound by bun or

braid, fell in fiery waves past her waist. A simple blue muslin skirt flowed around her hips and legs, with her saucy steps revealing a pair of slim ankles and calves. But there was nothing simple about the way she danced.

Without conscious thought, Ryan moved past Marrow, his feet carrying him through the crowd until he stood at the edge of the brightly lit circle of dancers. The fiddlers picked up their pace. More couples squeezed past him as they rushed to join the circle. People clapped their hands to the jaunty cadence. Rosy flags of color flushed Rachel's cheeks.

While growing up, she'd always been so staid and bloody virginal to him, never this lustful, pagan woman he was watching dance in abandon. She wore a long-sleeved blouse, her breasts straining the soft fabric, the hot flames of the fire highlighting the crests and exploring the sensual curves of her body. Glowing with carnal radiance, she resembled a flame-haired Gypsy, a nimble forest sprite, her wide carmine mouth set in a smile for the man who had looped his arm around hers. Ryan's gaze went to the man.

"Does Miss Bailey know you are coming?" Marrow asked, over the festive din.

She would know soon enough, he thought, his mood darkening to the strength of a thundercloud.

She would know as soon as he grabbed her by the shoulders and shook her until her teeth rattled. Rachel, who was not so starchy as he'd always framed her to be in his mind, with her spinster clothes and tightly bound hair. He was beginning to realize he didn't know her at all. She was no *spinster*, to be sure!

Until that moment, he'd been worried about her. Worried about the hastiness of her departure. About her grandmother. Why she would leave London the way she had. He'd been worried about her life and her future.

She was quite content, he realized. What a calculating little opportunist she had been while with him in London.

She'd lied to him about the Rathdrum project. Lied by omission. Violated his trust by not following protocol. She lied about her reasons for coming to London, departing just as quickly when he'd told her he wasn't going to approve her levee project.

Ryan tightened his jaw as if that alone could contain the sense of betrayal he felt as he watched her laugh, as carefree as a woodland elf.

And she no longer had the barrier of his regret or conscience to protect her. Watching her, Ryan could feel the flames hot on his clothes, feel his chest tighten, as his eyes, glittering with the heat of the fire, followed Rachel around the glen.

Slowly, he became aware that his was not the only interest tracking her movements. Someone else was also watching, he thought as he felt the tug of his gaze, and looked across the flames of the roaring bonfire directly into David's eyes.

So much like his. Dark pools of black and unerringly intimidating.

His brother had been watching him.

For some time, it seemed, judging from the expression pulling David's brows low. No greeting met Ryan's gaze. No welcoming sentiment. Only rampant censure as if he'd just gotten his knuckles slapped like a disobedient altar boy.

His self-control rapidly deteriorating, Ryan smiled faintly, acknowledging in that one arrogant gesture that he wasn't going to apologize for what was clearly in his thoughts as he watched Rachel dance. She thought she was safe in Ireland.

No way in hell was she safe from him.

Let David read *that* in his eyes.

As he watched, his brother began working his way through

the crowd. But Ryan had already stepped out among the dancers.

The music played to Rachel's soul. The scent of peat, geraniums, and parched earth mixed with the laughter to create a magical sense of well-being. She was glad David had forced her to come, and, breathless, she laughed into her partner's face as he swung her in a circle to the final chords of the jig. He was one of many she'd danced with, and didn't even know his name, only that most of the people there had come from as far as twenty miles to laugh and to drink. He thanked her as a young girl pulled him away for another dance. More couples rushed to join the circle of dancers.

"May I have this dance, Miss Bailey?" Allan Marrow bent over Rachel's hand.

Her breath coming in gasps, too shocked to note that he had taken her hand, Rachel stared in disbelief. "Allan?" She was hot and flushed, her nape damp beneath her hair. "You are supposed to be in Dublin—"

"The Rathdrum contracts have been paid."

The fiddlers struck up another lively gig. "I don't understand," she said, when he took her hands. "How?"

They turned directly into Ryan.

Rachel's world quit spinning.

Dizziness pulled at her equilibrium, and she thought she might faint from the heat. "Ryan . . ." Her voice was too breathless.

She couldn't imagine why he was in Ireland.

He looked into her flushed features, handed his coat and jacket to Marrow, and pulled her into the throng of dancers. The shadowy rasp of a beard darkened his jaw.

"Dance with me," he said, in that sensual drawl that might have made her heart beat faster if his eyes hadn't told her other things.

Rachel didn't feel well. His presence, his energy raged hotter than the bonfire. "You're . . . here."

"A conclusion you've deduced without spectacles? I'm proud of you, Rache."

"*What* are you doing here?"

His eyes dark on hers, he said, "I believe that you invited me."

The stinging set-down caused her confidence to waver. His body hot against hers, one hand on her waist, he danced with her to the end of the long circle, then without breaking stride, led her through the crowd. Rachel felt the wildest sensation of fear.

"Where are you staying?" he asked, over the din of music.

"At the base camp."

Ryan stopped with her at the edge of the crowd. "How far?" His hand on her arm remained uncompromising.

"Follow the river." She pointed to the forest behind him. "Less than a mile. Ryan—"

"Don't," he said flatly. "When we talk, it won't be with my brother hovering over you."

Confused by his actions but not the manner of his tone, Rachel allowed him to pull her through the heavy throng of drunken revelers, past a row of vendors hawking their wares, and into the thinning light that surrounded the woods. He was escaping David.

"Elsie is with me, as well as my cook." She walked in double time to keep up with him, lest he drag her. "I need to find them."

"I'm sure David will see to them."

She stumbled over her skirts, but Ryan's grip on her upper arm kept her from falling. "I have your satchel," she said, in light of his terrible mood. "I would have sent it back—"

"You are in a lot of trouble, Rache."

A burst of panic filled her.

A jester wearing bells on his floppy hat bounced behind them until, finally ignored, he turned away to annoy another couple. More than one woman had the nerve to watch Ryan as he passed the booths. Her spine snapping straight, Rachel resented the open attention paid to him or that he seemed used to the notice. He appeared out of place, with rich garments that stamped him as indelibly wealthy, his height, and a face handsome enough to turn any woman's head. A dark wing of hair lay carelessly across his forehead, his square jaw set with purpose as he marched her like some recalcitrant child toward the path leading into the woods.

Rachel tripped again, nearly losing a slipper this time, but when she stumbled this time, Ryan lifted her into his arms. All without breaking pace. She hit the wall of his chest, catching her arms around his neck. No man had ever carried her. Her body jolted with a heady primitive sensuality that melted lower in the juncture between her thighs. She felt ridiculous and shivery at once, pressed so intimately against him, her legs dangling over his arms like those of some damsel in distress.

She didn't like the feeling. "Put me down, Ryan."

"No."

"I mean it, Ryan. Put me down." She struggled in earnest as he carried her into the trees. "You are behaving like a . . . a barbarian."

With that declaration, he threw her over his shoulder. "I swear I'm going to make you pay for this!" She beat his back with her fists. "What is wrong with you?"

"Why don't you tell me? Maybe you can even explain why it is I had to find out everything from someone else."

The sound of the rushing river grew louder and surrounded her with noise. A vision of Ryan throwing her into the water made her scream. Her struggles grew more frantic. He knew that she'd been financing the Rathdrum project out of her own pocket, she thought in panic, or Lord Devonshire had told him the truth about her—or he'd found out that she'd been hiding behind Allan Marrow for two years.

Then Ryan stopped. She felt the flex of his arm against her upper thighs, and she straightened, ready to pummel him. Her breathing harsh in her chest, her palms pressed against his shoulders, she looked down at him, her hair framing his face in a scented bath of spiced apple and cinnamon. She pulled her gaze from his lips to find his eyes dark on hers, a whisper of heat in their depths, his mouth so close they shared the same air.

Caught like a bird in the jaws of a wolf, she was unable to look from his eyes.

They remained frozen by the silence.

Closing her eyes, she let herself experience the sensation of his touch.

"What do you want, Rachel?"

She wanted to breathe again. She wanted his tongue in her mouth. She wanted just once more to feel his arms around her. To feel cherished by him. Even if it wasn't real. Even if it could go no further than tonight.

She had wanted this forever.

She lowered her mouth and kissed him.

Kissed him as she'd tried to do in London. Only this time he didn't pull away.

Parting her lips, he kissed her back with the same shaky urgency that stormed her senses. Her palms slid over the wondrous tug and pull of hardened muscles on his shoulders before her hands climbed into his hair. His skin smelled faintly of smoke and sweet-scented soap. His arm around her thighs loosened. She felt herself sliding down every hardened inch of him until her feet dangled in the air.

"Jaysus, Rachel . . ." Ryan's voice seduced another groan from her throat.

He felt good pressed against her body, and she met the plunder of his tongue, aware of his powerful arousal. And hers. The rasp of his face against her tender skin.

Even as he walked her into the thick trunk of a tree, and she felt his hands go to her waist and her feet touch the ground, she could not get close enough. Climb high enough against him. Yet still the kiss went on and on, possessively claiming her will, climbing the hills and descending the valleys of their past, destroying barriers that seemed to crumble beneath the onslaught of her emotions.

Once long ago he'd shown her what this would feel like. She didn't know if he remembered.

Then his mouth moved to the long column of her neck, and she heard herself groan his name. Ryan knew how to kiss. He was hard against her. Her head fell back as his mouth played havoc with the pulse beating wildly at her throat. Her eyes sliding open, she stared at the canopy of leaves overhead, lost to the stroke of his hand as he slid his palm up her leg beneath her skirt. She moved again to claim his mouth.

Yet, it was Ryan who pulled away, if only a little distance, enough to slow the flames. He mouthed the tiny hollow on her throat. "Are you and Allan Marrow lovers?"

She choked, taken at once by a fit of coughing. "Are you insane?" she rasped. "He's . . . he's younger than I am, Ryan."

A low moan escaped her when his hand cupped her breast. "More likely he's just smitten and easily manipulated."

Her heart thundered with uncertainty, for she was back to remembering the probable reason he'd come to Ireland. If the contracts had been paid, then he'd been the one to see it done. He would know that she'd failed as a manager and a leader, and that she couldn't do anything on her own. "May I please explain—?"

"Explain what, Rache?" He slid his fingers to the nape of her neck, until he cupped each side of her face with his hands.

They stood alone in a wooded copse. The top two buttons on his white shirt were open at his throat. He wore a waist-coat threaded with moonlight in the half darkness of the trees. "Explain why you really came to London?"

She did not fail to notice the implacable warning in his deceptively calm reply and took an involuntary step backward into the tree. She could see a watch fob in his vest pocket. Then she realized he was silent. Waiting for her to speak.

For all that she had to say, nothing came out of her mouth.

"How long have you been hiding behind Marrow and doing the work at D&B?" Ryan finally asked, no anger, no fury in his voice. Only a question behind the words.

She felt her eyes close as his mouth whispered kisses over hers. "You never wanted to know the truth, Ryan, as if that would absolve you from making a decision about me."

His silence told her she had guessed the truth of his reaction.

"Except the levee project was my own, Ryan," she said, motionless as he looked down into her face. "I wanted you to recognize me for something that I did."

"Enough to kiss me in London?"

Rachel wet her lips but as he watched her, her chin came up with new resolve. "That was . . . personal."

"How personal?"

She regarded his expression, defined by the shadows that shaped his mouth, and oddly vulnerable, and wanted to kiss him again. "Extremely personal."

He pulled back, and his eyes caught the moonlight.

"None of it was a lie, Ryan," she whispered. "I swear."

The tree at her back, she could go nowhere. A gust of wind flapped her skirts against his legs. One hand bracing the tree, he held his head down as if that act could restrain him from touching her. "If I kiss you again, I won't stop again." His voice was no louder than a whispered caress. A promise. "It won't stop with only a kiss, Rachel."

Drawing the cool air into her shaky lungs, she did no more than breathe as she cast her gaze away from Ryan's compelling profile. A muscle bunched in his cheek.

The distant music had ceased as the bonfire burned itself out, leaving the sky a velvety morass of stars. "What do we do, Rache?" he asked her. "We dance around the other. We sway to the cadence of our own personal rhythm. We always have. Do we keep dancing until one of us goes insane? Or do we just *do* it."

Rachel's jaw eased open. "Do it? *It?*"

"I want it. You want it. You make me hard just smelling you." He pressed his nose into her hair. "I'll never be able to eat apple pie again without imagining my mouth all over you. No apple will pass my lips without me thinking of having wanton sex with you. I want to see you naked. Touch you. Taste you." He pulled back to look into her face, his mouth so close she could taste his breath on her lips. "Do we continue the same old dance, Rache?" He slid his fingers into her hair, his eyes on her parted lips. "Or do we sin?"

They stood together in the scented fragrance of the woods, not quite touching, yet so attuned to the other, Rachel could almost hear his heartbeat. "Are you mad, Ryan?"

"Completely." His voice had taken on an edge. "And I'm not even drunk."

"You should be," David said from behind him. "Because when you wake up in the morning you're going to have one big headache to contend with."

Paralyzed with shock, Rachel remained where she was between Ryan and the tree as she listened to David's footsteps in the leaves. "If you two aren't really, really careful, you are going to find yourselves married," he said, like a priest.

A domineering one at that, and Rachel stepped around Ryan. David's dark eyes fell first on her disheveled state, then moved to Ryan, who had yet to turn around she noted as he still leaned with his palm against the tree as if in pain. "Ryan no longer belongs to the Catholic Church," she said bluntly, in no mood for intimidation. "You *can't* marry us, David. Nothing happened."

"Yet," Ryan said, throwing his arms akimbo as if it were her fault that he had carried her off into the woods. "Nothing has happened, *yet*." He returned her stare.

Truly, she stood between two of the most domineering men in all the empire.

Then Ryan walked away and left her standing with David, who looked as benevolent and compassionate as a bolt of lightning.

Chapter 8

Ryan's nose itched. Somewhere in the farthest recesses of his brain, he sensed that he wasn't in bed alone and that he was suffering God's worst headache. A warm body curled next to his back.

With the sunrise, Ryan's senses continued to awaken.

He could hear panting, feel the lick of a wet tongue against his neck, the awful scent of dog breath. He groaned on an oath and turned his head. The hound beside him leapt to its feet, wagging its long tail as if Ryan had been asleep for a century rather than a few measly hours. He objected to dogs in general. Mornings in particular.

He lay on his coat atop a thick cushion of straw. He could still scent Rachel on his shirt. Taste her on his lips. His eyes focused on the heavy timbers of the ceiling. A white mass of spiderwebs competed with bird nests on the drooping crossbeams that stretched across the breadth of the roof. A dozen species of noisy finches fluttered about the eaves, sweeping in and out of the hole in the drooping roof.

Until this morning, he thought he was sleeping in an abandoned barn. Ryan turned on his side to pet the ugly hound, his hand freezing as his gaze caught movement in the corner of the stall.

David sat on an empty molasses barrel, his elbows resting on his knees. Ryan groaned as much from the tormenting ache in every muscle in his body as from the sight of a black-garbed priest looking at him with wrath flickering in his eyes. A fat chicken landed on the stall door in a flutter of wings, shedding feathers over Ryan's bed.

"Congratulations," David said, on a note tainted with amusement. "You found the only private quarters to be had within ten miles."

Ryan sat up and pulled his leg against his chest. His face itched with the start of a beard. "Good morning to you, too."

"I'm asking you to stay away from Rachel."

Succinct as always. Ryan shouldn't have been surprised. He had no intention of staying away from Rachel. "That's difficult to do considering the business we both share."

"You know in what way I mean. Rachel is more vulnerable than you think."

"Vulnerable?" he scoffed in disgust. "Like a slab of steel."

"Steel, for all of its strength, can fracture." David met Ryan's gaze, silently defying him to challenge the statement. "Before you accuse her of treachery, know that she used her entire inheritance to float this project and pay the laborers. She is the only reason twelve hundred people have not lost their jobs. She sold her estate in Carlisle to finish this project. Rachel is very popular among the locals, and her crew is protective."

Bracing an elbow across his knee, Ryan observed his brother in the dusty, hazy light of the barn. "How the hell did you find me anyway?"

"A lot of folk saw you leave with her last night and did not take kindly to any threat ye might be posing. They worry for her. So, I kept an eye on you." His gaze surveyed Ryan's sleeping quarters, and one corner of his mouth dimpled. "Did you have a restful night?"

At least he'd been able to sleep prone, which was more than Marrow had probably accomplished in the carriage. Ryan picked straw off his sleeve. "Is she happy living in Ireland? Hiding her passions behind books and other people's lives? Who are her friends?"

"Rachel has many gifts. She is generous in spirit and beloved by those who know her. Perhaps that is all she needs to be happy."

Reformed sinners made pious god-awful saints. Normally, Ryan didn't care for David's sanctimonious half-truths and propaganda. His brother had walked a wide swath of road when he was younger. But David's protective tone pulled at Ryan's conscience—and something else. There were entire years from Rachel's life that Ryan knew nothing about. She had practically disappeared after his wedding to Kathleen. Ryan would find letters every so often that she'd written to Kathleen.

"It isn't my intent to hurt her," Ryan said, dropping his gaze to the straw in his hand before resuming his posture and dusted off his hands. His impatience, the power he'd restrained for her sake, gave Ryan's voice a hard edge. His reasons for being in Rathdrum were far too complicated to launch into explanations now.

"Last night . . . if you want to know what happened, let Rachel tell you."

David scoffed. "Rachel fakes confession. She wouldn't tell me anything if I buried her in sand up to her neck at low tide."

"Rachel lies during confession?" Ryan was incredulous.

"Not at all. She just doesn't confess to anything." David unfurled his long frame. "You aren't far from my place of residence. Glenealy happens to be my diocese. Do you want to wash and shave?"

"Is that an invitation?"

"You smell like a hound. Besides"—David remained in the doorway of the stall—"you've earned the right, since it's your donation that just increased our building fund. I can spare the water and some breakfast for you and your men."

Ryan raised a dark brow. "Indeed." Obviously, David had absconded with the money Ryan had had in his satchel.

Marrow sat sleepy-eyed on the step of the carriage and came to his feet when Ryan walked out of the barn five minutes later, shrugging into his coat. "Sir." A thatch of blond hair stood straight on end. "Father Donally told us to follow him."

Adjusting his collar, Ryan turned to look over his shoulder as David climbed into a black buggy.

"Sir," Marrow said beneath his breath, "he asked why I was here with you."

Ryan turned his attention on Marrow. "What did you tell him?"

"That I'm here to take over Miss Bailey's duties."

Ryan stared at the sky, wondering why he'd felt it so bloody necessary to come to Ireland and handle this matter with Rachel when a dozen accomplished Ore Industries solicitors could have completed the task. Even if he hadn't begun to chafe under the moral bit of his quandary, the approaching clouds added an edge to his mood. He did not suffer dilemmas. Not when they applied to business decisions.

"She won't like your decision, sir," Marrow contributed further.

Ryan directed the force of his tone at the young engineer, for it seemed annoyingly obvious he was smitten with Rachel. But pity the poor fool who could not control her.

She would leave heel prints on his back.

Ryan reached around Marrow for his personal effects beneath the seat. "Follow us in this carriage. I'll go with my brother."

* * *

"Mum"—Elsie pushed aside the tent divider—"he is here."

Rachel's head was bent over the last of her buttons on her shirtwaist. "Who is here?" She yanked her jacket off the cot and shrugged into the sleeves.

The color rose high in Elsie's pretty cheeks. "Mr. Donally, mum," she whispered energetically. "He is here with Mr. Marrow. They have gone to the work site."

Marrow again. Rachel frowned. She had overslept for the first time in years.

She watched as a flustered Elsie hurried to straighten the tent as if Ryan would be coming inside her private quarters. "Elsie, please see to breakfast." Rachel's impatience with the flighty girl was evident in her voice. "We'll eat outside."

Rachel checked herself briefly in the glass before leaving the tent, aware that a pebble had somehow gotten into her boot. She'd had a wretched night's sleep. Freckles were clearly visible on her nose after she'd spent all day yesterday in the sun. Though why she should care at all she didn't know.

A dreary sky threw a canopy of gray over the treetops. The closer Rachel got to the river, the louder the sound of rushing water and the slower her steps until she reached the ledge. A mist rose from the forest floor behind her. Ryan stood balanced between two girders stretched over the river, looking at something near the bank below as he spoke to her foreman. Marrow stood beside them.

Ryan appeared much as he did last night when he'd taken her in his arms and kissed her in the moonlight. Dressed in dark trousers and a white shirt now plastered to his body from the river spray, he looked as if he could be a fixture to the steel-and-granite construction site. Clearly, he was a man straddling the banks of two opposing worlds, knowing both intimately. A crane was swinging its heavy load over the riverbed, the sound of the steam engines too loud to hear anything else. Then, as if sensing her presence, Ryan lifted his head and saw her standing on the ridge.

Her heart thumped against her ribs. She'd thought after he'd walked away from her last night that she'd mastered her emotions. She was wrong.

Rachel couldn't be within a hundred feet of him without experiencing some bodily reaction that sent her brain into a spin. *Doing it* had suddenly become a choice in her mind. Restless, she wriggled her foot in her boot, aware that the stone was bruising her insole. She dropped to untie the laces, so did not see Ryan's frown, only felt the slide of his gaze down her body. Her hands not entirely steady, she noted that her thick braid fell over one shoulder. She realized she'd forgotten her work hat.

Rachel yanked on the knot. "Damn," she muttered, when she discerned that she would need fingernails to loosen the laces.

The work crew was moving down the river. Turning back into the woods, Rachel let them go on without her. Embarrassed and furious with herself, she finally dropped upon a fallen tree stump and bent over her knee.

How was she possibly going to manage the rest of the day when she couldn't even dress herself?

A pair of dark shoes materialized in front of her.

Rachel's hands froze. Hands on her laces, she raised her head.

Ryan loomed tall against the gray sky. His gaze drifted down her attire, his eyes graphic with displeasure. Surely, he didn't expect her to climb around on crossbeams and scaffolding in petticoats?

He held a hat out to her. "Put it on before you go to the construction site," he said.

He was giving her his hat. "Don't worry," he said, reading her silence with amusement, "I'll borrow another."

She rejected the notion that he protect or coddle her, that any act of chivalry on his part only made her feel inept if not outright suspicious. "You don't have to do that. I can get my own hat."

"I'm not being nice. I'm being your boss. It's an order."

Rachel snatched the pithlike helmet from his hand, her fingers brushing his, and set the hat behind her.

"What is wrong with your boot?" he asked.

"I have a pebble inside. It's nothing."

"Let me see."

"Absolutely not. I can do this myself."

"Jaysus, Rachel." He straddled the tree trunk. "I'm not going to bite you. I'm not even going to kiss you. Just give me your foot."

His fingernails were smooth and buffed, in better shape than hers. "I don't want the laces cut," she warned him, knowing she would appear spineless if she refused his aide. "The lace is only knotted. If you can't untie it, I'll go back to the tent."

"Let me see."

Rachel brought her leg around and plopped her foot between his legs, causing him a moment's startled hesitation. She lifted her chin. A perceptible flicker darkened his eyes. He wrapped his hand around her slim ankle and slid it nearer to his pelvis.

Rachel swallowed hard as she tried to look somewhere else, a formidable task as he worked his long fingers over the laces with surprising proficiency. Her lashes drifted downward to his tanned, competent hands, dark against the white cuff of his shirt. Those hands had touched her intimately last night and made her feel needful things inside.

Looking at Ryan's dark head bent over her leg, she forced

herself to think of something other than his words to her last night. "Have you ever had a rock inside your boot?" she asked offhandedly.

If he thought her foot between his thighs the least evocative, he said nothing. "Many times when I used to visit sites." He politely attended the laces. "They can be a nuisance."

He smelled different today, more tame.

"I imagine it's been a long time. Climbing around a construction site like a common laborer. And in your churchgoing attire, too."

He ignored her. "You've been in Glenealy with David." She leaned nearer to inhale the clean scent of him. Her braid whispered across his forearm. Ryan had used David's shaving soap. She raised her lashes to see his wary eyes narrowed on hers. "Don't worry," she whispered against his cheek. "You won't find the ladies protesting the scent of his shaving soap on you."

He removed a knife and cut the laces.

"Dammit Ryan!" She stared in disbelief. "I told you—"

"I hope you have another lace," he said without apology, easing her boot off her foot and dumping out the guilty stone. "I would hate to see you don satin slippers with that outfit."

"Thank you very much, but I'm really quite recovered."

He held her ankle captured.

The temperature escalated between them. "Nonsense," he said politely, his hand a solid vise around her ankle. "You look flushed. My services are the least I can provide for all the endearing hospitality I've found among my Irish kinfolk."

She felt the first drops of rain. Suddenly, she wondered where he had gone last night after leaving the fair—or if he had slept alone. "Did you not find your quarters cozy last night?"

"I did." He leaned nearer and leered, no longer interested in appeasement. "And I didn't sleep alone in case you were wondering."

She tried to yank her foot away. Her palms fell back on the rough bark of the tree as she caught herself. "I wasn't wondering any such thing."

His hands warm on her calf, he caressed a thumb across her knee, rolling his palms beneath her legs and sliding her across the rough bark until her foot was again between his thighs. "Don't you want the sordid details? I thought you liked it when I talked naughty."

"Not as much as you like talking naughty." She opened her mouth and tasted the rain, feeling decidedly naughty.

"Does it bother you that I might have had company in bed?"

Taking issue with his smugness, she returned her gaze to his dark enigmatic one. His hair, troubled from the mist, lay across his brow. He grinned. "If I were to compare the way that you both kiss, you slobber less."

"I do not slobber . . ."

Then something in the glow of his black-brown eyes caught her retort and stilled any further rebuttal. That mischievous twinkle told her she had missed some vital clue to the joke. "I take it the lady in question was not human."

His scent surrounded her. Even through David's shaving soap, she knew Ryan's unique scent. Would know it anywhere. "Frankly, I had a dismal night's sleep, sharing my pallet of straw with a bloodhound." He slid the boot back over her foot, leaving his hands to linger where they shouldn't. "At least I wasn't cold."

"Straw?" Rachel laughed before she slapped her hands over her mouth to smother the impulsive outburst. Her eyes on Ryan's, he watched her with a hint of amusement behind his languid expression, the perfection of his broad shoulders constrained by his shirt. "I know it must have been terribly dreadful for you." Her words sparkled with mirth. "I shouldn't laugh." She laughed harder.

"Please, don't control yourself on my account."

Another drop of rain disturbed a fern that pressed against the fallen log where they sat. She was delighted that his night had been as miserable as hers. "Have you eaten breakfast yet?"

"David took pity on me. He found me this morning."

The misty light of the surrounding forest had painted his face in dappled shadows. "I'm glad." Her hand lifted and brushed the hair from his brow before she could catch the action and stop herself.

A hush fell around them.

The tender gesture had been her downfall. His fingers gently wrapped around her wrist, the action freezing her gaze on his. Her treacherous senses had finally cornered her. "I'm glad that you slept alone," she quietly admitted, the words strange and out of place since he was preparing to marry another woman.

The scenario, familiar in too many ways, dampened her smile and forced reality back into the equation of the moment. "Considering your future with Snow White."

"A business arrangement, Rachel," the casual words didn't even break his verbal stride. "Nothing more."

She wanted to throw rocks and shatter his mercenary attitude. Ryan had literally embarked upon emotional castration. He had no emotions. Only a ruthless sense of purpose and retribution against a society he too often despised. He was as conflicted as she was. "How can you marry without love?" Her voice was barely a whisper, an accusation. "After knowing a real marriage?"

"How can you ask me that? Never having known marriage at all? Other than your childhood fantasy about my brother, have you ever been in love? Or do you stand the high ground on romantic principle alone, thinking a physical relationship is more than what it is?"

A surly objection to his comment formed. His grip tightened on her wrist, and suddenly she was watching him turn her hand over in his larger palm, examining the lines and crevices with the stroke of his thumb. She had callused, work-hardened hands. Her fingers curled inward. She was ashamed by the ugliness he must see.

The act, out of place in her character, brought Ryan's gaze from her hand to her eyes. No condemnation, only assessing. "Have you ever been with a man, Rache?" Constraint in his tone and something else made her face hot. "Have you ever lain in a man's arms?"

Rain pattered on the leaves overhead, falling like pebbles on the ground. A heavy bough protected them from the rain, but not from her heart, or from the sins of her past.

Heat rising into her scalp, she dropped her gaze to his hand, too shaken to look up. He had removed Kathleen's wedding band almost before the funeral had been over. Even then, he was running away from his life. From his memories.

Looking away, Rachel would tell him no more than her actions had already revealed. She didn't care what he thought of her, whether he considered her a whore or not. She owed him nothing. Certainly no explanation of her past.

"When, Rachel?" Ryan's restlessness was subtly territorial and lifted her chin.

He tilted her face. She tried to remain composed when his touch aroused her. He refused to allow her to turn away. "When I went away to the university. After you married. I met him while you were still on your honeymoon."

Ryan's presence made her want things she would never have. The very conflict inside her threatening her autonomy, the balance of power between them, and all she had worked to achieve. "Is Allan Marrow here to take over this project?"

For once, she caught Ryan off guard. Either because he was not prepared to answer—or didn't want to answer.

He dropped his hand from her chin.

And whatever camaraderie had briefly blossomed between them vanished in the face of war. "I knew it," Rachel whispered between her teeth. "You are doing *exactly* what I predicted that you'd do."

"The problem is more complicated than you know."

"It always is, Ryan." Bending over her knee, Rachel struggled to lace her boot as an unexpected desolation swept over her. He would never grant her fair equity in their partnership. "You're permanently removing me from this division, aren't you?"

Ryan caught her arm as she stood, pulling her around to face him. His eyes on hers were no longer compromising. "Listen to me—"

"Let go of my arm." She couldn't bear to be near him. "I mean it!"

Ryan released her and stepped back, as if by doing so he divorced himself from her.

"Rachel." He stopped her from turning away.

"I've been fighting years to keep this division afloat."

The rain had strengthened and fell in sheets outside the shelter of the trees, dripping on her face and hands, soaking Ryan's shirt against his shoulders. "When this project is completed, there *will* be no more Donally & Bailey left in Ireland."

The statement sent an icy rush down her spine, the implication far-reaching. He was killing her Irish division. With it, he would kill her future and take the jobs of hundreds of people. "You can't." Rachel glared at his handsome face through a relentless sheen of tears. "I won't allow it. I won't."

She hated him.

Hated that he'd come to Ireland and, with his magical touch, fixed her financial ills only to take away her division. She hated that she could still be in love with him after everything he was doing. But more than anything, she despised that he looked at her stomping around the glade with sympathy. As if he were innocent of his part in ruining her life. She knew now why he had come to Rathdrum. Not for her.

"I only have one thing to tell you, Mr. Ryan Donally. This—" she balled up her fist and would have hit him in the jaw had he not jerked his head sideways. "Traitor!"

"Jaysus, Rachel." He grabbed her wrist and spun her around against his chest, nearly lifting her off the ground in her fury.

"Let me go." He was suffocating her. "Or I swear I'll scream. They'll throw you in the river for all that I'll stop them. You can't do this to me!"

"Scream all you want. Bring your men down on me, Rachel." His mouth touched her ear. "But it won't change the facts. This division has been losing money for years."

His body warm against her back, she shook her head back and forth, frightened by the awful intensity of her emotions, hating the tremor that slid over her body. "You're a bastard. No wonder so many people hate and despise you and write terrible things about you. How could I ever have thought you decent? You've *never* been decent."

Her words had been cruel and struck him, as she'd wanted them to strike. To the core of his being, but once voiced, she wished only to take them back.

Ryan's hand moved over her stomach. "I don't know, Rache." Spooned as she was against him, she could not evade the heat of his enveloping body. "How could you have ever thought me remotely decent? What did I ever do to give you that bloody idea?"

"I'm sorry." She was barely able to breathe. "I should not have said—"

"Too late." He touched his mouth to her hair. "Words are like bullets. Once out, you cannot take them back. Or maybe you're just bloody lying to yourself. Like you lied to me in London."

Rachel felt the fight leave her body. "I didn't lie."

"And that, too, is a bloody lie!" His Irish brogue thickened with the suppressed violence in his voice. "I don't even know myself when I'm around ye, Rachel. I never have. So spare me your self-righteous resentment. I've not the want to listen. Nor the desire to play the villain. No more, Rachel. No more. I'm finished."

He dropped his arms. She stumbled forward before turning, stunned.

"My accountants are going over your books in Dublin as we speak. You'll be reimbursed every shilling you've personally invested in this project."

And just that fast, a shudder caught in her lungs and tightened her throat. "Don't take me off this job, Ryan."

"It should never have gone this far. But I understand why you did what ye did."

"How can you?"

"Because I would have done the same." He took a step toward her. "Have done the same on more occasions than you know."

But how could he truly understand when what he wanted to take was everything she had? His wealth protected him. His status shielded him from irrelevance. He had a daughter that he loved. A sterling future on the horizon.

Rain dripped from the branches above her. She heard voices near the river.

"As soon as I finish the site inspection, I'm returning to Dublin," he said. "I will arrange for my solicitors to meet yours. You *will* listen to my offer."

Her jaw opened in disbelief. "You want to buy me out of the company?"

"I'm asking you to take my offer. You will never lack for

anything, Rachel." Ryan stepped out from beneath the sweep of branches and stood in front of her. "And if you're thinking about going to David or Johnny, don't. Marrow works for me. As do O'Roarke and O'Reiley. They will not let you back on the site without me."

Rachel crossed her arms against the chill. She hated her helplessness and the endangered feeling it gave her. He walked past her and out of the glade. "You'll need to inspect the west crossbeam beneath the railroad trestle," she called, and when he turned, added, "I found a problem yesterday."

He nodded.

He didn't tell her he would have found the problem anyway. His ease was an illusion, she realized, as she watched him stroll from the glade. Surely, he would not take this division from her.

"Mum," Elsie said as Rachel entered the tent a half hour later, Rachel's hat clutched in her hands. "I was bringing this to you."

"Thank you." Rachel took the proffered object and walked into her private quarters.

She stopped. Two worn trunks sat piled atop the other at the end of her bed. A man's frayed woolen coat lay atop her cot. "Mr. Donally ordered Mr. Marrow to be moved in here, mum."

Her jaw tight, she dropped her hat on a chair, reminding herself again that Marrow's post there was not his fault.

"Mr. Donally said that we would not be sleeping here tonight," Elsie said. "Someone will be taking us to Glenealy. Father Donally has given us a cottage."

"At least you'll be warmer tonight." Rachel dropped on her cot.

"Is there anything wrong?" Elsie asked, from where she remained in the doorway.

Rachel scraped a forearm across her brow. After leaving

the glade, she'd returned to the bridge to find Marrow, only to learn that he had gone on ahead to the second site. Had Ryan gone there as well? "We're leaving for Dublin as soon as I'm finished here." She thought of all the loose ends she needed to tie before leaving.

"But mum . . ." Else dipped. "All right, mum."

Rachel flinched as she slid to the floor, her back bracing the cot, her knees against her chest.

For just a moment, she laid her cheek against her knees and forced herself to take slow breaths. It wouldn't do to allow anyone to see her like this, she thought miserably, leaning on her elbow to pull out the small leather chest beneath her bed.

She couldn't manage one single portion of her life. Last night she'd considered doing things with Ryan that would send her to confession every day for the rest of her life.

Today she'd tried to punch him with her fist.

She found the scissors needed to repair the lace on her boot. Her vision blurred and watered with the frustrating task.

The Dublin division of D&B was a money-losing venture. Maybe Ryan had a right to discharge her from this job. And maybe he'd always done exactly as he damn well pleased without concern or apology to anyone. She needed to get back to Dublin to prepare her solicitors for the upcoming confrontation. She needed to know her legal options. Talk to Johnny.

Rachel needed to think. Yet, the last thing she wanted was to be alone with her thoughts. She had no doubt that she possessed the will and stamina to fight, but at the moment, she wanted something else more personal. Something nearer to her heart.

Closer to her soul.

Something the saner part of her intellect told her she would be better off forgetting.

But Rachel didn't want to forget. There would be time enough in the years to come to forget to oblivion's content.

"Damn you, Ryan Donally."

Then she damned herself for traveling to London in the first place and awakening needs she had put to bed years ago. She was also frightened because of his connection to Lord Devonshire.

"You want that I should throw his fancy lordship in the river, Miss Bailey?" The voice came from the entrance that separated her private quarters from the main section of the tent.

Bent over one knee, she smiled. Ralph Blakely, longtime Glenealy resident, teamster, and David's answer to British toll collectors, stood in his blue denim overalls observing her on the floor. His shiny gold tooth flashed.

Blakely and his loyal twin, if anything, were protective of her. "You'd probably end up in the river yourself." Rachel finally repaired the lace on her shoe and tossed the scissors back in the trunk. "Do not mistake Mr. Donally for being soft. If you know what is good for you, hide when he is around."

"The supply wagons are outside." He handed her a slip of paper as she strode past.

Rachel walked with him outside and greeted the other teamster who had driven the load from Rathdrum. He pulled off his hat and nervously crushed it in his big hands. "Mum." He nodded as Rachel approached, her thick braid swinging against her backside.

"Did the authorities take out too much in toll?" she asked.

"No, mum." Blakely snapped smartly, always proud of his cleverness when outwitting British authorities. "They'd have to find us first."

Pleased that this particular Irish criminal was loyal to David, Rachel lifted the tarp on the first wagon and looked beneath. "We brought two wagons here and took one through Glenealy to the second work site," Blakely said.

Dwarfed beside him and his companion, Rachel inspected the invoice. Flipping through the pages, she studied the rows of expenditures, using more mental energy than she'd spent on anything all day. She welcomed the distraction.

"Everyone is talking about last night," Blakely commented.

"What about last night?" She lifted her gaze from the columns.

Blakely shoved his hands into his baggy pockets. "My sister wants to know if Mr. Donally hisself will be back in town for the festivities tonight. She's decided a bit of handfasting should be in order."

Pressing her lips together in an unsuccessful attempt not to laugh, Rachel flipped a page. Twice Ryan's bulk, and strong as an ox, Blakely's sister was a force with which to contend when impassioned by a cause. She'd already outlived two husbands. "I'll be sure and tell Mr. Donally that he has an admirer." Lifting the tarp on the second wagon, she grinned to herself. Handfasting Ryan to Blakely's sister might be better than throwing him in the river.

It would certainly be more just.

"Father Donally let one of the cottages behind the church to his brother," Blakely said, offhandedly.

Rachel's mind quit tabulating sums. She had not inquired where Ryan had found a place to stay tonight. "The cottages?"

The same group she and Elsie were staying in tonight?

"Is it true?" Blakely's red hair looked brighter as he stepped into the sunlight. "Did Mr. Donally remove you from the project?"

"He did."

"What will happen to us?"

"Nothing. You will not lose your jobs. You can tell everyone that." Rachel dropped her gaze back to the papers in her hands. "Mr. Marrow will need all the help he can get. I trust you all to be respectful of him."

She intended to find Marrow and speak to him before she left. He would be expecting instruction.

"If you insist, Miss Bailey." Blakely sounded disappointed as he followed her around the second wagon.

"I do insist," Rachel said, without looking up.

"You should not be going back to Dublin alone," he said from behind her. "Do you want that I should take you, Miss Bailey?"

Rachel stopped working. "You can't," she said gently, then stopped his protestation. "Mr. Marrow needs you. And Father Donally would not know what to do without you."

"Father Donally does need us." He shuffled his big feet in the wet grass before looking up at the blue sky. "Perhaps it will stay dry for your trip back."

Her gaze followed his. The blue hurt her eyes. "One can only hope," she said, overwhelmed by the need to taste the rain again.

Chapter 9

⟨~~∽◦∽~~⟩

The lamp on the altar glowed beyond the darkness of the pulpit's gloom. Ryan's steps sounded loud and empty on the stone floor as he moved down the side aisle toward the rectory. He carried his coat. Burning candles layered the air with a hint of pungent smoke. Familiar smells to someone who had been an altar boy most of his youth. Ryan eased open the rectory door and stepped inside the room.

David sat at the desk, reading in the dull light of a lamp. He lifted his head from behind the papers and looked over his spectacles, which he removed at once. "Ryan . . ." He set the reading glasses in a drawer. "I wasn't expecting to see you."

Ryan's amused gaze moved from his brother to pass over the sparse stone interior and low-beamed ceiling before he shut the door. Ryan knew the hour was late. "Do I need an appointment?"

"Normally, you do." David stood. "Is the cottage comfortable?"

Ryan had moved into the cottage three days ago. He'd been poring over papers and notes from the project when he'd heard Rachel arrive in the neighboring cottage. He'd stood at the window, a glass in hand, watching Her Highness direct the masses to do her bidding as they moved her trunks inside. Rachel had seen him and shut her curtains directly. She'd had no idea how thin her bedroom draperies were. And Ryan wasn't gentleman enough to turn away. He'd stood at that window every night since.

"There is nothing wrong with my accommodations," he said, turning from David's probing gaze. "I wanted to say good-bye in case I don't see you tomorrow. As soon as my driver is finished making repairs on the carriage axle, I'll be returning to Dublin."

"For some reason, I expected you to stay longer."

Ryan felt awkward. As if he wanted to say more but didn't know how. David reached for a decanter of whiskey and poured a shot. "Would you like a glass?"

Ryan accepted the tumbler. David poured himself a glass, watching as Ryan found a chair. "Will Rachel be returning with you?" David asked.

"I'm sure she won't be returning anywhere with me."

David didn't reply. After a moment, he re-capped the flask, and said, "Did you know I used to drink a bottle of this stuff a day?"

"Are you content here?" The query was out of his character, and Ryan surprised himself by letting the question slip his guard.

"Aye." David tipped back the glass of whiskey. "As much as any man can be at peace. This is a nice place to live. And I find that I can at least do some good."

Ryan had been twenty-two when David returned to England nine years ago. Returning from whatever job he did for the government. He had walked away from the family and his entire life. Ryan no longer even knew him. But then, that was as much his fault as David's.

Bending forward, Ryan braced his elbows on his knees and studied the liquid in his glass. "What happened to Rachel after she left England?" He raised his gaze to find David's hooded. "What happened to her at Edinburgh?"

David leaned back in the chair and steepled his fingers against his chin. "What do you mean?"

His brother knew damn well what he meant. "Tell me about the man with whom she had an affair."

David sat forward with his forearms on the desk, his hands cupping the empty glass, and said nothing.

"Why didn't he marry her?" Ryan asked, managing to restrain the uneven rise of his temperament.

"That's a question you'll have to ask her."

"I'm asking you."

"And I'll not be answering in her stead."

"Does everyone *else* in the family know?"

"How *is* the family?" David changed the subject, his tone considerably more conciliatory than Ryan's mood.

"Your trust is sitting in the Bank of England," Ryan said, letting his gaze go over the simple surroundings. "Chris put it there a few years ago."

"Unlike some, money means nothing to me."

He looked at the ring David wore on his right hand. "It might one day when you quit punishing yourself for whatever sins in the past you committed and understand what you really want."

"Now that's a change." David laughed, coming to his feet in a swish of black robes and staid pragmatism. "The sinner lecturing the saint."

Ryan rose. "The last I'd heard you had to be dead to be a saint."

David walked around the desk. "Have you found what you are looking for, Ryan?"

"Yes, I have."

"Have ye now?" David leaned a hip against the desk and folded his arms. "And what has all of your wealth bought for ye? Do you sleep well at night? Do you enjoy the taste of the air that ye breathe, the feel of the sunlight on your flesh? Or are you still searching for your pot of gold, Ryan? Your reason for living?"

Ryan felt his jaw clench, but his eyes showed nothing of his mood. "My reason for living is waiting for me at home in London. She turned four last week."

"That is a lot of burden for a little girl to carry alone."

"She won't be alone much longer."

"Yes, we've all heard about your society wedding. Congratulations. It only took raiding a major corporation to purchase your blue-blooded bride. Very good, Donally. The family is proud of you as always."

"Jaysus." Ryan rolled his eyes in disgust. "Do I need your bloody approval? For once in my life, why doesn't someone just congratulate me and mean the sentiment? Is my life not my own?"

"The scandal sheets worship you. You live the kind of existence everyone wants to have but hates you for having. You're Irish in a British world. Here, you're a traitor to your kind. So, who are you really, Ryan Donally, but a man still searching for an identity?"

"I didn't come here to be lectured." Ryan set the glass on the desk and reached for his coat. "Frankly, my life is no one's business. I made that bloody clear years ago."

"So every member of the family has told me. Numerous times."

"You talk so freely about me. Why are *you* really here? In this place? In the middle of nowhere? Preaching the gospel?"

"Life changes a man."

"A memorable statement if ever there was one. I'll engrave it into your tombstone." Ryan swept a black-gloved hand through the air. "Life changed David Francis Donally into a hypocrite if there ever was one. Ask yourself if you've found what you're looking for before you judge my actions."

"Are you in love with her?"

Ryan paused, struck by the enormity of his first response. There were parts of his heart so private his thoughts stood known only to God Almighty Himself. "My feelings for Rachel are irrelevant."

David's expression remained unchanged. "I wasn't speaking of Rachel."

Settling his hat on his head, Ryan glared at David, feeling as if his brother had just tricked him into revealing something he shouldn't have.

"You're bloody in love with her." David laughed.

"Hell, she tried to slug me in the jaw. Why wouldn't she be on my mind?"

"The two of you got in a fight?" David's voice was mildly curious. "Really? Rachel is one of the most restrained people I know."

Ryan laughed at the absurdity of David's observation. "She has the temper of a she-cat." She was her most dangerous when she purred.

"Who won?"

Ryan didn't answer. He had thought of her every night since she'd appeared in London.

He had thought of her when he stared into the fire and burned in bed alone. He had thought of her with a sourness that fed his mood and dulled his senses until he'd slaked his lust with his own hands. And still she came to him in his dreams.

Ryan didn't want to pick a quarrel with David. One did not row with a priest, and Ryan had already said too much. He returned to the cottage to find his driver waiting for him on the walkway, only to learn that the carriage axle would not be repaired by morning for lack of adequate parts.

Ryan stripped off his coat and, snatching the bottle of whiskey off the sideboard, decided to finish what he'd started the night before. On the mantel, the ticking clock intensified his irritation, tapping into his head like a hammer. Disgusted with the continued tenor of his thoughts, his mood black as sin, he sat on the soft leather chair and stared at the dying fire.

Rachel's image lured him like a Lorelei and flooded his mind. His burning need for her consumed the whiskey's potency and kept him sober. He remained in a frustrated temper, unable to dispel his mood or the rush of lust that settled between his thighs.

Ryan imagined her hands touching him. He imagined more.

He imagined her hating him forever when she learned of his ultimate purpose there. Normally, whimsy played no part in his mood, but tonight he had a touch of conscience only because he was trying to protect her interests the only way he knew how. The business had changed since it had been a family-owned operation. But there were parts of the old he missed. The simplicity of developing one company rather than managing a corporation and, though he'd kept D&B independent, he knew he no longer could. Not even for Rachel.

Leaning his head against the back of the settee, he raised the bottle to his lips and drank, loathing his infernal preoccupation with her. Assuredly, he was mentally deranged.

Rachel leaned against the narrow casement, staring across the yard that separated her cottage from Ryan's. She had been in her bed, buttressed against the pillows, her paperboard propped against her knees, when voices outside had sent a jolt racing across her senses. The lamp beside the bed hissed in the late-night darkness.

Sliding her feet into her slippers, she'd grabbed her wrapper and hurried to the window, where she eased back the thin drapery.

Ryan stood briefly on the walkway leading to the cottage, talking to his driver, the chalky moonlight shimmering over his hair, making it black. Whatever was said made Ryan angry. When he entered the cottage, she'd heard the door slam even from where she stood.

Earlier that afternoon she had caught a glimpse of him in town with Allan Marrow. In the fading sunlight, Ryan had appeared weary and impatient before he'd looked up to see her coming out of the D&B office. Saying something to Marrow, he'd walked away in the direction of a waiting buggy. He'd been avoiding her these past days as much as she'd been attempting to avoid him. Rachel wondered if the effort was as difficult for him.

She had made a few purchases yesterday, necessities that would tide her over for the trip back to Dublin tomorrow. Later, Blakely had brought her to the cottage with her trunks and her books and papers.

Despite her talk with Mr. Marrow, he clearly did not relish the idea of her leaving him in Rathdrum alone. He was an Englishman, after all, in Ireland, and half feared for his life. She knew that Marrow was really only worried about his performance. Until now, she had always been there for him. A part of her wanted to feel smug and irreplaceable. Instead, she felt only worry for the people who worked for her.

Why wasn't that reason enough to despise Ryan for taking her off the job?

The light across the yard went out as she watched and, for a moment, she thought she saw a shadowed movement in the window facing hers. Moonlight filtered through the trees, laying a soft visible path across the ground between the two cottages. Her legs were unsteady. Closing her eyes, her mind wandering in reckless defiance to the night that Ryan had kissed her, she leaned her forehead against the glass to cool her face before she turned back into the room.

What was happening to her?

"May I speak with you, mum?" Elsie stood in the doorway, silhouetted by the light behind her, and Rachel nearly jumped.

"Yes . . . of course." She covered her heated face with her hands. Had Elsie seen her staring at Ryan's cottage? "What do you need?"

Elsie took a step into the interior of the chambers. "I'm not so blind or naïve as you think. You should know, considerin' where ye met me. I've not been the proper lady's maid. You've been patient with me while I've been learning the books."

"You're not with me to be a lady's maid forever, Elsie."

"And for that, I am grateful to ye for helping me with my studies." She raised a palm to her heart and suddenly looked younger than her eighteen years. "It is because I love ye . . . like you were me own mum. My own sister," she primly corrected with a blush, "that I wish for you to have what is in this box." Elsie shifted nervously before revealing a small wooden box the size of her palm. "God curse me to be sure, but I am glad to get this out of my keeping."

Rachel took the box, confused. "What is this about?"

"Sometimes when a woman's birthing is too much for her or if she has had many children . . . the midwives would secretly give her these. They are illegal," Elsie whispered. "But I was told that they work."

Elsie dipped out of Rachel's small chamber. Rachel turned up the lamp. She held the box in the light and removed the lid. Inside were four sponges with strings attached. She had heard of this form of contraception, and knew that such devices came from the Mediterranean. She lifted a sponge and held it to the light for further examination. Even as enlightened as she was about most things, she felt the crawl of heat into her face.

How had Elsie known?

Rachel shut the lid of the box and lay back on her cot with an audible groan.

Rachel's shoes were damp from running across the wet grass as she stepped into the church to find David. She'd tied her hair back with a yellow ribbon. She'd dressed in her most demure dress, but even so, the peacock blue bodice clung to her chest. Breathing in the calming scent of incense and beeswax, she crossed herself with holy water from the font and proceeded toward the rectory.

The door opened, and David stopped when he saw her.

"I need to make a confession," she blurted.

"Now?" He acted surprised, as if she'd never made a confession in her life. "Do you think we can do this tomorrow?"

Rachel's mouth opened. "I hope you don't treat all of your parishioners like this, David. This is hard enough to do as it is."

"Have you committed some grievous wrong?"

"Yes!"

His chest seemed to rise and fall with a narrow-eyed exhalation. He finally agreed to hear her confession. Rachel followed him to the booth and waited until the window slid up between them.

She'd not been to confession since leaving London. Even before then, she had managed to hide most of her sins from David. She hated people knowing her weaknesses. Now, she didn't know where to begin.

"Rachel . . ." David's disembodied voice came from the other side of the mesh screen. "It's late, and I wish to retire to my bed."

She squeezed her eyes shut. "Forgive me, Father, for I am about to sin."

"About to sin?" David leaned forward, and she glimpsed his face through the screen.

"I am going completely mad," she said to those probing eyes. "I swear I feel as if I'm going to lose control of myself."

"Trust me, you're not the only one," she thought she heard him say. Then he drew away, and she wasn't sure he'd said anything at all.

"You know more about me than anyone, David." Rachel drew in a shaky breath. "These last weeks have been the hardest in my life. I swear I am either going to have carnal relations with Ryan or kill him. I cannot decide."

The window slammed down, startling her. The booth shifted.

A moment later, her cubicle door was thrown wide. David stood like some fierce Jehovah, with his hand gripping the latch. "Out!"

"I . . . absolutely will not." Rachel pressed back against the wall, insulted. "Not until I confess."

"When did you last see my errant brother?"

"Yesterday. In the village. He didn't even talk to me. If we'd done anything at all, I would be confessing my sins. Not my intent to sin."

"Are you in love with him, colleen?"

Her voice paused if only for a breath, but David recognized the hesitation for what it was. She only knew that no other man made her feel as alive as Ryan had when he'd kissed her. Both times. No other man had ever made her laugh or cry with the same intensity. No other man had ever made her want to buy pretty bonnets and clothes or want a family.

"I may suffer some physical infatuation," she admitted. "But who doesn't. You know what Ryan is like?"

David cocked a brow. "Frankly, I have no idea."

The strength of her emotions caught her. "He's charming—"

"Aye," David scoffed, "when he chooses to be."

"Generous . . ."

"When he wants something."

Rachel frowned. Ryan was one of the most generous people she'd ever known. "He's beautiful," she said with squared shoulders. "He's like the sunlight on fields of clover. He warms me, David."

"He sounds a lot like you, colleen," David said quietly.

David's face had blurred behind her tears. "If I was truly in love, I would not have lost my temper a few days ago. I tried to hit him, David."

"You lost your temper because he is taking you out of Rathdrum, colleen."

"Yes," she said emphatically, regaining some of her equilibrium and purpose. He understood the dichotomy of her turmoil completely. "He wants to buy me out of D&B."

"And you've put as much blood and sweat into building D&B as any of the Donallys."

"As a matter of fact, if I saw Ryan, I'd probably shoot him."

Maybe she'd shoot him. Or maybe she'd make love to him. To her, either choice held the same element of catastrophe. "I *need* you to stop me from doing something I'll regret forever," she whispered. "I'm desperate. How could you allow us both to stay here? This is *your* fault."

"Is it now?"

Rachel stubbornly refused to apologize. "Yes."

David folded his arms, his eyes as black in color as his sleeves. "So you're wantin' me to save you from eternal damnation, are you?"

"Maybe a small miracle." Rachel fidgeted with the lace on her bodice. "In the form of a lightning bolt on his cottage, perhaps?"

David stood aside, inviting Rachel to step out of the confessional. "Follow me." The command seemed furtive with purpose, his robe swishing around his calves as he turned toward the rectory, expecting her to follow him.

Coming slowly to her feet, Rachel didn't like the set of

his shoulders or the dark expression in his usually warm eyes.

"Now," he called over his shoulder.

"Get your bloody hands off me." Ryan threw back his shoulders to dislodge the grip of the behemoth who had practically dragged him to the rectory against his will. His gaze shot to Rachel, surprised and concerned to see her standing with her hands clutched in front of her, her attention fixed on the floor, looking more like an erotic porcelain doll with her wild curly hair framing her face, rather than the capable, self-possessed woman he knew her to be. His eyes narrowed on the other man standing close behind her. With his bright red hair and worn overalls, he looked like a twin to the bastard who had dragged him there.

"What the hell is going on?" Abruptly, as if sensing his baffled attention, Rachel snapped her gaze up like a chastened schoolgirl. Candlelight caught in her dark auburn hair, and the urge to rip the man's hands off her overwhelmed him. "Are you all right?" he asked, his black gaze briefly touching on the bloke who had his hand on her arm.

"You're getting married," David said, with a casual bluntness that alerted Ryan more than any angry intonation and forced his gaze from Rachel's.

"Naturally." Ryan cocked a brow. He wished now he hadn't drunk so damn much. "And who is my fortunate bride this special day?"

David smiled like a wolf. "I'll allow you to pick from the women in this room."

Ryan had forgotten that grin, but recognized the danger of its presence. David used to smile like that before he kicked Ryan's ass or dunked him in the horse trough. Nearly five years Ryan's senior, David never let him forget it. "Your sarcasm stinks like bilge, David," he quietly warned. "You can't marry me to anyone. This is not amusing."

"Do I look amused, baby brother? I warned ye both I would do this if you couldn't resolve the state of affairs between the two of you."

"Do what? Hell, I haven't done anything."

"I am going to handfast you to Rachel. An ancient Irish wedding tradition that does not require the blessing of either church. You may have decided that you are no longer Catholic. But you *are* Irish, despite what you want to believe. These vows will do for now."

Rachel struggled with the man's grip on her arm. "You cannot do this, David."

"Not only can I do this; I intend to do it now. I am extremely weary and wish to retire to my chambers." David nodded to the man holding Rachel. "I'm finished with the problem the two of you pose. You can work out the details of this arrangement later."

Mentally circling for some way out, Ryan was torn between laughing at his brother and murdering him. "This is insane. You cannot coerce either of us to do this."

"I know a merchant captain in Dublin looking for able crew members. To make matters clearer, in case you still doubt my intentions, if you don't extend your hand, I will have you shanghaied to San Francisco. These men are here because I can trust them to see the job done correctly. We might not see you again for a year."

White-hot anger set in. Ryan pressed a finger and thumb against the bridge of his nose, fighting a fierce headache that was suddenly beginning to form. "Dammit, David." He lunged forward, only to have his arms caught by the behemoth standing behind him. His brother would do it, too. "You call yourself a priest? I'll have you arrested."

"Aye," David said, the twinkle in his eyes betraying the sage tone of his voice, "'twould be within your official right to do so. Kidnapping is illegal. Even between family members. But you'll still not be acting on the threat before a year is passed."

"It won't be a year for me," Rachel said, in a strangled whisper. "I won't do this."

For thirty seconds, Ryan had forgotten Rachel standing behind him. He whirled on her now, suspicious that she was somehow the cause of all of this. Wasn't she always the cause of every great disaster that hit him? "What did you tell him, Rachel?"

"Me?"

"Why else would he be doing this?"

"You two either put your hands together now or say good-bye for a long time. Right hands. The knot needs to be tied correctly."

Silence roared through the cavernous hall, bouncing off the stone wall and floor like hurled boulders of defiance.

Ryan finally shrugged off the meaty hands attached to his shoulders. "Do it, Rachel."

"I will not." Her green-brown eyes flashed. She'd bathed earlier, he realized. That special scent wafted all around her. He could be in a dark room with a hundred women and still know her. "This is ludicrous," she said. "David isn't going to send you anywhere."

"Would it make a difference to you if he did?"

"Yes." Her eyes fever-bright in the candlelight held to his. "I would not wish anyone sent off to San Francisco."

"Then you would at least miss me?"

"David won't do this, Ryan."

They both shifted their gazes to the aforementioned subject. "You're bluffing," Rachel whispered. "Aren't you?"

David's expression told her that not only would he ship Ryan off; he was definitely considering doing the same to her. "He can't marry us legally," Ryan finally said, holding out his hand if only to end this farce. "He is full of hot air as always."

"Put your hand atop his, colleen," David said, then added when she refused. "Touching him shouldn't be difficult considering what you told me less than an hour ago."

With a sardonic lift of his brows, Ryan shifted his gaze to Rachel's horrified face.

"Rachel . . ." David warned.

"All right! I will!" She set her hand atop his.

Her pale fingers trembled. Outside, rain beat against the stained glass of the church, and Ryan cursed himself for coming to Ireland. He cursed his stupidity a thousand times, half-listening as David spoke words over them before binding a blue cord over their wrists and tying the knot. The heat of Rachel's palm seeped into his skin, touching him in all the wrong places. Slowly, as his senses grew attuned to her, he became more aware of her standing diminutive beside him, to the faint blur of her blue skirt, which caught in his vision. She barely reached his chin. Despite his detachment, too many emotions at that moment rose out of the shadows to capture him. An odd sensation of reality lent volatility to the possessive instinct kicking him in the gut.

She was beautiful. Everything about her was soft and shiny, from the way the candlelight pulled the red-gold of the sunset from her hair to the liquid intensity of her eyes as she turned to look up at him and spoke the vows David asked her to say. With her cheeks flushed pink, her eyes bright, her fury eclipsed by distress, she might have been a Spartan waiting for death in the pass of Thermopylae for all the tragedy in her eyes.

In the end, the handfasting ceremony might have ended calmly if Ryan hadn't been drinking earlier. Or if the man behind him hadn't drawn a pistol on him in the first place and forced him here. David had always been a bully—a bloody tyrant.

Ryan's mood descended rapidly and, when David leaned over to untie his hand from Rachel's, Ryan hit him with his left hand. His brother went sprawling against the desk, sending books and papers scattering over the floor; then came back with considerable more force behind his fist.

Still tied to Ryan's hand, Rachel had grabbed his arm in an attempt to keep them separated, without realizing she was leaving him defenseless. David's fist smashed Ryan beneath the jaw. His head hit the pillar that supported the heavy-timbered ceiling, and he went down as if hit by a pole axe.

"Enough!" Rachel commanded. "This is your fault, David Donally!" she turned amid her billowing skirts, testing Ryan's scalp until her hands felt the lump.

Ryan remained unconscious.

"You've hurt him, David. How could you be such a brute?"

"You asked me to save you from damnation." His teeth showed pink as he withdrew a handkerchief from his pocket and dabbed his lip, unrepentant, as he studied his brother's fallen form. "The two of you have one year and a day to decide your future."

"Handfasting isn't legal." The thought of having Ryan in complete control of her life, even for a year, was obscene. "It's . . . pagan."

"Ah, but the custom is practiced widely all over the British Isles. And my boys will confess to your willingness to be here." David raised his gaze. "Won't you?"

Rachel glared at each of them until Ralph Blakeley finally shrugged, as unrepentant as David had been. "It's for the best, Miss Bailey. Father Donally says so."

"When my brother wakes up, he can decide what he wants to do with a wife and an affianced." His voice remained without humor. "Perhaps you can all share the same house. Become friends."

"I'll never forgive you for this, David Donally," she called after him, as he and his two Fenian bodyguards left the room.

"And you can be sure I won't be coming to you anymore for confession! Ever!"

The door slammed.

"That should worry him into his grave," Ryan muttered, from his place in her lap.

His eyes remained closed, and she saw him flinch when he moved his head. "Are you all right?" She touched his cheek. Then worked to untie the knot binding their hands. "Can you move?"

"If you don't count my double vision and jarred brain, I'm perfectly cheery." He tested his jaw. "Am I still in Ireland?"

"Yes, unfortunately." Rachel pulled at the knots on the rope. "I'm sorry that David did this to you."

His eyes suddenly narrowed on hers, and her heart leaped into her throat. "What the hell did you tell him anyway?"

"Nothing," she answered too hastily, thankful when the ribbed cord fell to the ground between them.

"Nothing?" Ryan sat up and draped his elbow across his knee as if to get his bearings. "Nothing? Like your affair was nothing?"

"*My* affair?"

She struggled to climb to her feet, but Ryan clasped her ankle. "Yes, your affair." In one furious movement, he slid her across the stone floor beneath him, dragging up her skirts. He imprisoned her flanks with his thigh. "That little piece of nothing in your past that no one wants to talk about."

"Don't talk about me as if you have such a pristine history."

"You don't know me, Rachel. And if everything you think you know you gleaned from the newspapers, you know very little about me at all."

For the first time in her life, Rachel didn't care if Ryan was right and she was wrong. She felt responsible for everything. For ruining his plans for his daughter. His future. She didn't know what to tell him. She'd never felt more like a coward than she did at that moment. "What are we going to do?"

"Don't look so tragic, Rachel." He cupped his hand over her chin and looked into her eyes as if to discern the cause for her concern. "David doesn't have the power he thinks he does. We're not married."

"Then everything is as it was between us?"

"There has never *been* anything between us, Rachel." His gaze touched her lips, and the touch sent a physical current through her veins. "Maybe if there had been, we could have saved ourselves the agony of today," he said.

"Agony?" She laughed. "Meaning I would have found you boring by now and would feel free to continue on with my life?"

"We could always find out." The corner of his mouth crooked, reminiscent of that naughty-boy grin that had always made her melt. "Just how boring things would have been between us."

Rachel ran her tongue over her lips, raising her gaze from his lips to embrace his eyes. He was always so sure of himself, of his influence over people. The heat from his body seeped through her clothes. "Or you could just leave Ireland as you found it"—her voice was breathless soft—"and go back to London."

"Even if I wasn't lying on top of you in my brother's rectory, I still could not do that."

A shiver hampered her ability to navigate her words. She braced her small fists on his shoulders. They were hard and sculpted beneath her palms. "I don't want an affair with you, Ryan."

"What *do* you want?"

He'd pulled back to look at her, and she found herself acquiescing to the intimate tone in his voice, the probe of his eyes. She was vain enough to think she could control the situation. "Are there rules to this sort of thing?"

"Not for what I want to do with you, Rachel."

She groaned. The sound forming deep in her chest. Just thinking about his hands on her body sent a frisson across her nerve endings. An exotic fog began to cloud her judgment.

"One time wouldn't officially be considered an affair," he whispered against the corner of her mouth.

"It isn't?"

"Not even close." His words were husky and dangerous. "One night. No business. No past. No future. Only you and me, Rachel."

She did have a way to prevent conception in her pocket, yet nothing was ever one hundred percent. But the power of Ryan's body, his words, and the promise of more set her heart racing. He'd still not kissed her.

She wanted him to kiss her.

"Ryan." Her voice was a whisper against his.

"Tell me what you want." His lips grazed the soft curve of her ear. "Tell me."

"I don't know."

"You do, Rachel."

Would one night be enough?

"No business." Her eyes slid closed. "No past. No future," she said, ready to quench the burn. "Then everything will be as it was?"

"I swear." His lips touching hers, she tasted her own restless energy. "Everything will be as it was, Rachel."

And opening her mouth to his, Rachel sank into the carnal promise of that one crushing kiss.

Chapter 10

Ryan thought about retracting his oath the moment he shut the cottage door behind Rachel. Normally oriented toward decisive action, he attributed his accelerated heartbeat to the fact that they'd just traipsed a hundred yards through a path in the misty woods. Silently, watching her survey the room, he leaned with his back against the door and let his gaze dwell on the picture Rachel made as she stopped and looked into the bedroom. Firelight traced her profile with inviting strokes of light and shadow. Her awareness of him never more visible as she turned to take in the simple furnishing, the papers he had spread over the table, his coat and jacket lying on the settee. Finally, she raised her gaze to his.

The air between them turned electric.

She looked wanton in silhouette, her hair unfettered and free flowing past her waist. He suddenly felt irresolute and knew he had methodically plundered her defenses to the very loss of his own.

"When did you last have your courses?"

"Pardon?"

"Do you want to take a chance that anything we might do will lead to a child?"

"You needn't worry about that."

"Pardon me for caring, Rachel, but yes thc hell I do."

His gaze held her pinned to the floor, his dark eyes penetrating. But one corner of his mouth lifted. It seemed even progressive women of means were embarrassed to talk about the subject even with the man to whom she wanted to have sexual congress.

"What I meant to say is that I have something . . . that should assure . . ." Nervous but determined, she faced him directly. "I have something that will aid against conception."

"Indeed." When he made no move into the room, she looked away.

"Elsie knew a midwife. Despite Elsie's age, she is far more experienced in dealing with these matters . . ."

"You and Elsie spoke on this subject?"

"Not on purpose." Flustered, she lifted her chin. "You think that I'm knowledgeable about such worldly things; I am not. But neither am I naïve enough not to understand the far-reaching ramifications of what can happen between a man and a woman." She moved against the back of a chair, and when he still did not reply, she lifted a brow. "Am I supposed to apologize that I should have left the cottage tonight prepared?"

The oblique statement settled the matter of any doubt in his mind. If he might be unsure of his own intentions toward her, he was no longer unsure of hers toward him.

His gaze holding hers, equally direct, Ryan reached behind him and twisted the key in the lock. "No apology is necessary."

He removed the key and set it on the table beside the door. His body was tense and aroused. A fire glowed in the hearth, all that remained of the blaze that had burned earlier in the evening. He laid peat atop the embers.

"Do you want anything to drink?" he asked.

"Not tonight." Rachel's hands slid into the folds of her skirts. "I want to know when I wake up tomorrow that this was real."

The words she spoke held him captive and, with an effort, he pulled his eyes from hers. He braced a hand on the mantel, fingers gripping the edge, and waited for the flame to catch and burn. A strange flutter pulled at his stomach, and with something akin to disbelief, he realized he was nervous, like a green lad in the throes of his first sexual encounter. The confidence that had become so much a part of him through the years had fled and left him raw and wanting, unable to comprehend the emotions that stirred in the passing currents of air much like the hot embers in the fireplace.

He looked over his shoulder. Rachel had not moved and seemed to be suffering the same hesitation that pulled at him. Yet the fire was there between them, simmering like the flames in the hearth, slowly consuming the air they breathed. He felt the heat go over him. The warmth infusing his veins.

There was no going back for him. He did not play the regret game, so did not question the actions that led him to this cottage. His adolescent obsession had become a palpable force in his mind.

She was beautiful. More beautiful than the verdant Irish hills she so loved. More beautiful than the ocean and the sky.

He had never understood himself when he was around her, but he understood now.

He'd once imagined this moment.

He'd wondered what she would feel like to his touch. Taste like to his lips. He wanted to know all of her.

As if the years had not passed by them. As if the journey they'd traveled had been the same. He could not change what had come before, but tonight she would be his.

They gradually migrated to the center of the room, and Rachel stepped into his arms as if she had always belonged against him. As if her thoughts lay parallel with his.

"Why are we doing this?" she whispered.

"When I find the answer, I'll let you know." Ryan laid his cheek against her fragrant hair, her feminine softness fitting the hardened planes of his body.

"I'm nervous."

"Will Elsie miss you?" he breathed against her temple.

She kissed his chest above his heart. "No."

Their feet moved to music only they heard in the silence of the night. A night that was not so silent at all and filled with the resonating rhythm of promise.

Chastely, he bent and kissed her lips. Tasting. Testing. Challenging.

Then he angled his mouth and took a little more.

Their breaths mingled.

"Stay with me." There was a husky tenor to his voice, a strange desperation. "Stay with me until dawn."

She looked up into his shadowed eyes. "I will."

Spreading his fingers across her narrow waist and back, he smiled into her hair. He'd already hardened to a libidinous length, but knowing he had all night, was in no hurry to take her. For consume her he would. His body ached.

He molded his hand to her ribs and traced the ribbing of her bodice to claim her breast. She groaned softly in her throat and closed the faint distance between their lips.

"You fit perfectly in my hand," he whispered into her mouth. "Do you know that?" He splayed his fingers across her stomach and slid his hand over her mons, claiming her through her skirts. "And here."

The kiss began to smolder, and what had been controlled and restrained changed into something more.

Something more powerful. More profound.

Heat pooled inside him.

He slid his palms up the curve of her back and cupped her jaw, holding her face between his hands, and the world narrowed to a pinpoint of auburn light. He fisted his hands in the thickness of her hair, pulling her head back to expose the curve of her throat to his assault. He began to lose the iron guard that kept his emotions bound close and private. She raked her fingers through his hair, avoiding the lump at the back of his head. Thrown off-balance, Ryan couldn't prevent himself from enveloping her with his arms, from taking a step forward as if to climb inside her, to swallow her. They came up against the wall or a door, he wasn't sure anymore where he was. The kiss turned primal.

His hands closed around the fabric of her skirt, and he yearned to rip off her clothes. Even as he no longer fought to hold back the scorching need that rose within him, he gripped her bottom, lifting her off the floor until she was pressed flush against his body. She raised her legs to wrap them around his hips. Her searing heat burned through his clothing until the cadence of his movement drove him hard between her thighs. Propelling him toward orgasm even as he remained fully dressed.

He tore his mouth from hers with a gasp.

Her chest rose and fell with her own heated exertion. Her lips were swollen and wet from his kiss, her eyes wide.

"We're going too fast." He pressed his forehead against hers, holding himself steady between her legs. "I'm in serious jeopardy of disgracing myself."

Her long slender fingers had worked the buttons on his shirt, and it hung open to his waist. "We should slow down," she amiably agreed, and tongued his nipple, sending scions of pleasure racing through his flesh.

"Slowing down would be wise." Gripping her hips, Ryan moved his hands up her calves and over the warm globes of her bottom. He moved her body against the hard length of him. "You feel so bloody good."

Rachel's head fell back. "Perhaps . . . you are right." Her back braced the wall. "We *should* slow down. I cannot . . . breathe."

Wearing her corset, she was seriously in danger of passing out.

He lowered her feet to the floor and turned her around. Bracing both hands on the wall, she drew in breath around her.

"Relax, Rachel. When you pass out it will be beneath me."

She choked on a laugh. His words were offhand as he divested her of her dress. Her thoughts were not. All that existed in this room stood behind her, swallowing her in his enormous shadow. She could not speak as he turned her around to face him. His dark head bent; he unfastened her corset with hands that seemed steadier than hers. A nervous pang fluttered through her stomach. "What are you thinking?" she asked him, when he stood back and gazed down at her.

His eyes raised to fix on her face. She touched his hair, nearly velvety black in the dancing firelight. "You have soft hair."

"Do I?" His tone was deceptively mild.

"Beautiful hair." She strove to sound dignified.

He filled his hands with her breasts. With the corset gone and wearing only her chemise, she felt the contact like a jolt of electricity against her flesh, a relentless wave pouring through her veins. She closed her eyes, enmeshed in the sensual contact. His mouth moved over hers. "I'm thinking that I've never seen you naked, Rachel."

He pulled her chemise over her head, and suddenly she was standing before him only in her pantalets. Not that she was resisting, but she was nervous, a fact he seemed to grasp. His hand cupped her cheek. "Are you sure you don't want anything to drink? This is going to be a long night."

She closed her hand over the sponge she'd pulled from her

pocket when her skirt had dropped to a puddle at her feet. "I need privacy," she blurted out.

"Rachel . . . we're getting naked together. There is no such word as privacy."

"Merely a momentary retreat." She stepped over her clothes and walked through the nearest door if only to breathe past the suffocating constriction that seemed to tighten her chest. Rachel had never been more nervous in her entire life. Not even before she'd taken her final civil engineering exams.

Halting, she stopped when she came up against the iron bedstead, and spun to see Ryan braced with his arms against the doorframe, watching her.

His eyes dark as jet, his shirt hung open, no longer tucked in his waistband. A deepening shadow hazed his jaw and matched the wildness surrounding him.

The restraint she'd sensed in him when they'd arrived at the cottage had been replaced by something far more compelling. Rachel couldn't read his expression but felt his awareness of her. She shivered, every sense attuned to his blatant sensuality.

He stepped into the room, increasing the spiraling tension a thousandfold. If he raised his arms, he would easily touch the ceiling. "Truly, Ryan . . ."

"Rachel—" He caught her wrist, gently but insistently turning her hand palm up.

Rachel inhaled the warm scent of him. She glimpsed the shadow of hair in his armpits. It occurred to her that she was far more undressed than he was. That fact penetrated her whirling mind as she opened her fist, struggling to draw breath before she lifted her gaze. "It's a sponge," she felt obligated to say.

"I can see that."

She caught only the briefest glimpse of his eyes as he bent his head and kissed her. "I even have an idea where it goes."

She met his eyes boldly, found breath enough to breathe, and lingered in his arms. "I suppose you've seen these before?"

His hand shifted to her face, long-fingered and solid against her jaw. "Lie down."

She backed away a step, dismayed that he would seek to perform such an intimate task. But she shouldn't have been. Her body thrummed with the desire to experience what she saw in his eyes, the blatantly erotic appraisal that laid waste to her senses. "You cannot do what you are thinking . . ."

His smile turned sinful and, slowly, without even touching her, he continued to stalk her backward, removing his shirt, balling it in his hand as he tossed it aside with his shoes. "And you cannot possibly understand how much I want to touch you," he said, as she sat abruptly on the bed, her wide gaze sliding over his chest. "Did you think to put this sponge in all by yourself?" he asked.

He was solidly built. Magnificent, with ridged muscles and black, coarse hair that trailed down his abdomen to disappear in the waistband of his trousers. His body bore the strength of a man comfortable with danger. She felt diminutive.

She felt feminine and alive.

On fire.

"I used to dream of this." He leaned over her and caught himself against his palms above her. "I used to dream of what you would feel like, look like, all naked and flushed with desire on my bed. What you would taste like."

His mouth suckled and teased her breasts, drawing each nipple between his lips. She groaned and thrashed, grabbing his head between her palms. Braced above her, he moved down her body. His lips hot against her stomach, his tongue circled her navel.

"Ryan—"

She felt strange. Wonderfully feverish, as if the hot flush rushing over her was not caused by anticipation.

"Trust me, Rachel."

There were those three little controlling words she hated.

Before she caught her breath and regained her senses enough to exert some control over this matter, he moved lower over her abdomen, taking her pantalets with him, leaving her body exposed, the most intimate part of her vulnerable to his gaze.

"You are so beautiful." He surrendered the word like a caress.

His broad shoulders gleamed with moisture, his jaw rasped against her tender flesh. A sudden burst of shyness made her want to clamp her thighs together. She had not been able to breathe when he'd touched her with his eyes. Now he touched her in ways she'd never imagined. His fingers entered the cleft between her legs, igniting her body, until she was on fire, half-mad with passion. No longer possessing any control, she let her legs fall open, granting him more access, until his mouth replaced his fingers, and the shock nearly drove her upright. She grabbed fistfuls of his hair.

He laved her, tortured her, did things that were so deliciously wicked, her head fell back, and her hands closed on his skull, encouraging and welcoming him.

She couldn't breathe.

Her body tightened with passion. Tightened even more with something devastatingly elusive.

"Not yet, Rachel." She could hear the grin in his voice.

"You are such a bastard," she uttered, boneless and frustrated by the ease of his domination. Her knees remained opened.

"Call me what you will." She felt him part her and slide the sponge inside her until it rested against her cervix. "But when you come, I'll be the one looking in your eyes."

Rachel struggled to her elbows and caught herself on her hair. He was standing above her, his deft fingers working the buttons on his trousers before he slid them off.

Hesitantly, she dragged her gaze over every glorious

length of him to touch the fire in his eyes, and the intimacy of the moment slid into her thoughts.

This was Ryan.

Her Ryan.

Shrouded in more than mystery, yet so familiar. The bane of her childhood, her dream lover, her hero in more ways than she had ever remembered. She marveled at his feral naked grace, unable to recall a time when he had not been part of her existence.

"I want to touch you—" She caught both hands around the width and length of him.

Ryan's grip manacled her wrists almost at once and drew her hands from him. "Not yet." He pressed her into the mattress, kissing her thoroughly, diverting her. "I swear I haven't the control to withstand it, Rache."

She felt the heat of his skin, tasted herself on his mouth. He moved between her legs, his voice a hoarse whisper. "Tell me that you are sure."

"Yes." Her heart pounded against her ribs. Her vision blurred. She needed to know that he felt the same rush of madness in his blood. The same vulnerability. "And you?"

"Jaysus, Rachel." His whisper touched her lips. "I have wanted you always."

Then he entered her, pressing deeper until she'd opened to take him all the way inside her. She was tight, and he was big. He was larger than she imagined. Though she'd held the full length of him in her hand, she had not imagined the feel of him inside her. Her body arched into his hips, joining his passion to hers, filling her completely.

She heard the deep primal groan that might have come from her or Ryan. She didn't know for sure. The muscles in his back were hard beneath her gliding palms.

"Rachel . . ."

Opening her eyes, she looked into his face, inches from

hers, their breath ragged, their mouths so close they touched. So many shadows played in his eyes. "Don't . . . stop," she cried out, feeling the rising tension climb, wanting him with her when she peaked.

She clawed her fingers in his hair and pulled his mouth to hers, opening him to her hunger. Her tongue moved in tandem with him, equally driven by the welling need fusing their bodies. He increased the rhythm of their lovemaking. Then he pulled back as if to watch her face, to see into her eyes. Her lungs grabbed on to his name, her gaze trapped in his, she opened her mouth on a scream, but the sound remained locked in her throat, coalesced inside her, sweeping over, until she was arching high against him, crying out, mindless. But he had not seen her. Eyes closing, his mouth came crushing down on hers, swallowing her cries where physical and emotional desires melded and imploded.

Together.

Where there was only Ryan.

Lost in his own climax, his British façade broken, he gripped her hips in his palms, and swore like a real Irishman. The heat of him poured hot inside her. He lost himself in the lips that plundered his, before he collapsed on his elbows, weak as she.

"I never knew . . ." she murmured against Ryan's throat, closing her eyes to exhaustion. "I never knew it could be like this."

It had never been like this for Ryan.

Conscious of the primitive need to take her again, he rolled her on top of him, desiring only to see her in the moonlight, her full breasts a silken invitation for his hands.

She made him swear and do things he'd never said or done around a woman.

They made love twice more that night, once on the floor in front of the fireplace, and again after they'd eaten a small meal in the kitchen, all with the same fierce mating that had driven them earlier.

It was long after midnight when Rachel turned in his arms and, smiling gently, closed her eyes. "I've never had such a memorable evening, Ryan."

The pads of his fingertips combed damp hair from her face, unprepared for the compliment or the playful tilt of her mouth. No one had ever thanked him for much of anything before. "I'm glad you were pleased."

She purred and nuzzled like a cat against his hand.

Ryan soon discovered that sleep eluded him.

It was the chaos of his emotions that rocked him. The fire in the other room had long since died from neglect. He disliked the darkness. He had never been comfortable with the darkness, for it equated to solitude, and he thought of his daughter's fear of the dark, wondering if he had not somehow imprinted his own fear of it there himself, with his insistence that a light remain on in her room. But tonight there was no light surrounding him. And tonight he no longer felt alone.

Moonlight angled across the bed, revealing Rachel's hand resting lightly on the pillow where he lay on his side watching her.

She had asked why they were compelled to do this.

When I find the answer, I'll let you know, he'd told her.

He knew the answer.

It lay between them like the moon-forced tide, impossible to contain or control, washing over them both. But like the tide, the undercurrent threatened to pull them out to sea.

Ryan only knew that he did not know how to navigate the waters he found himself swimming and still keep his head above water. For tonight had been a lie. While he attempted to gauge the more perceptible nuances between lust and whatever else he was feeling, he did know that one night with Rachel was not nearly enough.

Chapter 11

"I don't imagine that I should mention that men don't like women to tell them what to do in bed," Ryan said, against her ear.

Smiling to herself, Rachel lay as if drugged on top of Ryan, her thighs wrapped snugly against his hips, her damp body glued to his. "I don't imagine that you'll mention that fact at all." She sighed against his chest. A downy white pillow cradled Ryan's head, pale against the darkness of his hair and the heavy shadow that had formed on his jaw. "Do you think anyone will miss us this morning?"

He turned with her onto her back. "How are you feeling?"

Contentment was too tame an emotion for what she felt when he pulled back to look down at her. "Ravished."

They both smiled at the same time, concurrently. How many times had she awakened last night to find him curled against her? His arm draped around her. To find that she was as eager to feel the pleasures of his body as he was to offer. The morning light defined his nearly black eyes under thick lashes as he continued to gaze down at her. "Why didn't you marry him?" Ryan asked. "The man before me."

Rachel held his unwavering gaze. Perhaps had he attempted to force the issue, she would have been able to turn away, a silently bald declaration of her reluctance to dredge up the past. She could never tell Ryan the truth. Not all of it anyway.

"He married someone else."

A small silence fell between them, and she felt him mentally step back from the topic. There was caution needed when walking on glass, and he recognized it, too.

"Do you still dress up in feathers and play opera diva in front of your mirror?"

She looked at him, appalled that he would know that about her.

"You'd be surprised what I remember about you," he said, as if reading her mind.

"Tell me," she said. "What do you remember?"

"That you jumped your first hurdle on horseback when you were ten on a horse that was too big for you. You wept when that ridiculous goldfish I gave you died."

"I had that fish for a year."

"Your favorite flower is honeysuckle—"

"How do you know that?"

"You wore them at your first communion. While other girls wore wreaths of lilies, you wore honeysuckle cultivated from your father's orangery. You were a lot of trouble even then. Independent thinking was never encouraged by the nuns."

Rachel looked into his dark fathomless eyes, struck anew by him.

"You like Emily Brontë and Sir Isaac Newton's *Laws of Motion* equally. You liked men in scarlet uniforms, too."

She disliked that he'd brought up any reference to his brother and told him so.

"Forgive me for ruining the moment."

She didn't know if he was sorry or not. Maybe he had only wanted to get a response out of her. He brushed his lips against hers.

She came back for a second taste until only their breathing filled the awakening silence of the flowering dawn. Then his hand cupped her chin, and he kissed her deeply, delving his tongue inside her mouth. He consumed her with the same meticulous resolve he'd used to claim her memories. And blissful seconds later, the hard length of his erection pressed against her hip, and then his hand was between her thighs, touching her swollen softness intimately, her state of arousal obvious.

Her eyes opened to his. Only inches apart, their breaths ragged, he spread her legs wider. He moved three fingers within her body. The slickness of her body eased the passage, then something much bigger and harder breached the passageway.

"Take me deep, Rachel." His voice was husky.

She wanted more.

She wanted this complete possession. She wanted to lose control.

His fingers sinking into her hair, Ryan rode her, their rasping bodies the only sound in the room, the rigid muscles of his arms taking each powerful stroke of his body until she helplessly closed her eyes, her perfectly guarded control lost.

The direct undisguised well of emotion held her within its palm and rocked her against the reality that he was not truly hers.

He drank her keening cry, taking her as a conqueror. In this arena as well as all others. It wasn't fair that he had the ability to disrupt her hard-won peace of mind.

For a long time afterward, weak in the turbulence of her climax—and his—she didn't move, as if she had the power to fight against the sure surrender to the dawn. When at last their eyes locked, she knew that they both lay in the same tenuous place. He pulled her into his arms, cradling her head against his shoulder and, for just that moment, she let her heart go free.

It was the wrong thing to do.

"When we awaken, you and I need to talk about our agreement," he whispered, draping his arm over her waist. "I'm not letting you go."

Her eyes opened. She didn't want him to change their agreement. She didn't want to be his mistress or have some torrid, ugly affair that would ruin her memories of last night. She wasn't going to love him and watch him marry someone else.

Rachel listened to the growing noise of bird chatter in the trees outside. Listened as Ryan's breathing evened and slowed. After a while, she turned her head and chanced a glance at him. Bright early-morning sunlight spilled through the slatted window.

His hair brushed his nape, and, smoothing the lock from his forehead, Rachel remembered not too long ago when he wore his dark hair longer, the perfect image of a pirate, in his wilder, reckless days when defying conformity had been his measure of an erstwhile challenge. She had only to breathe to touch that flesh-and-blood memory now devoid of clothing.

Her impossible yearnings had begun to clash with her will.

Whatever the answer to her turmoil, she understood that their passionate interlude had to be over.

Restless to leave before he awakened, Rachel eased from beneath his arm. Her clothes lay all over the floor, testimony to the passion spent last night, and added a visual to the scent of sated lust on the sheets and between her legs. That Ryan now slept like the dead gave her a rare sense of triumph, especially since she could barely move.

She flinched as she eased her chemise over her head. Muscles she never imagined existed ached. Rachel gathered up her clothes and laid more peat on the fire to warm the room. When she straightened, she came face-to-face with his satchel. She had returned it to him earlier that week. It lay open beside a half-empty bottle of whiskey and a plate of cheese. Ore Industries papers were strewn over the table. Caught by the sudden find, Rachel bent over to read. She couldn't tell if the papers had fallen out when the satchel tipped or if someone had thrown them against the table.

Curious, she thumbed through the loose sheaf of papers, slowing.

Her mind blank with shock, unable to comprehend what she was reading and why, her hand lifted the top sheet, confirming what her eyes were telling her.

Icy cold rushed over her skin.

Dated two weeks ago, the statement of intent had been written to Ryan. Ore Industries was acquiring Donally & Bailey.

Ryan wasn't just dismantling the Irish division, but the entire company—to dismember, dissect, and murder.

He had not offered to buy her shares out of some noblesse oblige or loyalty to her. He wanted her out to eliminate the obvious problem she posed. The Irish division was only the first of the collateral damage D&B would incur with such an acquisition. Her hands shaking, she flipped through each paper, shock rendering her incapable of thought.

Fury shimmered and grew.

She dropped the papers on the table, her first instinct to shake Ryan awake and demand an explanation. Or to smash the clock over his head.

But fury had faded to fear. Shock to dizziness.

Had Ryan told her this in the glade beside the river? Rachel fumbled with her dress as she desperately tried to reconstruct the scene in her mind. Tried to remember what he'd said. Had she misconstrued his statements when he told her she would listen to his terms? *No*, her mind cried out adamant that she had misconstrued nothing.

Nor was this the first time a man had taken her for a fool, she thought, stepping into her shoes. She'd worn no stockings last night and wasn't going to return to the bedroom to retrieve her drawers. Her hands shook.

For one night, she'd allowed herself to forget.

Ryan had whispered tangible words in her ear, palpable in their possessiveness, which had made her heart race and her senses swim. She'd moved with him and been a part of him. She'd stepped out of time and into something that had been truly beautiful.

An inescapable passion made worse by the realization that not everything between them had been a lie.

Ryan stood in the salon of the cottage reading the papers Rachel had thrown all over the floor, a frown deepening his thoughts. He swore. Someone was knocking on the door, he realized as he looked up, aware that he'd been hearing the pounding for some time. He shoved the papers into his satchel.

Ryan flung open the door. David stood on the doorstep. "Somehow I didn't expect to see you still abed."

"Surprise, surprise." Ryan surveyed his brother grimly. "My valet took the day off."

He wore no shirt. Without suspenders, his trousers hung low on his hips. In a dark mood, he glanced around his brother's tall form, didn't see David's Fenian henchmen, so decided the call was probably social—though Ryan doubted harmless.

"Would you care to come inside?" Turning in invitation, Ryan strode back to the wooden sink where he'd been washing earlier before he'd seen the papers strewn all over the floor in the salon. His travel clothes lay out on the table, brushed and ready to wear. "I'd offer you tea and crumpets, but my other servants are also on holiday."

David walked to the bedroom door and peered inside. "You had a restless night, I see."

Aware that his brother was prowling, Ryan swished the razor in the bowl of water and scraped an edge of bristles from beneath his chin.

"I just saw Rachel off to the train depot," David said, his footfall drawing nearer.

"Did you?" Ryan scraped soap from his face with careful strokes, wondering what Rachel might have told David concerning their relationship, knowing she probably despised him this morning.

"I had an emergency to attend or would have returned to see you sooner. As it is, circumstances have arisen, and I will not be around for a while after today."

That sounded cryptic enough that Ryan paused in his shaving. He remembered that David had been bothered by something yesterday afternoon when Ryan had seen him in the rectory. Some letter perhaps. "I hope everything is all right."

"One cannot predict the needs of others," David replied, cordial but distant.

"That must be difficult for you." Ryan's blunt gaze touched his brother's in the glass. "To be so omnipotent yet not clairvoyant."

"How is your chin?"

Ryan washed the last spots of soap from his face. After dabbing his jaw with the towel around his neck, he looked at himself in the glass. His damp hair lay in strands. A bruise was visible where David had hit him. The knot on his head hurt more, but Ryan hadn't really noted the soreness until then. Not while Rachel had been in his arms, and he'd had his mind and his body occupied.

One solitary night had slipped into a provocative, bliss-filled morning. Even by his standards. They had spent their time together the very model of lovers, secluded in the cottage past dawn, unmolested by the outside world, unmoved by obligations, but not unaware that a dozen people were probably looking for them. He'd missed his appointments with the project manager and Marrow. He'd put aside the fact that he should have been in Dublin today and needed to be back in London by midweek. Ryan hadn't awakened until ten in the morning.

He'd awakened alone.

Tossing the towel into the sink, he turned to face his brother. He didn't need David to review his indiscretions or to judge Rachel's. Nor did Ryan want to be reminded of her reasons for racing back to Dublin before him. In fact, when he put his mind to the task, there was only one topic that remotely interested him.

"Do you want to tell me what you thought you were doing last night?"

"Protecting two people I happen to care about very much." The white clerical collar pulled against his tanned throat, but David looked far removed from humble as he leaned his backside against the settee. "Rachel isn't speaking to me."

"Imagine that."

Joining Ryan in the small alcove that served as the kitchen, David withdrew a folded sheaf of paper from inside his jacket. "I took the liberty of detailing the laws on handfasting for your solicitors to digest and mourn." He carelessly dropped the paper on the table, where it slid across an air current onto the floor at Ryan's feet.

His jaw tight, Ryan picked it up, skimmed the contents, and raised his gaze. His mood was surprisingly level, considering the fact that it was all chicanery. "Rachel read this?"

"Her reaction was more succinct than yours. She laughed,

then ripped it up and threw it in my face. I won't even tell you what she said about you."

David's dark eyes bore a hint of amusement. Hell, he was enjoying this. "She needn't have bothered." Ryan dropped the sheaf on the table in flagrant disdain. "English law won't recognize this."

"You weren't married in England. You were married in Ireland. Handfasting is permitted under the ancient Brehon law here and falls under the jurisdiction of common not canon law," David added. "But for the legal naysayer, I decided this morning after leaving Rachel to go one step further." He gave Ryan the special license secured from a magistrate. "Civil ceremonies *are* legal."

Ryan suddenly felt as if he were watching himself fall out a very high window only to be stopped by the pavement. The door opened, and Ryan looked up. "Are you bloody telling me Rachel is my legal wife?"

David settled his hat on his head. "She does not yet know just how completely. I'll leave it to you to explain."

If David had wanted to punish him for whatever sin he'd committed by leaving the Church, Ryan was positive the joke couldn't get worse. "This is laughable if not outright criminal."

"I'll be bidding you a fare thee well. It's been entertaining." His brother stepped out of the cottage and shut the door.

"I'm getting married in ten weeks!" Ryan shouted. He yelled something else a lot worse, caring little whether his arrogant ass of a brother heard him or not.

Scraping a hand through his hair, Ryan looked around him, impotent with incredulity, then padded barefoot across the floor and flung open the door. He wasn't going to let David ruin his entire life. "Where did you say you took Rachel?"

David turned in the grass. He'd reached the trees and shaded his eyes against the sun. "The train depot."

"I thought the floods wiped out the tracks around Rath-drum."

"She didn't leave from Rathdrum."

"You mean there's another train depot not far from here?"

"About an hour. Nearer to the coast."

"Bloody hell." Ryan's fist gripped the door latch. He'd been told in Dublin that there *was* no through train to Rath-drum until the repairs to the bridge were finished. To think he could have saved himself the torture of traveling over a rough water-bound macadam toll road better suited for vic-tims weaned on the Inquisition. "How long ago did she leave?"

"The train was due into the depot at noon." David pulled out his watch fob and flipped open the lid. "That means it should get to there around three."

A long whistle screeched through the outdoor station, jerk-ing Rachel out of her nap and nearly causing heart failure. Elsie occupied the window seat facing hers. By the look of the pages read in the book since they'd sat down, Rachel had not been asleep for long. People continued to loll in the aisles, shoving belongings on the upper rack above the crowded seats. Someone had brought chickens inside the coach car. Now conscious of the noise, the unpleasant smells, and her own unfamiliar emotions, all gathering in her head, her vacant composure cracked.

Rachel pulled her watch fob out of her skirt pocket. Brush-ing a feather from her emerald velvet traveling costume, she was tempted to go outside on the platform and shout at the conductor to get the train moving. "We are already three and a half hours late, for God's sake!" She snapped her fob shut.

Rachel needed to get to Dublin.

Needed to get in touch with her London solicitor and seek legal counsel before she confronted Ryan again.

And Lord in heaven, how did one go back to yesterday after an experience like last night?

"Pardon, mum?" Elsie shut the book in her lap. "Are you well?"

Rachel flicked a sideways glance at poor Elsie, who looked anxious, especially after Rachel's blasphemous verbal encounter with David that afternoon. She softened her expression. "I wanted to thank you . . . for what you did for me last night."

"Oh, mum." Elsie folded her hands over the book. "If only I did do you a favor."

"Elsie"—Rachel gently squeezed the girl's wrist—"you did do me a favor."

Pressing her pretty lips together in a tight line, Elsie drew nearer until her mouth touched Rachel's ear. "I forgot to tell you something important."

"About what?"

"I forgot to tell you that you're supposed to soak the . . . you know . . . what I gave you in lemon juice first."

"*Lemon juice?*" she rasped.

"I'm sorry, mum."

The very idea sounded as shocking as the intimate image of Ryan performing the detailed task of insertion, taking her easily to heights of sybaritic bliss with his tongue. He'd known how to touch her. Known things about her body that she'd never imagined. What would he have said if she'd tasted like lemonade?

She turned her face toward the large window.

Her cycle was always timely as clockwork, and she was sure her flow would start soon. Yet, as much as she sought to escape Ryan and the devastating effect he had on her, she had to force herself to consider the very real possibility that she might actually be his wife.

Another long whistle sounded from the engine up ahead.

The train wheels squealed, then jerked forward, the sudden momentum sending items crashing from the shelf above everyone's heads. Elsie jumped out of her seat with a terrified shriek. Passengers sprang into action. Rachel caught Elsie's carpetbag, filled with books, before it hit the floor.

Her arms outstretched, she stood on the balls of her feet as she tried to readjust the items on the shelf. She was wearing full travel regalia including a bustle and jacket that restricted her reach. "Elsie . . . help me, please."

A pair of gloved hands came over her shoulders and took the bag from her grasp, easily inserting it onto the shelf above her head. "Ryan!"

The train lurched again in an explosion of steam and cranking wheels, throwing her backward against him. "Rachel . . ." he said against her hair.

"What are you doing here?" she asked, beneath her breath.

Shaded by a hat worn low over his forehead, the steel in that gaze didn't escape her any more than the familiar warm scent of him flooding over her to bring the night rushing back in an inescapable flush. "We need to talk." His urbane tone did nothing to soothe her. "I think you know why."

He released her, and she whirled to face him, wobbling with the train's movements. "We've nothing more to say to each other, Ryan Donally."

"I'll move, mum." Elsie jumped out of her seat and collided with Rachel. "It will be no trouble for me to find another seat."

Catching her balance on her faux husband, Rachel pulled Elsie to the seat next to hers. "You're not going anywhere alone on this train." Not with the scurvy men she'd seen board earlier. "Sit next to me on the aisle. And don't listen."

"Yes, mum."

Without a word, Ryan removed his hat and sided past her toward the window seat facing hers. His height obliged her to lift her chin, his size impinging on her space before they both sat across from the other. Tugging off his gloves with his teeth, he removed each one, something in the manner of his movements revealing a barely contained violence.

That fast, her levity faded. David had told her she and Ryan were truly married, which she didn't for one moment believe. She had thought last night would have ended her obsession with Ryan, but it had only sharpened her desire and made her dislike him even more for his deception.

"Why are you here?" she asked.

"Why did you leave this morning without talking to me?"

They'd both spoken at the same moment.

Rachel was aware of an ink stain on her sleeve and folded her hand over the ugly mark. Today everything was supposed to have gone back to the way it was between them, and the fact that it hadn't alarmed her as much as her cowardice.

"We had an agreement for one night. You aren't supposed to be here."

The train grumbled over the tracks, the sound of the engine vibrating the walls of the coach. "Don't you think current circumstances trump all other agreements?" His words were spoken softly, his tone inflexible, yet she glimpsed a perceptible softening in his gaze as he read the panic in hers.

"What circumstances?" She glared with stormy eyes. "Or maybe you're incapable of honoring agreements that entail no profit."

His eyes grew equally stormy. "I forgot how well you know me, Rache."

Recognizing that it would be imperative for her to remain unemotional, Rachel folded her hands in her lap. He had always guarded his family dignity with an iron fist and would want to keep everything as circumspect as possible.

She forced her gaze out the window. The tracks had begun

to dip, and already the trees were thinning as the train neared the coast.

Secretly, she wanted to thrive on Ryan's dilemma. If her own dilemma were not worse. "I release you of any responsibility that you think you might owe this unforeseen occasion," she quietly said. "I don't recognize any marriage between us."

"Thank you, High Justice Bailey." Ryan leaned forward and braced his elbows on his knees. "But I doubt very much you have that kind of judicial power."

"You don't understand. David did what he did because of me." Disgusted by her maudlin yearnings, Rachel blurted everything out. "I went to him and told him . . . I told him that I was either going to kill you or sleep with you. Maybe both," she said in addendum, finding that her bottom was already sore on the hard seats. Or maybe she was too hot in the airless car. "I asked him to help me. I thought he would do something pious, like pray over my soul. Not handfast me to you."

She looked at the bow of Ryan's mouth, remembered the warmth and taste of him last night. She remembered other things, too. The soothing strength of his arms. The dark intensity of his eyes when he'd watched her release beneath him.

"I believe that we both agree this is not legal," Rachel said in a level tone.

"Hell"—scraping a palm over his jaw, he looked at her—"nothing is ever simple between us. Is it?"

And all at once, her defenses fled. "No one need know what happened between us last night, Ryan."

Casually, he edged his palm beneath her fingers. "A lot happened," he said after a long moment. "I'm just not sure what exactly."

"At least we are of the same mind." She did not attempt to

pull her hand from his larger one. Her surrender, fleeting as it was, raised Ryan's head.

He pierced her with those sultry eyes. Turning her hand over in his, he traced a thumb across the veins in her wrist. Skeins of warmth arced up her arm to play havoc with her lungs. "That is a first, I think," he said. "That we share a like mind on something. Even if you believe you hate me at this moment."

Her eyes shot to his.

"You read what was inside my satchel this morning."

Rachel slid her hands from his. "Yes."

"I didn't tell you everything because I didn't want you to be hurt more than you already would be, Rachel. You can believe that or not, but it's the truth."

She folded her hands tightly in her lap to keep from striking him, realizing now that she didn't know if his reasons for being on the train were personal or professional. "Then I should be grateful. Your conquests are not usually so fortunate."

Ryan sat back in the seat.

In the ensuing silence, she stared out the window at the untamed Irish shoreline, unable to speak another word. The land possessed a feral beauty, breathless in its natural element, changed through time only by forces greater than man's will. She had felt the same raw forces last night in Ryan's arms. Forces now restrained by the civil veneer he wore like a cloak around his life.

Rachel was conscious of his knees pressed against hers, of Elsie sitting next to her trying to look uninterested in both Ryan and the conversation. Mostly she was conscious of a sense of disappointment, amplified by an awful loss that grew and grew.

"I am not your enemy, Rachel."

"Then what are you?" She leaped to her feet. She had the

feeling that if she tried to hit him now, he wouldn't stop her. "Because you sure as blazes aren't my friend."

Rachel pushed past Elsie and stumbled into the aisle. Her movement drew the startled attention of other passengers as she grabbed the seats and wobbled like a drunk against the train's movement down the passageway.

She threw open the door. The wind and noise sucked a sob from her lungs. She stepped outside onto the metal grate. Below her feet, she could see the tracks whipping past. Rachel stepped forward and clutched the web railing.

Behind her, the door grated open and slammed shut. Her gaze remained focused on a flock of distant seagulls coasting with white-spread wings over the thinning treetops. She could see the coast through the trees. "You came to Ireland to buy me out of the company so you would have no opposition to the merger," she said without turning, her voice raised over the noise.

"That was my intent, yes." His coat flapped against her legs, but he made no effort to touch her as she finally faced him.

"You *built* Donally & Bailey! You worked hard. I *know* how hard you worked because I watched you. I watched you fight the status quo. I watched you take jobs no one else would. Plan projects no one else could. D&B wouldn't be what it is today without your dedication." Sounding almost admiring of him, and recognizing the interest sparking in his cool eyes, Rachel reined in her passion. "Where is that man, Ryan?"

He placed his hands next to hers on the rail and trapped her between his arms and his body. "Look closely, Rachel," he said. "I am that man. I haven't changed. Only your perception of me has changed."

Rachel didn't believe him. She remembered a day not so many years ago when he had rolled up his sleeves and walked the city's lower sewer grid in the heat of summer to trace the source of a problem. He'd never cared about society or the aristocracy or the manner of men the institution bred. Now, he had become the very thing he'd always despised. Her people would lose their jobs. Where was the man who used to care about those who worked for him?

"Need I ask Johnny his opinion on the acquisition? Or is he as powerless as I?"

Ryan straightened. "He knows what has to be done."

The wind pushed at her skirts. "Is that the universal excuse men use to justify inexcusable behavior? It has to be done because . . . ?"

"Ore Industries will put D&B out of business in less than a year. Taking my offer before the acquisition will benefit *you*, Rache."

She folded her arms. "If money were everything to me, then being pillaged by you would be more pleasant to endure."

Ryan's expression went dark. "You looked to be enduring just fine last night. In fact your endurance of my pillaging was endless."

"You're heartless," she whispered, when he slid his finger beneath her chin and tilted her face. "And knowing what I know today, I despise you."

Their eyes met. How could he ever have believed that after last night *anything* could go back to being as it was between them? "Certainly, your affection, no matter how candid, has always been refreshingly honest, Rachel."

"You mock me, Ryan."

"You mock yourself," he said, the true tenor of his actions locked in his gaze. "I pay my mistresses well, but I don't give them international corporations."

Rachel itched to slap his face. "You're not *giving* me anything!"

"My offer is a good one. I put it in your satchel. Packed in the baggage car with my valise." He stepped away from her. "I suggest that when you get to Dublin you take the time to read it carefully and accept the terms."

"Thank you." She tightened her arms over her torso. "For making my options patent. This is all so perfectly civil."

"There is no reason why it shouldn't be."

He was gallingly arrogant to think taking her to bed was within the bounds of normal negotiation, even for his ruthless tactics.

Indeed, she had not forgotten the truth about Ryan Donally.

He was a speculator who had made his fortune gambling. He gambled on stocks and commodities. On trade and commerce, and the buying and selling of people's futures. In his desire to crush those he despised, he'd destroyed human livelihoods. His character had suited his goals and made tycoons of those who had followed him, paupers of those who got in his way.

"I don't want to hurt you, Rachel."

Except he already had.

He reached for the door. "I'll move to another car until we get to Dublin."

Then he would return to London and begin the process of dismantling her entire life piece by piece until Donally & Bailey was as insignificant to him as she. "You know that you and I would never have worked," she called. "I am certain if we were ever to live as husband and wife, we'd strangle each other faster than I could spell *blushing bride*."

He'd opened the door, tall in the doorframe, his dark coat more than a cloak against the chill. It framed him with a cool detachment that set him apart from everyone else on the train. Especially her.

"Then it's fortunate for both of us we will never live as husband and wife. Take my offer, Rachel." His voice was soft. "It's the only one you're going to receive."

Chapter 12

"Rachel, are you still awake, dear?" Looking like Medusa with rags in her orange hair, Memaw stuck her head into Rachel's room. "I saw the light beneath your door."

"I'm not sleeping." Rachel stopped in the midst of folding a pair of stockings. Trunks lay open over her bedroom floor. Papers on her bed were scattered in disarray. She'd long since released her hair from its braid, and it fell over her shoulders. "But *you* should be."

"I brought you something hot." Memaw hobbled toward her with a cup in her hand. "You did not eat your supper."

As long as Rachel could remember, whenever she'd been upset, Memaw always brought her a cup of thick hot chocolate.

Her gaze fell on her satchel atop her counterpane, and she turned away. She and Elsie had arrived home late last night from the Dublin train terminal. One of Memaw's grooms had been at the station to pick them up upon their arrival. At least David had wired Memaw to let her know that she would be arriving.

She had not seen Ryan since he'd returned her satchel and changed seats on the train. That morning, she attended church, served punch at the afternoon parish social. Did normal things as if she weren't dying inside. Pieces of Ryan's business proposal lay scattered over the floor like huge white flakes of dandruff. Sometime before tomorrow, she would have to decide how she was going to rescue the rest of her life.

"I wish that you would consider going with me to London," she said.

"Nonsense." Memaw eased her frame into a chair beside Rachel's canopied bed. "I would only be in the way."

"You wouldn't."

"This is my home. It's yours as well, Butterfly."

"I wish you wouldn't call me that." Rachel scraped the hair from her face and immediately regretted the bite of her words. "It's just that I'm not a little girl, Memaw."

"Are ye so afraid of a wee bit of softness, Rachel?"

Softness was a luxury she could ill afford, especially now. But Memaw was familiar enough with Rachel's character to know that no matter how much pressure she'd ever been under, she'd never snapped at Memaw.

"He's thirty-one years old Memaw," Rachel whispered. "He's well educated, respected," she added, for heaven only knew the power he wielded over people's lives.

"He controls an international firm that employs thousands worldwide. He's about to be awarded a knighthood. He's one of the wealthiest men in England. How do I fight that?"

Her gaze fell on the floor. The London Times still lay where she'd tossed it earlier. His acquisition of Valmonts was yesterday's business news. Their paths were clearly marked. Futures staked. Both nonnegotiable with the softer side of life. "Taking apart D&B is merely business to him. Just like everything else since Kathleen's passing. Except for his daughter, Ryan no longer seems to hold an emotional connection to anything."

"Balderdash, girl." Memaw waggled her cane at Rachel. "I should take you over my knee."

Rachel looked at Memaw as if she'd gone mad. "Me?"

"He came to Ireland to see you, didn't he? And what did you do about it? Were ye pleasant? Sweet-natured?"

"He didn't come to see me."

"Ryan Donally could have sent a dozen men in his stead, dear. A man like that doesn't drop his business for a week without a reason."

Rachel rejected any idea except the obvious. He needed her cooperation to help make his next business acquisition go forward with as little trouble as possible. Ryan might be capable of passion, but she did not believe him capable of more, and she wanted nothing to do with him. "Truly, Memaw. Your bedside manner is appalling." She bent and snatched up the broadsheet. "Maybe you should grab your spectacles. His betrothal is even mentioned in the business column."

"Pah! Since when does society have anything over a Bailey? You've the blood of a queen running through your veins."

A famous pirate queen, Rachel laughed, having heard the old story about Grace O'Malley a hundred times. Rachel's strained emotions veered from laughter to near tears. She didn't think her pirate pedigree would count for much in the court of public opinion. But Memaw was proud of that lineage, so Rachel said nothing.

Finally, she set the mug of chocolate on her bedside table, and smoothed the lace doily. Not a thing was out of place. Indeed, she organized her entire life down to the color of stockings she would wear on any given day. Ryan was nothing but chaos in her life.

But Memaw seemed to want to champion him.

Her grandmother and David had grown close since his return to Ireland years ago, but Rachel suspected Ryan had always been her favorite Donally. Probably because deep
inside, past the hard-nosed bluster of his boyhood, he'd been
so needy for affection. Memaw had never liked Ryan's father.
He'd been on a project in Wales when his youngest son had
walked across the stage, first in his class in Edinburgh. But
her grandparents had been there. So had she. And Kathleen.

Rachel had been completely blind not to recognize that
Ryan had once been in love with her.

She thought of her own feelings for him, and attempted to
box up her reasons for sleeping with him into a tidy summa-
tion attributed to lust. The full realization of what they had
done together had not truly set in until he'd left her on the
train, and she'd arrived at the station in Dublin, walked outside beneath a perfect sky, filled with perfect stars, and realized how truly imperfect her life had become.

She had not slept with Ryan because of lust.

"Are you going to be working late, dear?" Memaw was
standing at the door. Rachel hadn't even heard her rise.

Staring distractedly at the papers she'd laid out earlier on
the bed, Rachel set her hands on her waist. "I've been working late every night for the past eight years. That's why I have
what I have."

"No, Butterfly." Memaw gave her a reproachful smile. "Ye
have what you have because you've fought for every inch for
your triumph."

"Have you ever been ashamed of me, Memaw?" she
asked.

"You can look me in the eye and dare ask me that?"
Memaw's tone took her to task. "You rolled over and played
dead once before. If ye do it again, ye deserve your fate, girl."

Frowning, Rachel watched Memaw wobble out of the room.
Later that night as Rachel blew out the lamp and lay down in

the moonlight-scented sheets, she stared at the inside of her canopy. She didn't want to be afraid of Lord Devonshire.

But Memaw had been right. She had run away from her life once before. She had done so to protect herself. She had done so because she was in love with her best friend's husband. She had filled that void with an education few women could only dream of achieving. And had attained independence at a cost greater than anyone could imagine. Now when it came time to fight, Rachel had capitulated to Ryan too easily.

The absolute realization of that fact struck her like a comet crashing down from the stars.

Walking away from her entire life was not an option.

Rolling onto her stomach, Rachel propped her chin on her hand and stared out the window. White lace curtains fluttered in the honeysuckle breeze. She was reminded of Ryan's memory of her first communion.

She'd worn honeysuckle in her hair that day because her grandfather had given her those tiny yellow flowers, and she'd wanted to honor him. Ryan was correct about one thing. She'd been punished severely for her disobedience.

But some things in life were worth the fight.

D&B had grown from the cellar of her father's house thirty years ago. It was as much her legacy as it was Ryan's to grow.

Maybe she only wanted Ryan to realize that Donally could coexist with Bailey. That D&B could coexist with Ore Industries. That it would be possible to go into the future without destroying the past.

Maybe it was time that she finally took a stand.

Women might never get the public vote, but they could own majority shares in international corporations and vote policy with their percentage.

How else did one beat a tycoon industrialist with well-laid

plans for his perfect future? But soundly and at his own game.

At least her actions guaranteed that he would not forget her too soon.

"Sir?" A knock sounded on Ryan's sitting-room door.

Snapping the cuff link closed on his sleeve, he glanced up, expecting the hotel porter. A fire warmed the outer chambers where he'd found lodging, awaiting his packet out of Dublin on Monday. There had been nothing leaving the city on Sunday. He'd spent two nights in the best lodging money could buy, and still hadn't managed to get more than a few hours rest. He wasn't in a patient mood.

"The chambermaid let me in, sir," his solicitor hastily explained his presence. "I didn't know if you would still be here."

Ryan stripped his jacket from the wooden rack beside him and slid his arms into the sleeves. "I won't be here much longer." He shrugged into the coat, turning to the glass to check his necktie, then walked out of the dressing room to the bedroom. A half-empty breakfast platter and coffeepot remained on the trundle cart.

Ryan poured himself coffee and, bringing the cup to his lips, regarded Smythe over the rim. "Why do I get the feeling I'm not going to like what you have to say?"

"You were correct," Smythe said. "Miss Bailey appeared at the office this morning."

Despite the fact that he knew she would, Ryan experienced a twinge of foreboding. His solicitors were supposed to meet hers this afternoon. Smythe shouldn't be here.

"She is a spitfire, if I can say so myself, sir. Must be the red hair." He chuckled, and Ryan continued to listen patiently. "Her employees admire her. Frankly, I've never met—"

"Smythe—" Ryan finished the last of the coffee and set down the cup with a *clink*. A glance at the clock on the wall told him that he needed to leave for the docks. "Is there a point to this?"

"She seemed to know I would be at the office, and gave me this—" Smythe set the envelope on the cart next to Ryan's cup. "She told me to thank you for the generous offer for Donally & Bailey stock. After reading your proposal, she was flattered that you would pay so much above market price, and that any *woman* . . . she emphasized woman, sir, would be faint with adulation over such generosity. She considered the offer above reproach and was honored, considering everything the broadsheets had written about you, that you had . . . a conscience. Her words, sir."

"No doubt she holds me in the highest regard," Ryan said, turning to face the window, his hands folded behind his back.

Smythe heard the veiled dry humor in his voice. "But she said you could take both your offer"—he cleared his throat—"and your person, and go to blazes. Only she didn't use blazes exactly, sir."

"Did she actually *swear* at you?"

"Not exactly at *me*, sir. She said that it would snow in hell before she ever sold you one share of D&B stock. She was so pleasant in her discourse, one could forget it was you she was talking about."

His well-honed composure blunted, Ryan stared out the window overlooking one of the numerous canals that snaked through Dublin, fighting the urge to laugh outright. She was a fool.

A knock sounded on the door, and a porter stuck his head inside. He wore a green uniform and round pillbox hat. "Your coach is here, Mr. Donally."

"Take my valise. I'll be there in a moment," Ryan said, then to Smythe, "Continue," he instructed.

"As you ordered, I offered reimbursement for the personal funds that she spent while at her job here."

"Don't tell me that she turned that part of the offer down, too?"

"No, sir. Just the opposite. She politely reminded me that you owed her interest." He set his satchel on the table and withdrew a folder. "Her accounting was more precise than mine on certain matters, considering we have not yet had time to go over every expenditure she made the last few years."

Ryan took the folder and flipped through the pages, impressed by Rachel's thoroughness in the short time since her return from Glenealy. No doubt, the arithmetic was correct. Rachel had the ability to add multiple columns of numbers as well as solve equations in her head that would leave most men gasping in reverence. Calculating interest would be elementary to her in comparison.

"She also gave me an accounting of her education costs, which she now considers a reimbursable expense." Smythe handed Ryan yet another folder of papers. "And miscellaneous fees"—another folder was added to the pair in his hands—"that include various bribes, transportation costs, and professional books. She told me not everything could be recovered, but that was the price of stupidity."

Ryan dropped the folders on the table, wondering what the hell that was supposed to mean. "Anything else?"

"I paid her, sir," his loyal solicitor said.

"Everything?"

"You told me to cooperate. And she presented her case well."

Leave it to Rachel to outtrump the trumpeter and abscond with more money than the Irish division of D&B was probably even worth. Admittedly, he was impressed with her little mercenary heart—which gave way to a greater worry that begged to ask the question why she didn't take the offer. There would only be one reason for that. She was going to make a bid for control—and with his own bloody money.

"Impossible," he said. "Bloody impossible circumstances."

He had gone to Rathdrum last week with the intent of taking Rachel out of the playing field and had managed to lose the first battle as easily as Smythe had lost his.

Ryan flicked open the lock on his satchel to add Rachel's folders. His satchel smelled like her, and he resisted bringing it to his face. He peered at the cloudy sky outside from beneath the low brim of his hat. Her complete disregard for her future overwhelmed any diplomatic inclination he felt to settle the political issues between them. He now accepted that this buyout would come at a price. Perhaps as penance for two decades of idiocy when it came to his utter frustration to make some logical peace between the paradox of his emotions when it came to her.

She should have taken his offer for her shares in the company when she'd had the chance.

And he should never have slept with her.

Yet, for one night in Glenealy, when Ryan had looked at the woman he'd once loved with his entire soul, he'd wondered what his future might have held if she'd fought half as hard for him as she'd ever fought for Donally & Bailey.

Ryan only knew he would not be losing any more battles.

Little did Rachel truly comprehend her circumstances—or her advantage if she figured out the truth. In the meantime, he had wired his solicitors in London to research handfasting laws and attempt to untangle the knot David had tied around his life.

"Finish your work here in Dublin." Carrying his coat over his arm, Ryan walked to the door, his hard-soled shoes marking his steps on the planked floor. "These quarters will be paid for until the end of the week."

Smythe glanced at the chambers. "Are you sure?"

"Try not to think of this as a vacation," Ryan said.

*　*　*

The weather couldn't have been more portentous of her future, Rachel thought as she sat on the Holyhead-bound packet, grateful that she'd made the ferry. Surrounded for the last few hours by her work, she raised her gaze from the table where she sat jotting down notes. The ferry was huge, with its double-decker tiers and windows on all sides. She estimated three hundred people on board. Once she was in Wales, the train would take her to London. She felt clever to have purchased the last two tickets out of Dublin for the day.

Attempting to return her focus to her work, she looked around the crowded salon before wisely capping the ink bottle lest it spill. Wind buffeted the ship, seeping through the glass behind Rachel, and she drew her cloak higher onto her shoulders.

Only the truly hardy people remained topside on deck as the storm proceeded to get worse. Whitecaps dotted the iron gray sea that blended into the horizon.

"It be colder than a wart on a bugger's ass." Elsie slid into the empty seat across from Rachel, bringing with her a chill breeze. Wrapped in a warm woolen cloak, she shivered. "Pardon, mum. I *am* colder than a wart—"

"You're soaked." Rachel leaned across the table to test Elsie's sleeve. "Where are your gloves?"

Elsie pulled a pair of woolen mittens from her pockets. "Wet, mum. It started to rain."

"Didn't you think you should have come inside earlier?" She reached for her reticule and withdrew her fur-lined gloves. "I'll not have you catch your death. Put these on until you warm."

"But what about you? Memaw told me I was to take care of you. If you were to come down with a chill . . ."

"I won't. Besides, we'll be in Holyhead in another hour."

"Will Memaw be all right without us, mum?" Elsie asked after a few moments. "Father David will check up on her, will he not?"

"God forbid," Rachel said under her breath.

She was in the process of returning to her notes when across the salon, the door flew open and the very flesh-and-muscle image of her thoughts blew in out of the cold. Frigid gusts whipped at his heavy coat as he turned to shut the door, his height setting him off from the crush of people surrounding him.

Almost as swiftly, Rachel dropped her astonished gaze to her papers. What was Ryan doing on the ferry?

"Move to your left, Elsie," Rachel whispered, pulling her hood over her head. "I fear the people milling about are distracting me from my work."

"Yes, mum."

All of her senses heightened, Rachel leaned to the right of Elsie's shifting body to better glimpse Ryan walking across the stateroom toward a bench that faced the picture window. Somewhere in her whirling thoughts, the realization that she could not be more cursed traipsed across her mind.

Rachel dropped her gaze to her papers. She hadn't expected that Ryan might still be in Ireland. Then he'd probably spoken to his solicitor. He would know what she was planning to do with all of his money.

She reread the letter she'd been composing to Johnny, frustrated when she'd discovered she'd lost the thread of her thoughts. Frustrated that in spite of the precautions with which she'd sought to fortify herself for the long road ahead, she had not been prepared for her reaction to Ryan. She couldn't believe that he was on board. That he had been on board for the last two hours without her knowing. He must have been sitting on the upper deck the entire time.

Rachel peered around Elsie. His back to her, his arms stretched across the back of the bench, Ryan had discarded his satchel and valise next to him on the bench. In front of him, rain rivulets trailed down the grimy window and obscured most of his view.

With *unapproachable* invisibly stamped across every hardened inch of him, his vulnerability was oddly striking in contrast. He appeared like some carved granite *tour de force* as Rachel wondered what he was thinking, staring out at the cold empty sea.

No longer wondering at the beating of her heart, she looked away. She knew that she wanted him enough not to pretend that she didn't, which only made her quest to defeat him harder.

But not impossible.

An hour later, the ferry arrived at Holyhead. Rachel disembarked in the crowd behind Ryan, never losing sight of him as he hailed a hansom to take him to the railway terminal. She stood a dozen people behind him at the telegraph office in the station. Not once did he turn.

Not once did he look over the crowd or seem to care that he drew attention wherever he went. He was beautiful and could make something as mundane as reading last evening's broadsheet tantalizing to watch. She saw him again just after dawn as the train pulled into a depot an hour outside London. He'd been sitting in the first-class coach, two cars down from where she and Elsie had encamped for the night. She'd opened her eyes realizing the train had stopped when the conductor walked down the long aisle outside her compartment announcing the station.

Ryan stood on the ramp nearly in front of her window, a shadow marring his jaw, his valise in one hand as he settled his hat on his head, looking as if he hadn't slept. Yielding to an immature sense of justice, she felt her mouth tilt, when suddenly he turned his head and looked directly at her in the window.

Startling her out of her sleepy complacency.

As if he'd known exactly where she'd been sitting on the train.

She felt the kick of her pulse. The telltale heat in her veins. She'd glimpsed the same intensity in his eyes when he'd made love to her, when his warm skin pressed against hers, and she'd kissed him with an urgency she had not been able to control.

"Where will you be staying?" The glass muffled his words.

A furtive glance at the other occupants around her reassured Rachel no one was paying attention. "Go away." She mouthed the words.

He put his hand to his ear.

"Go away." She mouthed the words more forcefully.

Without taking his eyes off hers, he moved to the window, his arrogance hardly surprising, considering he probably knew she was in London to put a halt to his precious Ore Industries raid on D&B.

She lowered the window and leaned outside. "You're the last person I would tell where I'm going, Ryan Donally." She attempted to keep her voice low.

For a moment, he merely studied her in exasperation. "You are the most stubborn, infuriating woman I have ever known in my entire life, Rachel."

"And you are the most infuriating, stubborn man."

"You have *no* idea what you're doing."

"I intend to talk to Johnny."

She knew exactly what she was doing and hoped Mr. Williams had the list of major stockholders in the company ready for her. She would fight him.

Ryan took a step nearer. He smelled salty and hot. Of sunshine and coffee.

"Go back to Ireland, Rachel. I meant what I said earlier."

Nearly eye level with him, she refused retreat. Faint embers of heat, remnants of Glenealy, burned between them. She knew he felt it, too. "Why did you wait so long to shut me down?" Her voice quieter now, she challenged him to answer. "You've had ample opportunity in the past."

The train gears released, shooting a plume of steam onto the platform. "Why don't you tell me your theory? Seeing that you've thought this completely out to the bloody end."

"Instinct," she said succinctly, feeling safer than she should with the glass between them. "Deep inside, you don't really want to destroy me . . . any more than you do D&B."

With a crank of screeching metal, the heavy wheels began to move. "Is that right?" Noting the flush on her pale skin, his amused gaze lifted to her lips and again to her eyes. "This is no game, Rachel." He walked beside the window, but the train began to pick up speed. "And there are no rules."

"Trust me. I never liked rules." He was making the worst mistake of his life, and she wouldn't let him do it.

Blowing him a kiss, Rachel slammed the window shut. She saw his mouth move. Then with a purely masculine gesture that only Ryan would dare execute in full view of a hundred people, he gave her a brief magnanimous salute. Out of the station, sunlight poured through the grimy window. Ryan remained on the platform, a lone figure in black, and she shut the shades, forcing herself to breathe deeply.

Rachel had lived in a man's world long enough to recognize danger when it opened its teeth and threatened to eat her alive—and, not for the first time since disembarking from Ireland did she appreciate that Ryan made a formidable enemy.

"He looked royally sore, mum," Elsie said.

Ignoring the disapproving stares of the elderly couple sitting in the cabin, Rachel dusted off her traveling dress and pretended indifference. Now all she had to do was find a place to stay. For all of her independence, she had never lived alone—certainly not in a place like London.

* * *

Johnny wasn't in residence. She'd learned from Stewart that he'd gone to Scotland to inspect three D&B sites. Moira and the children had gone with him, as if they expected to be there a while. A coincidence that did not escape her. Rachel disliked the idea of asking anyone else in Ryan's family for help. But she'd once been close to his sister, Brianna. They'd kept in contact, so it wasn't completely unheard of that she should find herself on the Duchess of Ravenspur's doorstep that evening after a fruitless search for a place to stay.

Standing outside the Bank of London that morning, she'd not realized the task ahead. Johnny had procured the rooms at the Palace Hotel during her last stay. Alone and single, she'd been unable to find suitable quarters for herself and Elsie, and she refused to stay any night at all in a place where she'd need to brace a chair against the door.

A butler answered her knock, and, after introducing herself, she stepped into the entryway before he could send her on her way.

A long moment later, a tall man appeared in the foyer. He wore a snowy white shirt open at the neck and black trousers. He was carrying a sleeping infant, its dark downy head resting on his shoulder.

Rachel had never met a duke before. She had asked to see Brianna and had not expected her husband. "May I help you . . . Miss Bailey?" he asked, her card in his hand.

Her gaze went to the tiny child in his arms. "I see that I'm interrupting."

"I've just returned from the ministry. Late meeting," he said, then when she didn't reply added, "My wife took our oldest and four of his cousins to the menagerie exhibit. She is staying with her brother, Sir Christopher, tonight, and won't be back until tomorrow."

Now, what would she do? "She sounds busy."

"Fortunately, so was I."

"I see." His glib humor made her smile. He looked as if he could be fearsome when setting someone to task. Yet, as she met his gaze beneath the high chandelier in the foyer, she thought only that there was a sparkle of deviltry in his gray eyes.

"You're the woman Ryan went to see in Ireland," he said, with subtle interest.

His obvious knowledge of Ryan's whereabouts this past week worried her. "And here I am, newly arrived in London, quite desperate to find someplace more civil to stay than what is currently offered. I swear I'm not penniless, and I do not intend to stay longer than it takes to find a house."

"Are you alone?"

"My maid is outside waiting in the hansom."

His gaze shifted to the man standing behind her. "See that the driver is paid and the girl brought inside," he told the butler before giving her his full attention. "You're exhausted, so I'll spare you the lecture on your lack of common sense for not coming here earlier, Miss Bailey."

"Thank you, Your Grace."

She appreciated the reprieve, and was glad that she'd finally found a haven among friends.

Chapter 13

"The bloody zoo?" Ryan crushed the missive in his hand, and glared at the young man who was unfortunate enough to carry the second message to him about his daughter's current whereabouts.

"She will return from Epping day after tomorrow, sir."

He'd arrived home yesterday to discover that Brianna had actually made a visit to this house and taken Mary Elizabeth back with her to London. After tearing into his staff, Ryan had managed to calm down. What was he going to do? Ride the wind to Lord Ravenspur's residence and snatch his daughter from his own sister?

Ryan instructed a servant to feed the unfortunate courier before the man trekked back to London. Carrying a towel, he returned to his dressing room. He'd finished dressing and was pulling the suspenders over his shoulders when Boswell entered.

"Lady Gwyneth and Lord Devonshire will be here in half an hour, sir." He joined Ryan. "Dinner will be served at eight."

Ryan slipped his arms into the sleeves of a jacket and,

looking in the glass, carefully readjusted his cravat.

"Contact Stewart in the morning at D&B. I want to know which site my brother went to in Scotland. I also have a stack of mail that needs to go out tomorrow. And I'm expecting Sir Boris in the afternoon."

His financial officer was in high dudgeon about Ryan's trip to Ireland and Johnny's inconvenient exodus on the eve of what would have been an announcement of a merger between Ore Industries and D&B.

"Anything else, sir?" Boswell inquired.

"Do you know anything about handfasting laws?" he asked arbitrarily, unaware of the direction of his thoughts.

Boswell's eyebrows rose considerably. "Are you planning an elopement, sir?"

"Nothing as romantic as that."

"Will this be a late night, sir?" Boswell asked after a moment.

"Just dinner."

"I imagine your new popularity will be the routine?"

Ryan's faintly bemused glance touched Boswell's in the glass. "That depends on whether I'm viewed as a social bounder or an accepted consequence of the spread of social democracy."

"Indeed, sir," his servant countered. "I believe that your sister's husband chairs that particular committee in Parliament."

Recognizing dissent when he heard it, Ryan kept his expression neutral. "Are you making a joke, Boswell?"

"I most certainly am not, sir." The older man cleared his throat. "I am merely making a facetious comment that there is no such thing as democracy, social or otherwise, sir."

Ryan walked out of the dressing room into his chambers.

"Permission to speak freely, sir." Boswell followed.

Ryan poured himself a snifter of brandy. "Obviously you've no aversion to speaking your mind," he said without looking up. "You've been doing it for years. Hell, you let my sister take my daughter to London. If I were going to rage at you, I would have already done so."

"As you know, Lord Ravenspur's house is not far from your London home," Boswell said, ignoring his tirade and getting back to the topic at hand.

"I know where my sister lives."

"I have visited her home on some occasions when you are in residence," Boswell said, reminding Ryan that Boswell and Brianna's elderly lady's maid were cousins. "I'd heard that just last month the Duchess of Bedford publicly cut Lady Ravenspur at the Green Lilly ball. If it weren't for the power-ful committee Lord Ravenspur chairs in Parliament, she would have no friends among the *ton*."

"I've no doubt of that, Boswell. Brianna is a suffragist, au-thor of scandalous books, and champion of education re-form." Abductor of small children. His younger sister could alienate anyone with the bat of an eyelash, and proudly so. He knew that she had not had an easy time with her new life since marrying a duke. "She just doesn't have friends in Lady Bedford's circle. I doubt I will either."

"I was out of line, sir. You are free to make your own choices about your future."

Boswell's attempt at humbleness failed. "No doubt you knew that when you spoke."

Clearly miffed, Boswell turned away. "Ring if you need me, sir."

After Boswell left, Ryan poured another drink, mentally consigning his valet to the night, his mood precarious at best. He was not unaware of what Boswell had been trying to tell him.

Yet, even as a part of him recognized his own hypocrisy, Ryan had accepted the necessity of allying himself to the genteel powerful. He'd known from the moment he'd inked the contracts that his future engagement to Lord Devonshire's niece would be of import to both London's business sector, which had been worried about the rift in Ore Industries, and to an upper-class society that, with the exception of a few, shunned his entire family.

Only now, he realized he was in danger of losing everything.

Ryan wore formal black dinner attire, his jacket buttoned at his waist. Walking outside onto the terrace, he could have been a shadow but for the slip of white beneath his sleeve. The sunset had turned the sky a dark indigo. With the exception of his housekeeper and valet, Ryan rarely saw any of the fifty-two servants and thirty groundskeepers he employed. Yet everything was always in perfect order. He looked over the sloping yard toward the rolling river and the distant pagoda where he had lunched with Rachel weeks ago. Faraway lights cast a dull halo against the horizon, and he thought about her somewhere in London.

He had not known she would be on the ferry from Ireland.

He had not discovered her presence until they'd docked, and he'd seen Elsie standing at the window. It had taken him a little longer to find her buried in the hood of her cloak, hiding from him at the back table in the salon. Watching her, holding her profile with his gaze, he'd realized one vital element at that moment. She was aware of his presence as much as he was aware of hers. He'd felt her gaze when he'd hailed the cab to take him to the rail depot and felt her presence behind him at the telegraph office. He'd been aware of everything about her, which was why he sat two cars from her on the train, as if distance had the power to separate her from his thoughts. She'd been asleep when he'd made his rounds down the aisle after midnight and looked into her compartment. When, for just a moment, he'd considered setting his hands firmly on her stubborn shoulders and shaking her awake for the pure shock value of seeing those beautiful hazel eyes open on him.

Though Ryan needed more answers to understand what David may have done to his life, and how to extricate himself from a complicated position—for now the options were all his. He smiled to himself, for Rachel had no idea the power he held in his hands.

"Sir," Boswell interrupted his thoughts from the doorway, "your guests have arrived."

Lord Bathwick's home rested in central Mayfair the second-to-last house among a row of twenty. An elderly butler with bushy eyebrows showed Rachel into the drawing room. Feeling rudely dismissed by him, she ignored his departure as she turned her attention to the room. The place smelled of brandy, cigars, and fading roses, as forlorn as any room when a party is over, and the guests have all gone home. She walked to the window and looked out over a small enclosed yard.

Two days ago, she had gone to Mr. Williams's house. He had given her the list they had talked about weeks ago of major common stockholders in the company.

Viscount Bathwick held shares, she thought, remembering the man who had approached her at the Telford ball. Lord Bathwick owned 17 percent of the common stock in the company.

She couldn't believe it.

"The Devonshire family owns the foundry that supplies steel to many construction firms, including D&B," Mr. Williams had told her. "Unfortunately, he has proven himself an adversary. Eight months ago he spurred rumors about production delays at D&B, and the stock fell 12 percent, which was how he accumulated the shares in the company that he has."

Rachel considered the practice highly unethical even as Mr. Williams laughed and explained that Ryan had been guilty of using the procedure himself. "I'm sure Lord Bath-wick considered it justice."

Turning over the calling card in her hand, Rachel thought about justice.

Lord Bathwick had given her this card the night of the Telford ball.

"Miss Bailey." Lord Bathwick's voice pulled her away from the window. "I apologize that I missed your call yester-day." He swept into the room and bent over her gloved hand. "Might I hope that your persistence is an omen fraught with good fortune and pleasure?"

Rachel resented the implication of that look. Dressed con-servatively in bone taffeta, there was nothing about her that implied she was there for anything but a business dialogue. "This call is many things, my lord, but pleasurable isn't one."

"She has a sting to her tongue. And no sense of humor." He was amused. Dressed in a bright red waistcoat beneath a chocolate velvet jacket that accentuated his deep blue eyes, he looked very dapper as he stepped back. "Your maid is sit-ting in the foyer. Would you like to summon her? I wouldn't want anyone to get the wrong impression about your visit. Not that one lone lady's maid could hold back the tide of gos-sip. These are bachelor quarters, after all."

Coming directly to the point, Rachel lifted her chin. "I wish to buy your shares in D&B."

He laughed. "Even if you said please, you couldn't afford my price. Would you care for something to drink?" He strode to a cabinet and withdrew a crystal decanter. "You look as if you could use one more than I."

Seeing Lord Bathwick in the fading daylight of the draw-ing room, Rachel realized his fawn-colored hair and tanned complexion bespoke a man who spent a great deal of time out of doors. That surprised her, for his nonchalant splendor clearly created a contradiction of personalities. He wanted her to think him a popinjay, when the calluses on his palm implied something else entirely. What kind of aristocrat had calluses on his hands?

After sloshing liquid into two glasses, he capped the decanter and returned with her drink. "If one is going covertly to plot the downfall of Ryan Donally, one should be expediently drunk. Capital stuff this is, too."

His words alarmed her. "I'm not here to plot anyone's downfall." Rachel accepted the glass only because she didn't wish to waste time arguing over trivialities.

"But of course you are." He peered at her over his glass. "The only question I ask is why you have waited so long?"

"You knew that night at the Telford ball what Mr. Donally had planned for D&B."

"My father sits on the Ore Industries board." Bathwick studied the glass. "His dwindling empire and all that's left of my great-grandfather's legacy. A company Donally took from us because Father is a conceited fool."

"Because he underestimated Mr. Donally?"

"You don't know. Do you? The sordid family history, as it were."

"I don't know you at all, much less your history."

He contemplated her more thoroughly before finishing off his glass. "You're a contradiction, Miss Bailey. A very beautiful one at that, but a contradiction nonetheless." Bathwick set down the glass. "On the one hand, you want D&B. On the other, you want to do this as cleanly as possible. What are your motives for fighting this merger when selling could make you wealthy?"

Rachel decided that he deserved an honest answer. "I have an interest in the Irish division. Mr. Donally has forgotten the people who have worked for him and who have made this company what it is."

"Donally is a businessman. If he has forgotten anything, none of us have ever seen it."

Rachel realized his animosity stretched way past any rivalry he and Ryan might have in the corporate world. "Why do you hate Ryan so much?"

"Hate?" The question seemed to startle him. "My dear girl, you're asking me that question when I'm sober." Peering at her, he folded his arms and leaned against the back of the settee. "Do you think Ore Industries was just some company Donally decided to take over one day?" The jackanapes in him had disappeared behind a sober face.

"Honestly, I don't know why he does half what he does, my lord."

"As you probably know, Ore Industries has always been D&B's biggest supplier of supplies and steel. The two companies rather grew up together in the marketplace."

Rachel knew that they had.

"Then once upon a time, Donally met Gwyneth at Ore Industries, when he was leaving a meeting with my father. My father turned down his request to court her, which in itself would have been within his rights considering Donally's lack of pedigree. But then Father decided to take Donally to task. In the tradition of big British business interests, Father decided to raise prices charged on goods. Donally refused to pay the exorbitant prices and took his business elsewhere, severing the contracts. Then, adding insult to injury, Father used his political connections to ban Donally from Regents and Cassavas, and a half dozen other exclusive clubs. D&B lost a summer's worth of contracts and failed to meet their deadline on two major contracts because Ore Industries delayed delivery of materials. One doesn't insult a man like Donally and expect nothing to happen.

"When the ashes settled, only Donally was left standing. My father holds the position he does now because he offered up Gwyneth to avoid complete annihilation." Pausing, Bathwick regarded Rachel's frown. "So, if you must know where my real hatred lies, look no further than his esteemed lordship, the Earl of Devonshire."

Rachel dropped her gaze to the brandy in her hand. She had not known any of this.

"Donally's newest acquisition would have one day been mine. That night of the ball, I had come to you about the possibility of our own business arrangement. Naturally, we bluebloods don't worry ourselves over something as trifling as money, but neither do I like the possibility of finding myself an impoverished lord. There are principles to avenge."

She set the glass on the table beside her. "Because you lost Lady Gwyneth to him? Or the means to your wealth?"

"Donally doesn't love Gwyneth." He pushed away from the settee and strolled back to the brandy decanter. "He's paying my father more than most people see in twenty lifetimes for the privilege of marrying into this family. My motivations for taking D&B from Donally may not be as honorable as yours, but they still put us on the same side."

Rachel laid her hands atop the chair. Did they?

The cool brightness of the morning suddenly seemed too hot against her back. "If you want your Irish division back, then we go into this as partners, Miss Bailey." Bathwick smiled, but his eyes remained observant. "I want a position on the board. It's the only chance you'll have of changing company policy."

"What about your father?" she whispered.

"May he rot. Unless you want to put in a good word for him."

She shook her head. She was remembering his threat. Then she felt her courage return and a lot more. "Even with your shares, I won't have enough to block the acquisition," she said, coming to a decision, for this fight was all that she had left.

That and her grandmother.

"But I have income sitting in the Bank of England to make up the difference."

"To a partnership then." He raised the glass. "If it happens."

"What do you mean?" She would have preferred his confidence.

"You have been in London over a week?" Bathwick asked. "Donally must know your intentions. So, why hasn't he already purchased the shares to stop you?"

Dropping the stack of folders on the desk, Rachel coughed at the explosion of dust. Mr. Williams stood in front of the window in her office. Behind her, Stewart helped carry in an armload of files.

"I'm a board member of this company." She dusted off her hands. "One would naturally think it should be a simple process to find out what this company is worth. Don't you agree?"

"I will be at my desk, mum," Stewart said, bowing out of the room and leaving Mr. Williams to her.

"Johnny could be in Scotland for a month." She removed her gloves and set them on her satchel. "D&B has a team of engineers who do nothing but inspect sites. No doubt he elected to head that team for the express purpose of fleeing London."

"I understand that Mr. Donally is none too content with his brother's absence either."

She walked to the window and looked out over the parkway that paralleled the embankment. She'd taken Ryan's old office at Donally & Bailey. If only temporarily.

"Why do you look as if I am suffering from a terminal illness, and you are trying your best to be cheerful?" She turned to confront Mr. Williams, who remained quiet. "Obviously, I'm not going to like what you are about to tell me. What did you find out?"

"Handfasting is similar to what used to take place in the Scottish border town of Gretna Green at the turn of the century," he said. "Marriage by declaration, another name for handfasting, still remains valid in much of the British Isles."

"But the British courts could not possibly recognize the tradition," she said, waiting for him to confirm this fact for her. Ryan had as much implied that to her.

"In your case, untying the knot will be more difficult than it was tying the knot."

Rachel pinched the bridge of her nose. "Why, dare I ask?"

"When Father Donally registered the marriage, it then became a civil union. You are legally bound to Mr. Donally, whether you accept that possibility or not."

Rachel brought her fist to her chest and forced herself to breathe.

"Miss Bailey." Mr. Williams was at her side. "Are you all right?"

"No, I'm not all right!" How else did one react to this kind of shock, she thought, except to have heart failure and die.

Returning to the door, she peered into the hallway. "This is utterly insane." But it explained Ryan's lack of action against her. She shut the door and closed the transom. "He's known all along."

Had probably known since he'd left Ireland.

"Perhaps," Williams said. "But it doesn't change the facts."

Rachel walked to the window. Not a cloud marred the sky. "I could own a hundred percent of D&B, and it will make no difference. Ryan will have control of it all."

This is what came from lust and an overzealous priest thrown together beneath one roof. If she ever spoke to David again in this lifetime, it would be too damn soon.

"What am I supposed to do?"

"That is between you and Mr. Donally. You need to talk to him."

"Then he's finally back in London?"

"Since this morning," Mr. Williams said. "He attended the Regatta yesterday. He does seem to be the man of the moment."

Rachel folded her arms and pretended that she didn't care what Ryan did with his time—or with whom. It went to the core of her pride that she remain impassive. Behind her, Mr. Williams approached.

"It would be unethical for me to counsel you to do anything illegal, but if you think about your problem from a business standpoint . . . Mr. Donally may not want this information known, and may choose to try to settle this matter as quietly as possible."

Otherwise, in layman's terms, blackmail went both ways.

Ryan would have to acknowledge her as his wife if he were to claim control of her shares. He would lose far more than she.

"I wish to begin buying company stock, Mr. Williams."

She and Lord Bathwick had just become official partners.

"I told you she was pretty."

Reaching for the last fragment of sleep, Rachel settled into her pillow. Somewhere above the *hiss* and *shush* of conferring whispers, wind chimes sang with the ebb and flow of the evening breeze that moved over her.

"Wake her," a little girl rasped.

"*You* wake her."

Rachel's eyes fluttered open.

Mary Elizabeth stood beside the bed, her blue gaze patiently intent on Rachel's face. Beside her stood a younger male version of Lord Ravenspur, his mouth covered in a sticky cinnamon glom of what once had been an apple pastry.

A glance at the clock on her bedside table told Rachel it was seven in the evening. She passed her gaze over the delicate floral chintz looped against the half-tester canopy and held in place by blue, tasseled cords. For a moment, she tried to remember where she was. She'd returned from D&B and promptly fell into bed exhausted.

"I gots a puppy," Mary Elizabeth proclaimed, while the creature in her arms wagged its nub of a tail.

Rachel rose on her elbow. The significance of Mary Elizabeth's presence suddenly alerted her. That Ryan had brought her to London surprised her. "Is your father here?"

The girl shook her head. "I rided the train with Miss Peapoo and Aunt Brea. Will Da let me keep my puppy?"

Amused that Ryan would rather suffer thumbscrews than be associated with such a caricature of a dog, Rachel did not have to pretend interest. "Let me see."

As she studied the dog with its wrinkled face, Rachel sensed that the girl was studying her. Clearing her throat, Rachel assumed the pose of a serious student as she looked at the puppy. "What is your puppy's name?"

"Button," the young Ravenspur heir burst out. Brianna's son stood a few inches shorter than his cousin.

"He gots a broke tail. Do you want to see?"

Rachel pulled back her covers and sat on the edge of the bed. Her hair, uncombed and wild, fell around her shoulders to her waist. She'd removed her slippers and stockings. "That's not broken," Rachel said, as Mary Elizabeth set the puppy down on the bed for display. "Someone chopped it off."

Rachel's gaze shifted back to the little girl's horrified face. "Many puppies have their tails bobbed," she rushed to say. "I predict that your father will let you keep the dog."

Mary Elizabeth squeezed the puppy to her chest. "I want him."

Ryan was disagreeable and difficult about everything in life, but when it came to his daughter, he was as soft as a bunny rabbit, and she told his daughter so. "With big fluffy ears," Rachel added. "And a handsome tail, when he's not an ogre with pointy teeth."

Mary Elizabeth laughed. Brianna's son whispered something in her ear.

"Do you like cats?" his bolder cousin relayed the question.
"Yes."

The girl turned triumphantly to the little boy, and whispered, "I told you she was nice." In a big-sister fashion, she wrapped her arm around her cousin's shoulders. "Robert is almost three."

"Free." The dark-haired imp proudly held up five fingers.

"I'm older," she sagely announced. "I had a birthday, and now I'm four."

"There you two are." A gray-haired woman bustled into the room. "Off with the two of ye now." She shooed the children away with a playful wave of her hands. "Your father is looking for ye, Lord Robert," she said. "And you, young lady. *Your* father is expecting you home now. He's come to London just to fetch ye back."

"Thank you, Gracie." Brianna entered as the two children left, screaming in excitement.

Rachel met her halfway, and they fell into each other's arms. Brianna wore a bright cobalt blue dress and jacket that matched her laughing eyes. "I'm sorry I wasn't here to greet you when you arrived. I've been with the family out of town." She untied the bow beneath her chin and removed the wide straw hat shaking her long hair loose. "Michael said that you had tried to find a hotel. Don't ever do that again, Rachel."

"Your husband has been very gracious to me."

"Don't count on finding a decent house or flat anytime soon. A place to live in London is difficult to find anytime of the year. Impossible until the Season is over."

"You're very kind to let me stay here."

Brianna smiled a cheeky grin as a dinner tray arrived. She plucked off a crust of bread. "Most people start out feeling that way, but they soon change their minds when they realize how persistent and annoying I can be." Plucky, unpretentious, the young Duchess of Ravenspur had changed little in character from the youthful sprite of her past. "Johnny told everyone about the acquisition before he left," Brianna said, slathering jam on the bread. "I'm sorry."

Unfortunately, that didn't change the facts, Rachel thought as she turned away to open the glass doors.

"Ryan went to Ireland," Brianna said offhandedly. "That was very unusual for him. Did he get to see David?"

"Why?"

Brianna's perfect brows arched. "David has been looking to take revenge on Ryan since our brother converted to the Anglican Church. The whole family was just curious . . . if they resolved their differences."

"You know David." Rachel sat. "He can be persuasive when he sets his mind to something. Did you hear from him?"

"Just the usual." Brianna licked the jam from her fingers. "You know David."

Bloody right, she knew that scallywag pirate. Rachel stirred the preserves and tried to look uninterested.

"Feel free to fatten yourself." Brianna gave Rachel another kiss. "I went through the entire strawberry jam stores when I was pregnant with my second. One would think James should have inherited a sweeter disposition."

"You have two beautiful sons."

"Alas, I've kept Ryan cooling his heels long enough." Brianna sighed. "I need to see Mary Elizabeth and Miss Peabody off safely before he comes storming to this house. He's in London, in case you didn't know. Shall I give him your regards?"

No doubt his social calender was already full.

"Ask him how he enjoys long betrothals."

"Da!"

Ryan lifted his gaze from behind a stack of papers on his desk. Blond curls bouncing, his daughter stood momentarily in the doorway. He'd barely set his pen down and stood before she bounded into his arms. All pinafore and ruffles, Mary Elizabeth smelled of apple pastry. "I was beginning to think you'd forgotten about me," he said into her baby-soft hair.

His sister stood in the doorway.

"Aunt Brea taked me to the zoo, Da. I saw a tiger."

He kissed her forehead, drawing back to look at the squirming bundle in her arms. "What is this?"

"Miss Peapoo won't let me keep him until I asked you," Mary Elizabeth said seriously. "He's a puppy."

"I can see that."

"Aunt Brea gave me a birthday party. Uncle Johnny was there and Uncle Michael, Chrissy and Megan and Rebecca and Robert"—she drew in a deep gulp of air—"and baby James, too. He stinked." She held her nose, her opinion of her newest cousin obvious. "But Uncle Michael gots me *soldiers* for my birthday! Lots of soldiers and cannons. Baby James tried to eat one. He cried when Aunt Brea took it away. And Uncle Colin, he gots me a saddle for my pony. And Uncle Christopher and Aunt Lexie gots me a *puppy!*"

"You've been busy, Mouse." Ryan lifted his gaze to Brianna.

"Christopher thought she might enjoy the puppy." Brianna smiled. "It's a very rare Shar Pei. We all agreed it would make a great addition to your household."

"I saw my fairy godmother." His daughter smiled up at him. "She said you would let me keep the puppy."

"Your fairy godmother?"

"She's pretty. I like her."

"Did she have a magic wand?"

"No, but she gots red hair. Uncle Johnny said leprechauns have red hair."

Ryan pulled back to look down at her. "Your godmother?" He looked at Brianna. "Rachel is staying with you?"

"It took her a day before she finally ended up on our doorstep."

"Robert waked her up." Mary Elizabeth said. "She was asleep."

"Is she all right?" Ryan asked his sister.

"She's fine."

"Do you like my dog, Da?"

With a wrinkled face and barely bigger than a rookery rat, *dog* was a term he'd use loosely to describe the strange creature in her arms. He'd never seen anything so ugly.

Miss Peabody tilted her chin. "Unfortunately, I found the creature in her bed this morning."

Mary Elizabeth's blue eyes narrowed mutinously. "He is afraid of the dark, Da. I has to sleep with him. Or he'll cry."

"Mary . . ."

"The mutt should be housed out back," Miss Peabody replied.

"He is not a mutt! He's the best puppy ever! I named him Button 'cause he gots a broked tail, and his nose is black like baby James's kitten."

The logic of a four-year-old lost on him, he listened as she chatted about the merits of a dog, and how she'd always wanted one—like she'd wanted a pony, kittens, rabbits and, last year, a parrot.

"I want him, Da."

"Well, I see matters are under control," Brianna announced with a flourish. "I shall go then."

"Brea," Ryan stopped her. "You were supposed to have had her back to me four days ago."

Mary Elizabeth pulled back to study her father's face. "Are you going to send Aunt Brea to the corner?"

"Now there's a thought."

His sister looked at Mary Elizabeth and smiled. "We had a wonderful time. She knows how to climb trees, Ryan."

Mary Elizabeth laughed and told him about the trees. Ryan was not impressed, and his eyes told his sister that they would talk later. "Oh, by the way," she said, as she applied her gloves to her hands. "Rachel hopes you enjoy long betrothals. I was under the impression that you would be married in October," Brianna said airily. "I wonder why she wanted me to tell you that?"

Ryan's gaze narrowed on her back, shifting to Miss Peabody when he realized she was still in the room.

"Do you like my dog, Da?"

Still carrying Mary Elizabeth, he walked outside onto the terrace and sat with her on the chair. "Let me see that thing."

"May I keep him?"

His daughter held the dog up for his inspection. As it wagged its stubby tail, completely unaware of its mortal shortcomings, Ryan took one look into Mary Elizabeth's hopeful, blue eyes, his one true triumph in life, and was aware of an enormous shift inside him.

"Please, Da," she pleaded. "Please."

"Shall I take the young miss?" Miss Peabody said from the doorway.

"No, that's not necessary. I'll bring her inside."

His daughter smiled. "My fairy godmother said you would let me keep the puppy."

"She did, did she?"

"She said you were a bunny rabbit and gots a handsome tail when you're not an ogre."

"I think I've read you one too many fairy tales."

"What is that star, Da?" Mary Elizabeth pointed to the flashiest, biggest star south of the moon.

"That is a very important star." Ryan sat with his feet propped on the stone balustrade overlooking his yard. His London estate backed against a park. He could hear a carriage on the other side of the trees. But for London, the night was peaceful. "In the olden days, seafarers used that one to help guide them over the oceans home."

A scented breeze moved over the terrace, wiping away the day's warmth. "Is that how you came home?" Her sleepy voice asked.

"No, Mouse." He smiled into her hair. "I took the train."

Mary Elizabeth nestled her head on his shoulder just below his chin. "Uncle Christopher says that you maked the train."

He tightened his arm around his daughter. "Not quite. Donally & Bailey helped lay the tracks the trains move upon. But I always wanted to build trains," he said.

"Aunt Brea said I could make things, too, when I growed up." Ryan frowned slightly. "Did she?"

"I had fun. Aunt Brea said that I can come back and visit. Can I?"

"If she can stand your talking." He smiled.

She snuggled deeper into his chest. "I love you, Da."

Ryan looked down at his daughter's upturned face, the power of that love nearly terrifying him. He was unfamiliar with the protectiveness that followed wherever she went. Familiar only with the purpose her life gave his. A purpose that suddenly seemed cloudy and surreal. A purpose he no longer entirely understood.

"I love you, too, Mary," he whispered.

But she was already asleep when he pressed a kiss against her forehead. The puppy lifted its head, wagging its stub of tail.

Ryan frowned. "What are you so happy about?"

Chapter 14

"**G**ood afternoon, Mr. Donally, sir." The uniformed attendant proudly held open the door as Ryan entered Ore Industries headquarters. A burst of wind and rain followed in his wake. "Welcome back, sir."

Carrying his satchel, Ryan continued past others into the marble-and-granite-encased lobby. He'd been out of the office three weeks, and people acted as if it were three years. The bellman cheerfully rolled open the lift door and stood aside as Ryan entered.

"It is good to see you back, sir." A jolt preceded the screech of cogs and wheels that set the lift in motion.

Ryan shifted his gaze to the back of the younger man's head as he spoke. No fewer than seventy-two people had thus far welcomed him back to London since his return. His private secretary had already accepted calling cards from two dozen visitors to his London estate only yesterday. He'd truly not anticipated this manner of frenzy since his betrothal announcement had made it to the broadsheets weeks ago.

"Your floor, sir." The lift jolted to a stop and, with a distracted nod, Ryan swept past the younger man.

"Mr. Donally—" His secretary shoved to her feet.

"Mrs. Stone." Ryan continued through the well-appointed reception area without noticing the magnificent Louis XIV décor, his shoes sinking into the luxurious carpet, muffling his footsteps. Mrs. Stone edged around the waist-high wall separating her paneled alcove from the anteroom, her heavy black skirts swishing in her hurried gait to reach Ryan's office door before him.

"Has my brother wired me yet from Scotland?"

Behind him, a staff meeting was breaking up, and he stopped to retrieve a handful of missives from two of his company officers. "Welcome back." Sir Boris fell into step beside Ryan.

Ryan threw open the door before he saw that Mrs. Stone had followed him. Impatient, he turned.

"If I may speak to you privately, sir," she said, pointedly ignoring Sir Boris.

Normally, Ryan wouldn't have agreed. Not when he owed every hour of his day to someone. Nodding to Boris to wait outside, Ryan motioned his secretary into the office and walked to the window to open the wooden blinds. "Speak, Mrs. Stone." He set his satchel and coat on the desk. "You have three minutes."

"I wish to take off two weeks," she said bluntly. "My niece is . . . indisposed. She has two small children. I was hoping that perhaps you would give me time to attend to her. I would even accept a week."

With his problems at D&B and the Paris acquisition in full negotiation status, Ryan needed her here. "Mrs. Stone—"

"My sister passed away ten years ago," she rushed to say. "Her daughter is my only family, sir. She lives in Manchester. It has been a long time since I've seen her. Or I would not have asked."

Ryan had never paid much attention to Mrs. Stone before, any more than he'd paid heed to any number of the people who worked for him. Strangely, it seemed as if he were noticing the smallest details in his life of late. His gaze passed over the salt-and-pepper-colored bun secured at her nape. She wore a black skirt and white blouse buttoned to her neck. He'd never seen her wearing anything different. Not in the four years since she'd talked him into hiring her to replace her husband after his passing. She knew the job, worked long hours, kept his personal books, and never faltered when he'd needed her to stay late. Nor had she in all those years asked for a day off work. For some reason, Mrs. Stone reminded him of Rachel. Perhaps it was the prideful way she carried herself.

He sat behind his desk. The thought of Rachel having to kowtow to any man the same way he was making Mrs. Stone do with him made him frown. "Two weeks?"

"Yes, sir. I'll not be a day longer—"

"Don't concern yourself, Mrs. Stone. Obviously, this is of importance. When will you be leaving?"

Her blue eyes brightened behind her spectacles. "This weekend. Oh, thank you, sir."

Ryan didn't know where the hell he'd find a secretary. "Mrs. Stone"—he stopped her retreat. "The train fare to Manchester is not inexpensive."

"I plan on taking the mail coach, sir."

Ryan removed a key from beneath his desk and slid open a drawer. "Take the train. It's faster." Hell, D&B had laid the tracks. "I want you back as soon as possible."

Mrs. Stone's hands wrapped around the money he offered. "I don't know what to say, Mr. Donally."

"Thank you will suffice. Your family is fortunate to have you."

"Bless you, Mr. Donally. I am the lucky one, sir."

Pulling out a pair of folders from his satchel, Ryan realized her words about her family were not lost on him. He thought of the yapping puppy his oldest brother had given Mary Elizabeth, and Brea's determination since Kathleen's death to see that his daughter was made part of her own family, despite his own arrogance and lack of cooperation. Johnny's loyalty had never wavered.

Then again there was David who, in his infinite wisdom to wed him to Rachel, had reminded Ryan that the man with the biggest stick held the ultimate power.

"Mrs. Stone . . ." he called as she opened the door. "I need my afternoon schedule. It's not on my desk."

"It is beneath the calendar." Her chin lifted at the implication that she'd forgotten such an important function of her job. Then proceeded to name off his itinerary, ending with a meeting Johnny had rescheduled with the head of public works—and the possible acquisition of three plump government contracts to expand Ore Industries' balance sheets.

Ryan sank back in the leather chair and, linking his fingers behind his head, observed her with a casual smile. "Thank you, Mrs. Stone. If you say anything else, I may realize how valuable you really are and decide not to let you go to Manchester."

She peered over her spectacles. "Then you won't mind my telling you that a writer from *Vanity Fair* was just here. I took the liberty of informing him that you were unavailable. Indefinitely. I didn't think that you would want to grant him a meeting after the last piece he'd written about you, and told him so in no uncertain terms."

"Thank you, Mrs. Stone." Amusement tinged Ryan's voice. "Tell Sir Boris that I need the second quarter financial report I ordered on D&B delivered to my desk."

"I believe it is on your desk, sir."

"It?" The report in question would fill more than one folder.

"A folder, sir. I put it on your desk."

Having had his fill of suspicious-looking folders, Ryan found and reluctantly opened this one.

You are such a bastard, Ryan Donally. I will not allow you to pillage D&B. Will return these papers after I have completed my analysis.

Love, R.

Written in her precise hand. A bouquet of forget-me-nots finished the sentence.

P.S., she added at the bottom, *Negotiation comes in many forms*.

She'd taken extra care to detail the flowers in purple.

"A love note, sir?" Sir Boris said from the doorway.

Ryan slowly looked up. "What is the status on D&B stock?"

As Sir Boris sifted through his papers, Ryan felt the kick of his pulse. The telltale heat in his veins that came when he recognized a hunt for what it was.

"D&B stock has risen 5 percent this past week, sir."

Ryan shut the folder. She was buying up stock and running the price higher.

He wondered if he possessed the willpower not to strangle her.

Negotiation comes in many forms.

So did blackmail, he considered.

"I need you to secure a list of major stockholders," he said, suspecting who might be behind Rachel's actions.

"At once."

He directed his gaze toward the window across the room. It had stopped raining. Rachel would not be at D&B this time of the day. He knew where she took her meals and when she left the building. He knew she went back to Ravenspur's in the evenings and remained there. Absently rubbing his fingers, he watched a pair of mismatched pigeons bobbing about the granite ledge outside the window.

"Where are we on the French deal?" he asked after a moment.

"Brendan sent a missive back from Paris two days ago. Valmonts' board is balking. But then that was to be anticipated. They'll go with Ore Industries' offer because no one else is going to bail them out of their financial predicament. They want to speak with you."

"Tell Brendan that they'll accept the deal. The terms are not negotiable."

"I already told him, sir. They will close the deal with you."

Ryan stopped the man at the door. "You did the initial assessment on that company," he said, shrugging into his coat. "They are bankrupt. What are they fighting so hard to keep?"

"Does it matter, sir?" The question clearly baffled Sir Boris. "We are not in the business of saving companies."

"No, I imagine we are not," Ryan said, with such ambivalence that Sir Boris didn't recognize Ryan's mood.

"Are you going somewhere, sir?"

Just some of his own business to attend to. "Cover my meeting at four. I'll be back in the office tomorrow."

Booths of sweetmeat-sellers, toymakers, and hucksters surrounded the fairground. Rachel tented a hand over her eyes and watched a raucous puppet show entertain a group of sticky-faced children. Every afternoon, she took a hansom to the outskirts of London to eat at a quaint inn where her father used to bring her as a girl. The family she once knew no longer lived there, but the inn still served the best shepherd's pie and ale she'd ever tasted.

There was plenty to entertain the idlers: jugglers, acrobats, fire-eaters, and fortune-tellers. She avoided the latter as she stopped in front of a stall selling lady's hats. Beautiful, stylish hats with fans of many designs to match. Rachel was not a collector of such feminine accoutrements, but her gaze kept going back to the frilly hat with a dainty brim and yellow ostrich feather that would lie just so over the cheek.

"It is of fine quality, *oui*?" the bald vendor asked.

"It is very beautiful," Rachel agreed.

"You have been eyeing this hat many days now." He smiled slyly, holding it out to her for further examination. A chilly wind gust caught her skirt, tugged, then slowly ebbed. "I will give it to you for a good price."

But she would not purchase it. They had this discussion every time she passed the booth, she thought as she moved down the aisle. To own something she'd never use seemed frivolous.

Finding an abandoned bench, Rachel opened her reticule and carefully unwrapped a piece of bread left over from her lunch. She tossed the crumbs over the grounds. Pigeons bobbed at her feet and fluttered around the tree branches behind her. She was aware, as the temperature wavered on the chilly side, that it looked like the morning's cloudburst was about to be joined by another. She wore no cloak.

Neither did she have a companion with her and knew she could never dally long near the riverfront before men began to call out to her. But she carried a reticule filled with rocks and a sturdy parasol. She didn't want to return to D&B just yet.

Dusting off her hands, she looked out at the ships on the river—and directly into Ryan's eyes. Wearing a long coat, he was leaning against the stone break-wall on the other side of the walkway, his gloved palms braced behind him as he watched her, the force of his presence filling the air like the thunderclouds gathering above her.

Yet, her heart did a flip-flop. She had not seen him since the train depot.

"You possess a remarkable ability to find peace in the most unremarkable places," he said, as if he'd been watching her a long time. "What exactly about this location do you find appealing?"

"Simplicity?" she said, calmly challenging him to argue the quiet charm of the secluded spot. "How did you find me?"

"Stewart told me where you spend your afternoons. Once here, all one need do is follow the trail of men in your wake. You glow."

She glanced down at her apple green jacket trimmed in black cording that she considered extremely conservative in cut, and saw nothing wrong with her clothes. "I've seen you with women dressed in far less than I'm wearing." Brushing a gloved hand over each sleeve, she lifted her chin. "Who was that countess?" She rolled her eyes at the photograph taken at the Ascot races only last summer. The woman had fairly spilled out of her bodice. "I won't even go into Lady Gwyneth. You're too easily seduced, Ryan."

The tension that lay between them was tangible.

Clearly, he knew that she was purchasing company stock. Maybe even that she'd visited Lord Bathwick.

His eyes also told her that she was his wife.

Before he cloaked the Irish predator behind a bland expression and smiled. "My carriage is waiting for us. You and I need to talk."

A flurry of sensations streaked through her. Fear. Panic. Lust.

And rebellion against all those emotions. She stood. "You knew we were irrevocably wed when we left Ireland," she accused him.

"David told me what he had done. But I had to make sure myself."

"You *could* have told me."

Neither of them expanded on what they were going to do

about undoing their vows. "Aren't you worried that someone might spill the news that you're wed? See us together?" She spread her arms and turned in a circle. "Ruin all of your plans?"

"But then if everything became public, that someone would no longer be a major shareholder in her precious D&B." He crossed one ankle over the other, his eyes amused as they swept her. "Ahhh, the dilemma with which we're both faced."

"Which one of us would lose the most, do you suppose?"

She knew she was an amateur playing a dangerous game. But she wasn't so weak-willed she'd fold and give him everything.

"I know what's important to your little mercenary heart, Rache." Raindrops plopped on the ground. "To play this dirty game of blackmail, you'll have to be willing to lose everything. Are you?"

Wishing to wipe that confident smirk off his handsome face, she folded her arms. When next she peered in his direction, his eyes were still on her, and dark. Hooded like a hawk's. He raised a brow at her. "Ooops. It looks as if blackmail is out."

He looked at her lips, lower to her breasts, until she felt the subtle shift of his eyes back to hers. He could touch her anywhere, and her senses responded. She took an unconscious step backward. "I imagine that we have much to discuss," she said.

He stood. "I imagine so."

Some age-old instinct warned her to keep her tongue to herself, and the temptation to know more of his thoughts abetted that instinct. She was willing to indulge him in some form of negotiation, but on her own terms, standing in the office at D&B.

They needed to decide how they were going to dissolve their vows. At least in that quarter they were united.

Weren't they?

Raindrops fell faster and pebbled on the bench.

"Why didn't you buy that hat in the booth?" he asked.

Caught as much by the strange tenor in his voice, she took another step backward, embarrassed that he would have seen her fawning over something so useless. "How long have you been watching me?"

He followed her retreat. "Long enough to know that you spend a lot of time alone."

When she realized she was retreating from him, she stopped abruptly. "I don't need anyone to make my life content."

"Your work is your only lover then?" His urbane tone mocked her.

"Yes."

He knew that she'd lied. He'd been her lover.

She put aside the fact that he was her husband.

And that every fiber in her being hummed with awareness of him.

The wind billowed beneath her skirts, but she did not take notice of the chill or the rhythm of rain against the leaves. He'd set his palm against the tree that was suddenly at her back. "Someone will see us, Ryan."

Recognizing the primal force of his thoughts aimed at her, she knew he was going to kiss her. Worse, she knew she would let him. She raised a hand to his chest. Felt the thump of his heart against her palm. "Damn you, Ryan."

"Aye, damn me as you will, Rache." His fingertips came alongside her cheek and, exerting only the slightest pressure, he tilted her head to meet his gaze. "I have no doubt that my unfortunate trip to Ireland will cost us both, one way or the other."

Rachel's gaze held Ryan's, stormy dark in the rain.

It always seemed to be her fate to appear in front of him at a disadvantage. Rachel was conscious of an entirely irrational feeling of annoyance. Somehow, she summarized in an equally irrational response, that everything happening to her was his fault—including her craving for him. How could she maintain control over her life, if she could not even control her carnal desires?

He turned as if he were looking for someone. A man stood discreetly just at the edge of the trees, facing another direction. "I've had the carriage brought to Whiteside Street. It borders this walkway. It's closer than traipsing to the mews."

She watched as he walked toward the man, obviously someone in his employ by the way the man's spine snapped upright at Ryan's approach. Panic infused the uncertainty riding her heartbeat, and this time she could not pull it back or rein it under control. Realizing that she was no longer safe from herself or the hazardous affair of her feelings whenever he was about, she was suddenly prepared to flee. The rain began to fall in buckets. Then she felt him at her back, and he pulled her beneath his coat.

They took the dirt path back toward the aisle of tents that backed against the walkway. Vendors were lowering their tent flaps, mothers gathering children. Rachel gripped her reticule as Ryan hurried her into a run. She saw that he carried her parasol, the tensile strength of his hand at odds with the feminine accoutrement.

"You may take me to D&B," she managed over her breath when they reached the carriage.

He bent and hoisted her into the carriage. "Get in."

Her slippers were ruined. He climbed in behind her and shut the door. Curtains covered the windows. Cold seeped through her soaked clothes to her drawers.

The carriage jolted forward. She sat on one side shivering and Ryan on the other. Her hair was disheveled beneath the hat she wore. He laid his long coat over her, enveloping her with his earthy scent. Almost reluctantly, Rachel lifted her gaze to his.

"Are you going to blame me for the rain, too, Rache?"

"Not at all." She clenched her jaw in a smile to keep her teeth from chattering. "You've enough delusions of grandeur, Ryan."

"Thank you for reminding me that I am merely human."

He hunched forward, rubbing his hands together for warmth. From her corner, Rachel watched him shift to find warmth and surrendered to the inevitable. "Why do m-men give their coats to women, and freeze?" she asked, burrowing beneath the wool.

"Isn't that what gentlemen are required to do?"

"The implication being that w-women are frail and help-less?"

"Or witless for leaving without a cloak in the first place." Ryan leaned forward. "Are we going to have an honest-to-God argument over this, Rachel?"

Her lips curved into a frown, but she couldn't argue with logic. "Only if you expect me t-to take your coat while you freeze." Reluctantly, she lifted the edge of the coat. "Can we call a truce? At least until we get warm?"

Ryan shifted seats and joined her beneath the coat, where he brought it up to her chin. He laid his arm across the back of the seat. They sat in silence.

"We can have a truce longer if you choose," he said.

She pulled back, unconvinced of the possibility. Her head pressed into the crook of his arm. "W-what are your terms?" Her teeth chattered.

"Quit purchasing stock." He tempered his concession with a subtle move of his body, encompassing more of her against him. "Both companies have too much at stake to drain re-sources in a public confrontation neither of us wants. We wait until Johnny returns."

She didn't want a public confrontation either. They had enough that was private between them to occupy her time. "What if I can get Johnny to take the company?"

"He won't do it. He likes the creative end of the business too much to give up his independence."

"But what if he does?"

"I'll wager the company he won't."

His confidence miffed her. "Why is Johnny in Scotland?" she asked after a moment.

"Why do you think? He's inspecting sites."

She rested her head against his shoulder. "So this has nothing to do with the fact that your entire family seems to be in collusion to throw us together?"

He gently nudged her face. "Did you get that feeling as well?"

"Will you allow me access to the company records, Ryan?"

"Do I have a choice?"

"No." Locked to a sense of contentedness by his camaraderie, she burrowed against him. "Why is it you're always so warm?"

"I'm a male. One of those nonhelpless creatures."

"Truly, Ryan"—she smiled against his shoulder—"you are conceited."

"I thought I was an ogre."

She closed her eyes sleepily. "Did you keep the dog?"

"What do you think?"

"I think that you're a lot softer than you let on, Ryan."

His mouth a fraction from her hair, silence hung in the moist air between them like a living, breathing thing. Everything about him was hard beneath his clothes. She started to retract her palm from his chest when his fingers wrapped around her wrist. "How soft do you really think I am?"

Determined not to let him bully her, she left her hand on the cool metal clip of his suspenders. She should have known that Ryan was incapable of playing the gentleman for long. "You have the morals of a tomcat."

"So do you." His mouth brushed her lips, and she slid her

hand lower, touching him where she had no business explor-ing. "Were you really going to blackmail me?" His voice was husky.

"I'm perfectly capable of a fit of adolescence between us. I've proven that my entire life." Along with the nervous flut-ter in her voice, her parted lips joined her rebuttal. Or maybe her mouth never left his. "But when it comes to carnal expe-diency, *you're* the one capable of tyranny."

"You like power as much as I do. Besides"—he leaned around her and shut the crack in the curtain—"this isn't busi-ness. It's personal."

Pressed against the crook of his arm, she could not escape the masculine warmth that pinned her against the seat. Her gaze rose to meet his, nearly black in the shadows. "Why aren't you visiting Snow White this afternoon?" she con-fronted him, her voice a breathy rasp.

"You tell me. Since you're so interested in my affairs."

Her arms relaxed of their own accord, doing battle with that traitorous vein of lust and something worse. Jealousy. "*Is* it an affair?"

His heavy-lidded gaze no longer held amusement. "Mar-ried men have affairs all the time. But usually not with their own wives."

She didn't want to be his wife.

And Ryan didn't want to be her husband.

But he felt the touch of her lips against his. His blood pounded in his ears and pooled in the most sensitive region be-tween his legs. His senses erupted beneath the heat of her mouth. He opened her mouth and took her in a full, deep kiss. Luxurious and alluring, the fluid exploration of his tongue, drawing a groan from his chest. He deepened the kiss a little more and stoked the embers between them. Part of his mind realized she was letting him stir fires that he'd wished to re-main cold. His hand left the line of her jaw to move to her breast. Her fingers speared his hair, and everything became an intangible reality, a communion of mutual desires. Slowly, he drew away.

"Jaysus, Rachel . . ."

Their breaths hot and mingling, she regarded him, unable to hide her confusion. Neither one of them were in charge. He could feel a tug-of-war inside her. A vague flash of uncertainty that preceded retreat, yet the image was fleeting, as she pulled him back to her mouth for another kiss.

Her lips were warm and soft and moist, her breath steamy, his body a hard contrast to her softer curves. Her arms tightened around his neck, and he deepened the thrust of his tongue, sinking with her into a hot sleepy abyss of sensual bliss. With a groan, she surrendered her back to the cushion of the seat.

His kiss became relentless in its demand, the token armor of her jacket rendered inadequate as he unfastened the buttons. Her nipples grew taut. He could feel her heart thudding against his palm. His hand wandered over her breasts and her waist, paying deliberate detail to every curve and hollow as he followed the arch of her hip and pulled her upright into his lap. He was so sure in his actions. So sure in the knowledge of her body.

Sure that he shouldn't be doing this.

It should always be like this between them. "I'm insane to be here wanting to do this with you." His lips touched her brow, her throat, the fragrant lobe of her ear. Her mouth. "You taste like ale, Rachel Bailey." His rasp penetrated the haze surrounding them both.

"Very heady ale it was," she said.

Pulling away, he looked into her flushed face. She gave him a coy smile, daring him to comment. She wasn't going to apologize for drinking a glass of ale with her meal. She wasn't going to apologize for anything.

His gaze lowered to the pale mounds of her breasts spilling over her lacy corset.

He dipped his head to suckle and taste her. He made his mouth a brand against her flesh. He drew each nipple into his mouth, his tongue moving over the crest of each breast, and he listened to the sound of her throaty moans. Slipping his other hand beneath her sodden skirts, he took more. She moved against his fingers.

"Do you like my touch?" He breathed in her scent, traced the outline of her cleft with his finger, and felt her body respond. He wanted her to say the words.

"Yes." She lowered her body toward his probe. "It's . . . nice."

The thought refocused his mind. "Nice is another word for polite." His other hand worked his trousers to free his erection.

With a sigh, she moved against him. "I . . . don't want polite."

Her knees hugged his hips. His finger razed her, spreading her. With a helpless cry, she dropped her head back against her shoulders. He steadied her, moving one hand against her nape, waiting for her to regain a moment of equilibrium. He opened his palm around her bottom and shifted her upward, pulling her higher onto his lap. Then he shifted slightly, and with one sure movement penetrated her. She closed around him.

Ryan didn't have time to think. Even if he could have thought at all. She opened her mouth to cry out, and he caught her lips in a melding kiss. A part of his mind recognized that he must have planned it this way. That she'd never had a chance.

That if he were honorable, he'd never have allowed this to go so far. The rasp of their breathing filled the interior of the carriage.

Somewhere outside he heard raised voices.

The carriage stopped and rocked in traffic. Slowly opening her eyes, she saw his gaze on her face. Self-consciously, she looked down at herself wantonly displayed for his eyes, her pale thighs spread wide over his, her skirts hiked to her hips, hiding what was beneath. But not the sensation. Heat flushed her cheeks. Her mouth looked swollen and ravished. Her vulnerability clashed with the possessiveness he felt for her. He leaned around her and pulled the curtain aside, but by then the carriage had jolted forward, bringing her to full awareness.

"Ryan—"

He was seduced by that single whispered utterance. By her absolute possession of his body. He slid the tip of his finger against her lip. "Shhh."

She tasted herself in that touch.

She tried to catch her breath. He could not.

The ends of her hair fell over her shoulders as she leaned forward and caught her hands against his arms, their corded mass hard beneath her clenched grip. His breath shuddered over an incoherent oath. Then he was thrusting inside her, his hands solid on her bottom, flagrantly carnal as he slid her against his sensitized flesh.

He ravished her mouth. She let him plunder her body. Or was she plundering his? His hands tightened on her waist, his hold on her restricting her movement, controlling her pace. She resisted, her every muscle moving sensuously to the melody and rhythm of his pulse. His head fell back against the squabs. He opened his eyes.

Their gazes met and held. Hazel green to black. Past to present. No farther, as neither had a wish to go anywhere but where they currently were. Then she was pressing her lips against his, drawing him deeper inside her body.

With a sound that was her name, he splayed his fingers into her wet hair, dislodging the pins from what remained of her coif. Her silly hat dropped unnoticed to the floor. Her mouth took his voice, his breath. Desire throbbed and seared. She seized what he surrendered. His hand gripped her scalp, and he suckled her racing pulse, her breasts, supporting her with his arm, before he was crushing her against him. He tried to halt his flight, but it was too late, for she was taking him with her into the fire.

She consumed all of him. A novelty that left him gravely exploring his own tenderized flesh as he lost himself to her in a shuddering orgasm.

When he opened his eyes, Rachel lay slumped against him, her every inhalation imprinting itself against his chest. He didn't know how long he sat listening to the return of reality: the carriage jostling over the street, the *clip-clop* of horses—and her weepy voice whispering against his ear. "I didn't have my sponge."

For the first time in his life, Ryan witnessed her collapse into tears.

What the hell?

"There is no sense worrying, Rache. We'll know soon enough."

She drew back, her direct regard watery and accusing. "I'm sorry." But her tone blamed him for her current state. She swiped the back of her hand across both cheeks, the movement contracting her muscles around him still deep inside her. "I'm not used to this . . . this manner of dominance."

Which meant that he had the power to make her come. "That's understandable." He could almost laugh at his own profound lack of logic—if he wasn't gritting his teeth, and nearly drunk on the arousing effect she was still having on his body. "I must be crazy to want you like this," he muttered hoarsely.

"This shouldn't have happened twice. Never. Not in a hundred million years." She pressed her lips against his temple and sniffled. Her body's movement continued to send jolting shocks through him. "We don't even like each other. To make a baby . . ."

He leaned his cheek against the cushion of her hair. "I imagine we like each other a little."

"We just don't want to be married to the other—for sound reasons. We would drive each other to murder before a year was completed." She turned her mouth to the lobe of his ear. "Wouldn't we?"

"A child . . . would certainly complicate . . . matters."

He caught her hard against him, thinking through that senseless haze that surrounded his growing erection, that he might have been insulted by the tragedy of Rachel's teary declaration had he not already realized the implication to himself. They were adults. Such things were handled discreetly, though thank Providence, he'd never experienced the problem. But Rachel was different.

Indeed, theirs was an interesting, if not unstable, predicament, to say the least, and the paradox of his emotions when it came to his feelings for her suddenly reeled his thoughts into focus.

How in God's name could someone who was so wrong for him on almost every level of his life feel so bloody perfect on this one?

His fists, filled with the wet fabric of her skirts, settled on her round, smooth buttocks. "Jaysus . . ." He pressed his face into her damp shoulder, the evidence of his desire now hot and hard inside her. "Just . . . keep moving," he finally surrendered the words, closing his eyes, half-stunned by the warm mouth opening over his because her kiss cut him to his soul.

Chapter 15

The sound of voices outside the carriage opened Rachel's eyes. She was lying cradled in Ryan's arms, with the coat wrapped around them. Despite warmth emanating from him, she was shivering. "You fell asleep," he answered the question in her eyes.

In the shadows, she couldn't read his expression. Didn't know his thoughts. But she felt his arms loosen, and she sat up. Her entire muscular structure ached as she bent to peer outside. The carriage had pulled onto a brick drive.

"Where are we?" she asked without looking at him.

"At my London residence." He adjusted his coat around her shoulders, covering her dishabille. "The least I can do is mend the damages to you before we talk."

She pushed his hand away. "I can do this, Ryan."

He caught her wrist. "You're like ice, Rachel." Her hands trembled and, for a moment as she looked into his hooded eyes, they softened. "Let me help you."

"Where is Mary Elizabeth?" she asked.

"With my sister." He opened the door and climbed outside.

Rain continued to fall in a drizzle. Rachel leaned into the doorway and reluctantly peered up at his house. Ryan lifted her easily from the carriage. He hurried her through the rain and up the steps. The front door opened as if by unseen hands, and he swept her into the entryway. He ordered a bath, sending the household into a flurry of activity. Without breaking stride, he walked her up a long staircase into an equally long corridor.

She stumbled on her dampened skirts and felt his hand tighten on her arm. A magnificent pair of Rembrandts hung on the wall. He was watching her take in the elaborate ceiling friezes, the beautiful fresco, and huge Venetian glass chandelier hanging in the tall foyer. "It catches the eye," she felt obligated to say.

"Money can buy anything, Rachel."

Had he bought her? Her cooperation? Her silence?

She looked at his stern profile, caught by the realization that everything surrounding him had its purpose. No doubt if something didn't meet his standards or expectations, it would find no place in his life.

Shivering from whatever it was that pervaded her bones, Rachel listened as he spoke to his valet and ordered tea. He left her alone in his private chambers. His bedroom was no less impressive than everything else she saw in his house. Royal blue velvet draperies adorned the long windows, and a matching canopy dressed the massive bed. No one seemed to question her presence.

"Let's get ye out of these wet things, mum."

She let a young maid undo the row of jet-black buttons on her jacket that Ryan had meticulously restored in the carriage. He'd repaired her garments and his, as if he had sexual congress with women in his carriage all the time—as if he hadn't taken her world and turned it wrong side out, upside down.

She could hear his voice coming from the connecting room as she slid out of her soaked clothes and stockings. Her corset and drawers followed, but for lack of anything else to wear, she kept her chemise. "We'll dry these at once, mum." The girl bobbed a curtsy. "They'll be good as new in no time."

Wrapping her arms around her torso, Rachel waited beside the window, shivering as the bathtub was filled. She'd wanted to rally together reasons for disliking Ryan, but the substance behind her emotions had dissolved. Still, anger was preferable to the confusion she felt. How could she have allowed this to happen at all?

A girl's shriek sounded from the next room, followed by a crash.

Rachel ran toward the connecting door. Quiet weeping drew her into the other room. Ryan sat on his haunches, a shattered teapot lying at his feet.

"Stop!" He held out his hand like a bobby halting traffic in the Piccadilly.

In dismay, Rachel looked down at her bare feet. She was standing among shards of porcelain and spilled cream.

"I didn't see ye there, sir—"

"It is all right," he was telling the distraught girl. "Just clean this up. Have Mildred bring another pot."

Ryan shifted his dark eyes back to her and paused. Beginning somewhere around her toes, his gaze ascended, taking its time, she thought, as he came to his feet. He was no longer wearing his jacket or waistcoat. She felt as naked and hot as she had when she'd sat astride him in the carriage, and the rest of the world receded in his eyes.

"Don't move," Ryan ordered her in a voice that brooked no disobedience.

Ordered as if he sensed her will to flee him.

He approached. "You're a lot of trouble, Rachel," he said, and lifted her.

With a gasp, she caught her arms around his neck. His heavy shoes crushed the glass like so many eggshells.

"Put me down." She wriggled, but his corded arms were like a vise around her. "Everyone will see."

"Everyone has already seen everything."

"What is that supposed to mean?"

"Stand in front of the mirror. Then answer your own question." He sat her abruptly on a chair. He walked to a cabinet. She listened as he poured something into a glass.

A moment later, he returned with whiskey. "Drink this. It will help with the chill, until I can get you more tea."

She looked into the bottom of the glass.

"Just drink it, Rachel."

She did as he asked, gasped, and choked on whiskey that was potent even for her. He took the glass from her hand and set it on the bedside table. She thought she glimpsed amusement in his eyes. "Did you step on any glass?" he asked.

She'd started to say no, until Ryan knelt before her, and she decided she liked having him on his knees in front of her. "I'm not sure."

He wrapped his hands around one ankle and turned her foot toward him. "Where?" His thumbs caressed the arch.

Her fingers tightened their grip on the chair. "Nearer to the heel, maybe."

Absorbing the sensuous glide of his fingers, she wriggled her toes to maintain stamina, but she was slowly sinking back into the chair. "Higher . . . lower."

"Here?" he asked, none too gently.

She closed her eyes. His flesh on her flesh mixed with whiskey for a potent rush of heat through her veins. "And the toes."

He raised his gaze. Rachel released her death grip on the chair.

"Why don't you hop around on both feet to make sure?" His smile was flat, and she realized he was annoyed with her.

"Though I wouldn't want you to impale yourself on shards of porcelain."

She wanted to impale herself on something else entirely, and it must have shown in her eyes, for his gaze grew dangerous. She felt desperately hungry and thirsty. Hot and cold. His very presence consumed her and panicked her. "Heaven forbid that I should ever know how to flirt," she said offhandedly, mortified by her behavior.

"Heaven help any man should you learn to flirt." He came to his feet. "I like you better honest."

She rose. They stood less than a foot apart, so close she could smell the heat from his body. "I've sent someone to bring back Elsie," he said, his voice taking on a discordant note. "She'll be here shortly to help you dress and get you safely from here." He slipped a finger beneath her chin. "I have work to do tonight. Lots of work, just so you can have unimpeded access to all the D&B records your heart desires. I'll have a team of bookkeepers and accountants make copies of everything tomorrow. Will that be enough for now?"

The concession left her momentarily speechless.

"What else do you want, Rache?"

She wanted to understand him.

"I want an honest conversation with you for once."

Swearing softly, he leaned against the bedpost. "Maybe that's what we've been having all along, and neither of us has figured that out yet."

Rachel didn't know what he meant by that, but she did understand the rift between them went deep. "Do you have a heart and soul, Ryan? Something . . . or someone that you would fight for to the exclusion of all else?"

"My daughter." He stared at the ceiling, drew in a breath, and met her gaze. "Do you understand the importance of that?"

She could not bear the pressure of his gaze. He intended to honor the contracts he'd signed with Devonshire. He'd never lied to her about that. Suddenly, the last thing she wanted was for him to see that today had softened her any more than it had him.

"I understand."

"I'm glad you do. Because I sure as hell don't. A temporary business truce doesn't nearly encompass the issues surrounding us."

"No, it doesn't. And if I were a man, we would not have even made that truce."

"If you were a man . . . I would not have taken you from the Rathdrum project. Hell, if you were a man, I'd let someone shoot me for what we just did in the carriage." He shook his head. "I've put the reputation of this company at risk all because I've allowed my head to get muddled with lust and friendship and a hundred other things I can't interpret. Or maybe I can, and I'm only just now beginning to understand them myself."

She'd been so accustomed to looking after herself for so long, of having to remain strong for other people, that she felt caught by his tenderness. Restrained by his kindness. Clearly, he knew how to home in on her vulnerability. By asking her to agree to any truce, he could not be asking her to aid and abet her demise more, or that of Donally & Bailey, she thought, thinking of all her workers and her agreement with Lord Bathwick.

"My fight isn't over a desire to chair the board," she said. "Even if the public could accept a chairman with bosoms, I have no experience—"

Ryan suddenly laughed. "You never cease to astound me."

"You can hardly deny that what is beneath my clothes is more important to everyone than what is between my ears."

Resting an elbow on his forearm, he scraped a palm over his jaw, finally fixing his gaze on hers. To her disbelief, his eyes were laughing. After a moment, realizing the humor in her comment, she laughed, too.

Ryan sensed the tension leaving her body.

"I've seen your work, Rachel. You have nothing of which to be ashamed."

And looking at her, Ryan recognized all that she'd overcome to get to her place. He understood her passion and her loyalty toward the people who worked for her. He understood it more than she knew.

Then as carefully as if she was made of spun glass, he touched her cheek. "For the record, I like what is between your ears equally as much as I like what is beneath your clothes." His thumb touched her mouth. "I'm *especially* fond of what is between your ears."

To her obvious horror, his teasing statement made her smile if only briefly. "That still doesn't make us on the same side," she pointed out.

Her statement was fact. He might be supportive, but he was not remotely close to seeing the future her way. Yet, for the few seconds they stood facing each other, the walls crumbling between them, he truly wondered what a future with her would hold.

Then he was no longer wondering.

His gaze found the fullness of her mouth, the mask of her displeasure no longer evident, her unbound hair a cascade of inviting warmth, and he knew a certain disturbing reluctance that she held the power to captivate him continuously in every way. A striking realization from a man who felt only a jarring foreboding at the direction of his thoughts.

He made no move to touch her and dropped his hand. He looked out the window, a perplexed thinness to his lips as he focused on the pewter skies that seemed to become the storm brewing inside him.

"Today wasn't supposed to have happened," she whispered.

"You're right." He turned, forcing her chin up. One step more, and he violated the invisible barrier separating them.

"Today shouldn't have happened. But it did. And therein lies the crux of the problem."

The backs of her knees caught the chair, and she sat abruptly. "There is no crux." Her voice was husky as he braced his palms on the armrests and leaned over her. "I won't fight a dissolution to this marriage." Her head pressed against the chair back. "You can have your solicitor draw up the necessary papers."

"Don't we need to think about this, Rachel?" he asked.

Her eyes liquid bright in the dim light held his. "A real marriage between us would be a disaster," her voice whispered.

"I'm asking you to consider a future with me."

She was so stunned by the implication beyond his declaration that all she could do was stare.

"We can both agree to disagree about the future of Donally & Bailey," he said. "We can also agree that if I stay married to you, my life will be altered immeasurably," he managed, with a barely exhaled abortive laugh as he sank to one knee in front of her. He was already considering what it would take to break the contracts he'd signed with Devonshire. "But we have to agree to agree that there is something between us worth exploring. Something that has always been there."

"We can't just divorce ourselves from who we are."

"Maybe we shouldn't try."

She turned her face away, or tried to, but he caught her chin, and wondered at her fear. No whisper of cooling air offered solace or refuge from emotions that hand-tied him to a disadvantage—that pumped through his body and filled his veins with fire and made him territorial, as if his possessiveness gave him some prerogative to his temper.

"Tell me you don't bloody feel something, Rache."

She held her palms against him. "Please, move away."

"Or you'll punch me?" He stood and looked down into her face. "Maybe you'd rather kiss me instead. If I weren't in the mood to play the gentleman, I'd show you just what it is you really want to do with me. Or maybe you'll just miss me if I walk away."

"I hate it when you turn into a tyrant, Ryan. I really do."

"You just hate it when I'm right."

"I can't, Ryan."

Looking into her eyes, he knew her feelings had to be inseparable from his. Yet, she wasn't going to allow herself to trust him. Perhaps she understood him better than he did himself, he acknowledged.

Even if what they shared on the erotic level was nothing short of staggering—one didn't base an entire future on the quality of a climax. Either he was acting impulsively, which he seemed to want to do around her, or deliberately, which was a known character trait—one that had made him hated by many. He no longer knew.

This fight was as much about them as it was about D&B. Hell, he'd give her the damn company if he thought it wouldn't be a foolish act blindly awash in noble sacrifice, but he knew their differences went deep down to the core of who they were.

Where he'd never found satisfaction to remain in one place, she'd never veered from her roots, never pretended to be anything but what she was. Never asked for more than she could deliver. Rachel didn't fit among the gilded, teardrop chandeliers and Heppelwhite armchairs he collected. She didn't attend soirées or wear beaded gowns and diamond tiaras. Lady Gwyneth fit into his vision of the future. Not she.

So why was he willing to throw away so bloody much for a woman who had been historically disposed, nay eager, to foist him off on other women her entire life.

The thought stumped him. He turned in the doorway of his bedroom and met the startled hazel of her gaze, half-veiled by a thick fringe of black lashes. She stood beside his bed. He let his gaze slide over her. The pale lamp glow at her back picked the warm hues from her red-gold hair. A pink flush had stolen over her cheeks. She was a conflicting blend of virtue and sin, her self-assurance a sham, her allure far deeper than physical beauty.

He was in love with her.

More deeply in love than he'd ever thought capable.

Men had laid sieges to cities and fought epic battles for that kind of love. He was no less motivated, but far more practical.

He wanted only to lay siege to what was in her heart.

For he saw in that raw glimpse, before she closed her eyes and looked away, that she loved him, too.

Ryan stood in the doorway overlooking the gardens surrounding the London Royal Yacht Club. The atmosphere was sizzling. Cassavas catered to an international clientele, a European consortium that included sheiks, princes, and an occasional American or British tycoon who had made his fortune on speculation—where old money continued to ignore the nouveaux rich. But if a man could pay the price, he could pass through the gilded doors reserved for the elite, dine on caviar, and wallow in his own self-importance.

Many looked up from their meals as Ryan passed. Dressed in black swallowtail coat and trousers as was befitting the formal dress required, he turned briefly to thank the attendant who had directed him to the gazebo, where he could see the shadow of a man inside. With his long legs outstretched in front of him, Lord Bathwick was holding an expensive Bordeaux in one hand and a cheroot in the other. The scent of tobacco drifted on the faint breeze and mingled with the river smell, which wasn't pleasant in the summer heat. A flash of lightning disturbed the distant sky.

"I'll announce myself," Ryan said.

Bathwick turned his head at Ryan's approach, his eyes widening in wary surprise before he adeptly screened his surprise behind a bland gaze. "Donally." He didn't move from his comfortable pose.

"Where is your father?"

"I am not his keeper, Donally." Bathwick sipped from his glass before setting it on the table. "But have you tried at his London home? He is known to be there on occasion."

Ryan felt the corners of his mouth tilt. He didn't bother taking a seat. He didn't plan to be there long. Bathwick had been a bone in his craw for years, even before Ryan acquired Ore Industries. They ran in many of the same social circles. There had never been any affection lost between them. Six months ago, Bathwick had been responsible for spreading rumors that sent D&B shares plunging, with a substantial loss that D&B did not have to sustain. In the process, Bathwick had gained a foothold into the door of his company, one that Ryan did not intend to allow him to keep.

He withdrew a bank draft and slid it beneath the small lamp sitting in the center of the table. "Twenty-two thousand pounds," he said. "More than your shares are worth. Go purchase yourself a nice country estate and retire away from the influence of your father."

The false smile faded from Bathwick's eyes. Whatever he'd been expecting from Ryan, receiving a bank draft clearly wasn't one. "Those are arrogant words for someone who doesn't know what I want."

"I know that revenge tastes sweet no matter which slice of the pie you eat. But I won't let you use Rachel to get to me."

Bathwick scraped his thumbs over the corners of the check. The breeze had picked up with the approach of the storm, and banners that rimmed the terrace flapped on their standards. "Did *Rachel*"—Bathwick emphasized Ryan's inadvertent use of her name—"send you over here to dispense with me?"

Ryan leaned both palms on the table. "She didn't have to. Your name came up on a list handed over to me today. Miss

Bailey is not part of the problem between your family and mine. Don't put her between something she doesn't understand."

"Or maybe you only want to halt her quest to take control of your company. She has the power to do that."

"Don't believe it, Bathwick."

"Then why haven't you stopped her? Maybe you don't believe she has the stomach for a fight. Or are you concerned she may actually grow to like me?" Amused Bathwick sat back in his chair. "Would that be a problem, Donally?"

The breeze had picked up with the approach of another storm and banners that rimmed the terrace flapped on their standards. He wasn't there as a businessman but as a husband. Bathwick didn't know that. "Take that draft to my personal banker at the Bank of London with the proper papers signing over your shares of D&B, and he will give you the funds. You'll surrender your interest in all of my holdings. If you are intelligent, you will persuade your father to do the same."

Bathwick peered at Ryan more directly. "I'm assuming this is the first salvo at something bigger aimed against my father. Something more direct. And not related to business."

"Good night, my lord." Ryan turned to leave.

"I hope you have a bigger arsenal than this." Bathwick called after him.

One foot still on the stairs, Ryan turned. A wind gust whipped the bushes, then faded. Lord Bathwick descended the stairs. "War with Father is an ugly thing."

He bid Ryan good evening, his coat flapping in the wind, and no amount of acquired social polish could hide the look behind Ryan's lengthening silence as he watched his lordship stroll away. Though Ryan had made his living in the corporate trenches and had not gained his reputation for nothing, when it came to the truth of the matter, he would pay whatever price it took to free himself of Devonshire.

* * *

"Purchase the hat, Miss Bailey."

Rachel stood on the busy Bond Street walkway so engrossed in her perusal of the beautiful items in the window that she'd failed to note Lord Bathwick's approach. Her startled gaze snapped to his eyes reflected in the glass before she turned to face him.

"You've been staring at it for half an hour."

"I said I would meet you at St. Anthony's tomorrow."

"I'm not Catholic." He shrugged. "One would only think our meeting clandestine."

"Of course, a meeting on a busy street is a much better place to conduct business."

Rocking back on his heels, he tipped his hat at two women as they bustled past. "What better place to make a clandestine meeting less obvious?" he asked with humor. "It is only my good fortune that I saw you leaving Hyde Park, left my cab, and followed." Turning to give his full attention to the object in the window, he said, "In my humble opinion, you should purchase the hat, Miss Bailey. You obviously want it."

Feeling a blush heat her cheeks, Rachel turned, embarrassed that he should always be catching her doing something that appeared desperate. They both surveyed the item in question. Unlike the bonnet she'd eyed at the fair, this one was a wide-brimmed French affair with red ribbons and a festoon of cheerful feathers. Nothing that represented practical. Maybe just once, she wanted pretty.

It had been over a week since Ryan had made love to her in the carriage. Eight days since she'd seen him. Eight measly days, and she'd vanquished her principles to the romantic mirage hovering over her. She had begun to miss him.

For too many years, she had followed his life through the scandal sheets, making these past weeks surreal. Like the way she felt about the frilly, feminine hat she gawked at today and in the booth at the fair, knowing that purchasing either one would be the same as admitting her life was a failure, that what she'd worked so hard to achieve was not what she really wanted. She didn't know why the hat was the unseemly metaphor, but it was.

She was afraid of wanting more. Afraid of sacrificing her soul for her heart.

She was afraid of Lord Devonshire.

"That is a lot of thought going into a hat, Miss Bailey. Perhaps, being the practical sort, you are asking yourself where you would wear something so extravagant."

"I'm not without a social agenda," she lied, not pleased with his observation, even though she'd said the same thing to Ryan at the fairgrounds. With the exception of Brianna's company and her morning whist games, Rachel had no social life in London.

"Let me guess. For lack of anything else to do yesterday, you joined Lady Ravenspur's whist club. You played with dowagers, spinsters, and other progressive thinkers. Today you've spent shopping though you've only purchased"—he lifted the lid of a red-painted box that she carried—"a doll."

Rachel pulled the box against her chest. "She's a gift."

"For Lord Ravenspur's two sons, no doubt."

"No doubt," she said behind a smile, eyeing him more thoroughly since his approach. He wore a dark blue frock coat, white morning waistcoat, and black trousers, looking quite dapper, as if he always appeared ready for public consumption. "How do you know what I've been doing?"

"I saw Ravenspur, yesterday. It was his wife's whist day." Looking at the box, he added, "The rest was an educated guess." He held out his arm. "The day is young, so count me your social agenda for the rest of the afternoon. We can do whatever you wish."

She looked up at the blue sky, felt the summer breeze on her face, and smiled. "I wouldn't mind finding something of an exhausting physical nature to do," she said, thinking she would enjoy a bout of horseback riding. Anything to help her sleep at night.

Bathwick threw back his head and laughed. When his blue eyes again met hers, they had warmed considerably from that last time she'd seen him at his Mayfair home, and they'd struck their bargain. She liked him. She liked that he had callused hands and an easy smile that she suspected was not as easy as he pretended, that despite his debonair, aristocratic front, he seemed to be as much an outcast as she was.

"You are not the stick in the mud as you enjoy letting on, Miss Bailey." Lord Bathwick observed her pleasantly through an eyepiece. "Your problem is that you are a woman in a man's world. A place where you can never compete—except as a woman. You would be amazed how cooperative a man can be in the right frame of mind."

"Are you, in your polite way, trying to tell me that I should take advantage of my charms—in a way that men will overlook my . . . ?"

"Brains?"

"Faults."

They continued to walk. "Have you considered that men are a perverse breed intent on their own pleasures? A woman who is smarter than they are is no pleasure."

"A man who is not as smart as I am needs to attend better to his studies." She smiled. "I care little for his pleasure."

"I've offended you," he said.

"Not at all." Only because he spoke the truth. Men looked at a woman from the chin down. She'd learned out of necessity not to be the wrong kind of target, which certainly made the array of feminine feelings Ryan had awakened in her unfamiliar. Ryan, whom she hadn't spoken to in days but dreamed about at nights, who made her feel as if she were seventeen again and alive.

"We have veered from the topic at hand," he said. "You wanted to see me at St. Anthony's for a reason, I presume."

"I hope I was not inconvenient in asking to see you." She did her best to remain calm. But under the circumstances, Lord Bathwick had to understand her position. "Some things have changed since our last meeting. Until John Donally returns and we can sit down and talk, Mr. Donally and I have agreed upon a truce."

The humor left his face. "Of course he'd ask you to do that."

"It isn't like that. This is a business—"

"As is ours." The walkway grew crowded, and he lowered his voice. "As such, we have agreed upon a course of action. One, by the way, of which Donally is already aware."

Her gaze widened on his, and she saw that he'd been waiting for that reaction. "Just a thought for you to consider," he offered with no solace. "This is what Donally and I do, Miss Bailey. If you have personal feelings that will interfere with the agreement we made, allow me to finish buying up D&B stock for you."

Their eyes remained locked. "Have you considered that we need John Donally?"

"If he won't head the company, as the former heir to Ore Industries I am more than familiar with the business. Unlike my aristocratic brethren, I am not averse to managing my own source of revenue."

The doll grew heavier in her arms.

Under the circumstances, she could not allow him to invest more than he already had, when a partnership with her now meant nothing in the wake of Ryan's legal claim on her. "You may withdraw from our agreement, my lord," she said, knowing she had to wait for Johnny. "I will understand."

Lord Bathwick murmured something and looked away but not before she glimpsed a frown beneath his usual urbane expression. "Your stubbornness will be my undoing."

Some of the tension evaporated. "How did Ryan find out about our partnership?"

He leaned both hands on the silver head of his walking stick and considered her. "Donally and I have a history. Even if he did not see the list of major stockholders in the company, he knew you couldn't make a bid for the company alone. He came to see me at Cassavas a few days ago and tried to buy me out."

"He wouldn't dare!"

"Ah, but he did. So, you see? If this entire issue didn't intrigue me so much, I might find it more profitable to opt out. You'll learn your error soon enough."

Ryan knew about her partnership with Bathwick and he had not come to see her.

Realizing that Bathwick had just said something profound, her mind suddenly stopped and lingered worriedly on the scenario of his words. "What does that mean?"

"Have you ever wondered how Donally found out about your Rathdrum project?"

Rachel swallowed her uneasiness. She'd assumed that Johnny had told him.

"It's Ore Industries' policy when confronting a hostile target to do an investigation on that target. By every account, my father considered you hostile *before* Donally went to Ireland. Why, Miss Bailey? Not that it matters to me." Lord Bathwick brushed aside his concern with an airy wave of his gloved hand. "But it might to Donally.

"You see, he is the only man who has ever beaten my father. Soundly. In the public arena. My father hates him, but he needs him—rather like a leech needs blood to survive, and has proven himself capable of using any means at his disposal to keep people in check."

Lord Bathwick bent over her hand. "Welcome to my world, Miss Bailey."

Chapter 16

The hansom pulled up to the curb of Ore Industries an hour after Rachel left Lord Bathwick. She dug into her reticule to pay the driver, frustrated because, for all of her composure, her hands shook. Grabbing hold of her hat in the gust, she let her gaze travel up the side of one of the tallest buildings in London. The door attendant and lift operator were present, which meant someone was still in the building at this late-afternoon hour.

Rachel had never been to the Ore Industries building.

No secretary greeted her entry on the eighth floor. The closed blinds covering the paladin windows impeded the light, but as she stood alone in the anteroom, Rachel heard the low rumble of voices from one of the offices and knew Ryan was there. A door was ajar. Recognizing his voice, she felt a keen awareness of him, and relief, unsettling in its novelty.

His presence carried security.

Standing in the anteroom, she could see three men sitting around his desk. If she moved to the left, she could see Ryan. He was leaning back in his chair, one ankle drawn casually

over his knee, his fingers threaded behind his head. He wore
no jacket, and his white sleeves were turned up to his elbows
as if he had been at the drafting board.

Remaining in the shadows, Rachel found a chair that allowed her an unimpeded view of Ryan. Because of the unusual summer heat that week, she had removed her jacket
before she'd left D&B. She wore a shirtwaist over a white
blouse and brown skirt, but even with less clothing, her skin
was damp beneath her corset.

Ryan's voice pulled her gaze. He was speaking about the
currently stalled negotiations ongoing in France. Valmonts
was once a prestigious engineering firm, with roots into the
past that went deeper than D&B's. She had never taken part
in meetings on this level, and despite her discomfiture with
their ongoing topic, she observed him with professional interest. In his office, high above London, fitting his station,
Ryan existed for the negotiation.

Pale daylight streamed into the room, complimenting the
white of his teeth as he grinned at something someone said
that made the group laugh. Then he leaned forward—his
shoulders contained by the pristine cloth of his shirt and
folded his hands on his desk. As she watched him speak, it hit
her with the flutter of her heart that this man was really her
husband.

Hers.

People listened to him. She listened. He discussed contracts
and projects on the same level that he entertained notable fig-
ureheads. She knew how he could lead an international corporation. Why the financials followed him.

There, in his element, he ruled from the clouds as she lived
with her feet firmly planted on the earth, among the greenery
and mists of Ireland.

Remembering Lord Devonshire's threat about scandal
toppling kingdoms, Rachel feared her presence in his life

would hurt Ryan. She had no idea the extent of Devonshire's knowledge of her personal history. How much of her past did he really know? It no longer mattered. She had come there today to tell Ryan the truth.

With a mental groan, Rachel leaned her elbow on the chair rest. Ryan must have seen the movement, for he turned his head and saw her.

She froze.

"If you will excuse me for a moment," she heard him say as he stood.

Rachel came to her feet when he entered the anteroom. Nothing in Ryan's gaze told her anything, except that he was surprised to see her. Indeed, he'd made an offer to her and managed to vanish from her sight completely for an entire week.

She apologized for interrupting him. "May I speak with you?"

"This isn't a good time," he said, his stance businesslike, but there was a glimmer in his eyes that warmed her everywhere as he took her elbow and pulled her farther into the shadows. "As you can see, I'm in a meeting."

"Mr. Stewart didn't tell me that this meeting was on your itinerary," she said, aware that what he did here did not belong in the realm of her jurisdiction with D&B.

"You only talked to *one* of my secretaries. I have three. Welcome to Ore Industries."

Feeling caged by the lack of light, she shifted her mind abruptly to look around the room. For a moment, neither spoke. She stood beside him, an inch from her past, seeking some place other than his face to rest her gaze. "I had heard that you paid a visit to Lord Bathwick . . ." Her voice faded as it occurred to her that this wasn't exactly the topic with which she wanted to begin.

At least that was one secret she didn't have to keep from Ryan.

"He didn't wait long before coming to you," Ryan said, his unconcern and total lack of alarm making her frown. "How close do you think you two are?

"We're business partners." She tightened her arms over her torso and peered up at him curiously. "He's in love with Lady Gwyneth."

"Quaint."

"I think he wants to fight you for both her and the company."

"I don't need to fight anyone for Gwyneth." Dark lashes framed the sharp edge of ice in his eyes. "And I will never let him take anything that belongs to me. I suggest you stay away from him, Rachel."

"You and I agreed not to purchase stock. I'm perfectly within my rights to wage battle on the rest of the business front as I see fit. Especially since I know you would do the same thing I'm doing in my place."

Ryan noted the warning in her eyes. "All is fair in love and war, is that your creed?" he challenged as if he considered her outburst amusing, if not fraught with gullibility.

Then she realized that her alliance with Bathwick did not threaten him, that he merely deemed it an inconvenience. "Clearly, Lord Bathwick is no different than you are in matters of business. You are both bloodthirsty. I feel as if I should be wearing a necklace of garlic."

"Is this what you came here to discuss?"

Noting that the men in the office had grown quiet, she looked around Ryan's shoulder. Without turning, he seemed to note the same thing. "I have to get back."

She grabbed his sleeve. "I just have one question," she said, when his eyes came back around to hers, and she suddenly floundered in her purpose.

She lowered her voice. "Why haven't you tried to see me?"

"I believe you made it clear where I stood in your life." One side of his mouth suddenly slid into a grin. "I thought I would leave you to contemplate your future with me. Do you miss me yet?"

She narrowed her eyes. "I see," she said, recognizing his conceit for what it was, "you thought by ignoring me, I'd want to see you?"

The fact that she was standing in his office answered her question for him.

His eyes touched her lips, and it occurred to her there was nothing indifferent or businesslike about him when it came to her presence. "To use your cliché, 'all is fair in love and war.' You want to make war. I am only interested in making love."

Unwillingly flustered by his outrageous reply, she opened her mouth, torn between shock and ire. "You're an ass, Ryan."

"Thank you, Rache." Bent slightly, he touched his lips to her hair. "My opinion of your charm is only superseded by that of your hat. Then again," he drawled, "everything south of that hat and north of your charm, reminds me of why I'm in love with you, too."

Rachel stared in disbelief. Did he even realize what he'd just said?

The noise in the office behind him grew louder as it sounded like the meeting he'd left had adjourned itself without him. "Mr. Donally?" A man from the office stood at the door. "We're nearly finished in here. Do you wish us to conclude without you?"

His hands still in his pockets, he turned. "I'll be there in a moment."

Covering her cheeks with her cooler hands, Rachel hastily sought to regain her composure. She was aware that she was in his way.

A strange tender light came into his eyes as he caught her staring at him. "Is there a particular reason you came by today, Rachel?"

Her gaze touched the doorway to his office, and she shook her head. She could not tell him about Devonshire here. "It can wait."

"I have a business engagement to attend tonight," he said, then proceeded to tell her he was busy for the rest of the week, which Rachel highly doubted under the circumstances of his earlier admission. She refused to allow him to manipulate her into missing him. Nor did she believe that he was in love with her, deciding his statement had surely been a figure of speech.

"Will you be going to Paris?" she asked, wondering about his other acquisition.

"If I did, would you come with me?"

Rachel looked into his eyes, started to tell him absolutely not, when he took her chin into the warm palm of his hand and bent over her mouth. "We could make love all night in satin sheets." His breath fluttered over her lips. "You can dine off silver and gold, bathe in chocolate. We could sin to our hearts' content."

She blushed hotly, and he laughed. Then his mouth lowered, and he was kissing her.

A hot openmouthed hungry kiss that pinned her feet to the floor. He tasted like rich coffee, and she went from uncertain to willing in the time it took for her to breathe.

No one kissed like Ryan. Not in her entire life had any man touched every one of her five senses as he could with only his mouth. He could make her hot and buttery—but instead of sinking against him in abject surrender, Rachel wedged her palms between them. His heart pounded in his chest. Dragging in a breath, she broke away.

"You haven't yet earned the right to ask me to go with you anywhere. I don't officially consider myself your wife."

"You are to me." His smile turned wolfish, a contrast to his temper when it came to managing everything about her.

"Maybe I'll unofficially give you a child, and in nine months you'll unofficially be a mother."

He eased his fingers around her jaw and traced the contour of her cheeks. Then recognizing her silence for the shock that it was, he lowered his hand. "If you change your mind about missing me, let me know, and I can do something about it."

Breathing hard, Rachel watched him walk back to the office, his gait fluid, an attractive figure in black, and knew exactly why he was so successful at high-level negotiations. "You don't play fair, Ryan," she whispered.

"I never did," he said over his shoulder. "You should know that about me by now."

Weary of dealing with accountants, bookkeepers, and her own heart, Rachel welcomed Johnny's telegram two days later asking for files on the Forth project in Scotland. At least his request gave her something to do in a company that ran with the efficiency of a Swiss clock and didn't seem to need her at all.

Ryan kept himself busy. So could she.

But her resistance to him was a hollow victory, she considered, as she closed the ledger on her desk. Behind her, the sun was beginning to set.

Stewart entered her office. He still wore an overcoat in the summer heat and carried his hat, prepared to leave for the day. "Are you sure you will be all right alone, mum?"

He liked to hover, and she tried to soften her censure. He meant well. "You're not obligated to arrive early every day and stay late because I am here."

Color crept up from his collar. "Perhaps not. But most of us realize what you are trying to do for the company, Miss Bailey."

His words touched her. For she was not sure of anything anymore.

"Not that I would disparage Mr. Donally. He has treated us—"

"You don't need to defend what you feel to me, Mr. Stewart."

Rachel didn't know what else to say. She understood the sentiment. She also knew that if Ryan dismantled D&B, she would never be sure that he would not do the same to her someday if he decided that she'd served her purpose in his life.

Not that she could serve any purpose in his life.

Truly, she could not be more conflicted. "Go home, Mr. Stewart." She smiled. "I will see the doors locked when I leave."

"I have not yet found all of the records for the Scotland sites that Mr. Donally requested," he said. "They're gone. Someone else has been in the vault."

The one thing she had learned about D&B's longtime senior secretary was that he was territorial about his space. "Couldn't the files just be misfiled? The storage cabinets were moved when the basement was painted in June. Perhaps something got out of order in your system."

He looked doubtful. "Maybe there is a chance—"

"You do not have to search now." Rachel sensed he was about to spend the rest of the weekend looking for lost files. "Tend to it Monday, Mr. Stewart."

"Mr. Donally requested my services on Monday. His secretary is out of the office—"

"Did he consider that you are needed here?"

"The arrangement is only for a few hours during the day until his return from Paris."

Ryan was going to Paris?

"Evidently, something has gone wrong with a business deal he is conducting, and he will be traveling there to close negotiations." Stewart replied to her expression. "I presume that is why he stayed in town rather than retire to the country as he always does on the weekend. He is leaving tonight."

"I see." Rachel folded her hands on the desk.

She wondered where Lady Gwyneth was, then remembered Brianna had told her yesterday at breakfast that her ladyship was visiting friends in Brighton.

When she looked up from her desk, Stewart had gone.

With the office silent about her, the clock on the shelf ticked away the minutes. The room was hot. Restless, Rachel walked the empty corridor to the back stairwell that led into the basement. She shoved open the door, welcoming the cooler air.

The walls were built from an old medieval rock structure and served as a firebreak between the irreplaceable records and the main building. She felt a draft at her feet and knew a ventilation system circulated the air to help keep mildew at bay. Ryan had designed this portion of D&B after a fire destroyed their Southwark office five years ago. Each floor accessed the stairwell through steel doors. The stones were cold beneath her palm. She lit a sconce at the first-floor landing, surprised to see the vault door ajar.

Once in the basement, she lit a second lamp and held it up against the shadows. The room smelled faintly of turpentine. Once every two years the basement had to be resealed and painted. Wooden file cabinets filled the length of the room. Every document, receipt, and bill of lading D&B ever created or received was here. She disliked the dark, enclosed space. It felt like a crypt, but she soon found the room less distracting as she worked her way through the first row of file cabinets, skimming the labels, looking for anything related to the projects in Scotland, curious as to why they would be missing. Certainly, project records were of no use to anyone but D&B.

The vault door clicked shut.

Bent over a bottom cabinet, she lifted her head. It had only been a faint noise, a vibration in the air, but in the silence surrounding her, the sound was immediately recognizable. She couldn't see the other end of the room in the shadows.

"Is anyone there?"

Silence.

After a moment, she walked around a long row of cabinets. She reached for the door—hesitated—then set her hand on the knob. Locked.

She jiggled the knob. The key wasn't in place.

She didn't remember seeing a key.

Telling herself she wouldn't panic, she calmly returned a moment later with the lantern. She told herself again not to panic as she set the light down and searched on her hands and knees for a key that might have jostled loose from the lock. Damn Ryan and his fireproof contraptions. She attempted to shove a cabinet away from the wall.

How could the bloody door shut of its own accord?

Already feeling as if she couldn't breathe, she knew she was panicking. Rachel slapped her hand against the door, more worried about being trapped in the basement for the weekend than she was about the possibility of any intruder.

Only through enormous self-control did she finally slow her breathing so she wouldn't pass out. Her reticule was upstairs. The lamp in her office burned. The night watchman would notice that she hadn't left when he did his rounds, she thought—pulling her watch from inside her vest pocket and looking at the time—in four hours. When she didn't return home, Brianna and Lord Ravenspur would know—except they were attending an opera tonight. Ryan was leaving for Paris. Rachel held the lamp up to examine the oil, mentally counting the hours before it went dark.

Monday morning was a long way away.

Chapter 17

Rachel lifted her head from her knees. Her legs drawn to her chest, she'd been sitting in the darkness. The lantern had sputtered out hours ago. A door slammed in the stairwell. The sound of descending footsteps brought her groggily to her feet.

A key jiggled in the door. The lock clicked.

Then Ryan was suddenly standing in the doorway. Backlit from the light in the stairwell, he stepped into the room and, at once, everything that had been dank and frightening no longer felt that way. She swallowed a sob and flung herself into his arms.

"Should I even ask . . . ?" He left the question in the air.

"What kind of awful place did you build?" His collar muffled her voice. He smelled heady and spicy. His arms closed around her, and she remained against his chest. "I thought I was going to be here all night. What are you doing here?" she finally asked.

"The watchman found your reticule," he said against her

hair. "He heard your pounding but couldn't find the key. Stewart wasn't home. So, he found me."

Holding her, he was so matter-of-fact. So utterly calm in the face of her panic, that she felt foolish to have burst into tears. Collecting herself, she stepped away from him, half-expecting recriminations for her stupidity. He didn't berate her.

"The door tends to close of its own accord." He held up a large key. "Stewart stores this in his desk. You're supposed to keep the key with you when you're down here." He turned and palmed the ledge above the door. Rachel watched as he revealed another key—as if she could have found the bloody thing in the rafters. "For emergencies, but Stewart is supposed to sign people into this room."

"I didn't know this room needed a key." No one had told her about the protocol. "The door was ajar when I came down."

"It shouldn't have been," he said, an undercurrent beneath his composure she hadn't detected before. "Rachel?" His tone lifted her gaze. "What are you doing here?"

"I was trying to find the Forth project records. Johnny requested them."

"And you had nothing else to do tonight?" She heard the frown in his voice.

Rachel looked at his clothes and realized he'd probably been pulled away from dinner. He should not look so good, she thought resentfully, aware that he didn't seem to be suffering the same trepidation as she was over their personal life.

"It isn't often I get to rescue you, Rache." His grin hinted of self-mockery. "Your self-confidence robs me of my reason to exist in your life."

Rachel dragged in her breath to speak. Movement on the stairwell above her drew his gaze. "The downstairs rooms are clear, sir," the watchman said from the landing.

Ryan took her elbow and climbed with her up the stairs. She glanced at his profile. "Then there *was* an intruder?"

"You're never to be here alone again. Do you understand?"

"I found a window open," the watchman said, when they reached the top of the stairs. "At least the bloke didn't steal or destroy nothing."

"How long did it take you to find Miss Bailey, McKinney?"

"Ryan"—she caught his arm to her—"it isn't his fault."

"No?" Four other men wearing blue uniforms were standing in the anteroom. "It's his bloody job to watch you while you're here. It's his *only* job." His hand went to her waist. "Get your things, Rache. My carriage will take you back to Ravenspur's."

Rachel looked at the men standing in the room as if about to face a firing squad. Then she reluctantly turned away, listening as Ryan ordered the men to go through the rest of the building. Outside, the moon was a pale disk over the Thames. She extinguished the lamp on her desk and gathered up her personal belongings. Ryan walked through the upstairs offices. Shutting each door as he checked the rooms. Sliding her arms into her jacket, she felt his movements in the next room.

Gravitating toward the security of Ryan's presence, she walked to the doorway of the adjoining office and stopped. No lamp lit the interior of the room. He was standing at the window, his hands clasped behind him, looking out across the river. The moonlight touched his close-cropped hair and lashes that were thick on a face quintessentially male—as distant as the stars—and she now recognized that his earlier restraint had been something barely contained and volatile.

"I hope I haven't delayed your departure for France."

"You scared the hell out of me tonight, Rachel," he said, his back still to her.

The words made her lungs catch on a breath. She'd been

perfectly adept at bravery in the face of his calm. When she didn't respond, he turned to face her.

His gaze traveled from the top of her square-shaped hat, down her throat, over the most passé garment he'd probably ever seen on a woman. It was licorice color, with a mustard stripe on the cuff of her sleeves and hem of her skirt. She suddenly felt ugly.

But he said nothing and, when he raised his gaze, she decided that she must truly be in love with him. How else did one explain this hot, ungovernable urge to have him? To believe that he might want her, despite everything else she knew stood in their way, despite wisdom and logic, and the fact that she knew nothing about being a wife or mother to anyone's child.

Her presence would complicate his life. Ironically, his own company policy had helped to mark her. Rachel blinked as a pair of shiny black shoes appeared in her line of sight. Blinked again when the owner of those shoes tilted her chin, and she was suddenly looking into his face. "Are you all right?" he asked.

A door shut down the hall, and she nearly jumped out of her skin as a constable approached. His eyes greeted Ryan importantly. "Everything is secure on this floor, sir," he said, like a military sergeant in training. "Is there anything else you need?"

"Send my driver up after you make a sweep of the building outside."

After the men departed, Ryan returned his attention to her. The room was dark around them. Warmly intimate. She marshaled her thoughts, determined to dispel the panic overtaking her. No one else was on the floor.

"Did you wish to say anything more?" he quietly asked, his tone reminding her that she'd come to his office a few days ago to tell him something important.

She blinked away the moisture in her eyes and looked down at his arm. "You don't have a French opera singer on the side, do you?"

He traced a knuckle across her cheek, and she felt a familiar jolt. "No, Rachel."

"Ryan . . ." She scraped a length of hair from her face and tucked it behind her ear. "You and I need to talk. I don't think you are going to like what I—"

"Don't." His fingers went to her lips almost as if he recognized her intent.

She gently grasped his wrist with both palms. "When we were in Ireland . . . you asked me about the man I was with before."

"Do I need to know the truth?"

"Does Ore Industries' policy involve investigating hostile business rivals? Did Lord Devonshire initiate the process against me before you went to Ireland?"

"Why would he do that?"

"But you do investigate business rivals?"

With an oath, he shoved his hands into his pockets and leaned against the doorjamb, already on the defensive, sure that whatever she had to say he wouldn't like.

"I had a child, Ryan."

Rachel took a step away from him to distance herself from the look that came over his face. But the words were out, and she did not wish to pull them back. He had a right to know the kind of woman David had forced him to wed and who was now his wife. "The man I was involved with was a university administrator and professor where I audited my classes. I met him at my admissions interview. He signed my acceptance into the program and later recommended me to take the civil engineering exam."

"Before or after you fooked him, Rachel?"

She blanched. He turned his head and stared at her with

flat furious eyes. "If that wasn't the way the scenario played out, then why are we standing here having this bloody conversation?"

Hot, stinging pressure built behind her eyes. "It wasn't like that?" Was it? she asked herself, had asked herself a thousand times in the years since. "We saw each other for two years. He liked books and art. I believed . . ." Shaking her head, she looked away, knowing it didn't matter what she'd believed about the relationship. "I was three months along when I'd learned he wed a London debutante. . . . I took the engineering exam behind my little curtained wall with my chaperone present. Then left Scotland. I met Elsie at the home David sent me to outside Dublin to have the baby. I eventually became a teacher for the other girls who were there."

Ryan still said nothing. Rachel rushed onward. "Lord Devonshire was on the university board of trustees." She toyed with the cording that edged her sleeve. "He must have found out about the affair. But I don't think he knows anything else. Will you at least say something?" she finally asked.

"What happened to the child?"

She pressed her lips together. "I came down with typhus in my eighth month. She lived for two weeks. She hadn't even been buried three months when Kathleen died. When I said those things to you that day—"

"Christ." Ryan bowed his head, rubbed his forehead with his thumbs, and quietly swore. "I'm sorry."

"That's all there is to dredge up for your company's files and the reason why we can never be together." She drew in a breath, any further explanation skewed with the impossible realization that her scarlet past could do irreparable damage to his future. He would know this without her elaboration. "I don't want us to hurt each other. If we can keep our personal life separated from our business—"

"Technically, everything you own is mine, Rachel."

"Technically, you're betrothed. There *is* no agreement between us." She stepped away, ready to leave the room, too exposed to separate the truth from his sarcasm.

Ryan put his arm across her path, trapping her against the doorframe. Her eyes were wet. The room was as silent as a graveyard. "What am I supposed to say, Rache? Your timing couldn't be bloody worse."

"Oh yes, you're leaving for Paris." She was incredulous. "You're pressed for time."

"Pressed for time?" He, too, became incredulous. "Is that what you think I feel at this moment? Trust me, what I feel would probably get me hanged for murder. What would *you* have me say to something like this, Mrs. Donally?"

The name slid off his lips and into her head like an incoming locomotive, shattering every trite reason she'd built to keep him at bay. She wanted him—and no sanctimonious platitude she felt about his character or hers or anything else could suppress that realization and what it meant to her life. "I would ask if you believe what we have between us is still worth exploring," she said.

His eyes were on her face.

She could not read his thoughts. He glared at the ceiling, his tall shadow black on the silver-washed floor. Moonlight spilled into the room from the window.

"Are you pregnant?"

"No," she whispered with less certainty than she should have felt. "Whatever you decide, it will not be because you are forced to remain honorable."

"Honorable?" Self-mockery evident, he shook his head.

Then he closed his eyes and leaned his head back against the door. "Whatever character traits I possess, honor isn't one." His eyes lost their abstraction and focused on her. "I love you, Rachel," he said in a whisper. "I've never believed those words meant anything. But I want them to mean something to you."

"But . . ."

"You want this to be confession time?" he asked in an uneven voice. "You want to know about me? You were right when you accused me of killing Kathleen."

Watching him, she could only shake her head. "No, I wasn't—"

"I was an abysmal husband. She deserved more. She'd been so eager, so needy, so bloody desperate to find meaning in her life that she could not find through me."

"You don't need to tell me this."

Ryan scraped his hands through his hair. "Don't I?" His eyes hardened on hers. "I thought I owed it to Kathleen's memory, never to fail our daughter. I swore that no one would ever shun Mary Elizabeth because she was the wrong religion or had the wrong color of hair. She would be welcome in *any* person's home. These things were all important to me until I looked across a ballroom floor and saw you standing on a balcony drinking champagne with my brother. I don't know why you came back into my life. But nothing has been the same since."

Rachel wiped at her face with the heel of her hand. "Did you love Kathleen?"

"I loved her. I thought I could love her forever. But I couldn't give her what she needed. Do you know what that manner of failure does to a man?"

"I know what the feeling of failure does to anyone," she whispered.

"I've never told another soul what I've just told you." He leaned his palm against the doorjamb behind her head.

"It is only fair that I know your secrets as well," she acknowledged.

"You scare the hell out of me, Rachel, because I don't want to hurt you either."

She gazed into his face and couldn't remember another time in her life when she was so completely without thought. Emotions moved through her. Vivid feelings. Light.

"Rachel?" His dark eyes held hers in a simple declaration of tender passion that drained the tension from her muscles. "I haven't slept. I drink a hell of a lot these days. I lie awake at night thinking of what it would be like to wake up to you every morning."

"I think about you, too."

They both shared a moment of solidarity in that regard, and Rachel, so naïvely new to every sensation cascading through her, felt a rush of new desire spill over her senses. He felt it, too—the incautious urge, the disquieting urgency to do more than touch hands.

"Smythe has already drawn up the papers to dissolve my betrothal contracts," he said against her hair. "Everything is more complicated than I first thought."

"Are you concerned Lord Devonshire can hurt you?"

She felt his shrug and knew he wasn't telling her everything. "I've spent enough years in the churning waters of corporate seas to know what happens when sharks smell blood." He touched a fingertip to her lips. "His fight is with me."

His driver entered the front room and stopped when he saw them. Ryan dropped his arms to his side and stepped back. "I have to leave." Resting his hand on her waist, he brought her downstairs and gave instructions to the two night watchmen.

"I won't be out of the country long," Ryan said, when he delivered her to his carriage.

"Am I still invited to Paris?"

One hand braced on the door, he leaned inside the cab.

"Have we settled everything between us then?" he asked.

Was he finally asking her to choose between him and D&B?

His hand wrapped around her nape and he took her mouth in a full kiss. When he lifted his head, she was breathing fast. Whatever they had between them, neither of them could deny the passion that seemed to ebb and flow in their veins like a force of nature.

His eyes on hers, he shut the door and stepped away from the carriage.

"Mr. Smythe is downstairs, sir." Boswell stood in the doorway of Ryan's private chambers. "He said that you sent for him."

"I did." Ryan finished knotting his tie.

"I'll see that our bags are loaded in the carriage, sir. I've sent word to the station to have your car ready."

"Thank you, Boswell. Send Smythe up here."

He reached down and grabbed the stud to pin into the fine cloth of his tie. The last train for the coast would be leaving in an hour. He'd sent his daughter back to the country earlier, a better place to be in this summer heat.

After Boswell left, Ryan removed a velvet case from the drawer at his hip. He opened the lid and stared down at the betrothal ring he'd purchased for Gwyneth. Eight small pearls surrounded a single three-carat ruby that drew fire from the room. His gaze lifted to alight on the black velvet jewel case containing the only necklace he'd inherited from his mother. A match to the ring.

He could give Rachel anything. Almost anything. He hesitated with uncertainty. He'd never outright given her a gift. How did one court a wife who was neither swayed by his charm nor unduly awed by the trimmings and superfluities of his personal dominion? A woman who was a romantic at heart, even if she didn't want to admit that fact. Why was it so appallingly imperative that he impress her? Yet, it was.

He had thought of nothing but her, everything they had both said to one another, since putting her in his carriage.

A knock on the door interrupted his thoughts. Smythe entered.

"I've brought Lord Devonshire's response, sir," he said, looking at Ryan standing in the lamplight and, perhaps for the first time in his life, completely uncertain. "His lordship considers your offer beneath him. Not only on the matter of the betrothal contracts but also on the matter of his business with you. He will take nothing less than Ore Industries."

The heat pressing down on him, Ryan looked out across the terraced yard.

Despite Ryan's bloodlust to commit a violent crime against his lordship, he knew that he had only himself to blame for his current situation. He had laid down the criterion that forged the alliance from which Devonshire could not wriggle, without considering the noose he'd put around his own neck. He'd already apprised Lord Ravenspur of the situation in case Devonshire would pay a call to Rachel. Gwyneth was in Brighton, and had probably heard that he'd been to see her uncle last week. At twenty, she now seemed very young to him—and he disliked the mercenary part he'd played in making her a pawn against her uncle.

"I'll only be absent as long as it takes to seal this Paris matter." Any other business he had planned while in France, he would cancel. "I'll manage the details of the settlement to Gwyneth myself and put everything in a trust." But there was a more important matter to which Ryan needed to attend. "I want to know who authorized an investigation on Miss Bailey's activities and everyone involved. I want them discharged. Devonshire is no longer to have access to company archives. Is that clear?"

"I don't understand."

"Call it internal housekeeping. Offer Devonshire my terms one last time." Only a fool out of his mind with greed would turn down fifty thousand pounds when the average workingman might make a hundred pounds a year. "Should he choose to remain uncooperative, I've authorized Sir Boris to initiate proceedings to have him removed from the board at Ore Industries. We'll give Devonshire ten days to consider his future." Unlike D&B, Ryan nearly owned Ore Industries outright. His board was appointed.

"As your solicitor, I must caution you—"

"How long have you been married, Smythe?" Ryan slipped into his jacket and shrugged it onto his shoulders.

Smythe's British façade faltered. "Is that pertinent to your betrothal agreement, sir?"

"I am married, Smythe," he said, having told his solicitor very little of the events that had transpired in Ireland. "There can be no betrothal agreement, hence no contracts with Devonshire. He's fortunate I'm offering to pay him anything at all."

Smythe's eyes went wide. "You never joke, sir."

Smiling to himself, Ryan closed the button on his jacket. "Miss Bailey is my wife. And I will not allow her to become fodder for the scandal sheets."

"Fifteen years, sir. In September." Smythe adjusted his spectacles. "You asked how long I've been married."

Ryan gave Smythe the velvet box containing the ruby ring. "Happy anniversary," he said. "Here is wishing you another fifteen years."

"Your Grace?" The Ravenspur butler bowed over Lord Ravenspur, who sat at the end of the table finishing supper.

Brianna sat across from Rachel. Paying little heed to the conversation, Rachel stirred sugar into her tea, not realizing that it was her fourth spoonful.

She listened to the hall clock chime the hour of nine and stirred more sugar into her tea with each slow, rueful *bong*. The last train to the coast would be pulling out of the station. She set down her spoon and lifted the cup to her lips, only to be yanked from her languor. The butler was standing beside her, presenting her with a silver tray.

"You have a special delivery, Rachel," Brianna encouraged. "Better to take the package than drink that tea, I think."

A brightly decorated box sat artfully arranged on the tray's center. "For me?"

"It just arrived," the butler informed her, all but tipping the tray into her lap to get her to accept the package.

Nervously aware that both of their Graces were watching her expectantly, Rachel plucked the package from the tray. "Thank you."

She stared at her name written on the card. At once, she recognized Ryan's bold script, and her heart began to race.

"Well?" Brianna prompted.

"It's from Ryan," Rachel said, aware that she was behaving like a complete noodle over a silly card, but as her gaze traced the *R* in *Rachel* with its flourish of curves and curls, it dawned on her then; she'd never seen her Christian name written in his hand.

Their entire professional lives, she and Ryan had carried on their relationship separated by a buffer; everything always filtered through secretaries and secondhand parties concerning some contract. They'd never corresponded on a personal level.

"Open it, Rachel."

"Brianna," Ravenspur said. "Maybe she wants privacy—"

Rachel tore the paper away and revealed a flat pearl case with a sturdy gold hinge. She flipped the latch, opened the lid, and stared in disbelief at the most beautiful, wonderful gift anyone had ever given her.

"What is it, Rachel?"

Tears filled her eyes. Finally, touching the beveled grooves carved into the gold filigree design that lay atop the velvet, she lifted her gaze and laughed. Proudly, she turned the box to display its beautiful contents. "Drafting tools," she announced. "Have you ever seen anything so perfect?"

Neither Brianna nor Lord Ravenspur replied. Both of them were looking intently at the box. "I believe it is a compass and divider set," Lord Ravenspur confirmed to his wife.

BRITISH ROYAL SOCIETY OF ARCHITECTS and the year 1863 had been engraved into the pearlescent lid.

"Not just any compass and divider set," Rachel said. Time and use had smoothed the edges of the box, as it held her heart. "These are part of his personal drafting tools."

Inherently symbolic. A declaration of intent. Intrinsically romantic. For a man who never shared his toys.

Chapter 18

❝**Y**ou look as if you want to jump.❞

Rachel gasped. Her hand clutching the collar of her pink wrapper, she turned from her place against the colonnade, overlooking the Ravenspur gardens.

Lord and Lady Ravenspur were sitting at the stonework table. His arm was stretched across the back of the chair, his ankle resting on his knee. Brianna held a sleeping infant. The scene was so intimate and personal that Rachel felt at once the intruder.

"My apologies . . . I must have walked past you."

"This is our favorite time of the day," Brianna said, looking like some elfin princess in a high-necked lavender dressing gown. "Just as the sun rises over the trees."

Rachel turned her head. As if on cue, sunlight glittered through the branches and pierced the treetops. A cacophony of birdsong began to fill the air. "They are a boisterous lot," Brianna said.

It had never seemed possible to Rachel that there could be any comparison between London and her home in Ireland, but the sunrise dispelled that notion. For thirty minutes every day, she loved them both equally.

It had been three days. Ryan would be in Paris by now.

Rachel turned and looked uneasily at Lord Ravenspur, trying to assess his mood. His gray eyes, nearly blue in the morning sunlight, remained hooded from her appraisal. "I swear I only bite on occasion, Miss Bailey." One corner of his lips quirked. "This isn't one."

Accepting his mood as a positive sign, she approached the table and placed her hands on the back of the chair. "I need to talk."

Lord Ravenspur sat forward. "Would you like for me to leave?"

"No," Rachel rushed to say. "You're the one with whom I need to speak, Your Grace." She sat in the chair across from him. "Without sounding impertinent, I wish to ask you about something that is weighing on my mind. It's . . . important."

"I'm sure if it wasn't important, you wouldn't ask," he said.

"What can you tell me about Lord Devonshire and his son, Lord Bathwick?"

His dark brows arched as he considered her request.

"I only ask . . . because you must know that Ryan has an extensive business association with Lord Devonshire himself." Among other things, she thought.

"Can you be more specific?" Lord Ravenspur.

"Are father and son estranged?"

"Since the death of Bathwick's mother some years ago, they've rarely been seen in public together. I do not know if they are estranged."

"What manner of man is Lord Bathwick?"

"Not typical," Brianna interjected.

"Bathwick once tried to do something few of his peers would consider," Lord Ravenspur continued. "He actually wanted to learn about the family business. Just after his mother passed away, he moved to Edinburgh to study mining engineering. Later, considering the learning of a trade abominable for a man of his son's rank, his father threatened the school's funding and had Bathwick removed from classes. I guess it's all right to sit on a university board of trustees, but another thing altogether to watch one's son mingle with the lower orders. Since then, Lord Bathwick has been a drunk and a fop, anything to get in the old man's craw."

"You know much."

His teeth were white behind his grin. "I know a great deal about many people."

Considering he worked in the intelligence branch of the government, Rachel wasn't surprised. Lord Ravenspur leaned forward on his elbows. "May I ask why you want to know?"

Rachel stood. "I would rather that you not know my reasons for now."

Lord Ravenspur came to his feet. He was tall, his stance casual, but his gray eyes were hardened perceptively on hers. "Devonshire is not a man with whom to trifle. If he has done something . . ."

"Is he capable of hurting Ryan?"

"Lord Devonshire is a pompous ass," Brianna readily volunteered. The baby cooed, drawing her gaze. "A year ago, he tried to ruin Ryan."

Rachel's fingers tightened on the back of the chair. "I have just one more question, Your Grace." This one she asked as she exhaled in frustration. "Was Ryan sober when he signed those contracts with Lord Devonshire?"

Lord Ravenspur cocked a questioning brow at his wife as if to convey a similar riposte. "None of us believe so." Brianna agreed with a tug of her lips. "But he's begun to change these past weeks. Did you know that last month was the first time he ever allowed me to bring Mary Elizabeth to London? Not that I asked, but I did not suffer his overprotective temper. He still hasn't returned to the Church, but we think it's only a matter of time. Months probably . . . maybe even weeks."

Rachel folded her hands atop the back of the chair. "What would happen if a marriage did not take place between Lady Gwyneth and Ryan?"

"That's really a moot point. Don't you agree, Miss Bailey?" His Grace asked. "A marriage can't take place."

Appalled, Rachel looked between them both. "You know."

"The entire family knows," Brianna said. "Ryan told us weeks ago."

Rachel looked away. Her thoughts scattered into a hundred directions. "Then this has been one entire conspiracy from the beginning?"

"We have conspired to do nothing, Rachel," Brianna replied, the certainty in her voice and eyes rocking her. "Ryan was thinking only of you when he told us."

Tears rushed and brimmed in her eyes. She felt trapped as if she was playing out a stage performance to an audience who already knew the ending. But they didn't know the ending, because no one knew her past, or anything else about her, for that matter.

"If you both will excuse me." She stepped away from the chair. "I should dress."

Rachel crossed the length of the loggia and entered her room, the breeze from her passing setting her drapes aflutter. She pressed a fist to her stomach and, drawing in a deep breath, sat on the bed.

Why could she not allow herself to be happy, she berated herself.

A cat leapt on the bed and, recognizing Brianna's spoiled Persian, she pulled it nearer. The old adage, "absence makes the heart grow fonder" took on meaning this past week—for she knew one way or the other, her life had irrevocably changed. Her cheek caressing the cat, she focused on the doll she'd set on the bedside table.

Four nights ago, the doll had been in the box tucked beneath her bed. Then it sat on the dresser. Last night she'd moved it to its present location. She reached out to touch the velvet dress—finally pulling it into bed with her, displacing the cat.

"May I ask if you are in love with my brother?" Brianna queried from the doorway of Rachel's room.

"No." Rachel pressed her nose into the doll's blond hair.

"No you're not in love, or no I can't ask."

"No." She sat cross-legged on the bed and laid the doll in the folds of her wrapper. She laughed. "You can't ask unless you have a few years to listen."

Brianna sat next to her on the bed. Her dark unbound hair flowed over her shoulders to her waist. "I do now."

"I thought that you and your husband ride every morning."

"He has an early meeting with the Foreign Secretary."

"Your children are probably looking for you."

"I'm sure they will when they awaken."

"Your servants?"

"All problems go to the housekeeper or the butler. So you see"—she held out her hands palms out—"I'm all yours."

Rachel fingered the soft ruffles on the doll's dress. "What would you do if you had things in your past that could ruin someone's life?"

"You're asking *me?*" Brianna laughed. "My reputation got me thrown out of England. But then I met Michael." She smiled. "Some things happen for the better."

"Trust me," Rachel whispered, feeling little vindicated by Brianna's words. "This is not for the better."

"Does this have anything to do with Lord Bathwick?" Brianna asked, looking anything but contrite in her prying. "It's just that you've been seen together. Not that I listen to gossip, but when it has to do with someone that I care about very much, I'm all ears."

"Ryan and I have already spoken words over Lord Bath-wick."

Brianna moved to sit on the edge of the mattress, and Rachel was suddenly laying her head against her shoulder. "I have been a terrible thorn in Ryan's side since I was a little girl. He has forever been getting into trouble because of me. Only now he has to think about his daughter. I don't want to hurt him, Brea."

"Don't you think you should let Ryan worry about that?"

"How can I when it's my responsibility?"

"Ask yourself what *you* want, Rachel."

"It's not that simple. I *know* what I want."

"Then make it simple." Brianna fluffed the frilly dress on the doll and set it directly in Rachel's lap. "Johnny once told me that a good engineer utilized his knowledge of science and mathematics and appropriate experiences to find suitable solutions to the problems at hand. I believe he was talking about building a bridge at the time."

Rachel smiled at the metaphor and, perhaps for the first time in her life, her goals became clear as glass. "The only question remaining then is what kind of engineer am I to build a bridge that will withstand the course of time?"

Rachel drew rein at the high wrought-iron fence, her gaze touching the carved pair of griffins facing each other across two stone pillars. Smiling to herself, she thought how appro-priate that she should be greeted by a mythical monster with the body and hind legs of a lion and the head, wings, and claws of an eagle. Tenting a hand over her eyes, she looked past the trees toward the distant towers before spurring the horse she'd rented from a village livery into a canter down the long tree-lined drive. As she passed from the grove of beech trees, she glimpsed the huge stone house just below the rise, and came to a stop. Until now, her calm had been laboriously contrived.

White stone architraves and columns framed large windows. From the garden level to the attic high within the gabled terraces and chimneys on the roof, the mullioned glass caught the sunlight and bathed the house gold. The horse did an impatient turn before Rachel continued down the long, winding slope.

As she neared the front entrance of the house, a groom came running toward her to take the horse. "Mum . . . We weren't expecting guests. Mr. Donally isn't in residence."

Rachel accepted the groom's aid to dismount. She was too sore to land on her feet with any grace or stealth. She was nervous, and it must have shown. She already felt minimized by the house. By the entire sphere of emotions surrounding her.

"Thank you," she managed. "But I've come to see my goddaughter."

"Miss Bailey." A uniformed footman appeared.

Rachel recognized him from her last visit. "Please see that someone cools down the horse, Jeffers," she ordered.

"At once." The groom bowed to her at the waist.

Neither man commented that she'd come with no groom of her own, and she didn't indicate that she'd not been invited. Mutual ignorance benefited them all.

"I will need to find Miss Peabody," the footman said. "Please follow me."

Pulling aside the edge of her riding habit, Rachel followed him up the stairs into the house. Every muscle in her body ached. She'd left London early that afternoon and taken the train out of the city. Holding the doll in her arms against her own insecurities, she turned her head and glimpsed a painting of a hunting dog. The complexity of her emotions exasperated her and, forcing her hands to loosen their grip, she had just taken a deep breath when a child's tortured scream sent a knife of terror through Rachel chest.

"Good Lord." The footman beside her blanched pale.

He and Rachel both hit the first flight of steps running. She could hear someone trying to soothe Mary Elizabeth, but she would have none of it, and her sobs grew more desperate. Rachel came to an abrupt halt on the landing in front of a sobbing four-year-old and three apron-wringing servants. "He's lost. He's lost!" Mary Elizabeth's tear-ridden sobs fell over Rachel. "I can't get him! He went into a hole."

Rachel heard the words key, monsters, and something about a Button that had fallen into a black hole. Standing barefooted no taller than anyone's thigh, Ryan's daughter wore a mismatched blue top and green skirt with a white apron hanging untied at her waist. Mary Elizabeth took that moment to look up and see her.

Something on Rachel's face must have inspired the child because she ran to Rachel as if she had the power to save the entire world. "He's lost!" Mary Elizabeth sobbed into her skirts and every doubt, every insecurity Rachel had felt when she'd stepped into this house vanished as Ryan's daughter clung to her.

Rachel crouched beside the child. "Who is lost?"

"Button." Her small fists were clenched at her sides. "I told him not to go into the hole." She wiped a hand across her nose. "But he is bad dog. He piddled on the floor"—she sniffed—"and I taked him to hide him from Miss Peapoo, and now he is lost."

Completely befuddled, Rachel looked for guidance from the others. "The dog went into the room Mr. Donally keeps locked, mum," Miss Peabody said. "In the attic."

"Then unlock the door for grief's sake."

"She is not supposed to be up there. We have been searching everywhere for her."

"What happened to your clothes?" Rachel asked, noting the child's state of disrepair and lack of knickers, worrying what other disaster had befallen her.

"I wetted them."

"I see. And how long have you been running free?"

"Since I waked up from my nap and sneaked out the window. Miss Peapoo locked my door." War drums hammered in her gaze when it fell on the older woman running up to them, who was obviously her governess. "I dressed all by myself. I wanted to make tea for Button."

"You locked her in her room?" Rachel asked the governess.

"The child needs discipline. And I will not tolerate her poor behavior. She needs bars on her window."

"Bars!"

Miss Peabody's dark eyes snapped to hers. "I am in charge of that child while Mr. Donally and Boswell are not here."

Rachel took Mary Elizabeth's hand. "Where is the key to the room upstairs?" she asked the gathered servants.

"You cannot go up there," Miss Peabody stepped in front of her.

Rachel eyed the woman. They were the same height. But Rachel had no doubt should it come to a fight who would win. "Move out of my way," Rachel warned.

"The key is in Mr. Donally's private chambers, mum," a servant hastily said.

"But we cannot be goin' into his private chambers, mum," another said.

Suspecting resistance from the troops, Mary Elizabeth tilted her chin. Rachel admired the little tyrant's spirit. Like her father—knock him down and he'll come back harder than before. "Show me the key," Rachel asked the girl.

Mary Elizabeth pulled her down the long corridor and into

Ryan's chambers. The windows and glass doors were opened to the lake, and a honeysuckle-scented breeze filled the masculine chambers. The chambermaid bobbed and pointed to the desk at the far end of the room. "In the desk, mum," she said.

Rachel walked past the four-poster tester bed next to the small writing desk. "There." Mary Elizabeth pointed excitedly over her hand. "The key! The key!"

Rachel grabbed the key and ran after Mary Elizabeth up two flights of stairs to the attic above the servants' quarters. She could hear a dog yapping behind a locked door.

When she ducked through the door to the upper attic, her jaw dropped open.

Tiny knickers were dangling on an old discarded lamp near an open dormer window. And then Rachel noted the ghastly disaster.

A maze of blankets draped an old table and bureau, held precariously in place by lamps, books, and anything else in the room that moved. Clearly, the girl needed fort-building lessons. The slightest movement would send the whole structure crashing to the floor. As she carefully edged to the side along the wall, she noticed that wasn't even the worst of it. Evidence that Mary Elizabeth had raided the bread pantry lay in an incriminating trail across the length of the room to a table set with teacups and surrounded by dolls.

Hers and Kathleen's dolls. The sight stopped her.

Mary Elizabeth ran forward and dropped to her knees in front of the hole, soothing the poor puppy that was too dumb to come out the same hole it entered. "He's in here."

After Rachel opened the door and reunited the two, she dismissed the servants, who had followed and stopped just outside the door. As she was the child's godmother, no one argued her authority. But she was more than that to Ryan and Kathleen's daughter and, as her gaze dropped to Mary Elizabeth's upturned face, she knew in that moment that she'd been given a gift: a precious, tender gift handed into her heart for safekeeping. Her emotions grabbed and tightened, and she turned to glimpse the shadows in the room where Button had strayed.

A bedstead leaned against the far wall. Trunks lined the floor beside an armoire and an enameled bath. Cobwebs clung to the rafters. There was a sense of pain to the emptiness. Ryan had put everything in there with the intent of never seeing any of it again. Mary Elizabeth leaned against her, clearly afraid. "Miss Peapoo said that the monsters will eat me if I go in there."

Rachel lifted the girl and perched her on her hip. Furious that an adult could say that to any child. She wasn't leaving this child alone with that governess again. "When?"

Mary Elizabeth shrugged her narrow shoulders. "Before . . . when I was bad and went in there to see the pretty dresses."

"It's just a room, Mary Elizabeth. There are no monsters in there. I'll take you in there one day, but right now we need to respect your father's wishes not to go inside."

She shut the door and turned. Rachel knelt beside the dolls around the table.

"Where did you get these?"

She pointed to the door that Rachel had just shut. Rachel wondered how it was that Mary Elizabeth's sudden bravery could convey such a vivid unmistakable impression of loneliness. At least she'd never contended with a wicked governess. And Mary Elizabeth had a father who loved her.

"This doll's name is Angela." Rachel lifted the first doll. She had played with all of them as a little girl. "And the others are Marsha, Dyanne, Josey, and Betsy."

Mary Elizabeth's eyes brightened. "What's *her* name?" She pointed to the doll with the blond tresses, nearly identical to the one she'd brought with her from London. Rachel had left it on the stairway downstairs when she'd heard Mary Elizabeth scream.

"That one is Victoria. Your mother and I used to play with these." Rachel gently lifted Victoria and turned up her skirt. "This doll was her favorite. One day, I accidentally dropped her off the roof of my house. We'd gone up there because that was our favorite place to go where no one could find us." She'd smoked her first cigarette behind the chimney with Kathleen. And drunk her first glass of real whiskey. They'd talked about love and boys and dreams. Kathleen had wanted nothing more than to be a wife and mother. Rachel had wanted to be queen of the world.

"I had to fix Victoria's leg before your mother would stop crying," she said, rubbing a finger along the broken hip joint.

"How did you fix it?"

"I took poor Marsha here"—she exchanged dolls—"and traded legs. Your mother never even noticed." Bracing her elbow across her thigh, her riding habit spilling over her feet, she looked around the cavernous room. "I like this place. Do you hide up here often?"

"Sometimes." Burying her cheek against the puppy's neck, she cradled Button.

"Does that fort actually work?" Rachel asked, tipping her chin toward the structure.

Mary Elizabeth turned her head to look at the edifice in question. She shook her head. "It's broke."

"Let us plug the hole to that other room, shall we?" Rachel stood. "Then I'll show you how to build a fort that will stay up for all eternity."

But first, she was going downstairs to discharge Miss Peapoo.

Chapter 19

Paris in late August sweltered. His thumb idly tracing the diamond design cut into the glass he held in one hand, Ryan sat back in the chair with his legs outstretched, ankles crossed, his eyes homed in on the men who sat on either side of the rosewood table.

Brendan droned on about the ongoing contract and the various assets the company had yet to put on the table. A window spanned the wall in front of him, providing Ryan with a clear view of the Parisian skyline, a mixture of old style and new architecture that spoke eloquently of both nostalgic grandeur and the direction of the future. Much like the timeworn glass and brass décor of this room spoke of this office.

His gaze touched the old Louis IV furniture and returned again to the old man nearest him, attempting to sit tall as if his life's work were not being taken from him. Monsieur Valmont had once been in competition with Ryan's father. He looked like someone's great-grandfather, with a head of gray hair and a suit wrinkled with sweat. Looking away, Ryan knew he had been in Paris longer than anticipated, certainly longer than he wanted.

He'd spent evenings poring over ledgers and paperwork Brendan had given him, more annoyed by the bureaucratic wall of nonsense leveled at him than he was by the spillage of red ink and the work it would take to tear down this company. Ryan felt an urgency to leave this room, this building, and this entire city. If he walked out of this meeting, he would not return. Either way, three thousand people were about to lose their jobs. He didn't know why he cared. But he did. Empty coffers did not build inventory or pay debts. Any sane businessman knew that.

"Sir?" Brendan had just asked him a question.

A dossier sat in front of Ryan. Written in French it was a very complex list of negotiable assets that he would merely claim later and which they had already discussed yesterday. He put his elbows on the table, raised his head, and met each man's gaze in turn. Frankly, he was glad they all sweltered.

"I believe you have had my proposal for some time, *messieurs*. You argue over trivialities. I have already tendered a stock offer to this company. If I leave, someone else will sit in this chair, and I guarantee the offer will not be as lucrative."

"Perhaps it is not money that interests us, Monsieur Donally." The man who spoke was Valmont's son. "Perhaps some things are more valuable than money."

Ryan tightened his jaw. Only someone with too much money would voice that benign sentiment. Ryan never believed it for a moment. He couldn't remember a time in his life when he hadn't been fighting for something—as if success was the only embodiment of all that he was. Money represented success, his comfort, and his escape. He did not trust a man who was not interested in wealth. But he respected knowledge, and the elder Valmont was one of the pioneers of the steam engine that powered trains. D&B had built thousands of miles of tracks which this man's engines traversed.

"Then tell me, Monsieur Valmont?" Ryan looked pointedly at both father and sons. "What *does* interest you?"

"Lord Devonshire won't like what you've done, sir."

Brendan sat across from Ryan in the carriage. The city lights had begun to awaken with the Parisian night life, and Ryan spoke without turning his gaze from the window. "You work for me, Brendan."

"It's because you pay me to do a job that I speak, sir. We are not in the charity business."

Recalling that he'd once thought those very words about Rachel, Ryan turned his head, his dark gaze cool; yet, he was utterly relaxed as he waited for Brendan to say more. The younger man removed his hat and sat forward, impressing Ryan with his directness and prestigious Oxford training. "I only meant that it was unlike you. *You* are unlike you. His lordship will not be pleased to know that you have established a partnership with Valmonts to build trains."

"Locomotives," Ryan clarified.

"Locomotives," Brendan echoed, with less enthusiasm.

"A faster slimmer version of today's archaic models. By dissolving the weaker part of the business, we can take advantage of their strongest asset and the original purpose of that company's existence. More than that, it will benefit Ore Industries, who would supply the steel and iron," and D&B, he realized, as they managed the labor that would lay tracks on English and Irish soil. "I see nothing but a profitable partnership."

Brendan listened as if Ryan had lost his mind. "That is what is important in the end," he conceded, with a little more enthusiasm than he'd displayed since Ryan's arrival.

Ryan grinned. Brendan had been correct in asserting that today he had exhibited behavior unlike himself. But Ryan liked the feeling.

The unexpected sense of accomplishment as if he were an adolescent again and just discovering his father's drafting table: the rush that came with the realization that action could give way to ingenuity.

He rested his elbow on a trio of frilly boxes all tied together with a red satin bow.

Earlier, when he and Brendan had arrived on the street after the meeting, Ryan had spotted a dress shop. Situated in the middle of a white satin-draped window, was the fanciest feathered emerald hat he'd ever seen. A pair of matching slippers, gloves, and the gaudiest most colorful fan had added to the charm. He thought of Rachel. His beautiful closet opera singer, who'd never wanted her father to know she played with dolls.

He thought about her life in the years she'd first left England. About the man who had abandoned her with child. She'd learned to survive on her own. She'd learned never to take anyone's help for a reason.

Maybe with his impending Valmonts contracts, they could reach a middle ground that would solve at least one of their problems. Ryan truly wanted to see Rachel's vision. He wanted to touch her passion. It was that very passion inside her he loved.

He knew now he would not ask her to give up D&B.

Later, after sending his packages to his room, he ate dinner in a small quaint restaurant down the street from his hotel. Devonshire would have received Ryan's final offer by now. He wanted only to get back to London and begin his life with Rachel.

Dabbing the napkin to his lips, he lifted his gaze and hesitated on an attractive woman he'd noted earlier at another table. She had thick dark hair piled high on her head and painted lips, with a daringly cut gown. Ryan tipped back the glass of wine and stood. He was tall and had to be cautious of the hanging lamp.

"Did you enjoy the soufflé, monsieur?" The server bowed over Ryan with his coat. He waited as Ryan shrugged into the garment before handing him the note in his hand. "From the mademoiselle, monsieur."

"Give her my apologies." Ryan refused the slip of paper.

He didn't look at the woman as he made his way outside the crowded room. Six months ago, he would have taken her up on the offer evident in her brown eyes.

Now he thought only of Rachel.

Ryan walked the two blocks to his hotel. The night was humid and rank, with the stench of unwashed streets, but he didn't care. The moon was high in a flawless sky. He thought of his purchase today. He'd had to squelch the desire to purchase the entire boutique of finery and present Rachel with every one of them. It was difficult, when he had the money to buy her anything, to buy her only what had been in the display case.

Ryan swept into the marble-and-granite lobby. He took the lift to his suites on the top floor. A single lamp lit the salon. Removing his coat, he walked to the window and looked out over the city. His hand worked loose the tie, and he tossed it on the settee. He was unbuttoning his waistcoat when Boswell suddenly appeared.

"Sir . . ." Ryan's valet stopped behind him. "One of your men brought over a missive delivered from your brother earlier."

Ryan met Boswell's gaze directly in the glass before turning and accepting the folded note. "Johnny? Has he returned from Scotland?"

"Mr. Brendan only said it needed your attention at once.

Also . . ." Boswell cleared his throat and Ryan wondered what had gotten into the older man. "You have a guest."

The note forgotten, he looked past Boswell toward his private chambers, in no mood for banal dialogue with his valet. Ryan's gaze fell on the opened boxes, where the hat and slippers should have been.

"It is Lady Gwyneth, sir," Boswell said. "She's asleep."

Shoving the note in his pocket, Ryan walked past his valet through his dressing room into his private chambers. A massive four-poster bed with swags of crimson velvet dominated the room.

Lady Gwyneth was sitting in a chair beside the bed. Her blond hair crumpled and falling over one shoulder, she was fully dressed in some sort of pale pink traveling garment. Her sister lay asleep on the bed. A maid was asleep in another chair.

Gwyneth's eyes were wide and liquid bright in the dark. "Please don't tell me to go." She held Rachel's fancy Parisian hat in her hands. "I know I shouldn't be here. It's terribly improper. I even opened your gift. It's truly the most beautiful hat I've ever seen."

"Jaysus, my lady," he whispered. "Did you all come here alone?"

She looked too vulnerable for him to let loose his temper. "Just my maid and my sister." Gwyneth burst into tears and flew into his arms. "I had to see you."

The hat he had purchased for Rachel in one of her hands, she stood on her toes and pressed her lips against his. "I had to."

Finally, he was able to edge her away. His hands continued to hold hers captured against her waist. "Gwyneth . . ."

"I heard that your solicitors have been to see my uncle. That the visit was about me." She stubbornly swiped at her tears with the heel of her palm. "I couldn't bear to think that I had done something to make you angry."

"Did your uncle ask you to come here, my lady?"

Gwyneth's eyes widened. "Why would you assume that? Despite what the two of you think, I agreed to this betrothal because of you. Not because of him." She lowered her lashes. "I see I *have* made you angry."

Ryan saw the flush on her cheeks. "You have not made me angry. Except by coming here. How did you find me?"

"I come to Paris all the time. This hotel is where we stay." She brushed at the feathers on the hat. "I would have found my own rooms had the hotel not been full. Boswell was most kind." She stepped backward and, holding the hat, smiled tentatively. "I have ruined your surprise. But I couldn't resist opening the boxes."

"We need to talk, Gwyneth."

"Then it's true," she whispered. "You do intend to break the contracts. That's why I came here. I saw the gifts . . . I thought I might be wrong—"

"Don't you think we should discuss this in the other room?"

Ryan stood aside to let her pass. He followed her through the dressing room and sat down beside her on the settee in the salon. She folded her hands around the hat, clearly aware of his dispositional frame of mind as he shoved his fingers through his hair.

"You can't break the contracts," she blurted out in a Joan of Arc sort of melodrama that made him flinch. "I'm in love with you, Mr. Donally."

"No, you're not, my lady." Ryan forced himself to turn his head and look at her. "I thought you were in Brighton. Or was it Bath?"

She chatted about her trip, and all the things she and her sister had done, while he'd been coming to grips with the mistakes in his life. "We traveled there to attend the function at the Royal Pavilion, with half the people from London present. I thought that you would be there. Or your sister and her husband. Despite the fact that the Duchess of Bedford publicly cut Lady Ravenspur at the Green Lilly ball. . . . I am happy to call her my friend and would have lent her my fullest support."

Ryan doubted very much that Brianna needed anyone's support, but Gwyneth had a good heart. "Have you considered that the same people who are so eager to snub my sister will treat me any differently? Or you, if we were to marry?"

"You are one of the richest men in all of England." Her voice grew stubborn. "No woman could possibly snub you. No man would dare."

Ryan laughed at her Byronic notion of reality. Most would gladly see him ruined. Her uncle the foremost on the list. "I think that you are very young, my lady."

"I am twenty, Mr. Donally."

"I am thirty-one. You don't want to marry me." His voice was soft and not unkind. "I don't even like to attend balls."

"But you dance so well," she protested.

"So do a lot of other more eligible men."

"But we've enjoyed our moments together." She leaned against him. Ryan felt no guilt. Their relationship had always been patently platonic. If Rachel hadn't appeared in his life when she had, things probably would have been different, he realized. "I would enjoy being your wife," she said, and blushed, before looking away.

"Gwyneth . . ." He took one of her hands in his. "I've offered a very substantial settlement to you."

"It won't matter." Her eyes were wet in the lamplight. She drew in a breath. "Anything you settle on me, he will only keep in the end, and it will not be nearly enough for his satisfaction."

"I'm aware of that and have taken steps to keep the settlement from his hands."

"You don't understand. He truly hates you. He has never forgiven you—"

"Are you afraid of him?"

She lowered her gaze to the hat. She'd already crushed one of the feathers from her kneading, and attempted to smooth the damage. Ryan tilted her chin and asked a second time. "Are you afraid of him, Gwyneth?"

"Seven days from now, I will reach my majority," she said, "and will no longer be under my uncle's control in accordance with my parents' will. I will then be able to keep my own money." The thought never having crossed her mind, she widened her eyes. "And he'll have no control, will he?"

"No. We'll only need to find someplace for you to go until then."

The possibilities suddenly became endless for her. "I can break the betrothal without recrimination. Quietly, of course. And he could not go after you."

"I've already put the house in Bristol in your name," he said, and for the next few minutes they discussed terms, and she became less and less bothered that she had been in love with him ten minutes ago.

"I *would* rather have a man who does nothing but pay attendance on me." She smiled. "I will be rich, won't I?"

"Very."

She looked down at her hands. "This hat was never meant for me, was it?"

Ryan considered telling her the truth. But something in the wobbly tenor of her voice forbade him to embarrass her. Or maybe he wanted only to protect Rachel. To keep her name as far away from him as he could until this was over.

"Do you like it?" He took it from her and set it on her head. Her blue eyes held his. "I like it very much."

Boswell appeared in the doorway with one of his bags.

Gwyneth looked up at him as he stood to greet his valet. "We have run you from your room," she said.

"It would appear that you have, my lady."

"Where will you sleep?"

Ryan looked out across the city landscape, positive that he was not going to enjoy anyplace that Boswell might have found on short notice. "As long as it isn't a pallet of straw, any clean bed at the moment would be acceptable," he said. "I'll be back in the morning for the rest of my clothes. Be ready to leave by noon."

He would be home in four days—feeling free for the first time in his entire life.

Chapter 20

"Suck it in, Rachel."

Glaring at Ryan's youngest sibling, Rachel gasped as Elsie yanked one final time with what Rachel was sure bordered on amusement. With both hands braced on the tall bedpost, she pulled in her breath. Her breasts swelled over the corset rim. "Is it possible that this thing might be too tight?"

From her place on the settee, her yellow morning gown spilling gracefully around her, Brianna popped a bonbon in her mouth. "Can you still breathe?"

"Barely." Rachel rasped out.

"Then it's perfect."

"Shouldn't I at least be comfortable?"

She looked at the clock on the back wall. Ryan's train was due into the station in an hour. She was afraid she would pass out on the way to the station.

Elsie tied the bustle pad around Rachel's waist. The frothy silk morning dress floated over Rachel's head before she could take a breath. Another young maid helped Rachel step into a pair of silk-lined ivory shoes with brass toes. Three

days ago, she and Mary Elizabeth had returned to London, and Rachel had asked Brianna to take her shopping. She had purchased two new gowns, one that had been discarded by an unhappy patron, but a gown that Rachel found to be the most beautiful dress she'd ever seen.

Elsie finished buttoning the row of tiny pearls up her back, then helped her slide into the jacket with leg-of-mutton sleeves. Black cording accented on the collar and sleeves matched the mesh containing her wealth of hair. Catching sight of Brianna's awed expression, Rachel turned in a rustle of peridot silk and soft white lace and looked at herself in the mirror. Today, she felt like something out of a Cinderella fairy tale, slippers and all.

"Elsie, make sure that Mary Elizabeth is ready. We'll need to leave soon."

"You're beautiful," Brianna said later, as she and Rachel climbed into the carriage. Elsie and Mary Elizabeth were already inside waiting. "Ryan won't even recognize you."

Had she changed so much in the two weeks of Ryan's absence? She wanted to laugh at the notion, as if a pretty dress could change who she was on the inside. She felt beautiful in her dress, but she didn't feel like herself. The carriage jolted forward.

While Brianna and Mary Elizabeth talked about Button's latest escapade in the fountain, Rachel stared anxiously out the window at the traffic, a shudder of longing pulling at her thoughts.

That morning, she'd sat at the table and opened the broadsheet to a story written about Ryan's trip to Paris. Instead of reading about lords and ladies sweeping through the final days of summer, she'd gone directly to the financials to find any news about investors' reactions to his trip to Paris. No one knew the details of the deal that had been reached, but Ore Industries stock was up, and the man with the Midas touch was touted to be on the verge of striking gold for his minions again.

The column went on to talk about his betrothal, his possible award of a knighthood, but she scarcely registered anything else. In the last few years, she'd grown accustomed to reading about Ryan; he'd long ago lost the freedom that came with anonymity. He was, after all, the sweeping embodiment of a dashing antihero, a commoner who dared encroach upon the ranks of society. The broadsheet columnists loved to write about him. They equally loved to hate him.

Turning away from the window, Rachel looked at Mary Elizabeth, sitting like a lady beside her. "I likes trains," she said, as could be attested to by her excitement when they reached the station thirty minutes later.

The Southern Railway terminal bustled. Rachel glanced up at the train indicator. The hollow noise of the station bounced off the four-story-high glass-and-steel ceiling.

"There is Dover," Brianna said. "The train arrived ten minutes ago."

Rachel took Mary Elizabeth from Elsie as they descended into the underground passageway that led to the correct platform. Mary Elizabeth had never been in a tunnel so asked questions about everything from the tiles on the walls to the way the tunnel smelled. People bumped her.

"Would you like me to carry her?" Brianna offered, but Rachel declined.

This was the first time she would be greeting Ryan as his wife. The little girl in her arms gave her something of an emotional buffer. "Are we late?" Mary Elizabeth asked.

There was no train on the near side of the terminal ramp. Rachel stood on the crowded ramp and looked up and down the walkway, then across the open station.

Ryan stood in the doorway of a railcar two ramps away. A hundred people and four sets of train tracks separated them.

His height separated him. He wore black traveling clothes and carried a woolen coat over his am as he turned back to the doorway. Rachel would have to retrace her steps down into the tunnel along the passageway to reach him. Then as she watched, Ryan held out his hand. An emerald green hat, bursting with festive feathers appeared first in the portal way. As Rachel stared, Lady Gwyneth descended onto the platform. The woman was smiling up at something Ryan said, a shared bit of laughter followed. He edged a hand beneath Lady Gwyneth's elbow only to stop as two people approached, one carrying a pad of paper.

Rachel tried to breathe. Her tightly cinched ribs would not expand. She managed to keep her chin high and shoulders back. Mary Elizabeth remained snug against her, the little girl's arms wrapped around her neck as she continued anxiously scanning the crowd for her da. She prayed that Brianna had not yet seen her brother, but knew she was too late in turning away when she felt Ryan's sister stiffen.

Rachel wanted to flee before Mary Elizabeth saw her father, but it was as if she was powerless to do anything but watch.

Finally, she turned and stopped when her gaze collided with Brianna's. She didn't know what was worse. Having Lord Bathwick witness her humiliation at the ball or now.

"Da!" Mary Elizabeth began to wriggle. "I see Da!" Both of her small palms went around Rachel's cheeks. "You gots to hurry," she said, as if Rachel was dense. "He's leaving."

Rachel handed the girl to Brianna. "I'm sorry," she mouthed the words, knowing if she spoke the sentiment aloud, she would only burst into tears. "Aunt Brea will take you to him, Mary Elizabeth." To Brianna she said, "You better hurry."

"You ask the bloody impossible, Rachel." Johnny dropped in the chair at the end of the rosewood table in the D&B conference room.

Still wearing his crumpled traveling suit, the shadow of a beard darkened his jaw, following a night of little sleep; he had just arrived late that afternoon after a tedious journey from Scotland.

"You've been in charge of the northern division since its conception, Johnny. You know this company."

"Does Ryan have any idea that you are leaving?" Johnny asked.

"All I'm doing is returning to my people in Ireland. I only want to be confident that they will have a job next year."

"Ryan hasn't abandoned us, Rachel." His voice was quiet.

Rachel sat across from him, her hands folded in front of her. Four days had passed since she'd seen Ryan at the Southern Railway station. Brianna had not been able to catch him before he'd boarded a train bound for Bristol. She knew that he had a house there that he'd bought for Lady Gwyneth.

Drawing in a deep breath, Rachel looked at Johnny. She wanted him to take responsibility for the company. She'd always prided herself on her ability to persevere. But she had not been feeling well lately and found a need to go home to Memaw. Strange that Ireland had become the embodiment of all that she considered home, especially since she had grown up with the Donallys in the North Country around Carlisle.

Johnny shifted his gaze from her and suddenly homed in on the elegantly attired man sitting at the end of the table. "Lord Bathwick," he acknowledged. "So, you think I'm qualified to step into Ryan's shoes?"

"What I think isn't important." He leaned an elbow on the table. "Miss Bailey wants me to give you my proxy."

Rachel returned her attention to the task of gathering up the papers in front of her.

"Maybe we should talk about this alone, colleen," Johnny said.

"Don't my shares pratically make me family?" Bathwick asked.

"Not when I consider how you got those shares, my lord."

"Surely I am no different from your own brother," Bathwick scoffed.

"Except he is my own brother, and you are not."

Bathwick's blue eyes moved to Rachel, and she felt the momentary softening beneath his bland gaze. He had visited her yesterday at Brianna's home, taken one look at her red-rimmed eyes, and taken her to the vaudeville theater on Gloucester Street. "I should go." He stood and brushed off his trousers with his gloves. "You two obviously need to talk."

Rachel lifted her gaze to check the clock on the wall.

Ryan was leaning against the doorjamb, one ankle crossed over the other. "Surprise. Surprise," he drawled, his voice more conciliatory than his eyes. "I see I'm late for my own hanging." His gaze touched the transom above the door. "Though no one else on the floor has missed the pleasure."

His cravat was loose. His unshaven face darkened his eyes. Exhaustion battled the proprietary expression in his eyes as he took Lord Bathwick into his gaze. He looked as if he'd been traveling all night to get back to London. "Tell him, Rache." He said the words slowly, social amenities aside. "Tell his lordship why his proxy will make no difference in the end."

She clamped down her jaw. "I won't."

"Tell him."

Rachel pressed both palms on the table and glared at her husband. He remained leaning against the doorjamb, one ankle crossed over the other, his casual stance an ominous companion to his gaze. She bristled. On what grounds did he have to engage in such draconian behavior? None!

And there was something else inside her as well, aided and abetted by her anger. She possessed a need to throw something at his head.

She twisted around to face Lord Bathwick, apology in her eyes.

"I think I understand the problem, Miss Bailey," Lord Bathwick said, then corrected himself. "Or should I rephrase, Mrs. Donally."

"Do *not* call me by that name."

"Deny it all you will," Ryan said, and she wondered if they were about to indulge everyone within hearing distance with a very public row, "but I have our marriage certificate. It's registered in Wicklow County, Ireland. David was very thorough."

Lord Bathwick stood at one end of the conference table and replaced his hat on his head, his eyes on Ryan. "My guess, since all of London knows you and Lady Gwyneth were in Paris together and she *did* return alive, I'm assuming that you've reached an accord without my father's approval."

"Lest he extrapolate the wrong conclusion from Lady Gwyneth's absence, let me assure you both she is nowhere she doesn't wish to be. If she holds any affection for you, she will tell you her whereabouts."

"Frankly, I wouldn't trust me either." Lord Bathwick eyed Ryan with expressionless eyes, then turned to Rachel. "My condolences on your nuptials."

Ryan took a threatening step forward. Rachel stood between both men, but it was Johnny who stepped in front of Ryan. "Maybe you should leave, my lord," Johnny wisely suggested.

"Stay away from my wife," Ryan warned, as if he had a right to say anything at all after cavorting all over France and England with his former betrothed.

"You are hot-tempered, Ryan Donally," Rachel shot back until Johnny turned to face her and, with a keen warning in his dark eyes, silenced her outburst. "No one owns me, Johnny." Her voice was quietly determined and aimed at Ryan. "No one."

Johnny glanced between them. "Did something happen that I should know about?"

"Nothing happened." Ryan's eyes moved to her. "I mean that, Rachel."

The sound of a bobby's whistle outside mixed with the traffic on the street. The heat in the room struck her. There had been no wind or clouds for several days, and she could feel sweat trickling between her shoulder blades.

"I will take my leave then." Bathwick bowed at the waist.

Rachel's gaze followed his departure before swinging back around to Ryan. "How could you—?"

"How could I not? What do you think you're doing—?"

"Maybe you two might want to know why I returned to London." Johnny interrupted. He slid a fistful of papers into the center of the table. "We have a potential problem."

Heart racing, her argument with Ryan momentarily on hold, she scraped up the papers. "A structural integrity issue has surfaced at the Forth site," Johnny said.

"Brittle fracturing?" Rachel's voice was unsteady as she handed the report to Ryan.

"The kind of problem that sends bridges crashing into the ground. I've put a temporary halt to any further construction at both sites."

"Which bridge span?" Ryan asked Johnny.

"The north span. Erected five months ago," Johnny said. "Had we not found the problem, we would have been faced with a disaster. As it is, we *need* those records I've been asking for to trace the foundry where the steel came from. We need to know if any of the other sites are affected."

"We've been on that for two weeks, Johnny," Rachel said.

"The recent renovations have caused some problems." Ryan returned the paper to Johnny. "Dispatch teams to begin inspections at the major bridge sites we've completed in the last year," he said. "I don't trust local governments to do the job."

"Neither do I," Rachel agreed, having had her fill of bu-
reaucracy in the past.

"I've already done that." Johnny's face remained expressionless, but his posture betrayed the tension evident in his
shoulders. "What else can I do?"

"Go home and sleep," Ryan said. "Tomorrow I'll have
Stewart bring up a list of the foundries that supply our steel.
Not one has alerted us to a problem, and I'm curious to know
why. On Monday, we'll put more people to the task of finding
the records."

Johnny turned to look at her, but Ryan had already moved
to the door and awaited his brother's departure. Clearly, he
felt the topic was finished. "What all of us want to know"—
Johnny asked her—"is how did David marry the two of you at
all?"

Rachel spared an involuntary glance over his shoulder at
Ryan. "He smashed your brother in the jaw and threatened to
shanghai Ryan to San Francisco."

"David did that to Ryan?" Johnny's eyes widened in barely
contained amusement. "This is too preposterous not to be
true. He always could best his baby brother in a fight."

"Very amusing, Johnny," Ryan said.

Rachel thought Johnny might strangle for lack of holding
back his laughter. "So did David catch you with your hands
in the cookie jar, brother?"

More like he caught *her* hands in the jar, Rachel groaned.
Eyeing her brother-in-law, she realized some things never
changed. Ryan could be a hundred years old and still be
treated like a guilty twelve-year-old by his family. "You
could, of course, try to congratulate him," Rachel pointed out,
annoyed. "Or me."

Johnny leaned over and kissed her full on the lips. When
he finished, he pulled away, a mischievous sparkle in his
black-brown eyes. "Don't tell Moira. But I always wanted to

do that." He chuckled. "Congratulations, colleen."

Ryan's dark eyes had narrowed perceptibly by the time Johnny turned, nodded, and strolled out the door, his sense of humor fully restored for the day.

After the door closed, Rachel felt the force and heat of Ryan's gaze as he locked his eyes with hers. They no longer stood beneath the guise of a truce.

"You could have told him the truth," Rachel said. "That I was the one caught with my hand in the cookie jar."

"And ruin his fun? When I'm already in enough trouble with you?"

Rachel walked to the window. If she left this office, he would catch her, which would only add more indignity to her already beleaguered stance.

"What did you do with Miss Peabody?" he asked after a moment.

"She was a witch. I discharged her." Rachel kept her chin high beneath the weight of his gaze. "I know that you think she was the best, but money doesn't always buy the best, Ryan. Elsie can stay with Mary Elizabeth until you find another suitable nanny."

Pinching the bridge of his nose, he shook his head. "I don't know why I'm not angry, considering that my daughter looked like something dredged up from the Thames when I arrived at Brea's house looking for you. She was playing in the mud."

Knowing his sensibilities had been shocked lent some measure of recompense to her mood. Ryan had always been highbrow to the core.

His back against the door, he crossed his arms over his chest. "I returned as soon as I received Brianna's wire. It was handed to me upon my arrival in Bristol."

Rachel folded her arms. "Thank goodness for the telegraph."

"I didn't invite Gwyneth to Paris."

"Fine." She faced him. "Then you only shared your private

rail car with her all the way back from Dover, then proceeded
to Bristol."

"With five other people," he pointed out.

Trying to conceal her reaction to that statement, she
shifted uneasily.

"We've reached an accord, Rachel. No matter what you
think of her or of me at this moment, I still have a duty to protect her. I owe her that much. Nothing happened. She's at the
house in Bristol."

"Hiding?"

"Apparently she is afraid of what her uncle will do to her
when he discovers that she has broken our engagement. He
should be receiving the news tomorrow."

For a moment, she could only stare. "She is doing that for
you?"

"She is doing this because I am making her very wealthy."

Despite herself, Rachel understood Ryan's position. Realizing what he was sacrificing for her, she dropped her
gaze to her hands. "Now that you aren't marrying Lady
Gwyneth, will you lose your nomination for a knighthood,
as well?"

"Whether I ever receive the orders or not will no longer
have anything to do with a marriage to Lady Gwyneth."

"I'm sorry," Rachel whispered.

"For what?"

"For always making your life so difficult."

"We're Irish, Rache. We make 'difficult' an art form."

She regarded him standing against the oaken door, startlingly handsome. Still not ready to concede to him full victory over her heart, she angled her chin, and asked, "Did your
deal with Valmonts close to your satisfaction? Have you suc-
cessfully annexed another territory into your kingdom?"

The growth of stubble darkening his jaw brought a preda-
tory glint into his eyes as she once again set him on their orig-

inal tack, for he had suddenly gone all dark and dangerous on her. "Something like that." No longer coolly taciturn, he pushed off the door and shrugged out of his jacket. "My business in Paris was quite satisfactory."

"Just once, I would like to be in your shoes, Ryan."

"No, you wouldn't."

The unexpected vulnerability in those words held her gaze to his. "At least you are considered important. That is something."

"Only because people are afraid of me or want something." He tugged at the knot on his tie.

Wary of his approach, Rachel stepped away from the window, and they faced each other across the conference table. "What are you doing, Ryan?"

His gaze traveled from her head to her toes. "I'm listening to you explain why you and Johnny were in here today talking about deposing me."

"That should be obvious."

Slowing in front of the window, he reached up and pulled the cord for the blinds. They cascaded to the sill, sending the office into a nocturnal twilight.

"So, what should we do about this difference of opinion between us?" His fingers working the buttons on his gray waistcoat, he again commenced pursuing her.

Her eyes, on the breadth of his shoulders, lifted to his face. "Competition is a fact of life." Rachel collided with a potted fig before she switched direction. "Don't you agree?"

"Yes." He shed his waistcoat.

"Great Britain is in the midst of the biggest construction boom in history," she continued, alarmed that at this rate, he would be undressed before she made another round of the room. "Ore Industries and D&B can actually complement each other if we manage to rearrange our resources. We pool our talent, yet our identities remain intact . . ." She paused abruptly when the door came up against her back. "We can work together."

He pressed both of his palms against the door, trapping her between his arms. "Would that make you happy, Rachel?"

Her breath caught in her lungs. The entire course of his behavior was at odds with everything she'd expected from him, and she was no longer sure that they were talking about D&B or Ore Industries. "Finding a solution to this problem would make me happy."

"Do you really want a partnership with Lord Bathwick?"

Rachel shook her head, unable to stop her gaze from misting, and it seemed that her whole world had been reduced to *this* moment. "I *want* a partnership with you."

He didn't speak at first. Then . . . "All right."

Her brows shot up. "All right?"

Amusement settled in his eyes. "I'm a pussycat, Rachel," he said, more interested in the flush on her cheeks than his concession. "Scratch my ears, and I purr."

Rachel stared at him speechless.

"Did you want to negotiate more?" he asked.

"No."

He reached above his head and shut the transom. It slammed closed. "Good."

His lips covered hers.

No simple kiss devoured her, but one filled with hunger and passion and a thousand other promises. His heat infused her and bonded to the length of her body. He eased his hands from the door and traced the contour of her cheeks, finally holding her to his plunder. And plunder he did. Her emotions converging into one feeble push and pull of her heart, Rachel raised her palms to his chest.

She broke away. Their breaths hot and mingling. Why had he capitulated so easily to her? "Do you have a fever?"

She felt his mouth curve into a smile. "Probably."

He pulled back and his eyes narrowed. "Did you really believe that I could have an affair with Lady Gwyneth after all the work it has taken me to get you to this point?"

"I had never felt the way I did when I saw the two of you together," she said. "I never want to feel that helpless again. I'm in love with you, and I'm terribly jealous of any other woman with whom you've ever spent time. I didn't think I would ever feel the way I do about you." Like she wanted to crawl inside his soul and stay forever.

"Thank you, Rache. Your words are poetry to my ears."

She held her palms against him. "When did you decide there would be no merger?" she whispered.

His lips caressed hers, lingering to taste and suckle. "In Paris."

"You did?"

He lowered his gaze from her eyes to the bow of her lip, and there was intensity in his eyes. "I did. But you put forth a compelling argument," he breathed against her mouth.

"I did?"

"You did." He reached behind her and locked the door. "And my only regret is that it has taken me so long to reach this point with you."

As soon as his lips touched hers, the world tilted, stopped spinning, and Rachel swayed. She moaned deep in her throat, all of his temperament and allure coalescing her desire in a hot pool between her thighs. Suffering the final departure of her will, she stretched her arms over his shoulders, her loss of objectivity resembling that of inebriation. Everything was becoming a blur.

Then she felt his hands shift, as if he were remembering where his palms had been headed when she'd broken away. His fingers eased down her spine, over her bottom, and back up the curvature of her waist, working the long row of buttons on her jacket. His palms were suddenly past her jacket and waistcoat and flat against her breasts. She closed her eyes. And simply merged with him as she breathed him deep into her lungs and became aware of her arms looped around his neck. Time slowed.

She wanted to stop it forever and ever. "Oh, Ryan"—her head drifted to the side when his mouth trailed down her throat—"this is not behaving with discretion."

Someone had to be the voice of reason.

Ryan pushed her jacket from her shoulders. His voice was hot and breathy against her ear. "I already sent everyone home. Except the night watchman, of course." Unhampered by any moral scruples, he encircled his hands around her waist. She'd never felt quite so petite, so feminine the way she did when his fingers enclosed her. "You should definitely refrain from screaming." He lifted her easily, swung her around, and sat her on the shiny, rosewood conference table behind him.

This was their office, after all, she told herself.

Their conference table.

His mouth returned to her lips. To the wet fullness of her lips. The kiss was hotter and, in an instant, everything in her world changed. His hands moved to her knees, and he pushed her legs apart. He slid his palms up her calves, traced the stockings on her legs to her thighs. Even higher, above the cinched garters, his thumbs stroked the split in her drawers. They stroked her and touched the damp apex of her thighs.

Her reaction was instantaneous. She grabbed his hands through her skirt and held them. "Ryan—" She was breathing hard.

So was he.

Their eyes held.

"What?" his voice rasped, when she didn't say anything.

Tears filled her eyes. She wanted to ask about Devonshire. But then he took her face in his hands and traced his thumbs over the delicate bones in her cheeks, and everything faded in the desire she saw in his eyes.

"You're not going to cry again?" He pressed his lips to her cheeks, her nose, and the space between her brows. "I'm apt to begin feeling inadequate. The only time you weep is when we make love."

She gave him a watery laugh. "I'm not crying." Her gaze briefly touched the transom; then her trembling fingers went to her waistcoat. "But maybe we should hurry."

"I don't want to hurry." He stepped between her legs and replaced her hands with his. "This is one conference this week I intend to take slow and enjoy."

But Rachel paid little heed as he removed her shirtwaist and blouse. She was soon lost to the scratch of his beard as he suckled her breasts. Her palms slid beneath his shirt and stripped him of the garment, sending it to the floor along with her skirt. Her tongue discovered the sculpted heat of his flesh. He tasted salty and sensual, and she soon relished her own unhurried find. Dark hair lightly covered his chest and angled downward into a V, disappearing beneath the waist of his trousers. Her lips tracing the corded delineations across his ribs, she dipped her hands beneath his waistband. A rasp of breath rewarded her study.

He tightened his hands in her hair. He was hot and pulsed with life in her palm. She stroked, caressed, and finally unfastened his trousers completely and freed him into her hands. Her finger encircled the milky bead that pearled at the tip of his sex, and she lapped it up with her tongue, her mouth needful, her body drugged with her own desire. His body coiled and tensed. Held by her need as she took him into her mouth and gave herself up to the wonder of discovery.

A low, anguished groan escaped his throat. "Jaysus, Rachel." He clasped her wrists.

Slowly raising her gaze, she looked up at him from beneath

lowered lids, her mouth wet from her explorations. His breath came in pants that made his chest rise and fall. A dark lock of hair fell over his forehead. Wrapping her legs around his thighs, she guided him inside her wet warmth, felt the swelling pressure of his probing entrance, the thrill of him filling her.

With an oath, he followed her down to the table and caught himself on his palms above her. His eyes opened. Raw, hot lust shone down at her, and they shared a charged moment, an intimate flash of helpless wonder. A declaration.

He pushed deeper, shattering the thin emotional barrier of her doubts. His tongue, hot and strong, thrust into her mouth.

Then his kiss consumed her. And she forgot to think at all because he was deep inside her, moving against her, already spurring her toward orgasm. Her hands traveled over his back. Corded, hot skin. She sobbed against the violent crest of her own climax. Cried out against his shoulder. Until he buried his hands in her hair and, with a final, possessive plunge of his hips, surged against her, filling more than her senses.

Her eyes opened, and when he finally raised himself and looked down at her, she smiled up at him wonderingly. For he was beautiful, and she braced her palms against his jaws, pulling him down to her lips, wanting only to tell him she wanted more.

Ryan was also thinking along those same lines that night after he'd brought her to his London residence, carried her over the threshold and up the winding staircase. What they'd begun and finished in the office, they started all over again on his stairway.

Ryan pressed her against the wall. His hands gripped her overjacket sleeves and pulled it off her, dropping it at her feet. Lips locked, she groaned and shoved her hands beneath his waistcoat, sending it the way of his jacket and cravat. They were breathing hard, and he was already stripping her out of her blouse. Her hair fell over her shoulders. Their mouths fused.

For a brief moment of lucidity, he recalled that Mary Elizabeth was still at Brianna's. Boswell had best keep the servants away. He dragged his lips from Rachel's, lifted her again into his arms, and carried her into his bedroom, where he fell with her to the bed. Landing on top of her half-dressed as he was, he caught himself above her and met her gaze, knowing she felt this gripping need inside her as well. Knowing and welcoming the sweet madness for what it was. For if he had lost control of the situation, so had she. Equality took no prisoners tonight.

The Y of his black suspenders lay over his shirt, and she shoved them off his shoulders, letting her fingers linger on his back. "Do you think people will wonder where we are?"

"God, I hope so," he said against her mouth.

He kissed her.

She kissed him back.

He had her trapped between him and the mattress. His breath came heavily against her mouth, her throat, and her breasts. They explored each other. Unfettered by time or interruption. He grabbed a handful of her chemise and stripped it over her head, savoring every inch of her body. She was wet beneath his hand. How much of that was him, he didn't know and, beyond the throbbing, sybaritic lethargy of his own groan as he released himself from his trousers, he didn't care. The blunt head of his erection pressed between her thighs. And only then did he feel the completeness he sought.

He held her still before he came too quickly.

Her legs wrapped around his hips, she opened her eyes.

"Wait," he murmured.

"I've never been in your bed." Her neck arched, she looked around her at the yards and yards of sapphire velvet canopy that draped the bed. "You have always had such beautiful things surrounding you."

"Have I?" Still wearing his trousers, he laid buried inside her, distracted, and did not understand what she saw that he didn't. Or perhaps that he took for granted. For there had never been a clear distinction separating who he was from what he had built.

"Here I was excited over one new dress." The whisper feathered his lips.

"I can buy you more than one dress, Rachel." He laughed shortly. "I wouldn't think any less of you if you took my money."

"And I am not some prize you can mount among your other collections, Ryan."

Breathing the words against his lips, she pulled his mouth down to hers, and he forgot to question the tenor of those words. Forgot everything but his ache to possess her.

His palms slid to her hips, then reverently to the flesh of her bottom. He moved, setting the rhythm. The very air between them crackled, but he made love to her that night in his bed, slow and easy, his gaze locked on hers, the urgency between them more controlled than in the office—but in the end, no less explosive.

Later, before he took his sweetly sated wife back to Brianna's house in his carriage, he told her that he wanted to marry her in a church before he made their vows public. He wanted that legitimacy, but deep inside he knew he wanted more. She'd been shocked when he said he didn't care which church, and even considered attending confession and seeking atonement, so a priest would bless them.

Something was changing inside him, and he wasn't entirely sure he liked the transformation. At least he'd always known where he'd stood with God and the devil. There was no arguing where he'd spend eternity. He could make unpopular and sometimes ruthless decisions in his life with no guilt. Kathleen had always warned him that he was too wild for his own good. Too ambitious. Too cynical. For a while in the beginning, he had wanted to change for her but could not.

He'd been faithful to Kathleen, but he hadn't been faithful to her memory. He'd been with more women than he could count. Beautiful women. Worldly women. Aristocracy or actresses. Most he never saw again. Most he never wanted to see again. He had never lost himself in a woman's body. Never shut his eyes and felt the freedom that came with the loss of his control. Or tasted the possessiveness he felt when he made love to Rachel. When he looked into her eyes and watched her come, knowing that he had done that to her.

And knowing that it was not enough.

He wondered if she would ever allow him to give her more than what she could buy or do for herself, and he felt robbed by her lack of appreciation for everything that he could offer her. No one except his daughter had ever wanted him just for himself. He was not used to the novelty. It left him feeling strangely exposed. Vulnerable. Searching for an identity beneath the trappings of his life.

Ryan, who rarely pulled himself out of bed before noon, was still standing at the window when the sun began to rise, and he watched the day awaken with an amber brilliance that overtook the shadows. There was beauty all around him in places he'd not looked in a long time. He touched the velvet curtains at his side, then turned into his room. He loved his daughter. He'd loved her mother. He'd always believed his heart rationed love like bread crumbs. And that he was not capable of feeling more than he had. Until now, he'd never known his heart had lied. For as his gaze fell on the bed, he thought of Rachel and knew that he had loved her his entire life.

Chapter 21

❦

It stinks like baby James." Mary Elizabeth held her nose as Rachel lifted her out of the landau in front of the D&B office building the next morning.

"It stinks," her cousin Robert enthusiastically echoed from Elsie's arms.

"That's because the weather has been hot, and we've not had much rain," Rachel said, without launching into the reasons why London could stink so fiercely in summers. She looked up at the darkening sky looming over the red brick building in front of her. "But I think we are about to find relief."

"I wants to go to the park," Mary Elizabeth announced. "Robert gots bread to feed the baby ducks and baby fishes."

Rachel smiled. "We're only taking a detour," she promised her.

"What is a 'tour'?"

Rachel put her back to the heavy door and pushed it open. "It means I am taking the long way from Aunt Brea's house to the park."

"Can Robert come on the 'tour,' too?" she asked, as the boy looked at her, his cherubic expression hopeful.

"I believe we are already here."

Rachel had slept late that morning. She never slept late. She still felt tired and sore in the most indecent of places. Ryan had been by the house earlier and eaten breakfast with his sister. When Rachel had finally made it downstairs around noon, Brianna was already out on her social calls—and she was left entertaining the children after she sent Robert's nanny upstairs to nurse her sniffles. Rachel had been about to venture to the park when she'd received a message from Stewart.

Once inside the building, she greeted the weekend watchman, a wiry former constable with a missing front tooth and eight children to feed. "How are Lara and your children today, Mr. McKinney?" she asked, shifting Mary Elizabeth on her hip, so she could sign the register.

"We enjoyed the fruit pies ye sent us last week, Miss Bailey."

Her gaze skimmed the list and noted Stewart was already upstairs. Johnny wasn't here yet. Upstairs, Rachel greeted Stewart, who was at his desk working over a pile of papers. "I'll only be a moment," she said, taking Elsie and the children to the drafting room in the back. "This is the drafting room," she clarified to the threesome.

She set out paper and charcoal, arranging the sticks in order of size and density. She set out wooden triangles, squares, and rectangles, explaining each piece as she went along. "All ready now." She handed the children a straight edge. Both looked at her as if she'd grown warts on her nose. "Can you draw a castle?" Rachel asked.

"'Course," Mary Elizabeth scoffed. Her younger cousin wasn't nearly so confident. "I'll show you." She patted young Lord Robert on the back in big-sister fashion as Elsie set him beside her on the stool.

Rachel paused briefly in the doorway. Watching the two

children, she felt as if she was looking at a rainbow that had materialized out of a stormy sky. It was as if she had breathed those colors into her lungs, and the entire world seemed a brighter place to be.

Outside, the clouds had darkened over the Thames, and a low grumble vibrated the walls and the floor. The ugly sky had no place in her mood.

"I'll see that she keeps the charcoal to this paper, mum," Elsie reassured her, misinterpreting Rachel's reason for remaining in the room. "They will be fine."

"Thank you, Elsie."

Stewart was waiting for her when she returned to the front. "I thought you might be interested in seeing what I'd found, mum. Unless you want to wait—"

"I'm not that patient, Mr. Stewart." Presenting him with a smile, she held out her palm, and he gave her a sheet of paper.

"Mr. Donally asked me for the list of foundries that supply our steel. I could only guess earlier. It has taken me most of the morning to make sure this is accurate."

The room darkened as clouds gathered across the sky. She held the paper to the lamp and read the list, not quite understanding what it was that excited Stewart.

"D&B has had three break-ins, maybe more that we don't know about," he said, his voice excitable. "Nothing of value ever seems to be missing."

"Yet, entire files on our northern sites have disappeared." Her gaze returned to the list of foundries.

"Six foundries supply our steel at any given project. This one"—Stewart pointed to the third name from the bottom—"is a subsidiary of Ore Industries in Wales. Lord Devonshire's domain. The family owns that foundry, mum."

Her gaze paused as her mouth went dry. "Ryan must already know about this."

"I believe that is why he asked for this list, mum. But you

see, he stopped all orders from that foundry in May, so I went back through our accounting records. Records not stored in the vaults, at least not until I move them down at the end of the year. Do you know where the last shipment from Wales went?"

"The Forth site in Scotland," Rachel answered.

"Exactly."

"When brittle fracturing problems are not discovered in time, people die," she said, appalled that even his lordship might knowingly hide information of that magnitude. "Someone at the foundry must have discovered the problem. And chose to say nothing."

The implication sent a chill down her spine.

Ryan would ultimately be held accountable if people died. They all would as board members. Maybe even prosecuted. It had happened before to companies accused of negligence where structures had failed and people died.

Stewart retrieved the list. "An accident of any magnitude would be like a tsunami rolling down the chain, crushing every firm involved," Stewart said, having already grasped the implication. "Which would explain Lord Devonshire's pressing interest for a merger with D&B. Our failure would percolate directly into Ore Industries' shares."

"In the process, Devonshire could then make a grab for both companies. Donally and Bailey would never survive."

"Except in this case Lord Bathwick owns a large portion of D&B, mum," Stewart said. "Mr. Donally already believes they have a foothold."

But that made no sense. Did it? Lord Bathwick wanted to stop the merger. She would not believe it of him. "Where did Ryan go when he left here?"

"He went to Ore Industries, mum. He believes that if files have been tampered with here, then they have there as well. The good news, if there can be any under the circumstances, is that it looks like we found the second site where the steel went. That's what I wanted to tell all of you."

Rachel wanted to go to Ryan. That someone could hate him so much frightened her to the core of her being. "Are you all right, mum?"

"I left my satchel here yesterday," she said, pulling her composure around her and finding a reason to remain and await Johnny. She would finish her correspondence.

Rachel walked down the corridor and into her office, attempting to stave off her uncertainty as she forced herself to think. Ryan must have already suspected Devonshire's involvement, or he wouldn't have been so specific in his requests. Her office was dark. Outside, the rain had started to pebble against the window and roof.

She glimpsed her satchel lying beside the desk where she'd left it yesterday and started forward. But as she moved into the room, the door slammed shut behind her.

Rachel swung around and nearly fell over her skirts. Her heart struck her chest, for she had been thinking about the thunder in the sky.

Lord Devonshire stood with his back against the door. Her heart went still. Reeking of spirits, he took in her gasp, recognized her shock, and clicked the key in the lock. "Is that Donally's daughter in the other room?"

Her breathing stopped. She would die before she allowed this man near that little girl. Her gaze swung to the second door that opened to the conference room, but Devonshire stepped into her line of sight before she could think of breaking for the other door. Aware of the danger, she took a step backward. "Get out of my way."

"Or what? I doubt you'll scream and chance bringing Donally's daughter in here." He advanced on her. "And I'll have any man who touches me arrested if he lays a finger to this suit. Indeed let them try."

Rachel stepped around the edge of the desk. "What is it you want?"

"Donally's head on a platter? Ore Industries? My niece's whereabouts? The possibilities are endless. Depending on how much he wishes to protect you." His height forced her chin up. Her heart hammered against her ribs.

"He was clever to get Gwyneth to break the contracts." He poked a finger in her shoulder. "Clever to hide her from me. But not so clever that I don't know his vulnerability. Did you know he killed two major mergers at a total cost of a hundred thousand pounds to my coffers? But of course you must. You put him up to it."

Rachel had no idea that Ryan had given up that much. Her thighs came up against the edge of the desk. "Now that bloody Irisher removed me from the board of Ore Industries." His voice seemed to draw venom from a new surge of energy. "From my own corporation! As if he has the right to take what belongs to me."

Her fingers probed the desk for a weapon. "You must think yourself invincible to threaten me," she whispered. "How did you get in here?"

"I told you what would happen if you got in my way. I bloody warned you. I told you I'd make you both pay."

"Get out of here!"

He raked everything off the desk. The lamp shattered on the floor. Books and papers scattered. "I want Donally to know what it feels like to lose everything in the world."

She lunged past him. He grabbed a handful of her hair and, without thinking, she slammed her palm against his face. "Don't you dare touch me!"

"Bitch!" He grabbed a fistful of her bodice.

She tried to swing her other arm, tried to fight. Her knuckles connected with his shoulder. He shoved her back against the desk.

His breath coming in gasps, Devonshire glared in disbelief at the blood on his hand. Immobilized by the violent weight of her shock, she'd momentarily frozen. Then he pounced on her, and she was fighting with all her strength. He jerked her around and pressed her face down on the desk. "Because of Donally, I have nothing! Nothing!"

A hand to her nape held her immobile. Her chest hurt. His weight pushed her against the desk and, finally she screamed. All she could think of was that Mary Elizabeth was in another room.

Please, God, don't let her come in here.

"He'll kill you." A sound like a sob escaped her.

Her hip burned from where she'd struck the corner of the desk. Somewhere she heard banging on the door. She slapped her hand toward the letter opener. It teetered, then toppled onto the floor. "Think about it, Miss Bailey." His lips pressed against her ear. "I could do whatever I wanted and he couldn't touch me without first destroying you. But I'm not going to rape you." He loosened his grip. "This is only a lesson. Take that message to Donally."

Her mouth tasted coppery. She caught her breath and started to twist around to face him, when he was dragged away from her. Johnny shoved him against a bookcase, his eyes darkened like a storm cloud. The door to the office hung on its hinges as if he had kicked it open. "You bloody, fooking bastard—"

"No!" She grabbed Johnny's arm. "He wants you to attack him!"

But Johnny wasn't listening. God in heaven, Elsie had run out of the drafting room, her eyes wide as Rachel yelled at her to go back down the corridor and shut the door.

"Get out of here, Rachel," Johnny snapped, when she grabbed his arms.

"No, Johnny!"

The watchman had come running into the office and stood

motionless. No one knew what to do. Lord Devonshire was a peer.

One didn't attack a peer, for God's sake!

"It's not worth it!" she screamed, holding on to one arm. "He didn't hurt me." The blood roared in her brain. She was still holding his arm when Devonshire came away from the wall, a derringer in his hand, and shot him.

Chapter 22

Ryan stopped in the vast doorway with its soaring marble columns as he scanned the tables, his height distinctive in the archway. His coat swirled around his calves. Rain had soaked the wool. A wet lock of hair hung in his eyes. He wore no hat, having lost it somewhere outside. He stepped into the dimly lit interior of a club he had not walked into since the establishment had removed his name from the exclusive list of clientele last year. Though he had been reinstated after his battle with Devonshire, he'd rather have been found dead in the Thames than spend one second in this room.

Devonshire sat in the corner, a painted oriental screen granting partial privacy. A single taper burned on the table. The club was nearly empty this time of the afternoon. His lordship was sitting with his elbows braced on the table, a drink in his hand. Ryan made a furious straight line toward the table. Despite the man's arrogance, there was about him a cumbersome sense of isolation as he cradled the glass with shaking hands.

Ryan only knew he'd kill the bastard.

Devonshire looked up with bleary eyes.

Seeing Ryan's approach startled him into instant sobriety. Seeing the murder in Ryan's eyes brought him to his feet. He might have called for help if he'd had half his wits. Without breaking pace, Ryan grabbed Devonshire by the velvet lapels and slammed him against the wall. "That was my *wife* you bloody attacked this afternoon!"

"Get your hands off me!"

"My daughter was in that building, you bastard. So was Lord Ravenspur's son!"

"I only defended myself from your brother! Ask her. She was trying to hold him back."

Shouts emanated from the room behind him. Ryan could find no balance between control and savage fury. "The constable won't arrest you because it's your word against hers, but you and I both know why you were in that building today. Did Rachel walk in on you while you were trying to pilfer more files—?"

"You don't want to do this, Donally," Devonshire choked out in fury. "I swear you will regret it. Check my pocket," he rasped. "She won't be testifying against me. Or I swear to God, I'll ruin her."

Some modicum of sanity reared its head and slapped manacles on his temper.

"The papers are in my jacket pocket. Bloody ask her about Edinburgh," he hissed. "Then tell me how much you are willing to pay for my silence."

Two men lunged toward Ryan, but he jammed his forearm against Devonshire's windpipe and, shoving his hand inside the man's jacket, retrieved the packet, the blind incaution of his emotions vanquished beneath something far more dangerous. "I swear on my life if you take this any further, when I've finished with you, you'll have only your entailed land on which to stand—or you'll be dead," he hissed in Devonshire's ear. "There won't be a place on this earth you can hide. Do I make myself clear?"

"I want my holdings returned. Everything you stole, I want returned."

His brother lay dying with a bullet in his chest. His daughter had been within fifty feet of the attack. Rachel had been within inches. "Just know that I am not my brother."

Ryan let himself be dragged away by the hands clasped to his arms. Devonshire stumbled forward, catching air in his lungs. His hands braced on his knees, he raised his head. "I could have you arrested, you bloody mick."

"You could try. But that was my wife you attacked this afternoon, and no man will argue my right to protect what is mine." Ryan jerked loose from the hands that held him. "Even from you, *my lord*."

"I'll have to ask you to leave, Mr. Donally," someone said, his voice timid in the chaos surround him. "We'll have none of this sort of thing in our establishment."

"Naturally, true gentlemen settle their differences privately, with a civilized duel to the death. Succinct. To the point. Is that what you want?"

"I've finally gotten you where you deserve, Donally." No longer guarded or wary, Devonshire's face was smug, a Sassenach pig when it came to venerating himself before his peers. "Such are the vagaries that go into winning and losing one's fortune and the company one keeps in bed. You'll be back to me on your knees, Donally."

Ryan rotated on the ball of his foot, his fist in motion when someone grabbed it in midair. Lord Ravenspur had appeared in the crowd beside him, his hand wrapped around Ryan's fist like a steel vise, looking as if he'd been traveling hard, his gray eyes warning him. "I've a carriage outside," he said.

Ryan felt the first semblance of rationality descend and

eclipse his muddled emotions. He shifted his gaze to Devonshire. "Stay away from my wife."

"An Irisher with airs." Devonshire straightened his cravat.
"I can't imagine whatever gives you people the idea you have
any rights at all."

Ryan pulled away from Ravenspur, his arm already in motion. But Ravenspur smashed Devonshire in the jaw first, the
fluid momentum of his fist driving him off his feet, against the
table, and sending him to the floor on the other side. His lordship dropped like a slab of beef on a chopping block. "An Irish
commoner who was the Edinburgh pugilist champion," Ravenspur said over the prone body. "Feel lucky he let you live at all.
And luckier still that I have for what you have done this day."

Ryan tore up the contents in the envelope and tossed the
pieces into the fireplace on his way outside. "I didn't bloody
need your help," he said between his teeth, as they walked
shoulder and shoulder out of the door.

"Perhaps not, but if you had hit him, then who would be
with your wife and daughter when the authorities carted your
Irish ass off to jail."

He stopped at the top of the marble stairs. The rain poured
off the eaves like a waterfall. Rain sheeted off the eaves and
poured in waterfalls over the walkway. Rachel was standing
at the bottom of the stairs, her clothes soaked, feebly clutching her cloak to her chest. "She insisted on following,"
Ravenspur said from beside him.

Her eyes were brilliant in the gray wet light, and Ryan
knew he could drown in that gaze if he allowed himself, if he
wasn't so appalled that his own actions had brought them all
to this point in the first place.

Rachel sat on the chair beside the bed where Johnny lay
unmoving. Wide strips of cloth bound his chest. She lay with

her head on the mattress folded against the crook of her arm, nauseated and frightened.

The door opened, and a nurse entered with a bowl of clean water. Earlier, she'd heard Ryan's raised voice downstairs. A slew of officials had dropped by in the last three days since Johnny was brought to Lord Ravenspur's residence. Ryan had gone earlier with the constable. Looking at her brother-in-law lying like death on the bed brought the tears all over again.

"Who is downstairs?" she heard Lord Ravenspur's voice.

He sat in the chair across from her. A shadow roughened his jaw. He'd turned his head to speak to someone who had come into the room with the nurse. "An inspector from Scotland Yard, Your Grace," the butler's quiet voice came from the other side of the room. "He wishes to have a word with Miss Bailey. Mr. Donally left a half hour ago."

After the butler had gone, she gave the full force of her gaze to Lord Ravenspur.

"You've already given your deposition to the constable." His gray eyes stark in his face, he looked at her from across the bed. "Let Ryan handle the authorities, Miss . . . Rachel."

"How can I?"

"Ryan knows what he's doing, Rachel. You have to stay out of this."

Outside the rain had ruined another sunset. She walked to the window and gripped the curtain, Devonshire's words ringing in her head like broken mantra. *I want Donally to know what it feels like to lose everything in the world.*

This was her fault.

Her fault for not being smarter. For bringing the children to the office when they should have gone to the park. Brianna had retreated to the nursery and not come out. Ryan had been with Mary Elizabeth. Rachel was afraid.

Not for herself. She didn't care for herself, but because she knew if Johnny died, Ryan would go after Devonshire, and, this time he would kill him. He'd already proven himself capable. He would get himself hanged.

She had not wept until she'd seen Ryan coming out of the club, until she'd touched him and felt his heart beating beneath her palm. She'd wept, with Ryan holding her in the carriage, unable to stop the tears.

Now she couldn't stop crying, and she gripped the velvet drapery and wept silently within its softness.

"Look at you, Rache," Ryan was suddenly beside her. His palm at her nape, Ryan pressed his chin against her temple, his clothes damp from the rain. "Don't cry."

"Was Scotland Yard here to arrest Johnny?"

"No one is arresting Johnny."

He tipped her head back to look into her wet eyes with a possessiveness that left her afraid for him. Rachel clung to him as he took her to bed. He undressed her and laid her beneath the blankets, and she fell asleep. Somewhere she dreamed she'd heard a little girl crying. When next she awakened, Ryan was gone, and it was night again.

The rain had stopped. The draperies drawn wide. Moonlight spilled into the room.

"Mr. Donally is with his daughter, mum," Elsie said from her chair beside the bed. "She had a nightmare."

Rachel wanted to go to her, but Mary Elizabeth's place was with her father. She pulled the cover to her chest and slid to the edge of the bed. "Johnny . . ."

"His missus and bairns arrived a few hours ago. Colin brought them. Sir Christopher and Lady Alexandra arrived just after you fell asleep."

God, they were gathering for a funeral.

"Do you know if someone has been able to reach David?"

"Her Grace has been trying, mum. She has sent a personal courier since they cannot seem to reach him by telegraph."

Rachel twisted around to her bedside table and dragged the silver-domed clock around to face her. Strange, it was only eleven o'clock in the evening.

Feeling as if she were coming off a wretched bout of drinking, she pulled herself out of bed and stumbled to the basin of water. She splashed her face, and then, bracing both hands on the basin, looked at herself in the mirror. She was pale as death as if she'd been the one to bleed her lifeblood all over the floor. Touching her swollen bottom lip, she examined the cut on the inside of her mouth. She must have bitten the tender flesh when Devonshire had shoved her against the desk.

Elsie helped Rachel dress in a simple auburn muslin gown. Ryan was still with Mary Elizabeth an hour later when Elsie finished braiding her hair. "Why don't you go downstairs and eat, mum," Elsie quietly said.

But as Rachel left her chambers, she only knew she would go insane if she stayed a moment longer doing nothing. She played out the events from the office in her mind. Over and over. Reliving what she could have or should have done. Dissecting, analyzing every awful moment from the time she'd walked into the office and seen Devonshire.

How had he gotten past the watchman?

Knowing now what she knew of the man, she questioned the circumstances that found her trapped in the vault weeks ago. There was no such thing as too many coincidences. And she was determined to find answers that could put Devonshire in prison.

"How long has she been here?"

"Nigh on two hours, sir," said the D&B night watchman, a stocky man in his forties who had acquired his shock of white hair only in the last year of the eight he'd been working for Ryan. "I was surprised to see her, sir. That's why I sent ye the message. She come in and asked to check the register.

Then wanted to see the books back for months. It took me nearly fifteen minutes just to locate them all. Then she checked the keys to the vault and to the doors. She wanted an accountin' of them all, sir."

"What did you find?"

"We're not missing a one. 'Cept the one you keep."

The one he kept in his desk at Ore Industries.

Clenching his teeth, Ryan sensed the uncompromising tone in Rachel's actions. He was still furious, but as much at himself for not noticing she'd been gone from the house for so long. What was she thinking, coming here in the middle of the night?

He jaunted up the stairs to the third-floor entry, pausing as he glimpsed a faint handprint of dried blood on the rail. Except for the area where carpet lay on the floor, Stewart had already seen the rooms cleaned. Ryan opened the glass door into the reception area. He followed the light down the corridor. A heavy *clunk* against the ceiling lifted his gaze. The rasping noise led him past the conference room and through another door that opened into a private dressing room. He walked into the lounging area in time to see a pair of stocking-clad legs wriggle from the trapdoor in the ceiling and dangle blindly as the owner of that body lowered herself from the ceiling onto the dresser.

Rachel clearly struggled with her grip, cursing her idiocy for not removing her cumbersome apparel. She levered downward, seeking a solid perch beneath her feet when Ryan wrapped his hands around her waist.

She might have screamed had she not slipped and tumbled into his arms. "What the hell are you doing?" His furious voice resounded in her ear.

"Mother Mary!" Her skirts rucked around her waist, Rachel unhooked herself from Ryan's death grip. She shoved away from him. "Don't *ever* do that again!"

Incredulous, he started to reply when he shut his mouth and glanced at the trapdoor. "I should be telling you that. Have you lost your mind or merely your way? What the hell are you doing coming here in the middle of the night?"

"There is a pathway up there that leads to the roof." Smoothing her bodice and skirts, she returned her gaze to the trapdoor. "An entire block of buildings connect to our roof. It could explain the break-ins."

"Rachel"—he clawed a hand through his hair—"that is the building's ventilation shaft. We've already—"

"I know what it is," she snapped at him. "But anyone could come into this building from that way. Have you considered that?"

"We put a lock on the grate eight weeks ago."

"Well it isn't there now." She leaned against the chair for support.

His eyes took on a steely hardness. "When was the last time you ate?" he asked.

"I don't know." She scraped her palm through her hair, then looked at the ceiling. "I left the lantern in the passageway. I have to fetch it."

"You're not going back up there," he said. "Stay here."

He raised his arms and gripped the edge of the trapdoor, stretching the cloth of his white shirt across his shoulders as he lifted himself into the crawlway. He was still wearing the same clothes he'd worn yesterday.

Ryan found the lantern. Then raising it, he crawled along the shaft and checked the grate. The blades of the fan were still as the eerie night beyond, which only meant no breeze moved the air. He checked the lock on the grate, frowning when he found it missing. Five minutes later, he lowered himself and brought the lantern down with him.

"Devonshire was in this office when I arrived," Rachel

said, when he secured the trapdoor and turned. "He did not sign in. So how did he get up here to my office? Maybe we can prove he is behind the burglaries. Maybe—"

"Rachel, I'm as interested in this as you are, but not at two o'clock in the morning."

She pulled out of his reach. "You must know Devonshire is guilty. You've already figured everything out. I know you have."

"Frankly, Rachel, it doesn't matter what I think. We have no physical proof to verify one single goddamn accusation."

"He had someone steal the files because he was trying to cover up the brittle fracturing problem we have in Scotland. He would have blamed you—"

"We caught the problem in time."

"You're not going after him because of me. And he knows you won't."

"Listen to me, Rachel."

She stepped backward, away from his hands, her breath laboring. Her hazel eyes filmed with tears. "I warned you this could happen. I told you." She dared him to remain silent. "What pound of flesh is Devonshire extracting from you?"

Even as he pulled her into his arms, she was still fighting him, and as he held her he didn't know how she would be able to live forever under someone's magnifying glass like a specimen spread out for dissection. "Look what you are doing to yourself, Rachel."

"Johnny should have stayed in Carlisle." She raised her small fists and hit Ryan's chest. "He should have stayed."

He held her face pressed against his chest as she wept in his shirt. "We're engineers," she said. "We're supposed to be able to fix problems."

Closing his eyes, he was shamed that he'd reduced Rachel to this. He held her against him as if he truly did have the power to fix all problems while silently berating his own lack of character, aware as the holy moral bugler blew a death knell over his entire future with her. She wasn't the threat to him. Just the opposite. The consequences of his own actions and associations had come back to bite the people he loved most.

Devonshire hurt her. He hurt her with his daughter only three rooms away. Sweeping an arm behind her shoulders and another beneath her knees, he lifted her. She wrapped her arms around his neck and clung to him as he bore her out of the private dressing lounge, through the conference room, and into the corridor.

"We can't just do *nothing*."

"I know, Rachel."

Ryan stopped at the bottom of the stairs as the watchman hurried forward to open the front door. "Turn off the lamps upstairs," he instructed, started to turn away, then stopped. Rachel's gown flowed over his arm. "Who was on duty this weekend?"

"McKinney, sir. He works the weekend shifts."

"Do you know if he left his post at all?"

As if sensing the sudden silence, Rachel turned her head. Ryan asked the question again. "It's important," he reiterated. "Did McKinney leave this post?"

"He's got them kids, ye know." The man rubbed his bristly jaw. "They come here, and he leaves to eat lunch with them out back near the thoroughfare. He never goes far and doesn't stay gone for long. . . . He never meant no harm, sir."

"I want to see him in my office tomorrow." Ryan's voice held a poorly concealed edge. "He's worked shifts at Ore Industries. He knows where to find me."

"Don't discharge him." Rachel's quiet plea vibrated against his shoulder. "Please."

"We'll discuss it later, Rachel." He shoved open the door.

A heavy fog was rising up out of the night, almost as if alive and breathing. He could hear the distant blow of a foghorn on the Thames. The *clip-clop* of horses' hooves on brick. An orange glow hovered over the gaslamp outside the door, picking out the shiny, dark shape of a carriage down the walkway. He'd brought Ravenspur's carriage and fancy blacks and was indisposed to be picked out as an easy target by some novice footpad. Especially with his wife in his arms.

"Ryan . . ." Rachel struggled to get out of his arms. "I fear I'm going to be unwell."

He lowered her feet to the ground. She turned her head away and was promptly sick in the small patch of flowers outside the door. It did not occur to him to leave her to her privacy. He held her hair off her face and, when she was finished, he accepted a glass of water and a damp rag from the carriage driver, who had gone inside the building to fetch them from the night watchman.

He patted her forehead. "You've made yourself sick. You can hardly stand."

"I haven't eaten. There's nothing inside me."

"Swish." He offered the glass.

As the carriage made its way back to Kensington, he pulled Rachel into his lap. Holding her against him, he bent forward and dimmed the light against the gloom.

It was nearing dawn when he finally left Rachel sleeping in bed. The door to Johnny's room was open. Ryan stepped over the threshold. Hesitated, as he saw the figure of his brother in the massive bed. A low fire burned in the hearth. Brianna and his oldest brother Christopher were sitting vigil next to Johnny, who lay unmoving, his chest and shoulders wrapped in swaths of white.

Christopher unfolded himself from the chair. He'd not shaven and looked like some brigand from the desert. Unlike the rest of the family, he and Brianna shared their mother's same blue eyes, and the contrast was stark in the shadows of his face. "Ryan," Christopher said. His dark hair was longer than Ryan remembered, a dusting of silver lightening his temples. They were the same height, the same build.

Ryan stopped on the other side of the bed as if he'd come up against an invisible shield. His hands shoved in his pockets, he peered across at his oldest sibling.

He had not seen Christopher in a year. They had never been particularly close, not like he and Johnny were—perhaps as much because they were so much alike as they were separated by years and Rachel's girlhood affection. But Ryan knew it was not simple to decipher his feelings. His relationships never were easy for him to understand. Yet, he felt a strange loss for allowing himself to become a stranger to his oldest brother.

"Moira fell asleep," Chris said. "Colin took her back to her room."

"No one can find David," Brianna said.

"I'm not dead, yet," the strained whisper came from the bed. "Spare . . . me David."

Ryan pulled his hands out of his pockets.

"Johnny—" Brianna was suddenly at his side.

"How . . . long have I been here?"

"Almost four days," Christopher said. "Plus or minus a few minutes."

Johnny asked about Rachel in a low raspy voice. Brianna answered his questions, then pressed his limp hand to her cheek. "You've lost a lot of blood. The bullet did not penetrate your lungs." Or he would not be alive.

"I feel like hell."

"I think he will go to any means to have us wait on him," Christopher commented, offering Ryan a vague smile, but there was a mist in his eyes as he dropped to the chair.

Johnny's dulled gaze raised to his.

Ryan had not spoken.

He had remained in the shadows, separated by more than

the width of the bed, unprotected by the layers of his life he'd carefully and arrogantly constructed through the years. He didn't know what was happening to him. His chest was tight.

"Don't blame yourself, Ryan." Johnny's breathing slowed, and he seemed to fade into the sheets, the words striking Ryan as nothing else had.

For Kathleen's last breath to him on this earth had held those very same words. "Don't blame yourself, Ryan."

It was as if he'd come full circle in his life—and the man in the mirror was not a man he liked.

Chapter 23

"**H**asn't anyone informed you yet that I'm not going to die, Rachel?" Johnny's voice rasped. "It's been nearly two weeks. You don't need to tiptoe around me."

"I'm not tiptoeing." Exactly.

Wide strips of cloth bound Johnny's chest. His face was no longer pale but flushed slightly with fever. Sitting on the edge of his mattress, her skirts spread around her, she attempted to pretend that his appearance did not affect her. Nor could the warm midday air and the scent of fresh-cut flowers disguise the reek of carbolic soap and disinfectant.

Still the physician had been optimistic and, since yesterday, Johnny's chambers were no longer a place of hush as it had been days before. Christopher stood at the end of the bed helping Moira with the tray as she settled next to her husband. Colin, who could have been Johnny's twin, sat with his long legs stretched out, joking with his brother about all the service he was getting. Amid the somber merrymaking, Ryan's absence was conspicuously glaring in a moment that the entire family had come together. He hadn't even made a brief enough appearance in her life this week for her to tell him that he was going to be a father.

"So tell me what you have been doing at D&B, colleen," Johnny asked.

"Stewart has traced every ounce of steel and materials procured from the Welsh foundry owned by Devonshire," Rachel finished their conversation as she adjusted the pillows behind her brother-in-law for his meal. "It will take a few more weeks for the results of the inspections to come in, but we are confident everything is in hand."

"Only because D&B is notoriously circumspect in its safety," Christopher said, and, as former chairman of D&B, not without experience on the matter.

"Ryan has kept this out of the financials," Johnny said. "How?"

"He's put all the focus on himself," Christopher said.

"As it should be," Moira said. "I lay the blame at his feet for what's happened to my Johnny. . . . Him and his high-handed ways."

Rachel glared at her sister-in-law. Her assertion illogical and ridiculous in the face of their current company. "You don't mean that, Moira."

"No, she doesn't," Johnny said.

But the words had already been spoken, and Rachel was angry. Ryan *had* managed to keep her name and Johnny's out of the news. A week ago, he'd taken Mary Elizabeth back to the country, away from the public eye. Then he'd returned and initiated an investigation into Devonshire's Welsh foundry in an attempt to subpoena records. While he'd been in Wales, the accusation of financial irregularities at Ore Industries brought in a slew of government auditors. Stocks plunged. Rachel was sure D&B would be targeted next for an investigation, along with all of Ryan's holdings. Deciding this was not the time to be intimidated by a fractious public when he was taking a beating on all fronts, personal and professional, she'd hunkered down this week with Stewart and others at D&B and managed to put the company's affairs in order.

She had every confidence D&B would survive scandal, though not completely unscathed. Her only desire was to spike a stake through Devonshire's heart.

But circumstances had changed everything.

Yesterday the physician had examined her.

"Perhaps you could all change the subject?" Moira asked, attempting to feed Johnny the gruel in the bowl she held.

"Wife," he rasped, his black eyes narrowing in a grimace, "get that stuff away from me."

"You're a wretched patient, Johnny Donally." She set the bowl on the tray.

"I'm starving to death, Moira," he grumbled weakly, looking pale and helpless among the sheets and comforter that Moira pulled to his chest. "Have ye no ken what that is like? I need sustenance. A fat juicy brisket—"

"Dr. Blanchard said you were to have nothing heavier on your stomach than mash for another week," Moira said, her thick black hair framing her face and blue eyes.

"Aye, what does he know? By the looks of him, he's never been hungry in his life." He turned his hopeful gaze on Rachel. "Do you by chance have anything to drink, colleen? Something real?"

Rachel moved to his bedside table and poured him a glass of water from the pitcher. "As real as water." She offered the glass.

Johnny peered up into her drawn face as he reluctantly accepted the glass. "How are you holding up, colleen? You haven't been looking so well yourself lately."

A quick gust of wind stirred the wind chimes outside the open window, and fluttered Rachel's hair. "That bridge would have become operational in October," she said quietly, still not reconciled to what Devonshire might have done to all of them.

"It looks like your appearance in Ryan's life was divine providence, colleen."

"How could you say that?"

"He wouldn't have returned to Ireland. I wouldn't have decided to go to Scotland. The merger would have proceeded as planned."

Everything happens for a reason, Memaw had told her when she'd returned from London, in her Confucianist wisdom and love of proverbs. A chill went over her. "Unfortunately, I see nothing positive in what happened to you," she said. "And Ryan is blaming himself for everything."

"As are you, colleen."

"He returned to London this morning," Christopher said, from his place at the end of the bed.

A knock sounded, and a servant entered, followed by the physician and an audible groan from Johnny, a cue for everyone to vacate the premises. Outside Johnny's chambers, in the sitting room, children's voices drew Rachel to the window. She pulled aside the heavy curtain, hoping just once that she would look outside and see Mary Elizabeth playing.

Christopher moved behind her. She saw him in the glass. "Are you sure that you know what you are doing, Rachel?" he asked her, his penetrating blue eyes observing the strain on her face.

She dropped the edge of the curtain and turned, annoyed that he would be standing behind her. He had insisted on going with her everywhere all week, she was sure at Ryan's behest. If he wasn't available, Lord Ravenspur had filled in as her bodyguard until she felt imprisoned by their protectiveness. Imprisoned by her desire for revenge. By her past. Most of all, imprisoned by her need for Ryan.

"I need to go home," she said, having made up her mind this morning to return to the green hills of Ireland.

She had her baby and her health to think about. The physician had warned her yesterday that she needed bed rest. Stewart had everything in hand at D&B and, for the first time in her life, she was thinking about someone other than herself. "Don't think about telling me I can't go, either. I've made up my mind."

"Don't you think you should talk to Ryan?"

"Chris," Lord Ravenspur said from behind them, handing Christopher a note as he turned. "This just arrived."

Christopher read the missive, then raised his eyes to hers. "Ryan's visit to the foundry must have yielded results. Devonshire has agreed not to pursue charges against Johnny."

"The man is beyond arrogant. It's insane to think he ever could or would file charges after everything he has done."

"Ryan would not have allowed you to be out on public display in any courtroom, Rachel," Christopher said. "As of now, it is Johnny's word against his. Even so, Devonshire would only say you invited him into your office."

Rachel utterly despised the defeat she felt at Devonshire's hands.

"It doesn't matter anyway," Ravenspur said flatly, ending the conversation with ducal flair. "For whatever reason, Devonshire will not file charges. It is over."

Rachel took the note. "In exchange for what?"

"You can't go inside, Miss Bailey."

Ryan's secretary stood like a granite sentinel in front of his office. Clearly strengthened from her extended holiday, she looked prepared to protect the Ore Industries' bastion from incursion.

Rachel looked around Mrs. Stone. The door to Ryan's office was shut—so symbolically parallel to their current relationship that she felt her throat tighten. She could hear his raised voice through the closed transom. "It is not going well for him?" she asked.

"Today alone, Mr. Donally has been in meetings with auditors, broadsheet journalists, board members, and Scotland Yard," Mrs. Stone replied in monotone. "This meeting is tame in comparison to the others. But then a roomful of accountants can have that calming affect on a person."

Mrs. Stone returned to her desk, and Rachel wondered if she had just made a joke.

A gray light lay against the shadows in the room. Tightening her hands around the doll Mary Elizabeth had left at Lord Ravenspur's house, she sat on one of the plush chairs in the dreary anteroom, determined to see her husband. As difficult as it had been to sneak out from beneath the guard of the Donally watchdogs, she found it even more difficult to see her husband today. She knew he was avoiding her and would probably continue to avoid her. He had truly convinced himself that he could only protect her by staying away.

The meeting lasted exactly an hour. Rachel looked up as five men filtered out of Ryan's office, their expressions somber in the face of whatever had occurred inside.

She waited until she was alone before reaching for her satchel and standing. Carrying the doll, she walked to the office. Her petticoat swished with her gait. She edged out her hand and opened the door wider. Ryan was sitting at his desk working over some papers. He looked up. Their eyes met and held.

"Good afternoon." She smiled tentatively.

He stood as she approached.

He looked as if he hadn't slept in days. "What are you doing here?"

"Are you going to avoid Johnny and me forever?" she

asked. "Or will you stay away and pile more guilt on top of everything else you're carrying on your shoulders?"

"I have no desire to fight with you, Rachel. And I'm really busy at the moment."

She looked down at the doll in her hands, because that was where his gaze had strayed. She had no desire to fight with him either. Not when the world was falling in on him. "Marsha is Mary Elizabeth's favorite doll." She offered the doll to him. A glass eye was missing, and she had taken on a cyclopic demeanor since she'd been buried in the mud twice. "I thought about putting a patch over her face and making her into a pirate."

"The doll is yours." He touched Marsha's worn, burnished curls, the act surprisingly gentle. Ryan had known that Marsha was hers. How?

"Where did Mary Elizabeth find her?" he asked.

"In a trunk in that locked room off the attic."

"The attic? At the country house?" His gaze lifted.

"Why do you keep that room locked?" she asked.

He set the doll on the desk. "Do you think we can talk about this another time?"

"You can't put your daughter in your big white castle and hide her from death or from the hurts in life, Ryan, any more than you are responsible for hurting me or Johnny. Any more than you can sell off your interest in Ore Industries to appease Devonshire or walk away from everyone who loves you because of some guilt you carry over your past behavior. Johnny doesn't expect that, and neither do I."

"Jaysus, are you deliberately trying to provoke me?"

"You need to be provoked."

"Not from you."

"Especially from me. If you act on something, then you better be acting for the right reasons."

"He's dropping charges."

"In exchange for what?"

"It's complicated, Rachel."

"Then ask yourself what is really important to you."

"I don't bloody know the answer to that anymore," he shouted at her.

Rachel raised her chin, for Ryan didn't intimidate her, and she could give every bit as good as she got from him. But it wasn't the time to take a stand. He shook his head. Inhaling a frustrated breath, Ryan walked to the window that looked out on London like a huge glass eye. He set his hands on his hip. For a long time, he didn't speak.

"When I was a little boy I used to live in Da's old office warehouse," he said, his back to her. "You probably don't remember the place. I used to watch him work and knew I wanted to be like him. He was able to create with his hands . . . I thought no one in the entire world could be as smart. But people treated him like filth. Not once did he ever put up a fight. I watched, hating the injustice of his treatment. Later, I swore I would be more than just Irish or Catholic. More than a third-class citizen. I swore that I would be one of those *other* people one day . . ." He paused. "I only wish Da could have seen what the back room in that old warehouse has become today." Shoving his hands in his pockets, he quirked his mouth and looked over his shoulder at her. "Funny thing is, he probably wouldn't even bloody care."

Rachel moved nearer to his side. "He was an inventor as much as he was anything else. He lived in his own world, Ryan."

"He never noticed one accomplishment in my life," Ryan said. "Everything went to Christopher. The company, the accolades . . . your heart. I still can't even look at my family without feeling as if I have to prove myself. I don't even know what it's like to walk a line and not care if I fall off.

Now, I'm no longer sure if I even want to get back on that line."

"You aren't walking that line alone, Ryan." Reaching into her satchel, Rachel withdrew a small bamboo case. She waited for him to turn before putting it in his hands. "This represents more than a token of my affection toward you. I want you to have it because you mean more to me than a hundred of these."

He opened the box to reveal her own professional set of drafting tools.

They weren't a gift or an award. Women didn't walk across a stage and accept diplomas, so she had never been able to celebrate her accomplishment except by this. "I bought them myself," she said with a smile, when his gaze lifted to touch hers—as if he knew what this meant to her. "I made choices in my life that could I do over again . . . I would do the same. You and I weren't ready to fall in love and live a life together ten years ago. We were too selfish and never would have appreciated what we had as a couple. You have a beautiful daughter. I would never wish that anything could have been different for that alone."

"Was the price you paid worth what it bought you then, Rachel?"

There was no animosity in the question, for he'd suddenly found himself facing the same stark questions in his own life that she'd faced in hers years ago, but the answer hurt. It hurt more than she realized, and she felt the first crack in her courage.

But at what point did they both stop running from each other's pasts. At what point was it worth it to them to begin all over again someplace new. With their own dreams to grow.

"I should never have had to pay the price at all." Her voice was determined to touch him because she understood that on some elemental level she was losing him. "Any more than you should for me or for who you are, though I don't believe you honestly understand who you really are anymore."

That forced a wry smile from him. "Is that your expert opinion?"

"Yes, from someone who knows you better than you know yourself."

"Then we have officially traded drafting tools." There was tenderness in his eyes.

"I want Donally & Bailey to be us, not some brick-and-mortar company. I don't care who controls Ore Industries or how many seats you hold on the stock exchange. There is nothing material here that I want. Come to Ireland with me, Ryan."

He returned his attention to the window in an office that was the extension of his empire, his wealth, and all of his holdings. She stood beside him, barely six inches separating her skirt from his calf. Her life from his. Their future from the past. "I'm asking you to give up a lot to be with me. I imagine that makes me a selfish person for not doing the honorable thing and walking away. But I *am* a selfish person. Your journey with me will not lead to gold, but it will take you home, Ryan, if that is where you wish to go."

"To Ireland," his voice whispered.

Rachel's eyes burned with tears she refused to shed. Though home was anyplace they could live and be free to love, Ireland was a nice place to begin. But she couldn't say those words or voice that sentiment, for going home to Ireland suddenly seemed like everything she wanted to do. She wanted a simpler life than what they had. She wanted him to want that life as well, knowing it was so different from everything he had here.

"To Ireland," she echoed, not realizing that she was throwing an ultimatum in his face, until two men had knocked at the door, and it was too late to say more.

He was suddenly busy, as others demanded his attention. Sadly, she watched him take the sheaf of papers, watched him converse, reminding her that he would never be hers completely any more than he belonged solely to his daughter. Perhaps this was what Kathleen had seen. What she had tried to change, and could not.

After a moment, Rachel left the office, walked past Mrs. Stone and, after exiting the lift, hurried out onto the street. The air was stiff and humid. Pressing a gloved hand over her black hat, she looked up at the sky, wondering if it was going to rain but decided to walk to D&B, unwilling to go back to Lord Ravenspur's just yet. Tomorrow she would pack. Tomorrow she would go home.

Tears filmed her eyes. Chastising herself for her melancholy, Rachel dashed a sleeve at her cheeks. She had given Ryan the opening he needed, thrown down her gauntlet as it were. No more discussion.

She refused to play the martyr. But she'd never reached the part, yet, where she told him that no matter what he decided, she wasn't going to give him a divorce or an annulment. If he'd wanted another Rembrandt in his life, he should have thought about that before they created a child.

She had not told him about the child!

"Mum?"

Stewart's voice startled her. He stood on the curb, as if he'd just climbed out of a hansom. Watching him hurry toward her, she hastily dabbed the moisture from her face.

"I was hoping to find you here," he said, his voice urgent.

"What is it?"

"This came an hour ago, mum." He handed her the missive. "From Lord Bathwick. A boy brought it. Said his lordship will only speak to you."

Rachel thought about throwing the missive away. Tearing it into a thousand pieces as it were. The impassioned thought paused her hands, if only for a moment before she read the note, considered the intent of the message, and deemed it important enough to follow. "Very well," she said, refolding the missive.

She looked at Mr. Stewart still standing in the walkway. "You don't expect that I should go alone, do you?" she asked him, when a familiar hand reached over her shoulder and plucked the letter from her fingers.

Despite herself, she jumped. "Ryan!"

"Tell the driver we'll be taking the carriage," he spoke to Stewart, his dark eyes narrowing on the note, his mercurial mood evident.

She was searching his face, her sluggish thoughts racing just to see him, even as his expression grew dangerous. "You're wrong about him," she said in some indecision, watching his lashes lift to reveal his eyes.

"As usual you are too softhearted, love." His gloved fingers tipped her chin, then gently slid into her hair, and his gaze moved over hers with such intensity, Rachel felt her knees go weak. "You don't expect that I would let you do this alone, do you?"

"I hadn't intended to go alone. I was going to take Stewart."

Stewart gulped visibly, his sense of chivalry never more evident as he bravely replied, "Of course, sir."

"Your sacrifice is not necessary," Ryan said. "Whatever his lordship has to say can be said to us both." Turning that implacable gaze back to her, he raised a brow. "Don't you agree?"

"I should have expected that you would not come alone," Lord Bathwick said when Rachel was shown into the drawing room an hour later, Ryan behind her.

His hands on Rachel's shoulders, he paused in the doorway and did a quick mental survey of the drawing room.

Lady Gwyneth sat on the settee, her hands folded primly in her lap. Wearing a white, billowy gown, she looked as if she were a bride sitting among the fragrant clouds. She wore a diamond-and-sapphire butterfly in her upswept hair, as glittery and bright as the smile she gave him. But as Bathwick stepped to her side, she lifted her hand to his, and her eyes spoke to the very depths of her heart. "We were married by special license yesterday," Bathwick said, immediately disabusing Ryan of the concern that Devonshire was presently hiding in some alcove.

"Felicitations, my lady," he replied, though curious why that should warrant a private conversation with Rachel.

"Won't you sit?" Lord Bathwick offered.

With an arm still possessively attached to Rachel's waist, he guided her to the settee across from the happy couple. "What is this about?" he asked.

"Before I go on, I want you to know that as of today, I have severed all ties with my father." Lord Bathwick looked down at Gwyneth, who still held his hand. "Tell them," he gently prompted. "She returned to London four days ago."

"There is a windowless room in the back of my uncle's library, set behind the bookshelves," Lady Gwyneth said. "Three months ago, I discovered the room. I remembered seeing papers and drawings at the time, but I never connected them to anything. After reading about everything that has taken place here in London, because of me," she erroneously asserted, smiling apologetically at Rachel, "I returned to talk to him in hopes that he would cease his ridiculous vendetta against you, Mr. Donally. This time when I went into the study, I found shelves of files that belong to you."

"She came to me," Bathwick supplied. "Father has known for a year that our foundry in Wales produced inferior steel prone to brittle fracturing. Steel too high in carbon," he explained to Gwyneth. "Which makes for brittle rather than flexible steel—"

"Lord Bathwick—" Rachel prompted, before he launched into the physics of the steel-making process.

"Father knew the bridge in Scotland would eventually fail, and had hoped to eliminate any trail back to us, thus hoping to prove your company negligent. I believe he possessed some scheme eventually to reclaim Ore Industries. Unfortunately for him, there never was a merger."

"People could have been killed." Rachel's voice was scathing.

"Except John Donally discovered the problem."

"Where is your father now?" Rachel demanded.

Lord Bathwick spared a brief glimpse at Gwyneth. "He came home this morning while she was in the room."

"My sister hit him over the head with a vase." Gwyneth wrung her small hands in her lap. "We shut the door and jammed the desk against it so he couldn't get out."

Having yet to speak, his elbows braced on his knees, Ryan rubbed a hand over his rough jaw. So far, nothing of this potential disaster had made it into the public. "You realize this is a criminal matter."

Lord Bathwick took the seat next to Gwyneth and faced Ryan directly. "In reality, the erupting scandal will only do more harm than good for everyone, and still doesn't solve the problem of my father. He can do irreparable harm in other ways. This doesn't have to become public. No one was killed. At least on that matter I have heard that your brother is improving. You have your records intact. I have set upon the matter of finding any other sites that may be affected by the steel that came from my family's foundry. Finally, when all is said and done, the worst that can happen to my father is a trial by his peers, which though humiliating to him would be far worse to the rest of us."

Lord Bathwick produced a document from inside his jacket pocket. "After a long discussion this morning, my father is willing to negotiate for his freedom. I believe you can still have your justice. You were the one who gave me the idea about a trust with your settlement to Gwyneth."

Rachel leaned over Ryan's shoulder and read the signed confession. Her sleeve whispered against his shoulder. The scent of apples and cinnamon touched him, then spilled into his veins. He turned his face, and her hazel gaze hesitated on his.

"If my father ever sets foot again in England, you have that document," Lord Bathwick said. "And he will never receive another shilling from Gwyneth and me. I wanted to give this to Miss . . . to your wife, so that she could talk to you."

Ryan moved his gaze to the younger man sitting across from him.

"You didn't misjudge me, Mr. Donally." Bathwick's mouth twisted with grim amusement. "But when I want to fight you it will be on familiar and legal ground."

Chapter 24

❝**H**ave you read this morning's financials?" Rachel stood with her fists clenched around the broadsheet at the end of Johnny's bed and looked between the faces of his two brothers. "Ryan has stepped down as head of Ore Industries."

"I know, colleen," Johnny said. "He told us."

Her jaw dropped open. "Ryan was here? When?"

Johnny looked at Colin and Christopher, who were sitting next to the bed, cards in hand, the game they were playing paused. "This morning."

"He didn't stay long," Christopher said, laying down a knave on the sheet that covered Johnny to his chest.

Rachel glared at each of his brothers and felt a surge of anger in Ryan's defense, despite the fact that she had not seen him since he dropped her off at Lord Ravenspur's after leaving Bathwick's three days ago. "Did you argue?"

Colin shrugged his wide shoulders. "I don't think so. Did we?"

"Only if ye count that wee discussion he had with Chris

about the dog he gave Mary Elizabeth," Johnny said. "I would call that an argument."

"Don't any of you care what he is doing?"

"What can we do, colleen?" Johnny asked, laying down an ace and swiping up the cards. "Ryan sets his mind on something, and that's the end of it."

"But he doesn't have to do this." How could they not care? "Did he say anything else while he was here?" Rachel looked between them.

"For instance?"

Clamping her jaw, Rachel turned and left the room.

She was leaving in a few hours to catch the train to Holyhead. Ryan had not been at his house this morning. He had not been at Ore Industries or Donally & Bailey. He had brought Mary Elizabeth here this morning and had not awakened Rachel. Now she had packed, and no one even seemed concerned that she was leaving.

"Maybe I shouldn't leave tonight," Rachel said, when Brianna joined her later on the terrace for tea. She'd listened all morning to the chatter of the ladies gathered around the drawing room, a familiar knot tightening in the pit of her stomach as she felt teary-eyed and in need of a nap, as if she hadn't slept enough these past days.

"Nonsense," Brianna quietly said, as if she understood Rachel's vexation and maddened frustration. "Memaw is expecting you back. You've already wired her."

Brianna was correct, of course. She'd settled her affairs at D&B yesterday. Cleaned out her office and prepared to return to Ireland. She had told everyone she was.

As soon as manners permitted, Rachel excused herself and walked out onto the terrace to find Mary Elizabeth. The afternoon silence drew her gaze around the yard. She walked to the edge of the yard and looked over the iron gate into the park.

"Lady Alexandra took them all to the zoo, mum," Elsie informed her when she'd walked through an empty house and up the stairs to her chambers.

Her peridot silk morning gown lay out in repose on her bed.

"Elsie, I cannot possibly wear this dress to Holyhead."

"Oh, but you can, mum." She fretted and wrung her hands. "It's beautiful."

Rachel narrowed her eyes, sure that everyone in this house had gone mad.

"My apologies, mum. But your trunks have already been removed to the carriage. Would you have them brought back?"

Rachel sighed. "No." She fingered the peridot silk.

The dress was too nice for travel. But it was beautiful, and she let Elsie dress her and fret with her hair. Elsie finished buttoning the row of tiny pearls up her back.

As Rachel slipped her arms into the waist-fitting jacket, she caught sight of Brianna in the mirror. "The train leaves at six o'clock," her sister-in-law said.

Rachel didn't bother glancing at the clock. She would get there early at this rate. She left the room and stopped as she met Lord Ravenspur at the top of the stairway. Wearing a nice suit of clothes, he didn't look dressed for taking her to the train station. Upon seeing her, he stopped pacing. One perfect eyebrow rose to peer at his wife, standing behind Rachel.

"Are you ready?" he asked Rachel.

"Does someone want to explain to me what is going on around here?"

"Mum," Elsie stood behind her. "I was told to give this to you."

Rachel looked at the wide velvet box in her hands.

"It's a hat box, mum," Elsie stated the obvious.

"Open it, Rachel." Brianna removed the lid.

Rachel stared at a beautiful wide-brimmed hat with a wondrous concoction of feminine ribbons, feathers, and flowers for trimming. It was made of pale blue silk, pleated beneath the brim. Elsie withdrew the hat and held it out to her. A long veil of airy Belgian lace cascaded from the back and flowed over Elsie's forearm as she offered the hat to Rachel. She couldn't move. Her arms remained at her sides. "I—" Rachel shook her head. "I don't understand," she whispered in reverence, afraid to touch the hat.

"He wanted to give you a church wedding," Brianna said. "But he hoped you would settle for this. He has been out all day looking for something special that would make you feel like a bride."

Tears filled her eyes. "He's here?"

Brianna took the hat from Elsie's hands and settled it on her head. "He's waiting for you in Johnny's chambers."

Rachel's hands trembled so much that Brianna was left to tie the ribbon into a fluffy bow at her chin. "Hurry," Rachel whispered.

Her defenses had crumbled completely. She rushed to the mirror. The hat didn't match the dress exactly, but she didn't care. From the neck up, she felt like a bride.

Lord Ravenspur snatched her elbow before she could run into Johnny's bedroom. "I would be honored." He turned her around.

They were standing alone in the corridor.

"I'm sorry." Rachel laid her palm on his forearm. "It's just that I never had time to think about being a bride. The last time I married him, I thought there might be violence. Indeed, there was violence, I suppose, if you count that David hit Ryan—"

"I believe that happens quite a bit in this family." His rueful smile was white and dashing, and Rachel glimpsed the rogue beneath the ducal façade of her aristocratic brother-in-law.

He walked her down the corridor, through the sitting room, and into Johnny's chambers. Rachel stopped. The entire Donally family was gathered inside. Ryan stood at the back of the room, Christopher next to him.

But her eyes caught on Ryan, and her lungs swelled.

He was standing in front of the fireplace, his hands folded in front of him. From his dark brows, the sweep of his hair across his brow, to his polished shoes, every line of his familiar body emanated the same magnetism that had pulled him into her dreams and kept her awake at night. That had forced her face into the pillow to muffle her tears when she thought she had lost him. His black coat fit his tall, splendid form, the dazzling whiteness of his shirt contrasting with the sensual black of his eyes, and everything about the moment caught inside her.

She felt the brim of tears behind her lids. Then she looked at Mary Elizabeth and young Lord Robert standing excitedly in their church attire beside her. One carried a basket of rose petals. The other a pillow bearing two simple gold rings. She looked at the faces of his family gathered around the furniture, touching each one in turn with her gaze. Christopher's twins stood with their mother. Johnny sat up in bed, his children around him. Colin next to the bedpost with his wife and his children. Rachel looked at each one as if they were her own, realizing that they had always been hers, and they were here for Ryan and for her, and she loved them all.

"Are you ready to begin?" the priest asked.

David wasn't present, she realized. She missed David.

But then her eyes turned to Ryan, the tears had suddenly become too real. She tried to breathe past her corset, past the escalating emotions. Past the panic.

Suddenly, she could no longer contain herself.

"I think . . . I think I'm going to be sick."

Had she said those words aloud? She must have.

Rachel pressed a fist to her mouth, backed a step, then turned and ran from the room, her feet carrying her down the corridor.

Ryan found her a moment later bent over the basin in her dressing room.

"Mother Mary and Joseph," she heaved. "I feel terrible."

When she was finished, he caught her tenderly in his arms. "You're supposed to walk down the aisle, not run away."

"This is not amusing. I'm so embarrassed."

He tilted her chin, and all she could think about was that she'd ruined her wedding day. Again. "It *is* rather disconcerting that you cry and throw up at the most inopportune times." His gaze touched her with tender solemnity. "You injure me, Rache."

"I'm going to have a baby, Ryan," she accused him, returning to the basin, miserable. "That does happen on occasion when one engages in the kind of activity in which we are so fond of engaging in carriages, which is entirely your fault." She groaned and tried to shrug him away. "I can do this myself."

"Ah, Rache." Ryan seemed inordinately pleased by her helplessness. "For once you're going to have to take my help." He held back the veil on her hat.

"We're in this together," he told her, handing her a toothbrush dipped in baking soda when she was finished. "Now, brush your teeth so I can kiss you."

"Are you sure, Ryan?"

"That I want you to brush your teeth?"

She let him hold and comfort her, but he knew what she meant. What they were doing today was permanent and real—and deliberate. "When I arrive with you at Memaw's house, I want no doubt in anyone's mind you belong to me," he said against her hair.

"Ryan—"

"Look at me, Rache." He brushed her hair from her face and tilted her head back. "Yesterday I went home to the country . . . and thanked God for every precious gift He'd ever given me. I took Mary Elizabeth to the attic, Rachel. I thought it would be harder than it was to say good-bye. But there was only peace.

"Today, there were loose ends I had to tie up before I came here. I wanted to do this right. Unfortunately"—he pulled out his watch and flipped open the fob—"we have to do this quickly. The train won't wait for us past six o'clock."

Movement turned their heads. Christopher and Brianna were standing in the doorway. "Are you two always this difficult?" Christopher asked.

Ryan's eyes darkly caressing her, he slid his hands up her arms and encased her shoulders with his palms.

"Always," they both answered together.

Rachel looked into his face. "But you gave up Ore Industries—"

"No, I didn't. Lord Bathwick negotiated a trade for his shares of D&B, and I sold him the rest. It's time Donally & Bailey officially became Donally&Donally&Donally. Maybe together we *can* make a difference in Ireland, Rache."

"But—"

He curved his hands around her face and framed the soft tenderness of her jaw with his palms. "We cannot see into the future. We cannot know that everything will be all right and turn out as we plan. We cannot keep questioning what we both know is right. I only know that wherever you go, I will go there, too, Rachel. I love you."

"I love you, too," she whispered.

She had always loved him.

• Forever.

And in the golden glow of the setting sun, with Mary Elizabeth at his side and his family around them, they spoke their vows. Then he closed his mouth over hers, proving in more than words that there was ultimate triumph in surrender.

For no matter where they went, they were going home.